Eventide

Eventide

SARAH GOODMAN

TOR TEEN

A TOM DOHERTY ASSOCIATES BOOK

NEW YORK

EVENTIDE

Copyright © 2020 by Sarah Goodman

A Tor Teen Book
Published by Tom Doherty Associates
120 Broadway
New York, NY 10271

www.tor-forge.com

Tor® is a registered trademark of Macmillan Publishing Group, LLC.

The Library of Congress Cataloging-in-Publication Data is available upon request.

ISBN 978-1-250-22473-6 (hardcover)
ISBN 978-1-250-22471-2 (ebook)

Our books may be purchased in bulk for promotional, educational, or business use. Please contact your local bookseller or the Macmillan Corporate and Premium Sales Department at 1-800-221-7945, extension 5442, or by email at MacmillanSpecialMarkets@macmillan.com.

First Edition: October 2020

Printed in the United States of America

0 9 8 7 6 5 4 3 2 1

To Hannah West,
brilliant critique partner and abiding friend

Eventide

Frigid wind howled across the empty fields, driving snow before it like frightened prey, rushing over sprawling farms and huddled little towns. The storm swept past a quaint parsonage nestled beside a country church. It had no concern for the girl kneeling by the winter-seared rosebushes.

Likewise, the girl paid no heed to the storm. She carried on digging at the frozen ground until a shallow hole lay before her. Carefully, she placed a hatbox in the cold earth and stared at it as the snow frosted her lashes.

She pulled a thin necklace from under her nightgown. With shaking fingers, she undid the clasp, sliding a gold ring off the chain and into her grimy palm.

She'd kept it concealed for months. Now it would be hidden forever.

The girl lifted the lid from the box. A scrap of fabric torn from an old quilt covered what lay inside. She didn't attempt to peek under its carefully tucked-in edges. She'd already kissed the perfect, tiny lips, memorized the shape of the closed eyes and the rose-gold of the baby's downy hair. The ring tumbled from her hand, coming to rest on the quilt. She replaced the lid, watching the snow begin to cover the small grave.

She stood on deadened feet. Then, without a backward glance, she walked away into the storm.

I

June 1907

Our passenger car felt cramped as a brand-new boot and roughly the temperature of Hell's sixth circle.

The orphanage had given us each a set of clothes as a parting gift, and because I was the eldest by several years, mine included an extra item: a fine hat in the latest wide-brimmed, beflowered style. I pulled it off, using it to fan my sweaty face. I doubted I'd need to look fashionable where we were headed.

Humid wind rushed through the train's open windows. I hadn't realized I was listening with half an ear to the scritch-scratch of a fountain pen on paper until the sound cut off and Lilah looked up from her work, a daub of ink on the end of her upturned nose. "I've just had the most wonderful idea for a story. I'm going to need more paper." She gestured with her pen to the small trunk at my feet.

"Again?" With a sigh, I shifted my boots so she could fling open the lid for the dozenth time. Papers shifted and slid off her lap as she scrounged for blank pages.

"I have to write it down this instant, before I forget," my little sister explained with an intensity only a girl of eleven could muster.

"Be careful. I don't want Papa's books all bent up. And get that ink off your nose."

Scrubbing at her face with her sleeve, Lilah shoved aside the battered copies of Beckman's *Treatment in General Practice* and *On the Prevention of Tuberculosis* before coming up with a folded ivory paper. "Can I use this?"

My acceptance letter to St. Lawrence University poked out from between her fingers. I swallowed hard, taking it from her. "Why don't you see if there's anything else to write on?"

While she rummaged, I looked at the stately letterhead, remembering the triumph I'd felt when I first read it. I was sure angelic choruses sang the opening line: "We are pleased to accept your application for admittance . . ." followed by details of the stipend I'd receive for academic merit.

All the late nights studying until my eyes burned and the candle guttered out, all the dreams of regaining our place in society—all for nothing.

Smoothing the pages, I carefully tucked the letter inside a faded book of fairy tales Mama and Papa used to read to me each evening. Nestled in bed between them, I would trace the words as they read, pretending my small fingers called the clever maidens and daring princes into being. Those days felt as distant and unreal as the magical tales that filled them.

I turned back to Lilah, who was scribbling away once again. "What's your new story about?"

Lilah tapped her pen against the fresh paper resting on her knees. "A girl who goes on a voyage across an unknown sea. She ends up in a land where everything is enchanted . . . even the sky. And the clouds are made of cotton candy."

I glanced around the crowded, dingy train car as we jarred along the tracks. "Why don't you ever write about things that could actually happen in real life?"

Lilah regarded me with lively hazel eyes. "It must be awfully dull inside your head, Verity. You've got no imagination to speak of."

"A vivid imagination can cause a world of trouble," I shot back.

I couldn't help thinking of our papa, as he used to be. Before the line between the real and the imaginary blurred in his mind, and horrors only he could see crawled out of every nook and cranny.

I retied the ribbon at the end of Lilah's strawberry-blond braid. Keeping us fed and clothed while dealing with Papa's deepening madness had left me no time for whimsy. "Don't bite your nails. Goodness only knows how many germs are on this train. It's a rolling petri dish."

Lilah sighed. "You're the bossiest sister in the world."

"Probably," I admitted, resting my head against the window. "But someone has to make sure we keep body and soul together."

Through the smudged glass, fields of sun-brittled grass spread as far as I could see. Without the towering buildings of home, the sky felt too near, like a giant lid trapping the heat of the day and us with it. Sweat slipped down my temple, stinging at the corner of my eye. The racket of the other children and the insistent click-clack-thrum of the train's wheels conspired to fray my nerves.

Wiping a damp strand of hair from my cheek, I scanned the train for Miss Pimsler. The agent from the Children's Benevolence Society sat near the front of the car, knitting a woolen scarf, of all things.

I stood, edging up the aisle toward her, skirts swaying against my calves. The train lurched around a bend and I banged my hip against a seat. A grunt escaped before I could capture it.

Miss Pimsler looked up, her round face shining with either earnest goodwill or perspiration. She wore the self-satisfied little smile of a person who is doing good and wouldn't mind if you noticed. "Do you need something, Verity?"

I did, in fact. But two tickets back to New York weren't an option. "Could you tell me how long until we arrive?"

Miss Pimsler fished an enamel pendant watch from her shirtwaist. "We'll be in Wheeler in just a few minutes." She closed the watch with a snick. "Did you know your parents spent some time in this part of Arkansas many years ago? That's why I decided to put you and Lilah on this train instead of one going elsewhere."

I tilted my head in surprise. "They did?"

Miss Pimsler nodded. "I believe your mother lived here as a girl, at least for part of her childhood. Your father visited briefly, too."

Curiosity fluttered through me, followed by an old familiar heartache. "Our mother died nine years ago, and Papa . . ." I trailed off. It went without saying he'd been in no condition to pass down family history, even before his recent commitment to the asylum.

Miss Pimsler tutted softly. "You're an intelligent, resourceful girl, Verity. You'll make a fine life for yourself with your new family, whoever they may be. Providence has a way of working these things out."

I smothered a scowl. "That's almost exactly what our aunt Susan wrote in her letter."

We'd never met Aunt Susan, our only known living relative, but her damning reply to my query said it was "absolutely impossible" for Lilah and me to come live with her family. The courts deemed it untenable for a girl of seventeen and her sister to be left to their own devices, so Aunt Susan's rejection had been the last shoe dropping, booting us into the Children's Benevolence Society Home three months ago.

"Your aunt sounds like a wise woman." Miss Pimsler patted my arm. "We must trust things will happen as they are meant to."

I bit my lip on a cynical retort, and moved back down the aisle. Miss Pimsler and Aunt Susan could trust in fate or destiny or starlight wishes all they wanted. I'd rely on myself.

My dreams of college had disintegrated, but in seven months I would turn eighteen. And I'd find a way to get us back to New York. There was work available for those willing to do it, as I well knew. Washing and mending had given us grocery money over the last year while I finished school. I could take that up again, and hire on as a shopgirl in one of the downtown stores, or join the typing pool at an office.

I slipped back into the grubby seat, considering my options. Lilah had returned her papers to the trunk and sat peering out at the open fields whipping by, her expression one of hopeful anticipation. "I think it will be wonderful to have a new mother," she said.

"Don't say that." My heart pinched at her casual tone. I pictured my mother, her cheeks bright with cold, laughing as the two of us skated together on the frozen pond in Central Park. "No one can replace Mama."

Lilah's voice dropped with an earnest ache that stole my breath. "Maybe not for you," she whispered.

My annoyance drained, leaving only dregs of sadness. She didn't know the Mama I'd adored. Lilah's one and only memory of our mother was of her white face in a satin-lined casket, with our baby brother, who'd outlived her by only a few hours, cradled in her arms.

With a shriek of brakes, the train lurched and slowed. Ash

and cinders drifted in through the window. "Children," Miss Pimsler announced, "we'll arrive in Wheeler soon." The other young passengers, a couple of dozen in number, turned toward the squat woman. She stood at the front of the car dabbing her forehead with a handkerchief. "Gather your luggage. Let's all do our best to make excellent first impressions."

I glanced down at my trunk and the two worn carpetbags that held all our worldly goods. We'd lost our home when Papa's medical practice failed, and I'd sold everything else to pay rent on a series of wretched tenement apartments.

The other orphans—I still couldn't believe we were counted among them—collected their scant belongings, smoothing travel-mussed hair and straightening wrinkled clothes.

I shouldered my carpetbag, handed Lilah's to her, and tucked the trunk under my arm. We stepped into the station, where a porter materialized from the dispersing cloud of steam. "Take your trunk for you, miss?" he asked, each vowel stretching like a lazy cat.

"No, thank you. I'll manage." I moved through the haze of coal smoke toward Miss Pimsler, my nerves swarming with countless worries. Everything was out of my hands now.

It was completely unacceptable.

Shuffling into a haphazard line, we set off on the short walk down a dusty trail into town. I felt my cheeks redden as I pictured how I must look, a nearly grown girl who should've been allowed to manage her own affairs, forced to go begging among strangers for a place to stay.

Shaking off the dour thoughts, I surveyed the town of Wheeler as it sat baking in the fierce sun. A handful of weathered buildings bordered a central square. In its center, an imposing redbrick courthouse rose over a spreading lawn, a small tin-roofed jailhouse squatting by its side. Across the dusty street stood a white clapboard church with a steeple that pierced the clear sky.

And at the edge of the grassy court square loomed a wooden platform.

"Wonderful!" Miss Pimsler exclaimed, directing us to leave our trunks beside the church. "It's much easier for families to choose their new children when they have a good view."

My blood tingled with humiliation, then flashed to hot anger as we plodded up the rickety platform steps like horses at a stockyard. We stared out over a gathering crowd. Solemn quiet descended over the square, and those who did speak cloaked their words in whispers. Each of us on the platform was being scrutinized, our merits and flaws silently parsed. Lilah's purposeful stride slowed. She tucked her hand in the crook of my arm.

Once we lined up along the stage, the milling townspeople ventured up the steps. A well-dressed man and woman neared. My heart thudded too hard and fast, then stuttered when they passed us by, stopping in front of a tiny redheaded girl of no more than four or five. Back at the orphanage, I'd overheard Miss Pimsler say older children were harder to place. Regardless, none of us had a say in where we ended up. If no one here wanted us, we'd be shipped off on another train to another state.

Sweat trailed between my shoulder blades, as much from nerves as the heat. I stared out across the square at a dark stand of trees in the distance, their silhouettes jagged against the painfully bright sky. A savage longing for New York—anywhere in New York, even the orphanage—throbbed in my chest. But there was no going back. Not yet, anyway.

I exhaled slowly, willing the tension out of my shoulders. My mother had lived in the area, or so Miss Pimsler said. The thought comforted me, somehow. Lilah and I would find a place for ourselves here, too, until we could go back north. "We're going to make the best of this," I said. Lilah nodded, her furrowed brow relaxing. "We're together. We'll be fine."

My attention snagged on the shrewd stare of an older man looking up at me with narrowed eyes. Perhaps it was the bald head, or the slight underbite that gave his jaw a bulldog quality, but for whatever reason, I felt sure he was not a person to be trifled with. I swallowed against the unease climbing up my throat.

The man crossed liver-spotted hands on the brass head of his cane and shifted his scrutiny to Lilah. She slid her hand into mine.

He mounted the steps, still watching us, his cane thumping with a hollow sound. Piercing gray eyes darted from me to Lilah with an unsettling air of expectation. "I'm Mr. Reuben Lybrand. What's your name?" He flung the question at her like a grenade.

"Lilah Pruitt." She squared her narrow shoulders in a show of confidence, but her hand in mine trembled.

I felt an instinct to step back, tugged by an instant distrust of Mr. Lybrand. If he took a fancy to us, we'd be packed up and taken to his home like auctioned furniture from an estate sale. We had no voice in our own futures. The indignity of it burned behind my ribs.

Mr. Lybrand rapped the end of his cane against the platform and called over his shoulder into the milling crowd. "She's over here."

A woman lifted her head in response to his gravelly voice. My attention glided over her magnolia-trimmed hat and ivory dress, coming to rest on an elegant face and eyes the color of a midwinter sky. Despite the heat, her skin remained fair and unflushed. She drew near, wisteria perfume wafting around her slim figure. The hair peeking from under her hat—even her long lashes and finely arched brows—was of the fairest silvery blond.

"Lilah?" she asked in a lilting voice. Lilah nodded, seeming a little dazzled. The woman's face lit with a relieved smile. She handed a sheaf of papers to the grim Mr. Lybrand. "Uncle Reuben, would you fetch Miss Pimsler, let her know we've found Lilah? Then you can start the car, if you don't mind." She returned her focus to Lilah. "Uncle and I prefer to be home before dark."

As Mr. Lybrand left, I noticed a woman avert her eyes when he went by, and I would've sworn a farmer in a tattered hat spit a plug of tobacco in his direction. Still, I felt much better about our prospects knowing he lived with this genteel, kind lady.

The woman continued with a delicate Southern drawl, still speaking only to Lilah. "I'm Miss Maeve Donovan. I wrote to Miss Pimsler when we heard the train was coming to Wheeler, to ask for a girl of about your age. She said a smart young lady with strawberry-blond hair named Lilah would be coming. From the way she described you, I knew you'd be just right." Miss Maeve's nearly colorless eyes never wavered from my sister as she spoke. "Everything is arranged. I'm here to take you home."

A slight dizziness came over me. For a hectic moment, I feared Miss Maeve intended to take Lilah and leave me behind. But no, Miss Pimsler knew our situation. She'd never allow such a thing. I was tired and overly anxious, sensing trouble where there was none.

Lifting my chin, I reached for a serenity I didn't feel. "A pleasure to meet you, Miss Maeve. I'm Verity, Lilah's sister."

The woman truly looked at me for the first time. I heard her sharp intake of breath as I adjusted my hat, wiping the back of my hand over my damp forehead. I must have looked a sight.

Embarrassment darkened my cheeks. "I hope you'll forgive the state we're in. Once we're settled, we'll both perk up." I repositioned the carpetbag on my shoulder. "Is it far to your house?"

Miss Maeve pressed her rosebud lips together and motioned to someone. Following her line of sight, I spied Miss Pimsler bustling onto the platform, smiling with horrible cheerfulness. "I'm sorry to keep you all waiting. I've been helping another family. There's always so much to do. . . . Verity, would you join me, please? I'd like a word."

Unease slithered over my skin. We moved a few paces away, but I kept an eye on Lilah, who carried on a bashful conversation with Miss Maeve.

Miss Pimsler placed a hand on my shoulder. "I would've liked to prepare you both, but the board of directors asks us to wait until a family is ready to take custody of the child before we explain." She took a bracing breath. "Please understand, this is the policy of the Children's Benevolence Society, and we stand by our rules. Like all new parents, Miss Maeve is approved to adopt *one* child."

I felt myself sliding toward a precipice, clutching for anything to stop the descent. Miss Pimsler fixed me with a determined stare. At her next words, I plummeted over the edge. "She's taking Lilah. And you won't be going with them."

2

I rocked back on my heels, the words slamming into me like a physical blow. They couldn't take Lilah from me. It was impossible. From the tumult of protests and arguments in my mind, a single question surfaced. "Why?"

"It's for the best." Miss Pimsler spoke each syllable with precision. "Adding only one child is less of a burden to new parents, both financially and emotionally. And starting with a clean slate is better for the children. No reminders of the past, you see." She nodded, the feathers on her ridiculous hat trembling. "Now, if there had been relatives willing to take you both, that might be different, but since there were none—"

"Take us back to New York," I demanded. Blood pulsed loud and wild in my ears. "I can take care of us. I always have." Curious eyes turned in our direction. "You have no right to separate us!"

"Mr. Lybrand and Miss Donovan agreed with the policy, as did all parents who applied to take in a child," Miss Pimsler said. "We typically don't send siblings on the same train, but in your case . . . well, after all you've been through, we made an exception. Be grateful for this opportunity, Verity. Some people have a difficult time welcoming strangers, children or not. Finding homes, even separate ones, is a blessing indeed."

I turned to Miss Maeve, who looked at me with sorrowful eyes. "Please, Miss Maeve. I can work to earn our keep. I'll do anything. I'll sleep in the stable if there isn't room in the house. Speak with your uncle." I looked around wildly for Mr. Lybrand. "Or let me talk to him."

Miss Maeve backed away, looking unsettled by my agitation. She twisted her hands miserably. "Verity, I'm so sorry. I tried—"

"Then try harder!" I shouted, grabbing the woman's sleeve. Beside us, Lilah's face was pale under her freckles. Miss Maeve gasped, trying to pull away, but I held my ground.

A heavy hand clamped down on my shoulder. I lashed out, throwing an elbow without stopping to see who I might hit. The blow landed against something hard and sharp-edged. Whirling, I found myself facing a barrel-chested man with dark eyes.

He straightened the badge pinned to his chest. "That's enough." He set his feet with a jangle of spurs. "I'm Sheriff Loftis, head of the adoption committee. If you can't behave yourself, young lady, I'll have you back on that train and shipped off in two shakes." His threat sent a wash of cold through my chest.

Lilah shook her head. "I don't want you to leave me, Very." Her voice hitched when she spoke.

Miss Maeve bent to Lilah's eye level. "Shhhh. . . . Don't fret. I'd be upset too, if I were in your place. But you'll be happy at our home. I promise. And Verity can come visit us."

As Miss Maeve comforted my sister, Sheriff Loftis leaned close, his breath smelling of snuff tobacco. "Miss Maeve's kind to offer visits with your sister, but they won't be allowed if you prove to be a troublemaker. This town isn't a place for those who can't follow the law and act respectable."

Lilah's eyes shone with unshed tears. I swallowed my own swelling panic, shooting a glance at the dwindling crowd of locals who might take me in. If I didn't wrangle my emotions, I could easily find myself kept from seeing my sister. Or worse, living in another state altogether.

I plastered on a smile. "Miss Maeve will take good care of you; I just know it." Miss Maeve shot me a grateful look. Being separated from Lilah shook me to the core, but in truth, I had no reason to believe she wouldn't be looked after. "And I'll see you soon."

Lilah's chin wobbled, just a little. At last she nodded, looking as stunned as I felt. Miss Maeve rubbed her back, easing her gently away from me. "You let us know where you're staying, Verity. We'll arrange a visit as soon as possible."

The grumble of an engine announced Mr. Lybrand's return. His dark green Model F Ford barely registered in my panicked mind as he pulled to a stop nearby. Miss Pimsler was talking at me now. ". . . and from what I've gathered, Miss Maeve Donovan is tremendously well liked. She's the teacher at the local school, you know. Lilah is a lucky girl. . . ."

Everything sounded muffled and distant. I stared at Lilah, tucked neatly between the smartly dressed Mr. Lybrand and the pristine beauty of Miss Maeve on the car's shiny leather seat. She looked like the happy ending to a sad story, the fortunate child rescued by wealthy benefactors.

Lilah waved a hesitant goodbye over her shoulder. I lifted my hand in reply, dazed, as a cloud of dust covered their departure. And in one fell swoop, I was utterly alone.

Sheriff Loftis watched the car disappear, then marched away, spurs jingling. Miss Pimsler's attention was immediately taken by a family asking questions about their new little boy. I snatched the opportunity and slipped away. Something she'd said had given me an idea.

My trunk sat forlorn on the dusty ground near the front of the church. I flung the lid open, pausing at the sight of pages covered with Lilah's looping cursive.

With no blank sheets left, I tore the flyleaf from a biology text. Damaging Papa's book felt almost sacrilegious, but it couldn't be helped. Using Lilah's pen, I dashed off a letter to our aunt Susan.

After folding another flyleaf to form a makeshift envelope, I gathered my few remaining coins for postage and hurried across the square to a post office I'd spied earlier. I borrowed some sealing wax from the postmaster and sent the letter off with a silent prayer. "Please let this work," I breathed.

Stepping back out onto the awning-covered sidewalk, I paused to let a buggy driven by Sheriff Loftis pass. A dark-haired girl of about my age rode beside him. The sheriff ignored me, but the girl gave a covert wave. I nodded my acknowledgment and crossed back to the churchyard, where Miss Pimsler was fluttering about.

She turned a mildly annoyed gaze my way. "Where have you been, Verity? There aren't many families left who haven't made a choice, and it's harder finding people to take the older children." She pursed her lips. "Especially those who don't try to make themselves agreeable."

"In that case, you'll have to excuse me." I gave a slight curtsy. "I need to mingle with the good people of Wheeler and find someone in the market for a disagreeable girl."

I made my way back to the court square, looking for any adults holding adoption paperwork who didn't already have an orphan-train passenger by their side.

A skinny woman with well-worn furrows on her forehead and a mountainous man sporting a white push-broom mustache appeared to be the only remaining couple. The woman picked a stray bit of hay from the man's overall strap as she spoke in an anxious voice. I moved closer, catching fragments of her words. ". . . supposed to have been older ones. The paper said all ages, girls and boys. If we'd seen that list with their names and ages before we came to town, we could've saved the trip."

I paused a few feet away from the pair and cleared my throat. The woman turned, crossing her arms. "Do you need somethin'?" She was a direct person, then. I could deal with direct.

"It looks like I'm the runt of the litter and nobody wanted to take me home." The woman set her lips in a grim line. "I'm Verity Pruitt, and I need a place to stay."

"Hettie Weatherington," she said. "And this is my husband, Big Tom."

A wordless exchange passed between them, and then the giant man said in a slow, deep voice, "We could always hire a hand from the next county over." The final few carriages rolled away, leaving me standing before my last hope, a couple who didn't seem to want me.

"No, please." I moved closer, tilted my head up to look the towering farmer in the eye. His shaggy gray brows lifted in surprise. "Whatever you need help with, I can do it, if you'll only give me a chance." I'd manage to spin straw into gold if it meant holding on to my last opportunity for staying near Lilah.

Hettie shot a glance at Big Tom. "What do you think?"

He raised one shoulder in a slow shrug. "I reckon it can't hurt to give her a try." He stretched the *a* in *can't* so that it rhymed with *saint.*

"You strike me as a girl with a lot of want-to." Hettie tightened the knot of graying hair at her nape, then thrust a sinewy hand in my direction. I tried not to wince at her grip. Hettie was short and thin, but strong.

"We'll do this as an indenture, on a trial basis, mind you," she said. "After a month, if you're doing well, you'll start earning a wage. It won't be as much as a hired hand would make, but it'll be something more than you've got now."

And enough, I hoped, to get back home when the time came. "Thank you. You won't regret it."

Hettie nodded, looking dubious. "Go on and tell that woman we're taking her," she said to her husband. Big Tom's mustache slid up with a hidden smile as he ambled away to do his wife's bidding.

When he returned a moment later, Miss Pimsler scooted along in his wake like a tugboat after a steamer. "I believe you'll find farm life suits you far better than you expect, Verity," Miss Pimsler said, rubbing a hand over tired eyes. "Hard work and fresh air are wonderfully invigorating." She looked suddenly weary, as if worn out by her own relentless optimism.

Big Tom proffered the indenture papers. We'd been told older children might be indentured rather than adopted, since we were close to adulthood and, theoretically, independence. If only the Children's Benevolence Society had waited a few more months, until I was of age, Lilah could've stayed with me and none of this upheaval would've been necessary. I stooped to rest the papers on the trunk that held the remnants of my former life, then crossed the *t*'s in my last name with a violent slash before handing the documents back to Miss Pimsler.

Despite my resentment toward the woman, a part of me understood she was doing what she believed was best. She just happened to be wrong. "Goodbye, Miss Pimsler. Have a safe trip back to New York."

"I'll see you and all the others when I return for a welfare check in the fall," she said, her face unexpectedly somber. "Verity, give this new start the chance it deserves. Try to bloom where you're planted."

I turned to follow the Weatheringtons, thinking how foolish it would be to put down roots in a place I'd be leaving soon.

My trunk left shallow trails in the dusty ground as I dragged it to Big Tom's buckboard. I heaved it in, hauled myself up, and leaned against the splintery wood of the side rails. Fatigue crashed over me. I yawned and didn't bother to cover my mouth. If Big Tom or Hettie cared to examine my molars to see if their new workhorse was a good one, now was their chance.

When Big Tom resumed his seat and the wagon was again in motion, Hettie gave me a bundled napkin and a Mason jar of water. "Figured you'd be hungry." She'd packed a slab of salt meat and a thick slice of fresh bread for the boy she'd expected to bring home. I wished Lilah were here to share it. Had she eaten yet? I chewed, forcing my eyes to stay open, and watched the tiny town of Wheeler fade until it was swallowed by the endless sky.

We followed a dirt road that was little more than wagon-wheel ruts, heading toward the woods I'd noticed earlier. But when the path drew within shouting distance of the tree line, it abruptly broke off, running parallel to the woods in both directions. In my weary state, I wondered why the road ringed the little forest instead of passing straight through. Perhaps everyone here was so unhurried, the circuitous route hardly mattered.

The ride from town took half an hour with the cart horse's leisurely pace. We reached the Weatheringtons' farm as twilight drifted down. Fireflies hovered low over the grass, their greenish-yellow glow winking off and on.

Big Tom stopped the buggy in front of a faded white two-story farmhouse. My legs had gone to sleep during the ride and I stumbled as I followed Hettie across the parched front yard.

"Your room is in the attic," she said, pushing open the squealing screen door. I mumbled my thanks, following her up a set of creaky stairs into a room with a sloped ceiling. She handed me a lit candle and bid me good night. "Get some rest, girl," Hettie said, her no-nonsense voice edging toward gentleness. "You look dead on your feet."

I could only manage a nod in reply as she left. Concern for Lilah took up all my remaining energy. Would the stern Mr. Lybrand be harsh with her? Would Miss Maeve have the courage to defend Lilah if her uncle was unkind?

But even my worries couldn't survive the siphoning fatigue, and I fell into bed. Consciousness blinked out like the lights of the fireflies in the field.

3

An agonized noise shredded the air. I sat bolt upright in the dark bedroom, adrenaline surging through my limbs.

For a moment, I didn't know where I was. Then the last few days came back in a rush: I was in Arkansas, on a farm, where I was supposed to be the new hired help. And based on the thump of feet hurrying up the stairs to my attic room, I feared I was about to receive a sudden initiation into my new job.

Hettie barreled in as I scrambled out of bed. She frowned at the candle stump still guttering feebly on the table at my bedside. I'd fallen asleep without putting it out.

"We've got a mama cow having trouble." Hettie tossed a bundle on the foot of the bed. "Here's work clothes and boots. Get on out to the barn, quick as you can," she said before rushing out.

I buttoned the short-sleeved work dress, tugged on the too-big boots, and clattered down the stairs with nerves humming. The screen door gave an indignant creak when I pushed it open. Shoulders back, I headed out across the dew-spangled lawn.

A heavy wash of stars covered the sky, pinpricks of light

against the inky blue-black. In the dim predawn, a huge barn loomed at the edge of the yard. The bellowing sound rolling from the open doors gave the impression that the building itself was screaming.

I hesitated in the doorway. The cavernous space was full of the scent of manure and the rusty tang of blood. Big Tom crouched in the center of the dirt floor beside a massive black animal. His hands moved expertly over the creature's distended abdomen. A lantern hung from a peg on the far wall, its feeble light shining on the cow's heaving side. I'd seen cows before, but only as sides of beef. This was my first encounter with the living, breathing article.

Another earsplitting bellow vibrated through the humid air. I felt my own eyes go wide when I saw two tiny hooves protruding from the cow's body.

Hettie emerged from a stall to the right, a thick coil of rope slung over her shoulder. She wobbled a bit under the weight before flinging it down beside her husband and motioning me over.

"It's full breech. We'll have to pull it," Big Tom said, securing a length of rope around the spindly legs poking out from the mother. Hettie stepped into place behind him. My breaths came quick and fluttery as I took up the rear. Big Tom gave a nod, and we pulled.

The cow groaned, and a bit more of the calf's legs appeared. Another tug brought the end of a tail into view. But on the next try, nothing happened. Big Tom's face went red with strain. "Can you pull any harder?" Hettie looked over her shoulder at me, and I saw real worry in her lined face.

"I'm trying," I grunted.

The sound of running feet carried over the cow's labored panting. From the corner of my eye, I caught a blur of motion just before someone pressed in close behind me. "Sorry I'm late, Aunt Het." The voice was deep, with a molasses-thick drawl.

"Where have you been?" Hettie sounded relieved in spite of herself. "I came to fetch you, but you weren't in the loft."

I shifted enough to see a tall boy with hair the color of straw wrapping the rope firmly around his hands. "I've got places to go and people to see," he said breezily. "Pull on three? One . . . two . . ." The "three" was cut short as we all strained in unison.

With startling speed, the calf slipped to the ground in a wet tangle of limbs. The exhausted mother stretched her neck out on the dirt floor with a soft lowing sound. When her calf bawled in reply, I dropped the rope and released a long-held breath.

The blond boy took down the lantern and knelt beside Big Tom. His brown britches were patched at the knees, but clean. A cotton shirt worn thin from countless washings hung open at the collar, showing a wide swath of suntanned skin.

"Let's see what we have here," he said, untying the rope from the calf's legs and carefully settling the ungainly, bloody newborn on its feet. Grabbing an empty feed sack from the ground, he murmured softly to the calf as he wiped it clean. His broad hands moved over the animal's reddish hair with practiced, gentle strokes. "You're a fine young fellow, aren't you?" He glanced at the mother cow, his eyes soft with concern. "We'll get your mama up and about in no time. Y'all will both be all right." A flutter of surprise lofted through my chest. I hadn't expected such tenderness on the farm.

The boy looked up at me, his light brows raised. "Are you the new hand come to help out?"

A little knot of defeat formed in the pit of my stomach. Big Tom and Hettie needed a worker who could make a real contribution. Until this boy arrived, my help hadn't been enough.

I had to improve. It was my only chance of staying and being near my sister.

I nodded in reply to the boy's question. His eyes locked on mine. "Well now, you're not exactly what I was expecting."

I watched Big Tom and Hettie go, noting the anxious tones of their hushed conversation. "I'd say that's the majority opinion here."

"I'm Abel Atchley. I'd offer to shake, but . . ." He lifted a hand, sticky with blood and Lord knew what else.

I accepted the challenge, gripping his hand tight and pumping it three times for good measure. "Verity Pruitt. Pleased to meet you." A smile touched his lips.

My skirt puffed out as I sank down next to him. The calf gave a pitiful little bleat and sprawled back onto the hay, knobby knees jutting at odd angles.

"Don't worry about helping out here," Abel said. "You can head on back to the house."

I thought I caught a playfulness in his eyes, a look I'd seen in everyone who smirked at my intentions of becoming a physician. "Would you say that if I were the boy you'd been expecting?" I asked sharply. "I'll be just as helpful as you, given time and practice."

"I was just trying to be considerate because you're new, not because you're a girl." He pulled a handkerchief from his back pocket, wiping his hands as he stood. Abel took in my ragged appearance and fidgety hands. "If you get this worked up over every little thing, you're going to run yourself crazy."

The remark was acid on a wound. I pulled myself to my full height, annoyed to still have to look up at him. He couldn't know my father was a madman, but my voice still came out low and dangerous, a snake hidden in the grass. "It's anything but considerate to poke fun at a person's sanity," I said.

"Are all Yankees this touchy?" Abel tilted his head, appraising me. "I meant it for a joke, that's all. Look, I stand by my offer, whether you like it or not. I'll get the mama and her little one situated by myself."

"I don't want your pity. And please don't talk down to me." My voice shook, like it always did when I was angry. Blowing out a hot sigh, I looked around the barn, suddenly furious that this was my new life. I set my face in stone. "I'm here to work, not to be coddled."

Abel's expression darkened. "Fine. I apologize for being friendly. I won't make that mistake again."

I nodded. "I'll earn my keep as long as I'm stuck in this place."

"'This place'?" Under a day's growth of blond stubble, Abel's cheeks reddened. "I see now. You think you're too good to live here."

"I most certainly don't think that," I retorted. Abel snorted in reply. "And don't make that noise like . . . like . . . some disgruntled horse."

"I can read your opinion of Wheeler all over your face, Miss Pruitt." He paused, frowning. "And yes, I can read. We're not all illiterate."

"If you're feeling inferior, that's not my doing. I certainly don't consider myself better than you, or anyone else." A half-truth, at best. My stomach twisted with shame, but I held my ground. I'd had bigger plans for myself than life as an indentured orphan, working on a farm, and I'd not apologize for that.

We faced each other, arms crossed and scowling, until the bawling of the calf diverted Abel's attention. He stooped to rub behind its ear again, then pointed to an empty bucket. "All right then. Haul some water in for the cow and calf while I get them into a stall."

I returned with my dress splashed from the knees down. My arm had gone rubbery with fatigue, and the bucket's metal handle left a bloody scrape across my tender palm. I set the water down with a slosh. Abel doffed an imaginary hat, sweeping into a facetious bow. "Much obliged." I gave a curt nod and marched out of the barn.

Sunrise broke over the tops of the distant trees, spreading a soft blush up and out from the horizon. A bank of low clouds trapped the glow and cast it back over the fields. I wondered if Lilah was awake to see this first dawn in our unexpected new lives. I turned a slow circle, taking in my surroundings for the first time.

The yard around the house was patchy, more dust than grass, with barns and sheds of all sizes cropping up like mushrooms across the property. To the east, a ring of spindly apple trees made a scant orchard near a rutted gravel road. Beyond, a barren field of wildflower-dotted grass divided the Weatherington land from the woods I'd noticed last night.

There were no other houses in sight. If I wanted to, I could easily pretend the farm was the only inhabited place on earth. Apart from the watchful inspection of a few goats in a nearby pen, I was alone.

I found I didn't like it in the least.

4

After a quick wash at the outdoor pump, I crossed the back porch into the kitchen.

A long table circled by three chairs sat elbow to elbow alongside a large porcelain sink and a hulking cookstove. Ducking under the cast-iron skillets hanging from a rack overhead, I made my way past the table, noting a mismatched stool drawn up next to one of the three straight-backed chairs. That would be mine, I supposed.

Hettie pushed through the screen door, a basket of eggs in the crook of her elbow. She stopped when she saw me, and I realized we were both unsure of what to say.

"I'm sorry for not being much use this morning," I began. "Anyone who wants to be a doctor can handle a little blood, but I'm afraid my muscles aren't as stout as my nerves."

Hettie took in the doctor remark with a cocked eyebrow, then considered for a moment. "Don't be too hard on yourself," she said at last, in what I was learning was her usual brisk manner. "You'll do better next time."

I mustered a smile. "I hope so."

Hettie finished cooking while I set the table. Abel strode in, a pail full of frothy milk in hand. He set it by the icebox without so much as a glance in my direction, then moved to the stove, swooping in for a piece of bacon. "Quit!" Hettie said, giving his hand a sharp swat. Abel dropped into his chair with a smirk. As Hettie pulled back, I noticed a cord of thin leather tied around her wrist. It ran through two stones, one a smooth, pale blue-gray, the other brown and knobby. Neither looked like my idea of a pretty accessory, but I asked about them in the spirit of making conversation.

"Where did you get your bracelet?"

"My charms?" Hettie's rough fingers strayed to the little stones. "Had them since I was a girl. Blue river rock for luck, and a bladder stone from a deer, to fend off sickness."

Hettie seemed like such a levelheaded person. I hadn't expected her to fall prey to superstition. "Do they work?" I asked, knowing full well they did not.

Hettie shrugged a scrawny shoulder. "Maybe they do, maybe they don't. But they can't harm nothing, the way I see it." Deciding that flights of fancy were true could indeed cause harm, as I well knew from my father's experience.

I pulled up my wobbly stool just as Big Tom lumbered in to settle at the head of the table. Hettie took her place at the far end. When they bowed their heads, I followed suit. There was an unexpected mix of folklore and faith in this place.

Big Tom's prayer was brief. "Lord, bless this meal to the nourishment of our bodies and our bodies to your service. And if you see fit, send some rain. Amen."

Hettie and Abel echoed his "amen." By the time mine followed, a beat too late, Hettie was already handing around a plate of fluffy biscuits. I grabbed one and reached for a second to pass to Lilah. My hand hung in the air for an awkward moment as I remembered that, for the first time in years, I didn't have another mouth to feed.

"My sister, Lilah, was taken in by Miss Maeve Donovan. Do you think she'll be good to her?" I asked, surprising myself with the question.

Big Tom looked up from his plate, nodding slowly. "If anybody was ever born to be a mama, I reckon it's Miss Maeve."

Relief seeped through my sadness. At least Lilah would have someone competent to care for her until I could reclaim her.

"I about dropped dead from shock when I heard old Lybrand was letting her take in a little one," Hettie went on. "Nicest thing he ever did, to be sure."

"They got a fine place to raise a child," Big Tom noted. "They live on the edge of the woods, about two miles from here. Nice, big house. Old Lybrand's got plenty of money."

Hettie's lips thinned. "I reckon we'd all live high on the hog if we were crooked as Mr. Lybrand. And Heaven knows he treats Miss Maeve bad."

"What do you mean by that?" My fingers tightened around my napkin, my momentary relief dissipating. "Is Lilah in danger?"

"Nothing like that. I only meant how old Lybrand keeps Miss Maeve on a short leash. And he holds the mortgages on three-quarters of the county, but he makes that poor girl work for a living," Hettie said, indignant.

I set my coffee cup in its saucer with a clink. "Miss Maeve may enjoy teaching. Perhaps she chooses to work because she finds it fulfilling?"

"Maybe," Hettie conceded, "but the point of the matter is he won't let her get married. She's had plenty of suitors, make no mistake, and he's run them all off. Every blessed one."

"The word around town is her uncle threatened to disinherit her if she ever married," Abel put in. In the clear, early light, his eyes were the same deep blue as the morning glory flowers tangling the fencerows around the farm. "Mr. Lybrand is what newspapers like to call a 'robber baron.' Makes it sound dramatic, almost piratical." I felt my mouth quirk in spite of myself at his choice of words. "But he's really just a sour old man from somewhere out east who made lots of money in the railroad business. And he owns a passel of banks. He travels some, but never takes Miss Maeve anywhere."

"Lybrand got the best deal of his life when Miss Maeve came to live with him after her folks died," Hettie said. "She cooks and cleans and keeps him company. Nobody else in their right mind would spend more than five minutes around the man. Stands to reason he wouldn't want her to leave."

"I'd like to go visit my sister." I needed to see for myself that Mr. Lybrand wasn't mistreating Lilah. "There's no need to spare a horse for me. I'm used to walking everywhere I go."

Hettie's face darkened, but I hurried on. "I'm not asking for time away from our work. If you lend me a lantern, I could walk over in the evening, after we're done for the day. I'm not bothered by the dark."

Big Tom and Hettie exchanged a troubled looked. "Best to avoid the woods," Big Tom rumbled.

Hurriedly, Hettie added, "I was going to send Abel to fetch some things in town tomorrow, but if you want to go, that'll be fine. You can stop by the schoolhouse and see your sister." Her smile was rusty from disuse, but genuine. "But not all day long, mind," she said, gathering the dishes. "We have too much to do for you to tarry overlong."

"Yes, ma'am," I agreed as I stood to help her wash up.

Big Tom left, his huge boots thudding on the wooden floor.

Abel followed him, casting one quick look over his shoulder to where I stood at the sink. I diligently pretended not to notice.

As I dried the last plate, Hettie disappeared into a tiny closet and returned holding a wilted straw hat. "So you won't blister," she said.

I put the thing on, the smell of sweat and hay drifting around my face. "Where are we going?"

"Cornfield, and we best get moving," Hettie said. "The men took the wagon on down to the fields already. They'll be waiting for us."

Donning her own hat, she swept open the back door, only to stop in midstride and look downward. I moved closer to peer over her shoulder.

Glossy green branches dotted with orange berries lay in a neat line across the porch, just outside the threshold. Hettie stepped carefully over them, frowning. When I followed, my hat brushed something hanging from the lintel. I looked up to find a bundle of dried flowers, tied with twine, dangling petals-down. Curious, I reached for one.

"Leave them," Hettie said quickly, eyes darting over the yard.

"What are they?"

"Summer's bride and buckthorn," she said, moving briskly across the porch and down the steps. "They're for protection. From evil spirits, curses, things like that."

"Where did they come from?" I asked.

"Big Tom left them, I'd venture." A worried squint deepened the lines around her eyes. I doubted she believed her own words. "Best let them be."

I dropped the matter and surveyed the sweeping landscape. It wasn't my longed-for home, but no one could deny the peacefulness of this remote place. Why did Hettie think dark forces would come to call here?

I tromped after her in my borrowed boots. Hettie's feet were bigger than mine, and the wad of newspapers stuffed into the toes made for uncomfortable going. We trudged in silence, our shadows marching beside us, thin black slivers on the dew-covered ground. So often, I'd wished Lilah would stop her relentless chatter. But in the company of the quiet Hettie, I missed my baby sister more than ever.

We walked through a pasture along a sunbaked track to the edge of a cornfield. The once-vibrant stalks, now gone brittle in the sun, rasped in a faint breeze. The silks straggling out from the withered husks were brown and crumpled like the legs of a crushed spider. "The heat got to the crop before we could harvest it all for eating," Hettie said. "But we can still use the dry ears. Big Tom will put some up to feed the stock this winter, and we'll grind the rest into cornmeal for cooking."

Big Tom guided a wagon pulled by a tall-eared mule several yards out into the corn while Hettie and I followed through strips of shadow. With care, Big Tom lowered his hefty form down between two rows of corn and began expertly breaking off the ears, tossing them over the high wooden sides of the wagon. I reached up to grasp one. My hands wrapped around the papery husk just as a long, dry leaf sliced the inside of my bare forearm. With a hiss of pain, I clamped a hand over the thin cut.

"You all right?" Abel climbed down from the wagon. "Those leaves are called blades for a reason. They're awfully sharp after they've dried out."

I jerked my sleeve down over the cut. "It's nothing," I said.

Abel stooped to gather the corn felled by the passing of the wagon.

"You can help me," Hettie said, moving to the opposite side from where Big Tom had disappeared amid the towering corn.

She bent one of the tall stalks and grabbed an ear. Her strong hands gave a quick twist, and it broke away from the stalk with a violent crack. "The down row's awful hard on the back." She gestured to where Abel bent over his work, breaking ears from stalks that had been crushed to the ground. "Especially when you ain't used to it."

Abel straightened, his arms loaded with corn, to give me a pointed look as he strode by.

"I'll help with the down row," I said.

Abel dropped his harvest into the wagon, then turned to face me. "Your muscles will be screaming in ten minutes flat," he said. "You sure you want to do this?" Boots crunching over the fallen stalks, he went back to his work.

I slid in shoulder-to-shoulder next to him. "I'm sure."

Abel's estimate had been generous. My back and shoulders tightened to furious, offended knots within five minutes, and stayed that way for the rest of our time in the field. The sun beat down, burning my back through the flimsy fabric of my dress as I worked. Sweat stung my eyes, slipping down my face to wet my cracked lips. I began to relish the short moments when the wagon moved to a new spot, because following it gave me an excuse to straighten up for a few minutes.

When at last Big Tom surveyed the field and announced it picked clean, I nearly buckled with relief. "Not bad for your first time," he said kindly. I felt sure that was a soothing lie. Abel's deft hands had stripped three-quarters of the ears we'd gathered in the down rows. Big Tom slid a canteen from around his neck and handed it to me. "There's a path to the spring just over that rise there," he said, pointing. "Why don't you fill this up?"

I found the little creek and filled the container with clear water. The first swallow lifted my drooping spirits. By now, it was nearly time to help Hettie with dinner. This was all foreign and uncomfortable, but there was no denying that the grueling day had started with excellent food, and I had hopes all the farm fare would be as delicious. My steps quickened, as if I could hurry the day along by moving through it faster.

I rounded a bend in the path, dried grass crunching under my boots. At the sound of Hettie's angry voice, I paused.

"That's where you were this morning when I found your bed empty?"

No, not angry. She was worried.

I ducked behind a pink-flowered dogwood and took in the tense scene. Big Tom had turned a stormy expression on Abel, who leaned against the wagon, staring down at the brittle earth. Hettie paced before him. "For pity's sake, Abel, why didn't you tell us before? We're family."

"I wanted to." Abel's voice cut over hers, high and strained. He rubbed at the back of his neck. "But this isn't y'all's burden to bear."

Big Tom spoke up. "I know you feel obligated to help, but there's a better way to go about it." He exhaled heavily, as if what he was about to say wearied him to the bone. "When's the baby coming?"

I felt my eyebrows climb. I swiped away a rivulet of sweat from my forehead.

"Soon. She keeps talking about marriage, but that's not going to happen." The derision in Abel's voice sent a streak of anger skittering through my stomach. "We need money, but I didn't want you two to feel bound to pitch in, so we kept it quiet as long as we could."

"I bet your mama is fit to be tied," Hettie said. "Guess this explains why she's been scarce lately. Didn't want me to suspicion something was wrong." Even the mention of his mother's distress didn't soften Abel's stony glare.

I'd heard enough. I stepped back onto the trail and made my approach with loud, deliberate footfalls. When the three turned my way, I gave the canteen a little shake. "Anyone thirsty?" I tried to assume the guileless look of a person who had certainly *not* been eavesdropping a minute before.

Big Tom took the water from my hand without drinking it and climbed into the wagon. "Time to head on back." Hettie joined him on the bench seat. Abel perched on the edge of the tall side panels, staring darkly at the field, lips pressed tight.

I chose a lumpy seat on the corn in the wagon's bed. I couldn't help sliding a look at Abel. To my surprise, Hettie swiveled to squeeze his shoulder. "We'll get through this rough patch," she said quietly.

I scraped dirt from beneath my fingernails, trying to decide if it was admirable or not that family love allowed them to sympathize with Abel when he was so clearly in the wrong. The girl carrying his child, the one he refused to marry, would need that kindness as she faced an uncertain future. Blood was thicker than water, they said.

Perhaps I was a little jealous of Abel.

I knew it was no fault of their own, but the people I was meant to lean on in times of trouble were nowhere to be found.

She walked for hours, over fields and valleys gone blank with snow. A jagged wind sliced through her thin nightgown, whipping her auburn hair into a noose around her neck. Bare toes, corpse-pale with creeping frostbite, crunched through a brittle crust of snow. All day she saw nothing but glittering white, felt nothing but black and broken loss.

The snow had stopped at some point. She'd blinked crystalline flakes from her lashes, uncaring, and walked on to nowhere. Under a sky bruised purple with dusk, she sank to her knees, ready to sleep and wake no more. The relief was immeasurable.

Then the woods called her. She felt a tug behind her crippled heart, a marrow-deep summons that pulled her attention to the copse of dark trees. Certainty settled over her. Perfect oblivion waited in the woods.

She forced herself up, stumbling on until she crossed into the forest.

Bare branches crooked black fingers to the sky, calling the night down. She moved in a dreamlike trance through the silent trees, until at last she found what had beckoned her.

At the heart of the woods, a circle of stones crouched in a clearing, toad-gray and splotched with peeling moss.

She trailed her fingers along the cold rock and looked into its shining black eye. A feeling of rightness swept over her like a warm sigh.

Gripping the crumbling edge, she pulled herself up onto the knee-high lip of rock. Blood traced its way down her leg, dropping onto the stone in a shocking red reminder of what had sent her into the storm.

She closed her eyes and thought of the baby girl. And of him. Then she stepped out into the welcoming void.

5

After we left the cornfield, I spent the remains of the day hoeing the vegetable garden and digging potatoes. "She's give plumb out," Big Tom muttered to Hettie when I at last made my slow way upstairs to the stifling attic. I collapsed into bed, a wispy concern for Lilah drifting by as sleep dragged me under.

Sometime during the night, every muscle in my body joined a union to protest the unfair labor conditions foisted upon them. I hobbled down to breakfast the next morning, the sorest I'd ever been. Wincing my way onto my seat, I glanced at Abel's empty chair.

"Abel had some family matters to attend to," Hettie said, placing a skillet of sizzling fried potatoes before me.

I stuffed my mouth with a steaming forkful. They tasted like bacon grease, an ingredient in strong contention for the prize of the most wonderful thing on the planet. "I hope nothing too serious," I said carefully.

"Time will tell, I suppose." Hettie fiddled with her apron strings, then rallied to do what she did best: dole out work. "I've got your day's chores lined out." She reeled off a list that made my aching back want to riot in advance.

"After we've mended the east fence, you can run into town," Hettie said. "There's a shipment of flour and salt in at the dry-goods store. Get me ten pounds each. Then you can go to the schoolhouse and see your sister, long as it's fine with Miss Maeve."

I forgot my aches and pains in a split second. "Thank you, Hettie." The emotion in my voice surprised me. I trailed off, closing my eyes for a moment to trap the welling tears.

Hettie gave a curt nod. I suspected she was as unused to accepting gratitude as I was to expressing it. "It'll be faster if you ride Lady May. She's real gentle and she knows the way." She frowned, adding, "Just make sure you don't leave the road, hear?"

I agreed, wondering why she'd felt the warning necessary.

I helped mend the barbed-wire fence and, looking like I'd just wrestled a wildcat and lost, followed Big Tom and Hettie to the barn.

I rubbed at my scratched arms and warily eyed the palomino mare Big Tom saddled for me.

At home, I'd walked almost everywhere. The last time I'd been this close to a horse was at a friend's sixth-birthday party, when a pony repaid my attempt to pat its nose by sneezing in my face. The experience had been both damp and startling, and I'd distrusted the entire equine species ever since. With a boost from Big Tom, I managed a shaky sidesaddle position. My perch atop Lady May's broad back seemed a shocking distance from the ground. I shouted a goodbye, too afraid to release my death grip on the reins for a farewell wave as I left the farm behind.

After a mile or so, I started to relax. Lady May kept her gentle, steady pace. A soft breeze stirred the sea of grass beside our path, bowing the blades like ocean waves. Birdsong floated across the open fields in high, happy trills. Even the warm, musky scent of the horse wasn't exactly unpleasant as we clopped along the gravel road that ran around the woods.

My gaze skimmed over the dense trees. The trunks, straight and close together, were very nearly black. I thought of the bars that lined the windows of my father's room at the asylum, and despite the growing heat, I felt a chill crawl down my spine. I was almost thankful for the belligerent sun.

Once in Wheeler, I tied Lady May to a hitching post and followed the directions Hettie had given to the Dry Goods and General Mercantile.

A bell above the door jingled as I entered. I stepped around a large barrel sprouting a bundle of brooms for sale, bristles up. Shiny brass cookware hung from the ceilings in neat rows, and the biting aroma of snuff mixed with the sweet, savory smell of gingersnaps. Signs on the rough plank walls advertised coal oil and Navy Star plug tobacco. Rows of tonics and bitters perched on a shelf under a poster proclaiming the virtues of quinine for curing the chills.

"Oh, hello." The clear, sweet voice drifted from the back of the store. I spotted a young woman dusting the glass-topped counter and recognized her as the girl who'd waved at me from the sheriff's buggy. Seeing her now without a hat, I realized she had astonishing hair. Shiny and black, it rose from her forehead toward high Heaven before sweeping back in a carefully rounded pouf. I schooled my face to neutral blankness a split second too late.

Her hand went to her coiffure. "Do you like it? Mama said rats are all the rage now. But I expect you know all about that, being from a big city."

I'd known my fair share of rats in New York. For a short time, Lilah and I had stayed in a tiny apartment on Mulberry

Street that had an entire colony living in the walls. I had to keep the cutlery closed tight in a tobacco tin if I didn't want to find droppings on the forks each morning. "Um . . . I . . ."

"I don't know why they're called rats either," the girl said with a laugh, misinterpreting my hesitation. "I think 'hairpiece' would do just fine, but I suppose that sounds like a man's toupee." She wrinkled her nose. "Still better than calling it a rat, if you ask me."

"Yes!" I half shouted the word, relieved to be at grips with the conversation. "Yes, I'd say so. And you look very nice," I added. It was true, in spite of the over-the-top hair. Her brown eyes sparkled and the apples of her cheeks shone pink, but not in the blotchy way mine surely did after a ride in the heat.

"I can show you how to make one, if you want. All it takes is old hair from your brush rolled into a little bundle." While I didn't fancy a style that made low doorways potential hazards, her offer was kind.

"It probably wouldn't work for me. My hair has a stubborn, hateful mind of its own," I said.

She tilted her head to one side, then quickly leaned over the counter and removed my hat. I blinked in surprise as she studied my tight, wiry brown waves like an architect eyeing a building slated for demolition. "It's not so bad as all that," she said after some consideration. "But I hate to tell you, this humidity isn't going to help a thing." She set the hat back on my head, smoothing my braid as though we were old friends. "Goodness! Where are my manners? I'm Della Loftis." She came around the counter and extended a delicate hand.

I shook it carefully, feeling my own was suddenly big and awkward.

"Listen, I'm sorry about the way my daddy acted when y'all first got into Wheeler," Della said. "You had every right to get upset, being taken away from your sister like that."

"No harm done," I muttered, feeling my face redden. I hadn't realized Della saw my outburst at the court square.

I cast around for any distraction, and noticed a family portrait on the wall. Sheriff Loftis frowned in sepia tones next to a blandly pretty woman holding a solemn toddler on her lap. At the woman's shoulder was a younger Della, sporting a gap-toothed smile. "That's a lovely picture. Does your family own this store?"

"Yep. Me and Mama run it, mostly, while Daddy's off sher-iffing." She twirled the feather duster. "The grapevine said you ended up with the Weatheringtons. They're good people. I bet Mrs. Hettie sent you to pick up something."

"Ten pounds each, flour and salt." I handed over the money Hettie had given me.

The cash register dinged as Della opened the drawer and counted my change. "Miss Maeve got your little sister, I heard," she said cheerily. "I think it's wonderful that y'all got to come here and start over." She stepped into the back room and returned carrying two burlap bags filled with Hettie's or-der. Della tied them with twine, her left cheek dimpling with a smile. "Anything I can do to make you feel welcome, you just holler, all right?"

"I appreciate that," I said, awkwardly hoisting the bags. "I should be going. I'm supposed to visit my sister at the school-house, then hurry back to the farm."

"Hold on a second and I'll get you something to carry those." Della searched under the counter and handed me a worn leather satchel. "This is Abel's. I'm sure y'all are ac-quainted by now." She must not have noticed the stiffness in my nod, because she said without any hint of embarrassment, "Abel and me have been thick as thieves since we were little bitty." The flush on her cheeks deepened slightly. I cast a quick glance at her slim waist. This wasn't the mother-to-be then. It seemed Abel got around.

"Anyway, sometimes I'll pick up his books when they come in at the post office, so he leaves the satchel here. He's forever ordering something new to read. Always said he'd love to be a teacher, if his aunt and uncle didn't need him on the farm." She twisted a loose curl around her finger absently. "When you came in, I was about to go deliver some things to a widow lady who lives outside of town. Do you want me to show you where the schoolhouse is on my way?"

"Thank you, that would be nice."

I shoved my purchases into Abel's satchel while Della grabbed a basket laden with bread and fruit preserves. Then she flipped the store sign to CLOSED and steered me out into the searing sunshine. We stopped to secure the satchel to Lady May's saddle, and I retrieved the pen and papers Lilah had left in our trunk from inside the saddle bag before we set out down the sidewalk.

Della greeted every person we met by name, and received replies that were just as familiar. I got polite nods and smiles until we encountered a lanky boy of about our age, who cut across the square from the direction of the courthouse, stuck out a hand, and shook mine like a one-man welcoming committee.

"I'm Jasper Ausbrooks," he said. "I just wanted to say we're all so glad to have you in Wheeler. You must be Verity."

"I am. How'd you know?"

"My father's the mayor." He pointed back toward the court-house. "I saw the list of everyone's names and ages. Sorry to hear about your sister and you getting split up." He withdrew his hand and pushed a shock of light brown hair from his forehead. His narrow shoulders rose in a shrug as he added, "And I'm also sorry that we're all in everyone's business around here. Small towns are like that, you know?"

"So I'm learning." It was disconcerting, after being essentially anonymous in a city of millions, to find that strangers knew details of my life.

"You should come to the county fair tomorrow," Jasper said.

Della was appalled when I said I'd never been to a fair before. "Bless your heart, you've been missing out," she proclaimed. "There'll be riding contests, a livestock show, probably a baseball game. One time we had a man from Texas come and wrangle rattlesnakes in a pen. It's the biggest event of the year, next to the ice cream social."

"I can show you around a little, if you want," Jasper said. "It would be a good chance for you to meet some folks."

I wasn't long for Arkansas, and anyone I met here would soon be a part of my past, but I might as well enjoy what the small-town summer had to offer in the meantime. "All right, I'll see if Big Tom and Hettie are planning to go."

Beside me, Della swung her basket, a subtle hint she wanted to get going. Jasper took note. "Guess I better head on back. I hired on with the revenue office after I finished school. It's as dead dull as it sounds, by the way." He grinned and stepped back off the sidewalk. "Who're you delivering to today?" he asked as he turned to go.

"Granny Ardith," Della answered. "Want me to get her to make you a potion or an amulet of some sort while I'm there?" To me, she added, as if it were nothing out of the ordinary, "Granny Ardith will do a little charm work now and then, if you ask her nice."

"She's a strange one, but nice enough," Jasper said. "We've got a stone she charmed to pull the heat out when I burned my hand on the stove last winter." Then his sunny smile dimmed. "Della, I still don't see how you stand going to her house, right up beside the woods like that. It makes my skin crawl." Without elaborating, he waved and darted across the road, back toward the courthouse.

Before I could ask more about this old woman's supposed abilities, or what Jasper had against the woods where she lived, Della pointed to a little red building tucked back several yards away from the street. "The Wheeler one-room schoolhouse," she announced. "It will probably seem quaint to you, but it's a good school. And Miss Maeve is real smart."

"Thank you for your help," I said, forgetting all about local superstitions or cabins by the woods as I stepped onto the dusty path that led to the schoolhouse.

"Happy to do it," she replied. "Maybe I'll see you at the fair." Della wiggled her fingers in a farewell wave and set off in the opposite direction. "When you see him, tell Abel I said hello!"

6

I approached the open door of the schoolhouse just in time to hear the scrape of chairs being pushed back for dinner break. About twenty students of differing ages came bustling out, pails in hand. I watched them stream past, searching for the telltale hop-skip step that gave Lilah away in a crowd. But she wasn't among any of the groups gathering in clusters to eat and holler and tease.

I stepped inside to find her at the teacher's desk, having lunch with her new guardian.

When she noticed me, Lilah leapt up, the contents of her lunch pail scattering across the desktop. The force of her running hug sent me tottering backward, and I nearly dropped the pen and papers clutched in my hand. I felt dizzy from the gust of relief that swept over me. "I'm so happy you're here, Very," she said, squeezing my middle. "Miss Maeve heard you were living on a farm. You don't know a thing about animals or farming! Has anything tried to bite you? Are you all right?"

"I'm fine now," I said into her hair. "Goodness, you're squeezing tighter than a corset." She eased her hold a little, but neither of us let go. At last, I handed Lilah her fountain pen, along with the draft of the story she'd been working on. "You left these in the trunk," I said. "Let me know when you finish. I want to read it, cotton-candy clouds and all."

"Deal," Lilah said, raising the top of a nearby desk and tucking the things inside.

"Hello again." Miss Maeve's pale eyes met mine. I couldn't help but return the smile she offered. I was struck again by her flawless porcelain complexion, the fairest I'd seen in this sunbaked country. Her beauty was not like Della's warm loveliness; it was cool and shimmery, like fine silver. Miss Maeve handed Lilah an apple. "I hope you're settling in well with the Weatheringtons," she said.

"I have a lot to learn," I said, surprised at how easy it was to be candid with the schoolteacher. Something about her invited me to say more than I intended. "The Weatheringtons are doing their best to make me feel welcome, but I'm afraid I'm more of a hindrance than a help to them right now." I looked at the well-swept floor, unsure of what to say next.

"I believe I know something of how you must be feeling, Verity. I was about your age when Uncle Reuben took me in. My parents and my dear sister, Aurelia, died in an influenza outbreak. I didn't know a soul in this town, but they all welcomed me as one of their own. Give yourself time, and you'll find your place here, too."

Miss Maeve reached out a slim hand and touched my cheek. I stiffened under her cool fingers, the unexpected contact straining the ease of our conversation. "I know it's hard to believe for a girl your age, but things have a way of working out, given enough time." She couldn't yet be thirty, but spoke like someone a good deal older. "Be easy on yourself," she went on. "You've had a great deal of upheaval and change in the past few days."

"Verity likes to run things." Lilah polished the apple on her skirt and bit down with a crunch. "She's always planning something or other."

"Not a bad trait," Miss Maeve said. "You can't let other people captain your ship. What if they run it aground?"

I laughed, a little uncertainly. Mr. Lybrand ran Maeve's affairs for her, and it seemed almost everyone had a say in what happened in my life except me. "Will you two be at the fair?" I asked. "Maybe we could all walk around together."

"Perhaps we'll stop by for a bit. The fair is so hectic and crowded, I'm afraid it's not really to my taste." Miss Maeve folded her slim hands at her waist. "But why don't you plan to come to our house for Sunday dinner? It will give you a chance to see Lilah's new home, and we can all become better acquainted."

"I'd like that very much," I said.

"You'll love it, Very." Lilah clapped her hands. "Miss Maeve had so many fine things waiting for me. I have a whole dresser drawer full of hair ribbons. Don't worry, I'll share." She paused to wrinkle her nose at my ragged braid. "Have you been doing your hundred brushstrokes every night? Because it doesn't look like it."

"Excuse me, Sassy Britches." I covered her mouth with a hand and laughed. "I'm the big sister. I'm supposed to tell you what to do, not the other way around."

Lilah's response was to lick my palm. I gave a startled yelp and my sister dissolved into peals of laughter.

"Lilah." Miss Maeve's voice was firm, but kind. Lilah clamped her lips together and raised wide eyes to Miss Maeve's face. "We must always think before we act. Do you remember what I told the class this morning? Every small choice we make helps create our character."

"Yes, ma'am," Lilah said, drawing a circle on the floor with the toe of one shoe. "I'm sorry."

"Tell your sister. She is the one your behavior affected."

"It's nothing, really." I didn't know which bothered me more: seeing someone else take charge of Lilah's upbringing and instruction, or seeing my boisterous, untamable little sister actually listening for a change. "She's done far worse. I remember once when she got hold of the chamber pot—"

Miss Maeve lifted a hand to stop me. "Lilah will be much more respectful in the future. Won't you?"

Lilah nodded, and I saw she was relieved to be in Miss Maeve's good graces again. Lilah, who tied my shoelaces together and once braided my hair around the slats of my headboard while I slept. Lilah, who pestered and harassed and pranked with abandon, gave Miss Maeve Donovan a grateful smile. "Yes, ma'am."

"Now, if you'll excuse me, it's time to call the children in. Lilah, don't forget to clean up your dinner things," Miss Maeve said before going to ring the bell.

"I'll see you soon. Sorry I have to go, but I'm on an errand for Mrs. Weatherington, so I can't stay long."

"That's all right." Lilah gave me another fierce hug. "Bye, Very."

I felt my smile fade as I watched her settle back into her seat. Truly, it was a relief to see her adjusting well. But did she have to do it so easily?

I retrieved Lady May and started back toward the farm in mellowed spirits. For a quarter mile or so, the path went straight toward the woods before veering north to skirt their perimeter. I found myself giving the trees sidelong glances, feeling as though I almost glimpsed something in their depths. I was telling myself not to be silly when Lady May abruptly

lifted her head, stopped, and stared into the woods. The muscles in her neck shivered, and she began an antsy sidestep.

"Easy there." I forced calm into my voice, hoping she
couldn't sense my anxiety. "Everything's fine."

Lady May pinned her ears back. She whinnied and pawed
the ground, backing away from the woods, her pupils ringed
in white.

"Now, listen," I said sternly, using my best "I'm the boss"
voice, the one I'd practiced with Lilah countless times. "There'll
be none of this foolishness. You're fine, do you hear?" I released
the reins with one hand to give the horse a reassuring pat.

With a frightened squeal, Lady May dropped her head and
bucked. The sudden motion pulled the reins from my other
hand, sending me sliding sideways. My sweaty fingers scrabbled for anything to hold, but I caught only a few strands of
mane as another buck sent me flying.

I hit the ground. My vision blackened with the impact. I
blinked hard, regaining sight just in time to see the spooked
mare spin and rear. Sun glinted off horseshoes above my head.

Hooves crashed back to earth right beside me. I had no
breath in my lungs to cry out, but Lady May let loose a terrified whinny. A spray of gravel showered my face as she wheeled
and galloped away.

When the sky stopped spinning, I sat up and watched the
horse disappear from sight. A fine goose egg swelled on the
back of my head. I pressed the lump experimentally, wincing.
I could only hope I didn't have a concussion. The sacks of flour
and salt lay nearby, still tightly tied, next to the open satchel.

Head pounding, I gathered the fallen items. My hip throbbed.
Shaking, I climbed to my feet and tried to walk. Each hobbling
step sent bolts of pain sizzling down my leg.

I forced myself to focus through the pain, and the

nauseating worry that I might've just lost the Weatheringtons' horse. There was a chance Lady May would return to the farm on her own, since she'd bolted in that direction, but there was no way to be sure what the spooked creature would do next. I had to get back and alert Big Tom and Hettie that she was missing. But walking the road back to the house with a banged-up leg would take ages. Lady May could be long gone before I reached the Weatheringtons.

I stood and squinted into the murky woods. It would be much faster to cut straight across, rather than following the far-flung road all the way around. The trees couldn't span more than a quarter mile across. I'd be through and back out onto the road in no time. If I were lucky, I might even come across the horse before I made it back to the farm.

With my jaw clenched, I stepped off the path and waded through knee-high grass until I stood at the edge of the woods. A cool breeze wafted from the shadowy depths, toying with the tendrils around my face.

It took only a few steps for me to leave the sunlight behind and pass into the dim forest.

The heat dissipated as soon as I moved under the outstretched branches. Patches of velvety emerald moss peeked out from under a thick carpet of fallen leaves. Ferns draped along low-hanging branches, kissed by green-tinged light filtering down from the canopy high above. I walked along, breathing in the damp earth scent, grateful for the cooler air.

For several minutes, I didn't notice the unusual quiet. Then, all at once, the silence seemed to mass into a nearly solid thing at my back. No hint of birds rustling in the treetops, not even the shush of a breeze in the canopy. My steps suddenly sounded too loud. I gripped the satchel close and, ignoring my aching hip, walked faster.

As I made my way closer to the heart of the woods, the trees began to change. Scrubby pines and spindly oaks were replaced by towering trees with smooth gray trunks so massive I doubted even a chain of three Big Toms could reach around them. I hurried along hard-packed black earth, absent of the scrubby bushes I'd been dodging until now.

The air grew cooler. Then cold. My breaths came faster as I realized each ragged exhalation hung before me in the air. I watched the impossible sight, breathing out frozen clouds on a summer day. A violent shiver racked my body. I had stepped into frigid midwinter.

Alarm trickled through my veins. Something was wrong. Every icy breath heightened my distress. It was too cold, too still. And too quiet. This was the charged silence of hide-and-seek, when I knew someone—somewhere—crouched in wait. But this didn't feel like a child's game. This felt dangerous.

I broke into a jog, looking over my shoulder, my injured hip pulsing with pain. Briars snagged in my hair and ripped at my bare forearms. The cold only intensified. Goose bumps raced down my arms. Something followed. I was certain. The unseen thing pressed at my back, pushing me deeper into the trees.

Herding me.

My pulse pounded harder, faster, so loud in my ears I could hear nothing except a primal part of my brain shouting a warning: *Behind you. Behind you. Look behind you!* I whirled around, eyes wide as I searched for my pursuer.

There was no one there. Only the watchful trees witnessed my panic.

The intense feeling of being pursued ebbed away. My hammering heart began to slow. The goose bumps dotting my arms faded, and the air felt less bitter against my skin. I exhaled and saw nothing in the air before me. Yet I knew I couldn't feel calm again until I'd made it through the woods.

Head down, eyes fixed on my feet, I kept up my brisk pace. I went only a few more yards before stepping into a clearing.

At the heart of the open space stood a well.

The posts and well wheel were gone, leaving only a ring of rock about knee high, its surface patched with moss and lichen. I guessed it to be nearly eight feet across, far larger than any well I'd seen before. I felt a stirring in my chest. The low, gray stones, worn smooth with age, seemed to call me. The need to place my hands on the neatly stacked rocks swelled.

I moved on noiseless feet, feeling dragged forward almost against my will. Hesitantly, I reached out. This well was far, far older than anything I'd ever encountered. I closed my eyes and pressed my palms against the stones. The hairs along my arms lifted. There was power here, something strong and ancient. I felt it snaking under my feet, lurking in the dark waters, seeping into the ground to be drunk in by the trees.

I jerked my hands back as though I'd been shocked.

Chafing my fingers together, I willed the ridiculous notion away. Reading so many of Lilah's stories must have caught up with me. Laughing aloud at the fancy, I shook my head and opened my eyes.

In my peripheral vision, a shadow flitted past.

Squinting, I peered into the dim woods and again caught the quick dart of a small figure. "Hello?" I called.

A face peeked out from behind a mottled gray trunk.

The shock of seeing the little girl nearly startled me into fleeing, but I found my feet rooted to the spot. Her eyes, set in a round face, were deepest brown, rimmed by bruise-dark shadows. Long black hair lay over her shoulders, the same shade as her knee-length dress. She emerged from the gloom, her small, white hands hanging limp at her sides.

I blinked hard, to make sure my vision hadn't deceived me. When I looked again, she was gone.

I scanned the forest to my left, then right, and spied her disappearing behind another tree. "Are you lost?" I called, going after her.

Slowly, she stopped. My heart jittered against my ribs. "Do you need me to help you find your way home?" My voice took on a hushed tone, the way one speaks in an empty church.

She shook her head. An explanation for this unexpected encounter came to me in a flash. The child must have followed me from the schoolyard. The feeling of being trailed through the trees made sense now.

"You can talk to me," I said with what I hoped was an encouraging smile. Her face remained blank. Some of the anxiety I'd dispelled crept back in. Her expression reminded me of the few times I'd seen Lilah sleepwalk.

"You need to come with me," I said, annoyance and unease mixing in a sour brew in my gut. No matter how odd the child was, I couldn't leave her alone in the woods. "You can't hide out here all day. They'll be worried about you at school."

I reached for her. Without a sound, the girl turned and moved swiftly away. She went straight into the forest, slipping between the trees on silent feet. The black of her hair and dress melted into the dark of the woods as she slid further into the shadows.

"Wait! Where are you going?" I hurried after her, but the laces of my right boot snagged in briars. With a groan of frustration, I sank to a crouch and began quickly untangling the knotted mess.

A creeping, slithering silence wound itself around me. Once

freed, I straightened and called after her. No one answered. The little girl was gone. I searched for a while, until at last, only the looming trees watched me turn to go. Hopefully she'd returned to the schoolhouse, scared out of her truancy by our meeting.

When I pushed out of the trees and stepped back onto the road, I inhaled the humid, sticky air with gratitude. I threw backward glances at the woods for the remainder of my walk. The farther I traveled from the trees, the less troubling the inexplicable cold and the encounter with the child felt.

Blanketed by the flawless June sky, I hurried on and let myself think only of delivering Hettie's groceries and finding the missing horse. I tilted my face to the sun, grateful for the relentless Arkansas heat.

7

Noontime next day found me wedged between Big Tom and Hettie in the surrey, jostling toward the nearby town of Argenta to attend the county fair. Lady May pulled us briskly along under the midday sun.

When I'd limped back to the farm after my walk from Wheeler, I'd discovered my erstwhile mount already there, knee deep in Hettie's rosebushes. The mare had plodded over to nuzzle my neck in apology. I didn't even mind the partly chewed rose petals stuck in my hair. Hettie had been less than delighted to see the state of her garden, but I felt only sweeping relief to realize I hadn't, in fact, lost the Weatheringtons' horse.

Today, Lady May tossed her mane as we rattled along between sprawling fields sprinkled with wildflowers. She seemed in high spirits, and she wasn't the only one. When Hettie had announced at daybreak that we'd need to hurry with our chores so we could get cleaned up and head out, she'd actually started whistling. Her cheerful expectation proved contagious, and I found myself excited to visit my first-ever county fair. Even Big Tom hummed a merry melody as we rode. This was, I decided, going to be a good day. If Fortune smiled on me, maybe Miss Maeve would decide to bring Lilah to the fair after all.

Before we were brought to Arkansas, Lilah and I had never spent a single day apart. If I felt ill at ease in this unfamiliar place so often, surely she must be at loose ends sometimes. Thoughts of all the new experiences I'd had in my short time at the farm reeled by—delivering the calf, working in the cornfield, fixing the fence, and slopping hogs. And that was to say nothing of my trek through the woods.

A startled little gasp slipped out. I hadn't told Big Tom and Hettie about the girl in the woods. Yesterday, after I came back late and on foot, I'd worked with reckless intensity as penance for my failure to even fetch flour and salt without causing added trouble. In my fervor to do better, the strange incident had been forgotten.

Hettie gave me a quizzical look. On her lap rested a small crate packed with Mason jars of pickles and her best pear preserves, carefully selected for entry in the canned-food contest. "What's the matter?" she whispered, leaning close. "Is your corset laced too tight?" I still wasn't clear why Sunday best was required for a county fair, but Hettie had insisted.

I shook my head, sending the tulle on my hat rustling. "Yesterday, on my way back from Wheeler, I saw a little girl in the woods." I felt Big Tom tense beside me. "I thought she might've come from town and gotten lost, but then she walked away into the trees like she belonged there."

Hettie focused on the jars in her lap. For a few seconds, their glassy clink and the crunch of Lady May's hooves against the gravel were the only reply. "You went into the woods?" she said at last.

"After Lady May bolted, it was the fastest way back." I adjusted my hat, wishing the circle of shade cast by its brim did a better job of cooling my face. "Are there any houses in the woods? Maybe the girl lives there."

"A few folks live *near* the woods—Reuben Lybrand, old Granny Ardith—but no one lives *in* them. There are stories about folks seeing . . . things out there." She cleared her throat, as if the next words had to fight to get free. "Unnatural things. What you thought you saw might've been something else entirely."

"What does that mean?" I asked, looking to Big Tom to elaborate.

His huge hands clenched and unclenched the reins. "Might not've been a girl at all," he said.

I lifted a skeptical brow. "You make it sound as though she were some sort of spirit." Eyeing Big Tom, I waited to see his mustache lift with a smile. Surely this was a joke on the newcomer, a little game to scare me. But he only shook his head slowly.

"The things in the woods ain't nothing to laugh at," he said.

Stolid, salt-of-the-earth Big Tom and Hettie Weatherington believed in ghosts? I supposed it wasn't such a leap from thinking herbs, plants, and rocks could protect or bring good luck to believing in a haunted wood, but a ripple of surprise rolled over me regardless. The child had been strange, but not *that* strange. "She didn't look ghostly." I winced, realizing that I claimed not to believe in ghosts, yet somehow had an opinion on what one would look like. "She skipped school, then got worried she'd be in trouble when I saw her, so she ran off." I spoke my theory with brassy certainty, yet the memory of the woods pressed in—that sense of being enveloped in something beyond my previous experience. My hands started to shake. I slid them under my knees. "I think we should go look for her."

"If there were a missing child, we'd have heard about it by

now. The whole town would've been out looking out for her," Hettie said.

Big Tom nodded. "A clerk from the corn mill rode over to bring our pay this morning, and he didn't mention anybody in town going missing." They took for granted that any unusual event would be the subject of immediate, widespread discussion throughout Wheeler.

"The best thing you can do is keep out of those woods," Hettie said. I opened my mouth to protest, but she held up a silencing hand. "If it'll ease your mind, I'll ask around, see if anybody's heard of a little one gone wandering. But you got to promise to quit messing around in the woods." The lines between her eyes deepened with worry. Whether I believed in something other-worldly or not, I was indebted to these people. They'd given me work and a place to stay, plus more patience than I felt I deserved.

"All right," I said. "No more shortcuts. I'll stick to the road next time." Big Tom smiled his approval and Hettie reached over to pat my knee with stiff sincerity.

"Good. We want you safe." Surprised, happy warmth hit my chest. It had been a long while since I'd had someone try to take care of me.

"We're here," Big Tom announced. A sea of wagons and buggies converged from every direction to pack Argenta's main street. The sidewalks thronged with people, all dressed up and streaming toward a sprawling field behind the train depot. A tall sign lettered in bright red proclaimed the pasture to be, at least for the day, the Pine County Fairground.

Big Tom steered the buggy into a shady spot under a stand of oaks and climbed out to tie the horse. All the hitching sheds were already occupied. It appeared the entire county really had turned out for the fair. Hettie stood, hugging her jars like treasure, readying to climb down.

"Let me hold that for you," I said, reaching for the crate.

"I've got it," a deep voice answered. Abel had ridden ahead on his own horse, a chestnut gelding with the unexpected name Merlin. Appearing beside the buggy now, he took the box in one hand, then extended the other to his aunt and helped her step down onto the wheel-rutted ground. "You look really nice, Aunt Het."

Hettie scoffed, but there was a light in her usually serious eyes. She'd dressed for the occasion in a high-necked burgundy blouse and gored skirt, graying hair coiffed under a ribbon-trimmed straw hat. Life on the farm seemed to offer few breaks from the grinding sunup-to-sundown routine, and it made me smile to see how much Hettie enjoyed this day of respite.

My smile faded when Abel reached for my hand next, his blue eyes sincere as he took in my white eyelet dress. "And so do you, Verity." I knew this was a peace offering, not a flirtation, but I couldn't help thinking of his left-behind love, or how Della pined for him, unaware of his secret.

I schooled my features to a neutral expression. "Thank you." His warm, callused hand closed over mine as I stepped lightly to the ground.

"You're welcome," he said as Big Tom and Hettie began filing down a trail worn through the grass toward the fair. We fell in line behind them, Abel with his hands in his trouser pockets, whistling softly to himself. His cream-colored shirtsleeves were rolled up to show tan forearms. I wanted to slap myself for noticing. Scoundrels shouldn't have such nice arms.

Dabbing sweat from my upper lip, I scanned the rows of white tents edging the western border of the field. From a livestock-judging area, the lowing of cattle and the fractious bleat of goats and sheep carried over the swirling crowd. Big Tom pressed a quarter into my palm. "Advance on your wages," he rumbled. I thanked him and pocketed the money, knowing I wouldn't be spending it on cotton candy or popcorn. I'd need to save every penny I got to buy my and Lilah's tickets back north.

"Y'all have a big time," Hettie said. She squared her shoulders, then marched proudly away to enter her wares in the contest, while Big Tom drifted off to watch Clydesdales in a plow-pulling competition.

"She's won three years in a row for her pickles," Abel noted. "They're always just the right amount of sour and sweet. Sort of like Aunt Hettie herself."

I only nodded in reply, looking away. Abel rubbed the back of his neck. We stood in a pocket of uneasy quiet. He stared off toward the far edge of the field, where a horse race was underway. Standing atop square hay bales, fans shouted their encouragement to a roan stallion making a come-from-behind charge at the black horse in the lead. A jubilant shout went up when the roan nosed his way to the win at the last second.

"Look, Verity," Abel began, "we got off to a rough start, and I'm to blame. I didn't mean to offend you that day in the barn. I'm sorry."

"Maybe I was a little touchy," I said, knowing full well I had been. But I found I couldn't make myself outright say I was sorry. Not to Abel. "I accept your apology." My lukewarm response earned a confused frown. Surely he hadn't expected us to become bosom friends. I had a feeling Abel Atchley had all the close female friends he needed, and then some.

I crossed my arms and began looking around for Lilah. Instead, I saw Della Loftis sweeping toward us.

"Abel! Verity!" A high lace collar accented her pretty, round face, and her dress was a deep periwinkle dimity to match the silk flowers on her hat.

Jasper and a girl I didn't recognize walked on either side of her. Matching sandy hair, gray eyes, and lanky forms marked them as brother and sister. Jasper loped along with loose-limbed ease, but the girl, dressed in a simple dark skirt and pin-tucked ivory blouse, carried herself as though she had a fireplace poker down her corset.

"I'm so glad you could come today, Verity." Della snatched me into a quick, unexpected hug. "This is my friend, Katherine Ausbrooks."

Katherine inclined her head, and I got the impression she was trying to appear dignified. "A pleasure to make your acquaintance." The words were kind enough, but her tone and the look she darted at me, standing there beside Abel, were anything but. "Abel's told us so much about you."

"Really?" I said. Beside me, Abel went still. I read embarrassment in his face, and wondered if he'd been saying disparaging things about the rude Yankee girl.

Della laughed, a buoy in the sinking conversation. "Nothing bad! Abel's really glad you came along. Big Tom and Hettie have needed help for ages. And it's good to have more young people around here," she said. "Y'all come on now, the music's about to start."

With that she linked arms with Abel in a familiar gesture. They fell into stride with one another. The back of Abel's neck was a suspicious shade of red. I frowned, wondering what *else* he'd said—or at least thought—about me. I followed a step behind, weaving through the crowd, flanked by the Ausbrooks siblings.

Jasper talked about the game booths he wanted to visit later and a sulky race we should all go watch. I couldn't help being a little touched that he'd included me in the group plans. We stopped near the center of the midway, where a quartet made of two guitarists, a tall man with a mandolin, and a plump bearded fellow tuning a fiddle stood on a pine board stage. The fiddler stepped forward with a grin to point his bow at Della. "Now that our soloist is here, we're going to kick things off with a special song by Miss Della Loftis."

The knot of onlookers clustering around clapped politely. Della took a nervous breath and smoothed her hands over her purple skirt. Abel nudged her in the ribs. "You'll be wonderful, Del. You always are." His words were all the encouragement she needed, it seemed, and she hitched her skirts and stepped onto the stage with confidence.

While Della and the band put their heads together on which song to perform first, Katherine sidled closer to me. "You're in for a treat. Della's got a beautiful voice. Prettiest in the county, I'd wager. Sometimes at church, she'll sing duets with Abel." She paused, giving me a sheathed dagger of a look. "They make a good pair. They've always matched up really well." Some current of meaning slid along under her words, and it took me a moment to catch the implication. From what I knew of Della, I strongly doubted she would appreciate her friend's snide insinuations.

And little did either of them know, I was far and away the least of Della's worries.

Katherine was still looking pointedly at me. I shrugged one shoulder. "If you say so."

"I do. So does everyone else in Wheeler. We all know they'll end up together. Della's had her eyes on Abel since we were little."

"Where are his eyes, though?" I said before I could stop

myself. Katherine gave me a look that could strip paint from a wall and turned her attention back to the stage.

The band finished the introduction to their song. Della lifted her chin and began to sing. Her voice rang clear and pure, running along the hills and valleys of melody with ease. The audience began clapping in time with the spirited beat. By the second song, I found myself toe-tapping along. Even Katherine loosened up a tad to nod her head to the rollicking tune. When Della launched into a song called "The Arkansas Traveler," Abel whooped in approval as an older man and woman stepped out of the crowd and began to dance.

When her song ended, the audience applauded with real vigor. Della flushed and waved her thanks, moving to step down from the stage. "Play something we can do the Virginia reel to!" the elderly dancer hollered, not ready for his fun to end.

"Nobody does the reel anymore, old-timer," a younger man in suspenders called back with good humor. The old fellow waved both hands in jovial dismissal.

"Della, didn't your granddad teach you the calls?" Abel asked. "Can you lead it?"

"Give it a try," the old man shouted, with his geriatric dancing partner chiming in her support. The chorus of encouragement spread over the gathered crowd until everyone was cheering for Della to call the reel. Della lifted a dark brow, giving Abel the kind of look only shared between friends who've known each other long and well. It said "look what you've gotten me into now." He beamed in reply.

Della threw her arms out wide, her voice ringing over the sawing of the fiddle as she shouted, "Ladies on the left, gents on the right."

A giggling girl of about my age grabbed a protesting

Katherine and me, hauling us to one side while the men and boys in the group lined up directly across from us. From the stage, Della met my eyes, slyly tilting her head toward Jasper. "Now bow to your partner." Jasper bent his lanky form double in my direction.

"I've never done this before," I said, trying to back away and finding myself hemmed in by the circle of boisterous onlookers. Still holding his bow, Jasper gave me an encouraging nod.

"It's not hard," he said. "Just follow my lead."

With no way to escape, I responded with the worst curtsy in history and resigned myself to my fate.

"Swing your partner," Della called as Jasper swooped over to link his arm with mine.

"Here we go," he said, spinning us in a high-stepping circle.

All around, other couples joined in the giddy spin, switching arms to repeat the turn in the opposite direction. The music bobbed along as we changed partners in succession, working our way down the line in dizzying loops of swirling skirts and stamping boots.

Before I knew it, the dance partnered me with Abel just as Della shouted, "Promenade." Abel lifted both hands, palms facing me. "Like this," he said.

I pressed my hands to his and joined in a bouncy side step that carried us between the rows of cheering dancers. Katherine gave me a disapproving shake of her head as we passed. Abel looked for the briefest instant into my eyes, then dropped his gaze to the trampled grass. Spots of color appeared on his cheeks. Maybe he felt ashamed of being here, dancing and having fun, while somewhere his abandoned girl had no such option.

The contagious vigor of the reel jostled aside those unpleasant thoughts. The fiddle took the lead, its twangy notes soaring into the pure blue sky like birds bursting into flight. As the song wound down, I partnered with Jasper again for a final twirl before the music swelled to a joyous ending.

Our audience burst into applause. I joined in, breathless and laughing all at once. Onstage, Della and the band took their bows.

"I'm a terrible dancer," I said to Jasper. That fact hadn't surprised me in the least, but it was a pleasant little shock to discover I'd loved dancing regardless.

At the edge of the knot of onlookers, amid the cheerful watchers, a white-haired man in a somber black suit fixed our little band with a mirthless stare. Under a sparse beard, his face was hollowed and lined. The narrow build and gaunt face spoke of frailty, but the look he swept our way held fire.

I had the feeling I'd just been deemed unclean. No mean-spirited stranger would squash my joy. Squaring my shoulders, I met his stare.

The man's gaze faltered, and a look of something I couldn't quite place—was it surprise? shock?—swept over his stern face. I broke the taut line of attention, looking away, confused at his reaction. When I glanced back, I caught a glimpse of the man's slim, dark-clad form slipping away into the crowd.

8

I watched him go, uneasy. My stewing was interrupted by Della throwing an arm over my shoulders. "Was that your first time dancing a reel? You're a natural."

Tearing my thoughts from the stranger, I looked to Della's rosy face. "That's a lie. But a sweet one."

"Come on, let's go get something to drink," she said, drawing hearty agreement from Jasper and Abel.

"I heard there's a stand selling Coca-Cola," Katherine offered.

Della's eyes lit. "Perfect." The others fell together, their voices and conversations overlapping one another. I followed a step behind, looking over my shoulder for the glowering man. His scrutiny had shaken me. The expression I hadn't at first been able to place, the look that had briefly wiped away the scorn and judgment, had been one of recognition. Impossible, for I was sure I'd never laid eyes on the man before.

When a lull fell between the others, I quickened my step to edge between Della and Katherine. "Did anyone see that man with the white beard watching the dance? He had on a black suit and hat. He looked . . . angry."

"Eyes as mean as a snake?" Jasper put in.

Della whacked his arm sternly. "Be nice, Jasper. That was Reverend Mayhew. I saw him from the stage. He preaches at the First Baptist Church here in Argenta. Dancing's a sin in his book."

"So are playing cards, going to movie theaters, and doing anything but sitting and reading the Bible on Sundays," Jasper said. We approached a wheeled cart with a red awning emblazoned with the white Coca-Cola logo, and Jasper began fishing in his pocket. "Me and Katherine got dragged to a few revival services Reverend Mayhew preached when we were kids. He had me about scared to breathe wrong or I might end up in Hell." He pulled out a fistful of coins. "My treat," he announced, turning to me first. "Care for a bottle, Verity?"

I wavered, not wanting to take his money.

"Father gave me and Katherine extra pocket money today. We've got plenty to share." I noted that Katherine hadn't volunteered, and when she heard her brother's generous offer, she scowled. That was enough to make me accept.

Jasper bought five bottles and handed them around, pointing to a stand of trees just beyond the perimeter of the fairgrounds. "Let's take a load off in the shade," he suggested.

We settled into the lush grass, all except Katherine, who sniffed and perched herself on the edge of a tree stump. I took a long drink, savoring the sugary fizz.

"This is so good, the reverend probably thinks it's wicked by default," Jasper said after downing half his cola in one go.

"You shouldn't be so hard on him," Della said. For my benefit she added, "He and his wife lost their daughter. It's been around nineteen years now, but folks say they never got over it." She gestured with the neck of her bottle toward a concession tent, where a middle-aged lady with graying auburn hair worked. The woman handed a paper bag of popcorn to an eager little boy, a tired smile deepening the creases around her light blue eyes. She watched her young customer leave, and a flicker of sorrow crossed her face. "That's Mrs. Mayhew."

I found it hard to believe such a gentle-looking person was married to the stern preacher. "What happened to their daughter?" I asked.

Katherine spoke up for the first time. "Her name was Mary. When she was about our age, she got in trouble with some boy. He left her and went away out of state somewhere." I couldn't help shooting a look at Abel, who seemed intent on watching beads of condensation slip down the sides of his bottle. "She hid her condition from her mama and daddy. They didn't have a clue why she was so melancholy, or why she kept to her room all the time."

"It might've all gone differently," Jasper said. "Except it was the worst winter in a hundred years, and her folks got snowed in at a church event in another town. That night, Mary's baby came. But it was too early, and it didn't survive."

"It drove Mary out of her mind," Della said, low and quiet. "All the hiding and secrets, going through it alone. Then the baby dying." A cloud lowered over our group. "I know when my little sister Josie died, it almost did our mother in. It was like all the stuff that was Mama got scooped out, and she was just this empty thing for a long time." I wondered what had happened to Della's sister, but decided it wasn't the time to ask.

Katherine took up the story again, with a little too much relish, I thought. "Mary Mayhew buried her baby in the parsonage rose garden. Then she walked off into the storm."

Jasper, stretched full length on the ground, propped himself on one elbow. "When I first heard folks whispering about the lost Mayhew girl, I remember hoping she'd just gone off somewhere and met up with her young man. Maybe he'd seen the light and come back for her, and they left together to start over somewhere."

His sister shook her head, lips pinched. To me, she added, "She died somewhere in the snow. Della's dad investigated her disappearance."

I looked to Della, who nodded. "She didn't take any warm clothes with her, not even shoes. They lost her tracks in the snow, and it stayed well below freezing for days after she disappeared. And I don't think she left with the father of her baby, either. When Daddy dug up the little grave in the garden . . ." Della paused, clearly troubled by the thought of this long-dead young woman's pain.

Katherine seemed less inclined toward sympathy. "He found a ring," she said. "One of those fancy hidden-message rings, with little panels all the way around that flip open so you can see pictures or words under them. One of the panels was torn off, but it's still really pretty. Della showed it to me once."

Della's apple cheeks flushed. "I shouldn't have, I know, but I always thought the story was so sad and . . . well, interesting. The Mayhews didn't want the ring, since they knew it must've been from the boy who got their girl in trouble. They told Daddy to get rid of it, but my mother wouldn't hear of it. She stuck the ring in a dresser drawer at our house. It has a little love note carved into it. And heliotropes." Her dark eyes flicked toward Abel, who had listened to the tale so far with a hard, flat expression.

A flare of righteous anger sparked in my chest, fanning the flame of curiosity. "Heliotropes? Why does that matter?"

"In the language of flowers, giving someone heliotropes means 'faithful 'til the end,'" Della said.

My mother told me once, when I was very small, that every

different flower held its own unique meaning. She always loved when Papa gave her a bouquet of purple crocus, because crocuses stood for cheerfulness. He'd bring them home when she was feeling low, which seemed to happen often. I remembered hoping that when their baby was born she would feel happier. It never occurred to me that neither she nor the infant would survive, and Lilah and I would be left motherless, with a father whose mind began sinking to deep, dark places.

Della's somber tone drew me back to an equally bleak story of loss. "Mary leaving that ring proves she didn't go off to meet her love. She buried that dream, right there with their little girl," Della said. She pointed to the distant spire of a country church. "The baby's grave is in the cemetery, behind the church. Mary doesn't even have a marker. They never found her body and Reverend Mayhew refused to hold a service for her. He was that ashamed of her."

I stared out toward the unseen graveyard, thinking of the iron cross we'd used to mark Mother's grave. When I returned home, I'd visit and lay fresh flowers on her final resting place. Hyacinths, for sorrow.

My somber mood turned to disbelief when Abel spoke up. "Whoever the fellow was that left Mary, he deserved a solid thrashing." Della and Katherine nodded along, completely suckered by Abel's blatant hypocrisy. This was the pot calling the kettle black if I'd ever seen it.

Before anyone could speak, a group of boys approached, calling to Jasper and Abel. "We're getting up a baseball game, Wheeler versus Argenta," said a stocky, wide-shouldered boy.

His companion pointed to me, Della, and Katherine. "Girls too, we need everyone to have enough. We've got gloves for everybody," he said, holding up a stack of weathered leather mitts. "Unless you're left-handed."

The gloom of Mary Mayhew's story fell away. Jasper leapt to his feet immediately, cracking his knuckles. "You're out, southpaw," he said to Abel, who shrugged, looking distracted. "Come on, ladies," he said, tugging his sister along. Della stood, too. "How about it, Verity? Do you play?"

I shook my head. "No, thank you." I'd seen baseball played by ragtag kids in the alleys around our apartments, and sometimes older boys at the orphanage organized a game in the courtyard, but I'd never had the inclination to join.

"Y'all come watch when we get going," Jasper said. "I'll be pitching for Wheeler. Nobody can hit my knuckleball." The two boys agreed and slapped him on the back.

"Sorry to leave you," Della said as she and Katherine turned to go. "Argenta beat us last year, so we've got to redeem ourselves."

I called a halfhearted "good luck" after them, already shifting to look at Abel. He sat propped against the trunk of a hickory, one knee bent. "That was an upsetting story, wasn't it?" I said. Not the most tactful opening, but I'd never been known for subtlety.

A muscle tightened in his jaw.

"Everything might've been all right if she hadn't been forced to go it alone," I went on. "Think of how things could've gone if the baby's father had stood with her. It seems to me his leaving is what pushed Mary to the brink." A drop of venom slipped into my words. "He's to blame, in my opinion. Do you agree?"

Abel's dark blue eyes locked on mine, and I saw him register my hostility. The wheels turned, and I fancied I could see Abel calculating just how much I knew. "Is there something you'd like to say to me, Verity?" he said at last, voice tight.

"I overheard your conversation with Big Tom. About the girl and . . . and the baby on the way." Abel's face went frozen-lake still. "I know it's not really my place to bring it up," I said, gaining confidence from the justice of my cause.

"Agreed," he gritted out.

"But I don't understand why you won't marry her. It's awfully selfish of you, if you'll pardon my bluntness. She shouldn't have to face this alone, just like Mary shouldn't have. That's all."

Abel's brows lifted in surprise. I expected the hot, shamefaced anger of someone called out on their misdeeds. Instead, a smile stirred one corner of his lips.

I scowled. "That's hardly the appropriate reaction, Mr. Atchley."

"Even sitting on the ground, I see you're still on your high horse." His short laugh was edged with ire. "First of all, she's only fifteen. And despite her current situation, I'm not sure she's ready to be married."

My jaw clenched. How dare he be so blasé?

He ran a hand through his wheat-colored hair. "To be such a know-it-all, you've missed one pretty crucial fact."

"And that is . . . ?" I asked, wondering what toothless excuse he could give for his behavior.

There was a glint in his eyes that turned their blue to ice. "I'm not the father of Clara's baby." He climbed to his feet, brushing bits of grass and leaves from his trousers. "She's not my lady friend. She's my little sister."

Understanding hit like a thunderclap. Abel's anger, and his hard remarks about marriage, weren't because he intended to shirk his duty. They were directed at the man who'd left his sister high and dry.

Nothing renders a girl speechless quite like realizing she's made a meddling ass of herself.

I swallowed hard, unsure of where to begin. "I'm sorry for

Clara—that is to say, I'm sorry she's in this—um—difficult predicament." My face blazed, but I stumbled on. "I hope she's all right." Even in my embarrassment, the seriousness of the girl's plight struck me like a blow to the gut.

As if we were back in the dance, Abel gave an impeccable bow. "Very kind of you." His gaze was back to its summery blue, but there was a hint of pique beneath. I couldn't blame him. I'd assumed the worst of him and been spectacularly wrong. "And now," he said, looking across the field to where the baseball game was in progress, "it looks like Wheeler could use a pinch hitter."

He glanced down at the half-empty bottle of cola in my hand and downed the last of his own. Tucking the empty bottle into his back pocket, he remarked, "You might want to finish that. I've heard it goes well with humble pie."

9

I wandered the fairgrounds alone for a long, long while. Pigs would fly before I ventured over to the baseball game. At last I decided to make my way back toward where the canning contest had been held and look for Hettie. The small-animal exhibition tent stood in my path, so I ducked under the sides and into its dusty, warm confines. Rows and rows of wire cages greeted me. Milling lines of patrons shuffled by, stopping to admire the sleek rabbits and glossy-feathered chickens. Indignant honking came from a cluster of geese who seemed to object to the judge prodding them around a show ring. Lifting my hem out of the dirt, I mumbled "excuse me"s and "beg your pardon"s. The tent was a muddle of sounds and smells and moving bodies. It was, in my current state of shamefaced confusion, all a bit much.

I was almost through the tent when I heard Lilah's voice over the crowd. "Look at this one, Miss Maeve." Stopping on a dime, I backtracked to spy my little sister, hand-in-hand with the beautiful teacher. Lilah's hair was plaited in an intricate braid that hung down her back like shining copper. She wore a lacy dress the color of new spring leaves, and somehow her wide white collar was still pristine. Beside her, Miss Maeve bent to admire a woolly-headed lamb. The little creature lifted its rounded nose and Lilah scratched behind its ears.

They made such a lovely picture. The fair-haired woman and the lamb, the happy girl enjoying her first trip to the fair. Jealousy spiked through my chest, followed by bitter guilt.

I should want to see Lilah this happy. It scratched at my mind, like a fingernail at a wound, this new and troubling worry that perhaps I was selfish for wanting to take my sister back to New York.

I slipped away, unwilling to face the possibility that I might suddenly be an unneeded visitor in my sister's new life.

After a few minutes of uneasy wandering, I spied Big Tom's wide frame parting the crowd. "I've been hunting for you," he said as he drew near. It was only then that I noticed Abel trailing in his wake. Big Tom hooked his thumbs in the straps of his overalls. "Me and Hettie are about to head back to the farm. You ride on ahead with Abel. There's a job waiting for y'all at the barn."

Meek as a kitten, I nodded and followed Abel out of the tent. He didn't slow his pace, so I sped to match his long strides until we were side by side. I couldn't help sneaking glances at his profile, trying to gauge just how angry he was with me.

"The mama cow isn't doing too well," he said, his tone neutral. We cut across the midway back toward where Merlin stood tied to a tree. "Big Tom thinks pneumonia. We'll have to feed the calf on a bottle until she gets better." He swung up onto the horse, settling behind the saddle instead of in it, extending a hand down to me. "Come on. We better get moving."

I felt my face heat as I realized precisely how snug our riding arrangement would be. Abel noted my unease with a smirk.

"Despite what you may think of me, I won't try anything untoward," he said. "But I can't promise the same for Merlin."

The horse, as if he were in on Abel's game, turned his long face toward me and nuzzled my sleeve. I shoved a foot into the stirrup, grasping Abel's forearm. His muscles tightened and, quick as a blink, I was perched on Merlin's broad back. I shifted so both my legs were on one side with my skirts spread over the horse's flank.

Abel's breath on my neck was warm and unexpected. I should start my apology now, but with him so close, it was hard to think properly. He nudged the horse into motion, and we set out for the farm.

We arrived as the sun dipped below the horizon. I fetched a bucket of water and Abel mixed it with powdered milk. "I should probably change," he said. "Hettie's not fond of trying to scrub calf slobber from my church clothes." He shot up the rickety ladder to the loft, leaving me alone with the calf.

I peered over the waist-high gate into the stall. "He's acting like that scene at the fair never happened," I said to the little bull, who looked at me with solemn black eyes. He sneezed softly, flapping overlarge ears, then licked his left nostril.

I glanced up to the square hole cut in the ceiling. Lantern light flickered down from Abel's loft into the gloom of the barn's lower level. I had to get this over with.

"Can I come up?" I called.

"Yep," Abel said. "I'm always at home to the company of pretty young women." He paused. "Or so I'm told."

Pretty? I swallowed hard, banged my forehead softly on a ladder rung, then skittered up.

Abel's bedroom, such as it was, turned out to be an open, hay-strewn space. A pallet of quilts and a feather pillow on a pile of straw substituted for a bed. There was no washstand or dresser, and his meager wardrobe hung from nails scattered randomly along the walls. A two-foot-tall tree stump served as a makeshift nightstand, with the lantern atop it beaming light into my eyes.

When my vision adjusted, my attention landed on the far wall, where the comfortable dishevelment stopped. A solid, neatly constructed bookcase stood against the rough-hewn plank wall. It held a surprising number of books, all neatly aligned, their spines straight as soldiers. On top of the bookcase, in a wooden frame, was Abel's diploma from the one-room schoolhouse.

From across the loft, Abel paused midway through lacing his work boots. I stood in awkward silence. Abel rose, gesturing grandly. "Miss Pruitt, welcome to my den of iniquity."

The laugh that bubbled up took me by complete surprise. His answering grin was enough to loosen my tongue. "I'm sorry for jumping to conclusions and sticking my nose in where it didn't belong." The dam broken, my words poured out as I crossed the loft. "Papa used to say when I get to Heaven, God will be relieved because He'll finally have someone else to run the world." I sucked in a deep breath and held it, waiting for his reply. A mourning dove cooed in the rafters overhead.

"It was big of you to apologize." He looked at me, running a hand through his tousled hair. "And I accept. You thought you were looking out for someone who needed it. I can appreciate that."

I exhaled in a rush. Suddenly, with my apology done, standing this close to him in this private space became overwhelmingly personal. I needed something bland to say, and fast. "You have a lot of books," I blurted.

"Much like friends, you can't have too many. I'd be happy to loan a few out. All you need to do is sign an oath in blood swearing they'll return unharmed."

"I prefer nonfiction." I pointed to the collected poems of E. A. Robinson. "And while I'm making black confessions, I've never been too interested in poetry."

Abel pressed a broad hand to his heart. His fingers were lightly sprinkled in freckles, barely noticeable in the lantern light. "Some truths are better left unsaid, Miss Verity."

I smiled. "I might be too outspoken at times."

"I'm not so sure about that. I think it's nice to meet a girl who calls it how she sees it."

A high-pitched bawl from the lower floor vibrated through the air. "Sounds like our little fellow is getting impatient." I shoved the lace-trimmed sleeves of my white dress above my elbows. "Shall we get started?"

Abel eyed me, then reached for a cotton shirt hanging on a nearby nail. "You can wear this over what you've got on," he said.

I slid my arms into the sleeves, rolling them up several inches until my hands reappeared. Abel nodded his approval, then swept deftly down the ladder. I grabbed the lantern and followed.

When I joined him on the packed-dirt floor, the calf was wobbling to his feet, still bawling indignantly. I pressed my palm against the wide, flat space between his eyes, and he leaned into my hand like a puppy wanting to play.

"Since he's warmed up to you, I think you should do the honors." Abel handed me the bottle.

I bent low, holding it in the calf's direction. He gave the rubber nipple a skeptical sniff, and turned his head. I tried again with the same results. "I know he's hungry. Why won't he eat?" I demanded. "He reminds me of Lilah. She never knows what's good for her either."

"Lilah is your little sister?" Abel asked, coming to sit on a saddle rack near me. I nodded, rolling the smooth glass between my palms.

"Yes." A memory forced its way forward: A knock on the door of our shabby apartment. Lilah, looking up from a book with a worried frown as I greeted the tidy-looking social worker. "Your father has been taken to the asylum," the woman had said in a voice bland as porridge, launching into a dispassionate summary of how Papa had been apprehended while brandishing a knife on a crowded street, shouting and flailing at attackers no one could see. "I'm here to escort you both to the Children's Benevolence Society Home," the woman had said. "Everything will be all right now."

Part of me was surprised we'd managed to avoid being taken into state custody for so long. But Papa's decline had been gradual, the spells of delusion coming in fits and starts. He'd even managed to hold on to his medical practice, though it was greatly diminished, until around three years ago. Since then, the dark days far outweighed the rational ones. Rumors reached me, casting his delusional public ramblings as the actions of a man too deep in his drink. Some whispered behind gloved hands that Dr. Pruitt had taken too freely of the Bayer pharmaceutical company's latest medicine, heroin. That wasn't the case, but no one could credit that such a brilliant mind had disintegrated all on its own with no outside interference.

"Lilah's all I have left," I said, forcing my mind back to the present. Abel likely took my words to mean she was my only living relative. At times, with the father I'd known when I was a little girl long gone, I almost felt that it was true. "I never dreamed we would be taken to different homes."

"That doesn't seem right to me, splitting up family," Abel said.

The calf's curiosity and hunger had started to win out over his fear of the unknown. He started toward me, skinny tail flicking from side to side. "I agree. But no one asked my opinion." I poked the bottle toward the calf again, but he once more turned up his velvety pink nose.

"There's a trick to it, you know," Abel said.

"You didn't bother telling me before I started?"

"You would've insisted on trying it your way first anyhow." He reached out with the toe of his heavy work boot and playfully tapped the end of my shoe. "Tell me I'm wrong," he challenged.

"Just show me this magical secret," I huffed, trying to hide a smile.

"You've got to straddle him. Get his neck between your knees and hold him still."

The calf butted my knee with his head. "If you're trying to make me look foolish, you'll regret it, Abel Atchley." I captured the creature's neck between my knees. The little beast struggled, flinging my skirts about. A flush stole over my cheeks. "Turn your head, if you don't mind."

"You're awfully concerned with propriety for a girl who showed up in my bedroom not five minutes ago," Abel said.

The calf bucked, nearly toppling me over. "Quit smirking and come help me!"

Abel came over, took the bottle from my hand, and unceremoniously shoved it in the calf's mouth. There was a garbled noise, followed by a gurgling. "Did you drown him?" I asked.

"Just watch," Abel said. The calf swallowed, fluttered his long dark eyelashes in surprise, and took another gulp of milk. He flicked his ears in contentment, then began to drink with gusto.

I took the bottle from Abel and, still keeping the calf pinned with my knees, watched him finish his meal. "We need to give him a name," I said.

"Any suggestions?" Abel asked, leaning against the stall door.

I patted the small rusty spots that dotted the calf's white forehead. "He reminds me of a freckle-faced boy who lived at the children's home. I believe his name was Edward."

Abel propped his chin in his hand. "I've always thought that name sounds like a direction. . . . Backward, forward, westward. Edward."

I laughed. "Your mind works in unusual ways."

Abel shrugged in reply. "I'll take that as a compliment."

The newly christened Edward sucked air from the empty bottle. "That's all for now," I said, looking up to find Abel perched on top of the stall gate. He held out a hand, and I scrambled up beside him.

We balanced on the narrow edge and looked down at the little bull, who butted the wall to show his displeasure. "I guess there's a reason stubborn people are called bullheaded," I said. Edward mooed loudly, deeply offended.

"Lilah would love Edward. I think they're kindred spirits." Unintended words tumbled out into the quiet, warm night air. "When our mama died, I became more a parent than a big sister. I worry about Lilah still, even though there's no reason for it now."

Abel nodded slowly, staring out the double doors into the dark pasture. Shadows massed over the fields. "I know the feeling, except I've got plenty of reason to be concerned for my sister. I can't imagine what'll become of Clara, or her baby."

I hastily dropped my eyes from his handsome, tired face, only to note how our hands rested side by side on the rough wooden beam. "You'll do what you can for Clara. Just like I will for Lilah. Then we'll figure out a way to do even more. Because they're family." I had a sudden, fierce desire to place my hand over his. I banished it as best I could. Now that I knew he didn't have another romantic entanglement, I wondered if he might return Della's affections.

A restless cloud wandered across the moon's face. "It's getting late," I said, realizing how unwilling I was to leave the barn. "Morning comes early around here. I should go get some sleep."

"I think I know just what you need before you turn in for the evening," Abel announced, sliding easily to the ground. I hopped down as he disappeared back up the ladder. He returned moments later, a book in his hand. "Now, don't turn your nose up at a little make-believe," he said. "Sometimes, you need to be someplace else for a while. Even if that someplace exists only in your head."

"My little sister is of the same opinion. You two would get along famously." I sighed, taking the book. "All right, I suppose it couldn't hurt."

❧

The moon shone brightly as I trekked back to the farmhouse. Across the fields, the woods stood like dark, distant sentinels.

The lamps had all been snuffed out in the house. Trying not to wake Big Tom and Hettie, I took off my heeled boots and crept up the stairs. Big Tom's snore rumbled from the back bedroom, reminding me in a strangely affectionate way of the grunty sounds of sleeping pigs.

At the door to my room, I paused to brace myself for the attic heat. It felt like each smothering day never truly ended, but rather bled into night-after-stifling-night. Time passed slowly here. Already it seemed ages ago I'd visited with Lilah and met her new guardian.

I changed into my nightgown and, lighting a candle, sank down onto the hard desk chair and opened the book Abel had lent me. It was a battered copy of *Old Country Fairy Tales*. I leafed through the gilt-edged pages, smiling when I encountered stories my parents had read to me when I was little.

I came to one I'd never heard before. Lifting the book closer to the candle flame, I examined the illustration of a witch beside a red-roofed cottage. The little house perched on barbed rooster's feet. Under the drawing, a caption read, "The witch Baba Yaga lurks in the woods, waiting to prey on unsuspecting children."

Baba Yaga leered up at me, hair bristling white and wild under a kerchief, knobby hands reaching out. Wrinkled lips peeled back to reveal iron teeth, meant to eat children lost in the forest. Chills raced along the back of my neck. The image rose unbidden—a little girl thrashing, panicked, in the grip of gnarled hands tipped with cracked, blood-caked nails.

I slammed the book shut, willing my mind away from the grotesque tale. But a creeping, cold sensation spread over my shoulders.

Certainty surged through me, as sudden and sure as it had been in the woods.

Someone was here.

10

"Abel?" I asked, going rigid in my chair.

No reply.

"Hettie, is that you?" With every muscle tensed, I turned to scan the empty room. My neatly made bed stood in the corner across from the door leading to the stairs. Beside it, the small wardrobe was closed tight.

Heart hammering, I took the candlestick from the desk and rose from my chair. My bare feet slid across the gritty floor toward the wardrobe. With trembling fingers, I reached for the handle. I braced myself and flung open the door.

There was nothing inside but my few dresses, now swaying gently, and my work boots. The sweat-stained straw hat I wore to the fields hung on a nail, looking sad and limp as ever.

I lowered the candle and sighed.

From behind came the barely perceptible shush of fabric moving: a curtain being drawn back.

I whirled to face the intruder. My candle flickered and went out, leaving only the moon's glow to show the figure of a man climbing through my window.

The urge to run swarmed though my limbs. I beat it back,

swallowing sour fear as I raised the candlestick. I rushed forward, aiming for the back of his head.

A rough hand shot up and grabbed my wrist. I gave a cry of alarm, but the man was through the window now. He clamped his other hand firmly across my mouth. I jerked back, freeing my face from his grip, and sucked in a deep breath to scream for help.

The scream died in my throat when I heard the familiar voice. "Hush, Very." The candlestick fell from my fingers to roll in a slow arc near my feet.

"Papa?"

The shock of seeing him washed over me like plunging into icy water. My heartbeat faltered, then picked up a staccato pounding as he held out his arms to gather me into a hug. Stunned, I collapsed against him, resting my face against his coarse jacket.

"Thank God you're still safe," he murmured into my hair.

"How did you get here?" I asked. "Did the doctors say you could come?" A confused hope sprang up. Perhaps he'd gotten better. Maybe a miracle had occurred in the asylum, and through some perfect mixture of the right medications and treatments, he'd been cured. I looked hard into his shining eyes, willing it to be true.

"You mustn't leave your windows open. I've done my best, but I can't promise my wards will be enough." He stepped away, dragging a hand down his haggard face. "The malevolence is near." His eyes darted toward the window. "It's coming closer." My fragile hope withered. The same delusions of wicked, unnatural threats remained. He was as unwell as ever.

I retrieved the candle from the floor and fumbled in my desk drawer for matches. Questions rioted through my mind.

"It was you who left the flowers on the Weatheringtons' porch?" I knew Hettie hadn't believed Big Tom scattered the flowers, but she could've never guessed the true identity of our mysterious benefactor.

Papa nodded, sending a lock of greasy hair into his eye. "Are they working? Has anything sinister touched you?" His eyes continuously scanned the room for danger.

"I'm fine. Nothing bad has happened."

"I'll have to take some wards to wherever Lilah is staying, eventually. First, though, I'll need to go away again for a while. I don't want to leave, Verity, but I must, to throw them off my scent. If I stay on the run, it will confuse them."

I ignored the familiar, paranoid rant. There was no *them*—no pursuers, in this realm or any other, that wanted to harm my father. "How did you get here, Papa?" His commitment to the asylum had not been voluntary. By leaving, he had become a fugitive.

"A nurse told me my girls were in new homes in a little town called Wheeler. As soon as I was left alone, I snuck away and came to find you." Papa licked his cracked lips. "Verity, I know there's a young man living here. I saw the two of you going into the barn. Don't let yourself be led astray. Share a bed with that boy and it will spell disaster." Papa fixed me with a level stare. His pupils dilated, the black swallowing all but the thinnest edge of color. "The wages of sin is death."

I felt a ferocious blush race up my neck. "Papa, you needn't concern yourself about that."

He began pacing like a caged animal. "You never listen to my warnings about the evils unseen, and now you ignore me about the boy?"

"I'm not ignoring you," I said, trying to soothe him. I had

to keep him quiet so he wouldn't wake Big Tom and Hettie yet. I couldn't present him to the Weatheringtons in his current mental state. "It's just that Abel and I are—"

"We were so young, then," he burst out, his gaze growing distant. "So very young when we fell in love." Papa went silent, and I had the notion his blank stare looked into a long-gone time and place.

I held my breath, waiting to see if a moment of lucidity would rise to the surface. If a glimmer of reason showed itself, there might still be hope. Sometimes, I could latch on to a commonplace statement in his ramblings and use it to haul him back to the here and now. "I never thought she would die," he whispered, lips trembling. "And the baby, too. What does a young man know of loss and sorrow and grief? All lifetimes ago, yet I feel it still." He drew a shuddering breath. The candle flame shadowed his eyes, deepening the gaunt hollows beneath his cheekbones.

I moved to sit on the bed, never taking my eyes off Papa. Mama's passing was not something I wanted to dredge up. But at least his thoughts were bending toward the past as it truly was, and not to one of his fevered imaginings.

"I know. I miss Mama still, too." I fought against the memory of my mother, her skin grayish against the ivory satin inside her coffin, the tiny body of my baby brother resting in her lifeless arms.

"My daughter," Papa murmured. His gaze shifted aimlessly around the room. "My little girl." His voice dropped to a gravelly whisper as he added, "Child of my indiscretion. I knew from the start I'd lose her."

"Papa, you're confused again," I said, a chill dancing over my skin. "I'm right here. And Lilah is safe at her new home." I hesitated, unwilling to tell my father where to find Lilah. Miss

Maeve might possibly be sympathetic to his condition, but I doubted Mr. Lybrand would understand. "Neither of us are lost."

Papa rushed forward and knelt before me. He rested his clasped hands on my knees, looking into my eyes with feverish intensity. "Two have been taken, and two left behind. It is right that I should pay for my iniquities, young though I was. I suffer for them daily. But I hope against all hope that you and Lilah might escape." He bowed his head. "You'll have to protect her for me, Verity. It's too late for me. My day of reckoning will come soon." He looked up at me, sad and small and lost.

One of the few unbroken bits of my heart shattered.

I swept the fragments aside, as I always did, and tried to think clearly. "Why don't you lie down and try to get some rest?" I pulled him to his feet, turned to the bed, and fluffed the pillow. "You can have my bed for the night."

Once Papa fell asleep, I'd go down to wake Big Tom and Hettie. He seemed no worse than he had before he was committed, and for that I was grateful. He'd come only out of a delusional need to protect his children. The Weatheringtons could help me get him safely back to New York. I'd need an advance on my pay to buy a train ticket, and it would be best if Papa got on at the station in Argenta or another nearby town to avoid drawing attention.

"No!" Papa's shout broke into my planning. "The nightmares will come again if I sleep." Before I could draw breath, he slipped out the window and ran nimbly across the roof.

"Papa, wait!" I clambered out on hands and knees behind him, cursing my long gown for slowing me. The tin roof still held some of the day's heat, and my feet burned as I hurried on shaky legs across the steep pitch. "Stop! You're going to fall!"

Papa rushed straight toward the edge of the roof. For a

horrific second, I thought he meant to jump. Instead, he made for the spreading boughs of an overhanging oak tree. He was halfway down before I reached it.

I wrapped my hands around a branch. Rough bark bit into my palms. Gripping the limb for all I was worth, I swung off the roof and looked down in time to see Papa's feet hit the ground. He was off like a shot.

Taking a deep breath, I let go.

Hot pain lanced through my left ankle as I landed. I gritted my teeth and hobbled after my father. "Papa! You'll be safe here, I promise." My words came in gasps. "Don't leave."

He was barely visible now, a shadowy form rushing into the black. I ran on, falling behind, watching Papa slip farther and farther away.

I kept my eyes fixed on him until he became one with the night.

At last I limped back to the farmhouse, my face wet with angry tears. I met the Weatheringtons coming out onto the front porch. Big Tom, shirt buttoned wrong and gray hair standing up like a rooster's comb, peered into the dark. "What's the matter?"

"My father," I said around the lump in my throat. "He managed to leave the asylum and make his way here."

"We'll go after him," Hettie said.

"It's no use." I winced as I climbed onto the porch. "If he wants to stay hidden, he'll be impossible to find. He's had a lot of practice."

"What does he think he's hiding from?" Big Tom asked.

I shrugged wearily. "Everything. All of it imagined. He's the one who put the flowers on your porch. He thinks they're wards against evil."

Hettie chewed a thumbnail. "That's a load off my mind. I

couldn't figure out who'd left them. What exactly is he warding against? That Miss Pimsler lady told us a little about his . . . problems, but not much, seeing as how we didn't expect to ever meet him."

"He gets confused about what's real and what's not," I said. "For several years he's been convinced that Lilah and I are in danger from something wicked that he can't quite explain. He came to warn me, so I'd stand guard against the . . . whatever it is he thinks is out there." And also against Abel, although I wasn't about to mention that part.

"The sheriff could track him down, I bet," Hettie said. "We should tell him. And let Miss Maeve and Mr. Lybrand know he's about."

I imagined Sheriff Loftis's distaste for me turning to suspicion when the inevitable question occurred to him: Was Dr. Pruitt's condition hereditary? Would the madman's daughter be next to lose her mind?

"Could we keep this private? Please?" I couldn't stand the thought of Papa being grist for the town gossip mill. And I didn't like the idea of having to tell Miss Maeve, and especially the compassionless Mr. Lybrand, about my father's presence. "He said he's going away again, and I don't think he's figured out where Lilah lives, anyway. He gave his warning. Now he'll keep moving, to lead the darkness away from us." The weight of talking about my father's condition in this much detail pressed down so hard I felt I might sink straight into the ground.

"He's your daddy. We'll handle it however you want." Big Tom's deep voice was soft. "I'll see if I can find any sign of him in the daylight, in case he didn't really leave. If you think he'll be all right, I reckon he will."

I closed my eyes and listened to the night song of a thousand frogs, peeping and chirping in their small, trouble-free world. Exhaustion swept over me. "Doesn't it make you angry when you can't fix things, but you still feel like it's your place to try?"

"It sure does," Hettie said. "Makes me goldang furious." The screen door complained as she swung it open and waved me toward the kitchen. "Now come on inside. I'll warm some milk, to help get us back to sleep."

We circled wordlessly around the table, heads bent over our steaming cups. Big Tom and Hettie didn't speak, but their solid, steady presence soothed my nerves. Against all odds, I began to relax. Quiet wrapped around the candlelit kitchen with the comfort of a well-worn quilt.

I closed my eyes, and let it enfold me.

The water was everywhere, driving spikes of pain through her ears and crushing her chest. She clawed her way through it, up from the slime-slicked stones at the bottom of the well. She dug herself out like a revenant from a grave, and all the while, she tried to forget. To push back the memory of empty skies and blackened trees. She swam harder, fighting away thoughts of a dark river, of blanketing fog and smothering loneliness.

Her fingers shattered a thin sheet of ice as she surfaced in the center of the well. She moved to the stone wall, searching for any gaps in the rock large enough to offer a handhold. But the well circled her in its smooth embrace, and no matter where she grasped for purchase, none could be found. Her white gown billowed around her as she treaded the frigid water. She was trapped and alone, just as she'd been before she threw herself into the depths of the well.

High above, a sound broke the morning quiet. The girl tilted her head back and peered into the circle of sky far above. She held her breath, listening to the telltale crunch of snow underfoot as someone walked through the woods.

When she cried out, her voice rang hollow off the stones.

The steps faltered. She called again, louder this time. The approaching footfalls resumed, with a hesitant shuffle. At last, the tail of a red woolen scarf swayed gently into the void of the well's mouth, and a woman's face leaned into view.

The girl blinked, sending cold drops of water slipping down her pale cheeks, and looked up into the startled eyes staring down. From behind the vivid scarf, the woman uttered a shocked oath and whirled away. She hurried out of earshot, calling for help with every breath.

The girl felt sure the older woman would return with a rope and another set of hands to help pull her from the well. A slithering dread eased up her spine, reminding her of the place of fog and shadow she'd just escaped. Some unnamed, unwanted instinct warned her that she would return there, that she would never be truly free.

For the first time since she'd awakened in the black water, the girl shivered.

II

A persistent thumping under the floor woke me from a fitful
sleep. I threw on a housedress and descended to the kitchen.
Seeing me, Hettie stopped poking at the ceiling with a broom
handle. Sausage links, bacon, eggs, and biscuits sat on the table while a big cast-iron skillet bubbled away on the burner.
The Lord might have commanded rest on the Sabbath, but the
message hadn't gotten to Hettie Weatherington.

"Sorry 'bout that," she said, propping the broom-turned-
alarm-clock in the corner. "I've got to stay right with these
dewberries or they'll scorch. They're for the cobbler." She
stirred the contents of the skillet. "You can't show up to Miss
Maeve's for dinner empty-handed."

In the confusion of last night, I'd forgotten the invitation.
I joined Hettie at the stove to taste a spoonful of the mixture.
"It's sour."

"Dump in another half cup of sugar and stir it up good
until it thickens. Mind it well." Hettie laid a faded scrap of
paper on the counter and untied her apron. "Use this recipe
for the crust. I'm going to get dressed for church." She seemed
determined not to mention my father. I appreciated her sparing

my feelings, but I felt Papa's appearance was too shocking to ignore.

I cleared my throat. "About my father . . ." I hid behind the open pantry door, retrieving flour and shortening. "Thank you again, for understanding. I know it was unnerving. I'm sorry he's—"

Hettie's face appeared as the pantry door swept closed. Her brown eyes were fervid. "Don't ever apologize for your daddy. It ain't his fault he got sick, nor is it yours."

I managed a nod, touched beyond words by her kindness. "Papa used to be a fine physician. He was respected, even admired. I was young, so I didn't really notice the way people tipped their hats to him, or how other men always wanted to shake his hand. Until they stopped doing it, and started crossing the street when they saw us coming." I shook my head. "I decided when I grew up, I was going to be the new Dr. Pruitt. I would regain that respect for our family."

Hettie seemed almost as taken aback as I was when she wrapped me in a sudden, bony hug. "You don't need to do anything for people to respect you except be respectable." She stepped back, holding me at arm's length. "As long as you do right, folk around here will treat you right."

I remembered Sheriff Loftis's cold black eyes and Katherine Ausbrooks's hostility. "You might give people too much credit."

"You might not give them enough. Now, finish the crust and get that cobbler in the oven or it won't get done before we have to leave for church," she said, disappearing down the hall to her room.

Abel's voice came from behind me. "Aunt Het gives the worst hugs. It's like being squeezed by a rake." I looked over my shoulder to find him leaning against the kitchen table.

"But they're rare as hen's teeth, so if you get one, you know she means it." He removed his straw hat and sat down, drumming his fingers on the table with the sound of galloping horses.

"Big Tom filled me in on what happened last night. We searched the property as soon as the sun was up, but there's no sign of your father."

I looked away, unable to meet his worried eyes.

"You could've told me about him. About his problems," Abel said.

"Sometimes people look at me differently when they find out."

"They shouldn't." Abel's gaze grew thoughtful. "And for what it's worth, I think you'd make a fine doctor." He paused, a crooked smile tilting his lips. "Doctors need grit, and you've got that in spades. It almost makes me think you're a Southerner at heart."

I thought of the people I'd met since coming to Wheeler. Of Big Tom's steady resolve and Hettie's determination. Of Della's good-hearted sweetness and Abel's open, easy smiles.

"Well then," I said, stirring the berries one last time, "I suppose that might be all right."

As soon as we walked into church, Della linked her arm in mine. "You're with me today, and I don't want to hear any fussing about it." I smiled in spite of myself as she tugged me along. Della Loftis was a crashing wave of friendship, and there was no fighting the riptide.

Congregants packed the little church like sardines in a tin, and I didn't spot Miss Maeve and Lilah until the service was over. The teacher lifted a slim hand in greeting, and started in our direction, pausing to speak with everyone she passed along the way. Lilah broke free and hurried over, making sure not to full-on run in my direction. Before, she would've pelted pell-mell without a thought.

"You'll love our house, Very," she said, slipping her arm around my waist. "I could stay there forever." Her attention shifted to Della, standing by my side. "I'm Lilah, Verity's sister. How'd you get your hair so fancy?"

Della patted her soaring locks and smiled. "Practice." Lilah nodded appreciatively. "And I think I could do something with your sister's hair, if she'd let me," Della said, brown eyes alight as she examined me. "Verity, how do you feel about curling tongs?"

"How do I feel about heating metal rods in the fireplace and placing them inches from my scalp? I'm against it."

Della waved a dismissive hand. "They're just the thing to take that kink out. I've used them lots and only ever burned myself twice. The second time didn't even leave a scar."

Lilah shot me a look of wide-eyed amusement.

"I think Verity is quite pretty, just as she is," Miss Maeve's silvery voice said. There was something odd in her tone, but I couldn't say what. Her pale eyes wandered across my face, and I felt myself flush under her attention. "We're happy to have your company for Sunday dinner, Verity. Lilah has talked of nothing else all day."

On the church porch, Abel spoke with a short, thin woman who looked so much like Hettie I decided this must be her sister, Mrs. Atchley. A passel of children ran circles around her feet, making it hard to tell exactly how many offspring she had. "A lot" seemed a decent estimate. There was a solemn-looking girl of about thirteen at her side, but Clara, Abel's sister who was in the family way, was noticeably absent. Abel leaned down to kiss his mother on her worn cheek, then came over, the dewberry cobbler I'd made balanced carefully on his wide palms.

"Don't want to forget this," he said, handing me the dish. "You know, it's partly my doing." He held up a hand, the tips of his fingers faintly purplish. "Hettie made me pick the berries for her yesterday."

"Don't be pitiful," Della said. "I can't count how many times you've made me come along to gather berries. I always end up with briars stuck in my arms, and when we picked the patch down by the creek, I got poison ivy on my face." She dropped her voice, adding darkly, "And other places. You can't imagine how that stuff spreads. What kind of gentleman would ask a young lady to come along on such a fool's errand?" From her barely concealed smile, I knew she would've followed Abel through a briar patch in the pits of Hell if he'd wanted her to.

Abel fished a white handkerchief from his trouser pocket and waved it like a tiny flag of surrender. "Hold your fire, Miss Loftis."

Miss Maeve watched the little exchange. "You two should join us for dinner. Abel earned it with the sweat of his brow. And I'm sure he'd appreciate it if Della came along." Miss Maeve looked to me, expectantly. It seemed my reaction to this invitation was of great interest to the teacher.

"The more the merrier," I said.

"Wonderful." She smiled to herself, absently smoothing the tumbling heap of ribbons atop Lilah's Sunday hat. "We'll wait while y'all get permission." Abel and Della walked away, laughing together in their easy manner. I watched them, realized I was frowning, and quickly looked away to find Lilah waving excitedly at a skinny, redheaded boy.

"Cecil!" she called. "Your agate marble is mine come Monday. I'll win it just like I did the cat's eye." A competitive gleam sparked in her hazel eyes.

"Oh yeah?" the boy said, grinning as he came over. He pulled a shiny marble from his pocket. "We'll see about that."

"Maybe I'll take it right now," Lilah boasted. She grabbed the boy's hand in hers.

"Doubt it," Cecil retorted. He trapped both their fists with his other hand and tugged her toward him, laughing. "Got you now," he said while Lilah giggled.

"Let her go." Miss Maeve's voice was clipped and cold.

I looked up, surprised. Cecil dropped Lilah's hand and stepped away. He glanced at Lilah, who flushed with embarrassment.

"They're just playing, Miss Maeve," I said, rankled by the overreaction to a harmless crush.

"No," Lilah said. "Mama's right." I felt my shoulders stiffen. Miss Maeve was already "Mama"? "A young lady should conduct herself with discretion," she said, as though reciting from memory.

The tension dissipated from Miss Maeve's face. "We should always be on our best behavior, especially on the Lord's day." A warm smile crossed her lips, but in the shade of her hat brim, her eyes remained chilly.

"Run along now, Cecil. I'll see you at school tomorrow," Miss Maeve said. The boy nodded and scampered away. "I've left the yeast rolls rising, and they should be just about ready to bake by now," she added, her composure restored.

We traipsed after her to where Reuben Lybrand sat waiting in his car. Della swished over to say Abel had gone on ahead with Merlin, leaving room for the rest of us in the vehicle.

There was a good deal of "No, you sit up front," with some

"Oh, I wouldn't dream of it," and a smidge of "Can we all just hurry up and go?"—that was from Lilah—before we all settled in.

Despite my best efforts, I ended up in the front next to Mr. Lybrand. "I'm looking forward to visiting your home," I said, raising my voice over the growl of the car's engine.

"Delighted to have your company," he replied, with all the delight of a man about to have a molar extracted. His fingers in their fine driving gloves tightened on the steering wheel as we pulled out of the churchyard and headed away from the town.

We sped along the road that skirted the woods. Pleasant conversation not being an option, I lapsed into silence and studied the passing trees. Today, they struck me as peaceful, even lovely. Sunlight skipped through the breeze-tossed upper branches. I had a fleeting idea that the woods beckoned, calling me into their shadowy embrace.

I shook my head, scattering the fancy. Perhaps the little girl in the woods had felt a similar tug, tempting her to come play there. The trees whipped by as we sped along, and I strained to catch a glimpse of her. The child never appeared, but something else caught my attention.

A thick layer of fog hovered near the ground at the edge of the tree line. As I watched, it swelled, rising like a tide. The fog swirled about, lofting and diving as if in the power of a strong breeze. I turned to see if anyone in the back seat had noticed the unusual sight, but they seemed intent on their own conversation. Behind the steering wheel, Mr. Lybrand's eyes were fixed straight ahead, his bulldog jaw set. When I looked back into the black crush of trees for any sign of the roiling mists, they'd already thinned to tattered wisps. Within seconds, the fog had evaporated to nothing.

Mr. Lybrand turned onto a short drive, grassy from infrequent use, taking us closer to the forest. I chewed at my left thumbnail, still trying to understand what could've caused the fog.

Miss Maeve noticed my fixation. "We aren't going into the woods, exactly, just to the edge," she said. "Uncle Reuben built the house many years ago. Had I been living with him then, I would've suggested we settle right in town, so we'd have close neighbors. But he's never cared for the busy town life."

I pushed away a smile at the idea of Wheeler, Arkansas, ever being considered busy, and turned my attention to the grand house rising before me.

Mr. Lybrand's home was a stately, three-story affair painted a deep gray and trimmed in white. Black shutters framed picture windows along a wraparound porch. A widow's walk ringed the upper balcony beneath turrets that gave the place a castlelike appearance. But anything of the imposing man's taste ended with the architecture. The rest had to be Miss Maeve's handiwork.

The porch dripped with hanging baskets of petunias in shades of purple and lavender. Hydrangea bushes drooped with clumps of sky-blue blossoms along one side of the house. A dozen crepe myrtle trees bordered a brick pathway through well-tended grass, white petals dropping from their branches like errant snowflakes. One entire wall of the house supported a trellis of dainty cream-colored rosebuds, and a towering magnolia with glossy leaves and pearly blooms stood sentry over all.

Mr. Lybrand parked the car in a carriage house nearly devoured by climbing roses. Lilah had the car door open before we even stopped rolling. "Isn't it pretty here?" Her short skirt lifted as she leapt out.

"It's gorgeous," I said, noting Miss Maeve's proud posture as she took Lilah's hand.

"I've always wanted to see where you lived, Miss Maeve," Della admitted, drinking in the scene as we strolled the neatly groomed lawn. "I'd heard Mr. Lybrand had a nice place, but this is . . . it's . . ." She turned a full circle, as if the right description might be hiding behind her.

"I'd say vibrantly verdurous," Abel said, appearing from the stables.

Della sighed. "You and those five-dollar words."

Lilah walked backward, pointing out her favorite spots. "I helped trim the dead blooms off the roses," she said.

"Sounds better than picking bugs off the potato plants and dropping them in kerosene to kill them," I said. "That's the sort of gardening I've been doing at the farm." Lilah lolled her tongue out in dramatic disgust. I knew she was impressed.

Miss Maeve led us across the wide porch to massive double doors. She pushed one open to reveal a soaring foyer. "Welcome to our home," she said warmly. "I hope you'll treat it as your own."

"And take that for the polite bunkum it is, not an invitation to move in," Mr. Lybrand groused as he brushed by and marched down a hallway. The rest of us filed in, our steps echoing off the polished hardwood floors. I ran a finger along the patterns of twisting leaves and vines swirling through the burgundy wallpaper. I hadn't been in a place this grand since I was a little girl.

Lilah charged up the stairs, calling down that she was going to put her hat away.

"Change out of your church dress, too," Miss Maeve said, hanging her own hat on a stand. Light spilled in from a transom window high overhead, turning her hair to shining platinum. "Uncle Reuben's probably in his study, third door on the right," she said. "Why don't y'all sit and visit while I set the table?" She vanished through an open door into a formal dining room.

"I'd like to help you, if that's all right," I called after her.

"Me, too," Della added quickly. We exchanged a knowing look. Neither of us wanted to visit with the charming Reuben Lybrand.

"I'll go keep Mr. Lybrand company, then." Abel passed between Della and me, giving us each a gentle jab with his elbows. "Thanks a lot," he whispered.

In the dining room, Miss Maeve swept a sterling pitcher of iced tea from a credenza and poured six glasses, placing them on a large oval dining table that gleamed with a mirror-finish shine. Della and Miss Maeve talked comfortably as they laid fine bone china on the table. When Lilah returned, she set to work folding napkins with intense concentration, her tongue poking out of the corner of her mouth.

I did my best to help, but my focus was drawn to the clawed feet of the dining room chairs. The fairy tale of Baba Yaga and her rooster-footed house in the woods flashed through my mind, dragging along thoughts of my father's bizarre visit.

"Are you all right, Verity?" Miss Maeve asked, dumping a spoonful of extra sugar into a glass of tea. She gave it a stir and handed it to me with a concerned look.

"Fine, thank you," I said with a start. "Maybe just a little tired." I sipped the syrupy drink. "We spent the day at the fair yesterday. I saw you and Lilah as I was leaving." I took a sip, not wanting to mention that I'd purposefully avoided them. The caffeine in the tea must've been stout as a draft horse. Already, I felt a little better. "Abel and I had to leave early for chores."

"We didn't stay long, either, I'm afraid," Miss Maeve said. "Uncle waited in the car, so we had to hurry."

"I don't care to travel after dark." Mr. Lybrand's imperious voice came from the doorway. "My niece and I spend our evenings at home." Miss Maeve's smile tightened around the edges as her uncle spoke.

"I'd like to say grace," she said, sending a quick look at Mr. Lybrand, who scowled.

We took our seats and bowed our heads. Through one squinted eye, I watched Lilah's primly clasped hands creep apart. Sneaky fingers eased toward the plate of rolls until, with a lightning-fast strike, she snatched one and shoved the entire thing in her mouth. To my right, Abel made a sound suspiciously like a laugh pretending to be a cough. Miss Maeve's head stayed bowed with perfect piety.

Sipping my tea, I found myself relaxed and happy throughout dinner, something I'd never imagined possible. For me, small talk had always been the social equivalent of breaking out in hives—it made me feel itchy and squirmy and all-around bad in my own skin. But Miss Maeve was a charming hostess who made everyone feel welcome.

As the meal wound down, Lilah shoveled in the last forkful of cobbler and wiped her berry-stained lips. "I want to show Verity the arbor. May I?"

"That would be all right," Miss Maeve said, loading a tray with a coffeepot and cups. "We'll move to the back porch. Della, would you mind helping me carry everything?"

Della darted a look at Abel, but rose from her seat with a gracious smile. "Of course."

"You can come with us," Lilah said to Abel, as if he'd just been invited to visit with royalty.

Abel inclined his head solemnly. "Thank you most kindly."

The arbor rested at the edge of the lawn near the woods, its domed roof supported by sturdy white columns. Lavender blooms clustered on rich green vines so thick they formed solid, living walls. "This is as far as I'm allowed to go in the yard," Lilah said. "I'm not supposed to get too close to the woods. Nobody will tell me *why,* though."

She bounded up the three steps leading into the arbor and disappeared behind the curtain of pale purple flowers. I pushed back the fall of blooms and ducked into the shade, Abel at my heels.

He settled on a stone bench. "Here's what I've heard from some of the old folks." He pitched his voice lower, and took on the rhythm of a fairy tale. "Once upon a time, maybe a hundred years ago—"

Lilah interrupted, "'Once upon a time's are supposed to be long, long ago. When there were castles and queens and things like that. A hundred years ago isn't far enough back to make a good story."

"Hate to disappoint, but when it comes to tales about the woods, about a hundred years is as far back as the stories go. That was when some settlers came over from Ireland, looking for farmland. When they got here, they found a well in the woods. Nobody knows for sure who built it, but it might've been the French fur traders who passed through in the seventeen hundreds."

"Or maybe it was *always* there," Lilah said, pleased by this potentially mystical origin.

"Maybe," Abel allowed, hiding a smile. "Regardless, the Irish brought their stories from the old country, about how there are certain places where the earth's magic congregates. And when you go near one of those places, you just *feel* like you're close to the edge of something big. Sort of like if you stand on a cliff with your eyes closed. You can't see it, but you can sense the open space before you. It feels big and grand, but also dangerous."

"Powerful," I said, quietly. Being near the well felt like standing outside before a lightning storm, when the air was charged.

Abel nodded. "The settlers decided not to use the well, and to steer clear of the woods altogether. The whole place gives me the creeps, so I don't blame them. Nowadays people sometimes see weird things in the woods. Like glimpses of something white moving through the trees, or a cold fog even on the hottest days."

"Maybe someone should properly investigate. There's a scientific explanation for everything, if we only know where to look for it," I said.

Abel's eyes were bright. "'There are more things in heaven and earth, Horatio, than are dreamt of in your philosophy.'" On seeing my puzzled expression, he laughed. "Don't tell me you never read *Hamlet* in school? I'll gladly hand over my copy."

"Anytime we're together, I end up with a reading assignment," I said.

A bee flitted through the blooms, industrious and unworried, its fat body flecked with pollen. I watched its progress, lost in thoughts of fog and cold and legend until Lilah's voice pulled me back as she fired a question at Abel. "Are you and Della sparking? I saw you two talking at dinner."

"Lilah," I snapped. "That's hardly your concern."

Her retort was drowned out by Abel's surprised laughter. "I talked to Verity, too. Does that mean we're sparking?"

Lilah put her hands on her hips and cocked her head. "Mama answers my questions with other questions, too." I cringed inwardly, as I did each time she called Miss Maeve her mama. "Are you and Della sweet on each other or not?"

Miss Maeve's voice floated over the sultry air. "Lilah, Della and I need your help."

"Yes, ma'am," Lilah called over her shoulder. She gave Abel a look that said "you haven't heard the last of this" and dashed away, strawberry-blond hair flying. Miss Maeve had terrible timing. Despite what I'd said to Lilah about minding her own business, I was just as curious as my sister to know whether Abel was taken with Della.

"That girl's a pistol," Abel said, strolling over to sit beside me. The familiar sun-warmed-straw scent clung to his clothes. He pulled a mint leaf from his pocket and stuck it in his mouth.

Maybe his nearness addled my reason, but the words were out before good sense had time to wrestle them down. "I think Della would like it if you two were an item."

Abel leaned forward, resting his forearms on his knees. A lock of blond hair slid forward. I couldn't see his expression, only a tense flicker of muscle in his jaw.

"I'm sorry," I said hastily. "That's none of my concern."

"It's all right. If you assume Della and I are a couple, you're like ninety percent of the town. There's always been 'Della and Abel.' I hardly remember a time when we weren't side by side." He studied the leaf-strewn ground. "How could anyone not love her? She's kind, and thoughtful. Easy to be with."

Abel lifted his head, and I felt him shift slightly to look at me. I stared down at my hands in my lap, wishing I hadn't pried. Of course he had feelings for Della, his lifelong friend who'd grown into an attractive, good-hearted young woman. The realization sent an unexpected twinge through my chest.

Abel stretched his long legs and crossed his boots one over

the other. His right hand rested on the bench between us, square and strong, tanned by hours in the fields.

"Do you plan to farm all your life?" I asked. Della said he'd wanted to teach, and I found I could picture him in that role.

He looked surprised by the tangential question. "I don't think I've got the luxury of making plans. I really loved English in school. If things were different . . ." He paused, shook his head. "Life runs in a pretty deep rut around here. You find a girl, you get married, raise a family, and do whatever your father did." His light brows lowered into a frown. "Except I won't follow in my father's footsteps. Drunk and gambler aren't exactly reliable professions."

"Not exactly," I agreed.

Abel's eyes on mine were rueful, with a hint of real loss behind them. "Everyone needs me. Mama and the other kids, Big Tom and Hettie. I'm not sure it really matters what I want."

I'd heard the same bitterness in my own voice when I'd told Lilah we would be leaving New York, and no, we didn't have a choice.

"It does matter, Abel." Without thinking, I reached for his hand. My fingers rested atop his, the heat of his skin matching the warmth in my voice. "If there's something else you want, you can find a way to have it. I know you can."

Abel's eyes dropped to where my hand lay over his. I pulled it away, embarrassed by my outburst. "I didn't mean to be forward," I said. "But I hate for you to think you have no options. It's a terrible feeling."

A mockingbird lit on the arbor steps in a flurry of white and gray, singing its ever-changing song, a mimicry of other birdcalls. We listened to it for a few minutes, both lost in our own thoughts. "They don't just sing the songs of other birds," Abel noted, rising to his feet. "They have their own unique sounds, too. Most people just don't listen long enough to recognize them."

"Let's go to the porch, before Lilah comes back out here," I said. "With Miss Maeve nearby, she won't pester as much."

Abel chewed his mint leaf, pushing back the curtain of wisteria. He leaned down, bringing his lips close to my ear. "I'd offer you my arm, but we'd never hear the end of it from a certain little sister."

I whirled and hastened toward the group on the porch, thankful the high collar of my dress hid the flush creeping over my skin. Abel strode beside me, the ghost of a smile lingering on his face.

12

As we drew near the house, Miss Maeve looked between Abel and me with a knowing expression that vanished so quickly, I wondered if I'd imagined it.

I plunked down in the porch swing next to Lilah. Miss Maeve handed round coffee, then joined us on the swing. She opened a fan to wave in front of her face. "Uncle Reuben has gone inside to rest. He often does during the heat of the day." She worked up a false smile, and I suspected Mr. Lybrand simply couldn't be bothered to socialize. I wondered, not for the first time, how she'd convinced the ill-tempered man to let a child come live with them. "Lilah, why don't you go find your new doll? Verity might like to see it."

Lilah leapt up, sending the swing rocking on its chains. "You'll love her. She's got a porcelain face and hands, and real leather shoes. . . ." She disappeared into the house, still talking.

Miss Maeve planted a delicate foot on the porch to calm the swing's motion. "Lilah is a darling girl," she said. I smirked at her choice of adjective, and Miss Maeve's laugh bubbled like spring water. "Oh, she's spirited, to be sure. But she'll mellow, in time. We have many happy years ahead of us."

I pressed my lips together to trap a hasty reply. Had Miss Maeve been more insistent with her uncle and Miss Pimsler, perhaps I'd be here with my sister, together, as family was meant to be.

And perhaps it was this thought and the persistent bit of anger I couldn't quite bury that spurred my confession. "Miss Maeve, I don't want to sound unappreciative, but I plan to take my sister back one day. When I'm eighteen, my indenture will end, and I'll return to New York." I looked hard into her pale eyes. "There's no way I would ever leave her behind for good."

Across from us, Abel and Della exchanged a nervous glance. Miss Maeve studied my face. Absently, she toyed with something at her wrist. A bracelet peeked out from under the edge of her frilly sleeve. Made of brown, twisted vine, it didn't fit with the woman's otherwise elegant outfit. A closer look showed a lock of rich auburn hair entwined in the strange jewelry. It must've been a superstitious charm, like the one Hettie wore.

Maeve's fingers worried a tiny bit of polished gold that hung from the braided vines. "I'm not surprised that you would have such hopes," she said. "But life has a way of deciding matters for us. Fewer things are in our power than we think."

The muscles in my shoulders tightened. "I've never adhered to the 'things will work themselves out' school of thought."

"That doesn't surprise me." Miss Maeve held my gaze, her expression unreadable. I shifted on the hard swing. Why did the woman speak as if she knew me well enough to predict my attitudes and plans?

The front door opened, breaking the strangeness of the moment. Instead of Lilah returning, Mr. Lybrand stepped out.

"Ladies, I'll be taking you both home now." He went off toward the car without waiting for our agreement.

Della sighed, rising from her chair. "Thank you again for having us, Miss Maeve."

"There's really no need for Mr. Lybrand to drive Verity all the way back," Abel said. "We can both ride Merlin."

The cacophony of metal gears spinning and the engine backfiring announced that Mr. Lybrand had the Ford cranked and running. "I suppose it'll just be Mr. Lybrand and me, then," Della said.

"I'm sorry," I mouthed.

"I won't pitch a fit for you to ride with me, but you owe me," Della leaned in to whisper. I laughed nervously, wondering at Della's unconcern that I'd be riding alone with Abel. Either she didn't have a jealous bone in her body, or I wasn't worth thinking of as a threat. Did I suddenly consider myself a rival for his affections?

Della took her leave, climbing into the front seat beside Miss Maeve's dour uncle with a tragic look in my direction.

"I'm going to tell Lilah goodbye," I said to Miss Maeve, not stopping to ask for permission to reenter her home. I stepped into the foyer, stilling at the sound of Lilah singing somewhere far above. My fingers trailed against the silky wood of the banister and, as I climbed, the words of the song became clearer.

"Abide with me, fast falls the eventide
The darkness deepens
Oh, with me abide . . ."

The sad, strange lullaby drew me onward. At the top of the stairs, I pushed open a door and peered inside a spacious, airy bedroom. A white wrought-iron bed, draped in layers of frothy, gentle pink fabric, sat against one wall. Brimming shelves of trinkets and overflowing toy chests ringed the rest of the space. In one corner stood a little writing desk. In the center of the room sat a white rocking chair with a high, intricately carved back. The faded velvet of its cushions looked worn, and the braided rug underneath showed signs of heavy wear.

Lilah leaned over a crib, gently untucking crocheted blankets from around her doll. "I was just about to come outside," she said, noticing me for the first time. "But since you're here, come see Winifred." I oohed and aahed over the porcelain doll while Lilah turned the handle to a silver music box. The eerie song she'd been singing filled the air.

"That's a bit melancholy, isn't it?"

"It's a hymn from church. It's supposed to be about God abiding with you, but Mama changed the words just a little, so now it's about us." Lilah plunked down into the thronelike chair. "I told her she didn't have to sing to me. Eleven is too old for lullabies."

"But not too old for dolls?" I joked.

Lilah's skin pinked under her freckles, and I felt instantly ashamed. Lilah had missed out on many typical childhood things when she was younger. If she wanted to dote on a special plaything now, what did it hurt? This life with Miss Maeve would be the first time Lilah had ever been truly mothered. I'd done my best, but I'd been just a child myself.

"Mama says I shouldn't rush to grow up," Lilah said. "But I'm practicing for when I'm a lady. I'm going to be a mother one day."

"And a writer," I added. I moved to the writing desk and rolled her shining gold fountain pen under my finger. "Don't forget that."

Lilah took the pen and spun it deftly between her fingers. "I'm going to do both," she said with such certainty I knew she would.

"Good. And I'm sorry I teased you about the doll," I said. "I'm glad you have Winifred." Absently, I opened the closet door. "And such a lot of lovely dresses."

"Let me show you the one I'm wearing to the ice cream social on Saturday. Are you going to be there? Mama's head of the Ladies' Aid Society, so she's in charge of everything. If you come, wear that white dress from our trip down here. It's your best one by a mile."

"I'll try to be there, but it depends on what needs doing on the farm that day," I said. Lilah shoved aside dresses with abandon until she laid hands on a sea-foam voile creation. She held it against herself, admiring the effect in a cheval glass.

"You're getting to be quite a fashion plate," I said. "That's a pretty color on you. It brings out the green in your eyes."

Lilah looked bashful at the compliment. She hung the dress hurriedly, then whirled away to rummage in a chest of drawers. "I've got a ribbon to match somewhere."

The frock slipped from its wooden hook. I bent, then shifted the tightly packed clothes aside to rehang the dress. A glint of metal caught my eye.

"Lilah, what's this?" I asked, running a finger along a hinge in the closet's back wall. "Where does this door go?"

Lilah turned, a clump of ribbons twining through her fingers like snakes. "Mama said it's a room where we can be safe, if we ever need it. She keeps it locked." Her eyes sparked with their usual mischief as she stooped and flipped up the edge of the rug to reveal a brass key. "But she's not very good at hiding things." With a flourish, she inserted the key in the lock.

"Why on earth does Miss Maeve think you might ever

need to hide in your own home?" I felt my heart go heavy. Did Miss Maeve think her uncle was dangerous? Or was some other threat lurking near their home? I glanced out the window to the woods.

"Mama's a worrier, just like you. She says it's best to be prepared," Lilah said as the door glided silently open under her fingertips and we passed single file into a dark, windowless room.

I blinked around at a space nearly as large as the downstairs parlor.

"Nothing much to see," Lilah said, stepping over a pile of newspapers. "I think she puts old, broken stuff in here, mostly." She nudged a cracked terra-cotta flowerpot with her toe, sending a shower of blackened leaves raining down from the withered plant inside. A plain worktable stood against the wall to the right, a cluster of empty glass bottles and unused candles neatly arranged on its surface. A little Primus stove squatted nearby. Hints of something earthy mixed with the sharper scent of recently burned kerosene. I wiped sweat from my upper lip, wondering at why Miss Maeve needed extra heat in the stifling upstairs room.

"You're probably right. Miss Maeve is just overly cautious," I said, recalling that I'd had bolt-holes scoped out at a few of the places we lived in New York. "But if you ever feel unsafe, tell me right away. Deal?"

Lilah exhaled sharply through her nose. "I will. Now stop worrying." She turned and pushed back through the dresses and into her bedroom. I carefully shut the door to the strange room, unease nagging at me.

"Would you like to have a tea party? Mama got me a nice set of china all my own. Della and Abel can join us," Lilah said, locking the door and slipping the key back into its hiding place. "I like Abel a lot," she added. "He has nice teeth."

I relaxed in spite of myself. "He does, doesn't he? But we can't stay. Mr. Lybrand wants us to leave. I came to tell you goodbye."

Her face went stony. "Mr. Lybrand can sit on a tack."

"Don't let anyone hear you talking like that," I said, worrying more about her safety than her manners.

"I heard him arguing with Miss Maeve yesterday. He told her I had no business being here, and she knew it," Lilah said. "She told him it was her choice to make."

"Good for her," I said.

Lilah bit her bottom lip. "He kept saying 'you know this is wrong.' Like it was some awful thing for her to be my mother now. He said it wasn't meant to be, and she shouldn't tamper with the natural order of things."

The music box wound down, plinking a tinny, discordant note. "You've got to ignore mean people, Lilah. Don't let him make you unhappy."

"I won't," she said, firmly.

I envied Lilah's buoyant spirit. Mine seemed to sink with any change in the currents. With a final hug, I slipped out of the room.

I crept down the stairs, expecting any moment to be dragged under by a wave of loneliness.

13

"You're awfully quiet." Abel's comment startled me from a brooding silence.

I half turned in the saddle, taking in the way he wore his hat shoved back with careless ease. He'd spent our ride thus far whistling in a merry, out-of-tune way. I was more than a little jealous of his good spirits. And of how easy it looked to ride astride while I wrestled skirts and petticoats to sit sidesaddle.

"I'm just tired," I lied. But the pesky urge to tell Abel what I was really thinking buzzed in my brain like a mosquito. "Also, I should feel relieved and happy for Lilah, and I do. But it bothers me that she doesn't need me anymore."

"There's nothing you *should* feel," Abel said. "Your family's been torn apart. Just because y'all survived doesn't mean it didn't hurt. Don't apologize for still being sad. Or incandescently angry, even."

I sighed. "The past few months have felt like an earthquake. It'll be better when I get back to New York and find work. Once I turn eighteen, I can be Lilah's legal guardian."

Abel glanced quickly away. "Sounds like you've got it all

figured out." He flicked the reins, and Merlin picked up his pace as the farm came into view.

We ducked our heads and rode into the musty stable. Thoughts in a murky swirl, I barely noticed when Abel dropped to the ground and reached for me. Without stopping to think, I placed my hand in his callused palm.

I landed facing him, suddenly aware of how warm his fingers were over mine. Powdery bits of straw dust rose to swirl around our legs. From the small window, a square of light shone in, setting bright fire to the gold in Abel's hair.

I had to fight the desire to pull him closer. He held my gaze for a long moment. My heart beat a staccato rhythm that was almost painful. The temptation to lean in, to brush my lips against his grew, but I held back. These feelings could be entirely one-sided. Abel might view me as a new friend, and nothing more. That thought was enough to make me let go of his hand. "Thank you," I said, stepping away.

"My pleasure," he replied. I recalled that breathing was essential and inhaled deeply.

"It's about time y'all showed up," Hettie said, poking her head into the stable. A basket of eggs swung from her wrist. "I had to get these myself before the hens took to breaking them." The warmth in her voice belied the snippy words. "How was your visit? Your baby sister doing all right?"

"Yes, ma'am," I said. "She seems well." Maybe a little too well, if that was possible.

Hettie sidled closer, dropping her voice and looking around the stalls as if we might be overheard. "I didn't hear no gossip at church about any strangers around. I'm guessing your daddy really did leave town."

"Are you going to tell Mr. Lybrand and Miss Maeve he

was here?" Abel asked. "Just in case he comes back to call on Lilah?"

My stomach dropped when I thought of explaining my father's condition to Reuben Lybrand. What if he decided providing a home for Lilah, child of a madman who might show up on his doorstep at any moment, was far too much trouble? He could send her away, and she'd be shipped off on another orphan train to who knew where.

"I think we should leave it be, for now. If he's even still here, he won't stay long. He truly believes he has to keep running." The burn of sudden, unshed tears stung my eyes, but my tone was brisk and sure. "Hettie, I know you've got chores that need doing. Let's get started."

❧

Days passed with no further word from Papa. I spent my time working side by side with the Weatheringtons and Abel. Big Tom gave me a hatchet and tasked me with turning a fallen tree into firewood for the coming winter. Despite the splinters in my palms, stacking the wood in the woodshed left me with a sense of accomplishment. In this small way, when I went back north I'd leave the Weatheringtons a bit better off than they'd been when I arrived. However, my sense of accomplishment was less significant after the days I spent hauling and spreading manure for fertilizer.

Under Hettie's tutelage, I managed to pluck a chicken, churn butter, and wrangle the horse-drawn plow as it tilled furrows in the rich, dark soil. Any time I worked outside, Abel had a way of turning up. Together we fed and watered the horses and slopped the hogs. We worked as a team to tend the sick mama cow, and both shed tears the morning we found she hadn't survived the night. And when it was my turn to feed Edward, Abel always seemed to wander into the barn to join me.

One afternoon, Hettie and I were in the kitchen, up to our elbows in bread dough, when Abel entered. He'd gone to Wheeler with a load of potatoes to sell to the store, and stopped by the post office to pick up a new book he'd ordered. He laid a slim envelope on the table. "This came for you today," he said before retreating back outside. Hettie shot me a curious look, but didn't pry.

I could just make out the return address. I tucked it non-chalantly in my pocket and continued working the dough, trying hard not to think that this note could change my future.

It was Aunt Susan's reply to the hasty query I'd sent that first day in Wheeler. I'd asked if she had any knowledge of other relations Lilah and I might have. Blood relatives would be allowed, per the orphanage policy, to take both of us in together.

I kneaded until my knuckles were sore and my shoulders ached, thoughts straying over and over to Aunt Susan's letter. When evening approached, I ate a hasty supper, then rushed outside, saying I needed some fresh air.

The sun melted toward the horizon. I made for the dark recesses of the barn, settled on a pile of feed sacks, and lit my lantern. With shaky fingers, I unfolded the single sheet of paper and read my aunt's spidery script.

Dear Verity,

I hope this letter finds you well. While I understand you are troubled at being separated from Lilah, remind yourself that finding families willing to care for you both is a blessing, and keep a grateful spirit.

In answer to your question, I do not know of any Pruitt relatives who might be living in Arkansas. Our family has no connection with the state, besides your father's brief and ill-advised stint in the summer of 1888. In answer to your curiosity regarding his time there, I suppose it does no harm to tell you of your father's foolhardy decisions of the past, although they were a great source of distress to our dear parents.

When he finished school, Matthew defied our father's wishes and did not begin medical training right away. He went south, with a frivolous desire to "be his own man." He traveled about, finding work as a manual laborer, a station far beneath our family's dignity. We had a letter saying he had settled for the harvest season on a farm in Arkansas, then heard nothing more for months, until he abruptly returned with a change of heart regarding his career.

Mother and Father were delighted Matthew suddenly wanted to begin medical school, but I noticed he was greatly changed—moody, withdrawn, sometimes sullen. I believe now this was the first sign of the madness that would befall him, although I did not realize it at the time.

His agitation intensified when he began receiving letters from your mother. Yet it seemed he longed for more of the very notes that caused him obvious pain. He haunted the front hall, waiting for the postman to deliver the mail each day. That winter, Elizabeth appeared on our doorstep. They were married soon after.

Perhaps, as you read this, you might wonder if you have relations on her side near your current abode. That I cannot say. Our parents, rest their souls, never spoke of your mother's background. It was not their place, but—forgive me if this offends—I have always suspected they knew something

*unseemly about her past. I know very little of who Eliza-
beth was before she came to New York. I do remember she
was from a small town called Argenta. Elizabeth said the
name was taken from the Latin for silver, and I found it
odd an uneducated girl from a rural community would
know such a fact.*

*I married my dear Phillip soon after your parents wed
and, in rearing my own little family, never found time to
spend with Matthew and Elizabeth.*

*Dear niece, I do pity you and Lilah. We can only hope
your father's condition was not passed down to either of
you. It is a shame I was unable to let you stay here and
attend school as he wished. You and Lilah would have been
most welcome, but Phillip and I have suffered financial
reversals that made it impossible to add two more to our
household.*

I keep you both in my thoughts and prayers.

Your loving Aunt Susan

I bit my lower lip and tasted blood. I was sure Aunt Susan's
"financial reversals" were nonexistent. More likely, she didn't
want her reputation sullied by taking in the children of her
lunatic brother.

But Aunt Susan had proved more help than she imagined.
My mother came from Argenta. How strange, to realize I'd
wandered the county fair in her hometown, unaware of the
connection.

Argenta, a little farming town, was the perfect place for a
young man to find work. Papa had done just that, ceasing his
travels to try his hand working on a farm. And, according to
Aunt Susan, when he returned to New York, he'd gotten letters of an upsetting—and apparently very personal—nature

from my mother. It was obvious that they'd had a relationship during his summer in the South.

I wandered from the barn into the dusky evening, lantern dangling in my hand. Papa's disjointed words came back to me. *"We were so young then . . . so very young when we fell in love . . . child of my indiscretion."*

I strung the pieces together: Papa and Mama met in Argenta while he worked the harvest. Then he returned to New York, she followed several months later, and they were married. I'd never known anything of their earliest history, only that I'd come along about a year into their marriage. Mama had kept a photograph of the three of us on her bedside table my entire life: Papa, young and clean-shaven, with his hand on Mama's shoulder as she cradled a lace-draped infant me in her arms. They'd hired a man with a Kodak box camera to take the shot, an extravagance to celebrate the arrival of their first child.

But what if I hadn't been their first child? I stopped in my tracks, thinking. *"My daughter."* I'd assumed he meant me, but recalling his next words chilled me. *"I knew from the start I'd lose her."*

Aunt Susan talked of his growing distress after returning from Arkansas, and upsetting letters from my mother. Something deep in my gut twisted. A new narrative played out in my head, and when combined with Aunt Susan's information and Papa's own words, it made sense: My mother became pregnant during the time Papa had been in Arkansas. Then he'd gone back home and the messages he received from her, the ones that troubled him, broke the news and kept him informed as the weeks went by. The pregnancy must have been a difficult one. *"I knew from the start I'd lose her"* replayed, over and over.

At last, Mama had journeyed to New York that winter, but without the baby. Their first little girl didn't survive.

An empty ache hit my chest as I thought of my mother, close to my age, having a baby in a bleak midwinter. Losing that baby girl, then leaving her home, and—

Familiarity crashed down.

I'd heard this story before, only with more detail, and different names.

Images danced behind my eyes, flickered and froze, then came into stark focus: A snowcapped church with a parsonage next door. A young girl kneeling in an icy garden; then rising and fleeing, disappearing without a trace into a blizzard, leaving behind a tiny grave. I sank to the ground remembering Jasper, Katherine, and Della telling a sad story as we sat under the shade trees at the fair. They'd talked about the preacher's daughter who'd gotten pregnant, lost her baby, and fled into a snowstorm. Mary Mayhew vanished nineteen years ago. That would be around 1888, when Aunt Susan said Papa returned to New York. The same time my mother had arrived from Arkansas, after months of corresponding with my father, who'd been distraught and anxious over what her letters contained.

The similarities were too stark. There was no way two young women could've had the same tragic loss in the same little town, and both fled during the same harsh winter.

I'd listened to the story of a troubled young woman and her lost baby, not knowing I was hearing my mother's own history.

I placed a hand on the dusty ground, trying to quell the sudden vertigo that overcame me. Could I tell the Reverend and Mrs. Mayhew their disgraced daughter hadn't died in that long-ago snowstorm? That she'd let them think her lost for years, when she'd actually gone to be with her beau?

The next realization stole my breath. Here was the solution I'd sought from the beginning: blood relatives who could take Lilah and me together.

I thought of Reverend Mayhew's hard eyes and judgmental air. He was surely the reason Mama felt she could never return to Argenta. But why had she let her own mother suffer for years, believing her daughter had frozen to death?

I pressed my fingers to my temples, thinking of Lilah. The Mayhews were her grandparents, too. But even if they welcomed us, would it be right to take her from Miss Maeve's home? They both seemed so content. So happy.

I rose in a daze and walked out of the barn, heading down the lane that divided the farm from the woods. Gravel crunched under my boots. In the gloaming, a barn owl's shriek rang out from the woods. I stared into the trees, my thoughts in a spiral.

For several seconds, the shape lurking there did not register. Then the figure moved stealthily between the trees, shoulders hunched forward, head bowed low. I squinted into the shadows, not trusting my own eyes.

Dimming my light, I moved toward the woods, eyes fixed on the body weaving between the trunks. As I walked, a sense of recognition grew. The gait was familiar, along with the shape of the man's shoulders. I caught a glimpse of the profile.

The trespasser stopped, turning to face me.

I took a deep breath. "Papa, I need to talk to you."

14

My father blinked slowly once. Twice. He tilted his head at an angle, a terrible smile stretching his lips. I took a step back, then forced myself forward. "Come back to the farmhouse—"

Still grinning, he put a finger to his lips. The lantern light flashed off his teeth. His eyes were huge, unblinking. I held out a shaking hand. "Come with me. Please."

Papa dropped into a silent crouch. Hunkered down, staring up at me, he looked like a wild animal.

With startling speed, he leapt to his feet. In one swift motion, he was up and running, sprinting away into the forest. I hiked my skirts in one hand and gave chase. Branches crackled like fire under my feet as I ran. He would not leave me again.

I ducked and wove through the underbrush. Limbs and briars snagged in my hair and tore at my clothes. I fell farther and farther behind. When Papa slipped out of sight, I kept going. And going.

Panting, I burst into a clearing and stumbled to a halt. The gray stone well waited before me.

I sat down among sodden leaves and doused my lantern light. It was already dark as night under the thick canopy.

Perhaps if Papa thought I'd left, he'd give his position away. It was another sign of his disordered mind that he had ventured into the woods without a light of his own.

I shivered in the blackness, sudden goose bumps dotting my arms. Willing my breath to slow, I drew in the scent of earth and trees. A damp chill circled me. The fog had returned. I hugged my knees to my chest, listening hard.

A branch snapped. I tensed, rising slowly, preparing to make a grab for my father.

It was only when the dim light of a lantern shimmered into view that I realized it wasn't Papa returning.

Hide. The voice of instinct was loud in my brain. I crept back from the well into the shadows, pressing my spine against a tree. A figure drew closer, and I recognized the silvery hair and slight build. I nearly laughed aloud. I'd been scared into hiding by Miss Maeve Donovan. But curiosity closed my lips before I could announce my presence. What was the school-teacher doing in the woods?

She walked slowly, her head bent over a lantern. In its soft light, her cobweb-gray dress looked almost white as she stepped gracefully through the trees. The fog swirled and dove, rose and shifted. It seemed to move with her, as though it were a part of her somehow. The temperature continued to fall, until my lungs ached with each breath. Miss Maeve paced slowly toward the well, her expression unreadable.

She placed the lantern on the well's edge, pressed both hands on the stones, and raised her face to the sky. When she exhaled, her breath hovered like a vapor. Then the tide of fog swelled, so thick it smothered the lantern light.

In that featureless gray, I felt completely alone. Abandoned, even. The expanse of empty woods at my back loomed over me until I could stand it no longer. I sprang up, gathering my unlit lantern. "Miss Maeve? It's me, Verity."

A sudden gust of wind, bone-breaking cold and sharp as a blade, swept by. I gasped at the wintry onslaught. The fog parted, and for one instant, the view ahead was unobscured.

Miss Maeve was nowhere to be seen.

Her lantern sat on the well's edge, its light a sickly yellow. "Miss Maeve?" I fumbled for the matches in my pocket and relit my own light, trying to make out anything in the murky woods. My pulse thrummed in my ears as I shuffled forward. The well was within arm's reach when my foot struck something at once solid and alarmingly soft. I looked down through the fog.

My scream tore through the clearing, echoing off the trees.

Miss Maeve lay on her back at my feet. Pale, unseeing eyes stared out from her white face. I dropped to the ground beside her, my lantern throwing slashes of light into the dark. "Miss Maeve! Can you hear me?"

Her hands were crossed at her waist, like those of a body laid out for viewing. I shook her shoulder, gently at first, then again with more force. A lock of platinum hair slid across her open eyes.

Reason shouted over my rising panic, reminding me to check for signs of life. I slid my fingers under her sleeve, pushing back the vine-and-hair bracelet I'd seen at Sunday dinner. No pulse. I placed my ear close to her lips, praying for the slightest stirring of breath, but found none.

I had to fetch help. I turned in a circle, gathering my bearings. When I'd stumbled upon the well for the first time coming from Wheeler, I'd emerged just beside a massive, smooth-trunked tree. I spied it and rushed away in what I hoped was the right direction.

Limbs and leaves whipped against my face as I ran. Every breath burst from my lips in a frosted cloud. An ache spread from my numbed toes, through my feet, into my legs. Was my father still in the woods, suffering in the creeping cold? I pressed my free hand against the lantern for warmth.

It was so hard to think. Where had I been going? I staggered to a stop, blinking heavy lids. When I opened my eyes, there she was.

The little girl stood at the edge of the lantern's glow, the light hollowing dark circles under her eyes and shadowing her round cheeks. I fumbled with the lantern, trying to make it shine brighter. My fingers wouldn't work, as though the commands from my brain weren't getting through.

The child moved at a steady pace, weaving and ducking between trunks and vines. I staggered after her, wondering if I was dreaming, wondering what I'd been doing in the woods before she came along. Why was it terrifyingly cold?

A violent tremor shook my body. The lantern slid from my fingers, its globe shattering with a sound like sleigh bells. I stared at it for a long moment. When I dragged my gaze up again, the girl was gone.

I sank to my knees and slid beyond caring, to a place of blissful unconcern. Only sleep mattered now. I felt myself slump to the ground. My last thought was of how perfect the leafy earth felt pressed against my cheek as I watched the icy cloud of my breath drift away into the dark.

15

Sunlight kissed my closed lids. I stretched, coming awake slowly. Hettie must be distracted, to let me sleep this late. Surely it was well past time to start breakfast.

A honey-sweet smell wafted by. I opened my eyes to find Carolina jasmine blossoms floating down through the trees. They shone bright yellow as they passed through slanted shafts of morning sunlight. For a moment, I thought I drifted in a lovely dream.

Then I turned my head and saw my broken lantern. I shot up, wiping dirt from my sweat-dampened skin. The shards of glass glinted with an ugly truth—last night's impossible events had actually happened.

Alarm raced through my stomach when I realized hours had passed since I fled the well to find help for Miss Maeve. With a pounding head, I resumed my run toward town. There had to be an explanation for what I'd seen, for Miss Maeve's sudden crisis. She might've had a pulmonary embolism, or a ruptured cerebral aneurysm. Had Lilah alerted anyone when she woke to find Miss Maeve gone this morning? My heart clenched to think of how frightened my sister must be.

I stumbled out of the woods, bits of twigs scattered in my hair, and crossed the grassy acreage that separated the trees from Wheeler. The little girl I'd seen must live in the woods, perhaps even unknown to the locals. She'd probably been frightened away by seeing me succumb to the cold. I tried to blanket the night's events in warm, comforting reason and logic. But underneath the hastily thrown cover, I felt the stirring of the inexplicable, felt it creeping out from its hiding place like a spreading frost.

I reached the town, expecting to find the sidewalks crawling with distressed citizens. School should've started already. By now, the teacher's unexplained absence would surely have caused alarm.

But the town drowsed in a placid heat haze. A woman passed into a store, shopping basket over her arm, glancing with surprise at my disheveled appearance. As I rushed by, two wizened old men looked up from their checkers game in front of the barbershop. I made for the courthouse, determined to find the sheriff. I needed someone in authority to deal with what I'd seen in the woods.

As I approached, the man himself strode down the wide courthouse steps, spurs jingling.

"Sheriff!" My skirts flapped loud against my legs as I ran to him. "It's Miss Maeve." I bent forward, hands on knees, struggling to draw enough breath to speak. "I know where she is."

The man lifted a gold pocket watch and peered at it. "So do I. She's teaching right about now."

I shook my head. "She's in the woods. And I'm almost certain she's dead."

"What are you talking about?" he asked, already moving at a fast clip down the sidewalk in the direction of the school. I rushed along beside him, matching him step for step.

"She's lying on the ground in the woods, beside an old well. I couldn't find a pulse," I said, forcing myself to speak calmly. "And I saw a little girl wandering out there." I didn't mention that my father, escapee from an asylum, could possibly be in the woods, too. The terrible thought that he might not have survived the cold threatened to overtake me. I shook it away. "We have to do something."

"What did the child look like?" he demanded.

"Maybe six or seven years old, dark hair and eyes. Round cheeks." A shiver raced over my skin when I thought of her pale face as she'd walked away into the night. "There must be people living out there, even though Big Tom and Hettie say there aren't."

The sheriff's posture went rigid. "No one lives in the woods," he said. We turned a corner at the end of the sidewalk, and the red schoolhouse came into view.

Sheriff Loftis's eyes darted toward the open front door. I stepped up behind him onto the porch to look inside.

There, writing sums on the chalkboard, was Miss Maeve.

My feet went to lead, dragging me to a stop. "It can't be," I murmured.

Miss Maeve stood at the front of the long, narrow classroom, her back to us. The busy space fairly hummed with the tap and scratch of chalk on slates as the students bent over their mathematics lesson. "Carry the one," she said, "like so. Is everyone following along?" She glanced over her shoulder and, instead of catching the eyes of her students, met my confused stare instead.

"Verity? And Sheriff Loftis. Come in, please." Heads popped up, borrowing and subtraction forgotten, as the class took note of our intrusion. Miss Maeve's pale gaze flitted over my face, worry darkening her brow. She put down her chalk and dusted her hands on her skirt. "Students, you've all worked very hard today. I think an extra recess is in order."

Amid the excited shuffling of children filing from the room, Lilah broke from the line to come to my side. "Is something wrong, Very? You look peaked."

"No, I'm fine. I was in town, and I wanted to thank Miss Maeve again for dinner," I invented. "The sheriff was walking this way and offered to join me. Why don't you go on out and get some fresh air?"

Lilah looked to Miss Maeve for confirmation.

"Run along," she said with a reassuring smile. "I'd like to visit with your sister and Sheriff Loftis for a bit." Lilah nodded, a little reluctant, then went off to join Cecil under a shade tree at the edge of the schoolyard.

"What brings y'all by today?" Miss Maeve clapped the eraser against the board, sending billows of dust into the air. The sight reminded me of the fog, drifting around her pallid face the night before.

"I saw you in the woods last night, by the well." I couldn't take my eyes from the purplish veins lining the backs of her hands, the same color her lips had been as she lay on the ground in the cold. "I thought you were dead."

She turned, confusion dancing over her features. "I beg your pardon?"

The sheriff tucked his thumbs into his gun belt. "I don't know what you're trying to pull, Miss Pruitt, but I won't stand for it. Were you trying to cause a panic? Play some mean-hearted prank?"

"No," I stammered. "No, I saw her. She was by the well. There was no pulse. I—"

Sheriff Loftis cast a look toward Miss Maeve, standing before us, the very picture of health. "Outright lies," he said.

"I can't imagine your motives for spinning such a tale, but they can't be good."

"Can you tell me what you saw?" Miss Maeve asked. I gave a brief account of the night, caught between her deepening frown and the sheriff's accusatory glower.

"And then I fell asleep. When I woke up the little girl was gone. And, here you are. And . . ." I waved my hand in her direction. ". . . obviously, you're alive." It wasn't a shining moment of deductive reasoning.

"Sheriff, Verity's clearly had an upsetting night," Miss Maeve said, gently. "Whatever she saw has deeply unsettled her. Would you give us some privacy, please?"

"If you insist. But be on your guard. I don't know what this girl's angle is." Sheriff Loftis nodded in my direction. "I'm keeping my eye on you, Miss Pruitt. You've shown yourself to be a young woman who can't be trusted to tell the truth." With that, he stalked away.

I settled into the desk Lilah had vacated, eyeing Miss Maeve closely. She pulled another desk close and slid gracefully into it. The sharp scent of chalk dust hung heavy in the air. When her clear eyes searched mine, I saw apprehension and, to my surprise, sadness. "I know this will be hard to accept, Verity, but for your safety you must listen. Don't go back in the woods. Some people, like the sheriff, might never believe it, but the woods are an eldritch, dangerous place."

"You mean haunted?" I wanted to sound brusque and dismissive. To my chagrin, my voice wavered.

Miss Maeve nodded. "You've experienced it yourself now. The strange fog, the cold. What you thought you saw"—she gestured to herself—"and the little girl are all part of it. The woods play tricks on your mind, especially near the old well. Someone should've warned you when you arrived in town," she said, suddenly the stern teacher. She tapped her toes on the pine floorboards.

"Big Tom and Hettie tried. I saw the same little girl there once before. They told me to stay away without getting into much detail. But I'm not sure anything could've fully convinced me something otherworldly was really happening until . . . well, until I saw the thing by the well." I pressed a hand to my forehead. "It's hard for me to believe still. I've never put stock in anything supernatural."

Miss Maeve nodded. "I understand. But you aren't the first to encounter unbelievable things in the woods. The people who've lived here for decades tell me there was always an eerie feeling there, especially at the old well, but since the Loftis girl drowned—"

"Loftis girl?" I asked. "Was she related to Della?" I remembered Della saying her mother had been gutted by the loss of a child.

"Josie was Della's little sister," Miss Maeve said. "About a year ago, she wandered into the woods to play, and fell into the well." She broke off, pressing her lips together. "It's a terrible thought, imagining her spirit is not at rest. After such a tragic death, she should at least have peace."

"But what about the thing I thought was you?" I frowned. "Was that some sort of . . . specter?" I couldn't believe that I was speaking such nonsense, much less that a growing part of me wanted to embrace it as fact.

Miss Maeve sighed. "I wish I could say. There have been occasional sightings over the years of an apparition, a 'white lady,' as the people like to call her. But even living as close to the woods as I do, I've never experienced anything there. Perhaps because I have sense enough to stay away."

She ran a finger along the spine of a well-worn reading primer sitting on the scarred desktop. "It's troubling, hearing that whatever you saw looked like me. All I know for certain is this: I wasn't by the well last night. And I'm very much alive." Her smile was careful, as if waiting to see if I'd accept the obvious truth—she was alive, plain as day—along with the nearly unbelievable: that the woods held something otherworldly.

I cast my eyes up to a neatly written cursive alphabet tacked just below the plank ceiling, as though the curling letters could spell out the answers to my many questions. "Miss Maeve, I don't know what—"

A little boy burst through the door, bottom lip trembling, a rip in the knee of his overalls. He leaned dramatically against the black potbellied stove that stood in the center aisle of the small room. "Samuel pushed me down," he whimpered.

Miss Maeve rose in one smooth motion and began fussing over the boy's scrapes. "I'll have a word with him. It doesn't do for friends to fight. Now, I could use a helper. Would you like to ring the bell for me to call the others in?" She took a brass bell from the windowsill and handed it to the boy. He scampered away, injury forgotten. Miss Maeve watched him go with a fond smile.

I rose on wobbly legs. I had responsibilities at the farm, and a lot of explaining to do to my employers. "I should go. I'll just say goodbye to Lilah and get back to the farm." Heaven only knew what Big Tom and Hettie had thought when I hadn't returned last night. And Abel. What had he made of my unexplained absence?

Miss Maeve took my hand in hers. Her fingers were cool and soft. "I know I've given you a good deal to think about, and much of it seems impossible. It always bothers me when I can't give solid answers, but in this case, I fear there are none to be had." She looked at me with an almost maternal worry. "But please, Verity. Don't go into the woods again."

I looked back into her pale eyes. "Of course not, Miss Maeve."

Dawn trailed amber fingers through the trees, tugging ribbons of light over the girl's motionless body. She lay on the mossy ground beside the well, eyes closed, her right hand clenched in a fist around a small linen bag. She felt the rigor mortis ease from her joints as her consciousness returned, dragging a familiar despair in its wake.

She flung away the little bag of failed spells. It landed at the feet of a solemn-faced man and an older woman, who watched her with expressions of defeat and dread. "Let me try cutting it. Just once more," said the woman. She bent down, a pair of heavy silver shears in her hand. "I did a new working. Maybe this time . . ." The blades snicked together beside the girl's pale wrist. A bracelet fell away.

A coil of black smoke swirled to life around her wrist. Twisting and snaking along her skin, it circled her arm for a few moments. Then it drifted away to reveal that the bracelet had returned. The man cursed, reaching out a hand to help the girl he pretended was his family.

She got to her feet, shaking away the offered hand of help. The sympathy made her furious. She knew he'd come to think of her *as a daughter in their short time together, but she was sick of his pity. And sick of the old woman's useless attempts to fix the disaster she'd caused.*

The girl felt the blank despair of the past few months twist inside her. It flared hot and wild, then hardened into something cold. Something pitiless. She locked eyes with the man, and saw him suppress a shudder. With a surge of satisfaction, she realized he was afraid of her.

The older woman tugged a tattered shawl around her slumped shoulders, her chin wobbling, unable to meet the girl's eerie, angry gaze. The girl began to walk away, deeper into the woods. Her mind was ablaze with plans for righting wrongs, plans for revenge.

"Something will work, sooner or later," the woman called, her voice wavering. "Please be patient, Mary."

"That's not my name," the girl replied, still walking deeper into the woods. Before the green and gold of the trees took her, she paused, looking back over her shoulder to where the man and the old woman stood motionless by the ancient well. "Not anymore."

16

I trailed back toward the farm, trying to reconcile myself to the notion that things of murk and darkness, of shadow and evil, lurked in the woods. I didn't want to believe that unseen beings like those my papa feared could actually exist.

I didn't want to believe that his demons were real.

The sound of hurried steps on gravel drew my focus. I peered down the dirt road to find Abel running toward me. He was unshaven and his eyes looked weary, as though he hadn't slept. But when I lifted a hand in greeting, a smile radiated across his face.

"Verity!" He said my name with an unabashed joy that stopped me in my tracks. He halted within arm's reach and I thought for one wild moment he would hug me. Instead, his eyes lingered on the dirt on my skirts and the scrapes on my hands.

"Where in the world have you been? Hettie said she went up last night to ask you how the calf was doing and found your bed empty. We've been worried to death." He rubbed at the back of his neck. "She figured you'd run away. I wasn't so sure about that. But then I thought maybe your daddy had shown up and . . ."

The words tapered off, and worry clouded his blue eyes. His fingers brushed my cheek as he pulled a leaf free from my tangled hair. My face tingled from the sweep of his skin against mine. "Have you been in the woods?"

"It's a long story, and one that makes me look pretty foolish, so I'd rather only tell it once." I started forward, unable to look him straight in the eye any longer. As we walked, I unbraided my hair and began to weed out the remaining greenery. "Are the Weatheringtons terribly upset with me?"

"Big Tom said maybe two words all morning."

"Down from his usual four, then?" I said, trying to lighten the mood.

"And Hettie cried." Abel let the statement hang in the hot air. I swallowed hard, unsure of how to respond. "But don't fret," he went on, the hint of a smile poking at the corners of his mouth. "It only lasted for a minute. Then she got mad as a hornet after she decided you'd run off. She's been hoeing the bean patch like she's trying to dig a hole to China."

The house came into view, and I spied Hettie and Big Tom kneeling in the kitchen garden. With their heads bent, they reminded me of two supplicants bowed in prayer, but their hands were in constant motion pulling weeds from around the squash plants.

I cleared my throat, then realized I had no idea what to say. I chose a feeble "Good morning." I immediately regretted how casual the words sounded.

Hettie sprang to her feet, dark soil showering from her skirt, while Big Tom began the laborious process of getting his large frame back to standing. Hettie darted forward, took my shoulders in a tight grip, and looked me up and down.

Her work-weathered features showed annoyance and worry in equal measure. "Where have you been?"

"This isn't going to boost your confidence in my good sense," I began. "But I went into the woods last night. I was chasing my father. I never found him, and then things took a . . . strange turn." Big Tom and Hettie listened to my story in tense silence. I knew I'd given them firm grounds for sending me away by disappearing all night without warning.

"I was on my way back when I met Abel," I finished. "I'm sorry for the worry I caused. Please don't write to the Children's Society. Don't send me away."

Hettie breathed in through her thin nose. "I ought to ship you back north, before you get your fool self killed. That would be the smart thing to do." Somewhere overhead, a crow rasped a raucous caw. I stared dully at the discarded weeds lying scattered in the garden, their leaves already curling in the blistering sun. "But nobody ever accused us of doing the smart thing," Hettie said. "We ought to have told you all about the woods."

Big Tom cleared his throat. "We've never had to tell an outsider about the haints and whatnot in there. Nobody likes to talk about it." He cast a solemn look toward the woods. "It's a mercy nothing worse happened to you." His eyes were soft with relief.

I swallowed against an unexpected lump in my throat. "I probably wouldn't have believed they were haunted anyway," I said. Did I even believe it now? I wasn't sure. I wasn't sure of anything anymore.

Hettie broke the uneasy silence. "Traipsing all over creation to find you put us behind. We've got beans to can. Come along to the canning shed directly."

She and Big Tom turned to go, leaving me standing at the

edge of the garden with Abel by my side. Hettie looked back at me, her voice gentler than usual. "Don't linger too long."

An oddly light feeling fluttered in my chest. "I never expected them to be so upset about me being gone." I picked up a hoe and chopped at a weed near my feet. The lightness turned leaden. What would they think if I took Lilah from Miss Maeve's home and moved in with the Mayhews? "Big Tom and Hettie were more worried than angry," I said.

"I was pretty upset myself." Abel's voice was quiet and deep. His wide hand covered mine, stilling my restless work. I looked up, startled. "Something else is on your mind, besides seeing your father and all that stuff in the woods. Something's troubling you."

"How do you know?"

His callused palm was warm against my fingers. "It's hard to explain, but I get a feeling what you really want to say is between the words that actually come out." His face was serious and so, so close. My eyes darted up from his hand to the cleft in his chin, then to his lips. I quickly looked away.

"The letter you delivered was from my aunt Susan, my father's sister. I'd written to ask if Lilah and I might have any relatives in the area who could take us in. Together."

Abel went still.

"Aunt Susan told me that, as a young man, Papa lived briefly in Argenta. He met my mother there. Mama never spoke of her parents, but some things my father said when he came to the farm, and a few details in Aunt Susan's letter . . ." I took a steadying breath. "The Mayhews might be my grandparents. I think their missing daughter, the one who delivered a stillborn baby and then vanished, was my mother."

Abel's lips parted in surprise. I could practically see the

questions forming. "If your daddy has trouble telling reality from fantasy, can you trust anything he said?"

"I don't know. That's why I need to talk to the Mayhews. The reverend wouldn't be my first choice for a grandfather, but Mrs. Mayhew looks like a kind woman. And family is family. Anywhere I can be with my sister is better than being apart."

Abel's frown deepened. He opened his mouth to speak, then seemed to reconsider his words. "What about Miss Maeve? She cares about Lilah. And Lilah is happy in her new home, don't you think?"

Here was the thorn in the rosy plans I'd made. The more I saw Lilah and Miss Maeve together, the harder it was to feel sure pulling my sister away was for anyone's benefit but mine. Lately, when I thought of returning to New York with Lilah, I had to ask myself: Was it selfish to want my sister back?

I sighed. "I don't know. But if the Mayhews truly are our grandparents, they have a right to know."

Abel looked down. "We need you here, though. You're becoming a big help on the farm."

I snorted. "That's a generous fib."

He went on as if I hadn't interrupted. "Is living with the Mayhews together really that much better than living a short way from Lilah, like you do now, and staying with us?"

"It's not just that. I was supposed to go to college in New York, then medical school." I gestured to the open fields. "I can't do any of that here. I don't want to leave you and Hettie and Big Tom high and dry, but I want to give up on my dreams even less."

He glanced around at the empty landscape, his eyes full of sad understanding.

"I have to know if the Mayhews are my grandparents," I

went on. "Once I get confirmation, then I'll figure out the next step."

Abel moved closer. "I hope you find what you're looking for." I felt his sigh as a soft stirring against my cheek. Being this near to Abel draped a spell over me. My thoughts went blurry at the edges. I felt myself leaning in, close enough to feel the heat of his sun-kissed skin.

I drew in a short breath and stepped back. The moment splintered.

Too much of my future hid in a haze of uncertainty. I needed clarity to see my way forward, and getting involved with Abel would leave me anything but clearheaded.

"I ought to get to work," I stammered.

"Guess I should, too," Abel sighed. He adjusted his hat and looked down at me, his gaze intense. "I don't know about you, but I get tired of all these 'should's and 'ought to's." His voice was low and rough-edged as he added, "I'll see you later, Verity."

I forced myself to turn toward the dusty path to the canning shed. I glanced back once, to see Abel striding across the sunlit field, straight-backed and strong. It shouldn't have sent a giddy thrill through my stomach when he looked over his shoulder and met my eyes. It shouldn't have mattered that he was as unwilling to walk away as I'd been.

But I was learning it was harder to tell my heart what mattered than I could ever have guessed.

17

A hush lay over the woods, just as it had each time I'd entered before. The absence of rippling birdsong—the trills and warbles that so often followed me about my morning work on the farm—felt like an additional warning to stay away. I wound through mossy trunks, a carpet of rotting leaves deadening my steps. I was breaking my promise to Big Tom and Hettie, and to Miss Maeve. Guilt nagged like a slight headache, enough to make me uncomfortable but not so severe I couldn't carry on with my plans.

I had to know if Papa was still here. Maybe I could find the little girl again, and prove to myself she was only an adventurous, wandering child. And a twin desire lurked in my heart: to know if the figure in white still lay by the well. Clearly, it hadn't been the corpse of Miss Maeve Donovan. But I wasn't completely ready to accept her explanation of some unhallowed being impersonating her.

I wanted to see it again. I wanted to see it and *understand it*. And so, when Big Tom told me to go to the far eastern field and cut a fallen tree off the fence, I'd taken my chance to slip away.

I patted my pocket, making certain my candle and matches were in place. It was broad daylight, but I'd come prepared should I somehow, by unforeseen ill luck, stay after sunset. A heavy woolen cloak lay over my shoulders, pilfered from among the mothballs in Hettie's cedar chest. If the cold came for me again, I was ready.

I made a careful search of the woods, calling Papa's name as I went. The trees caught and smothered my words. Once, I'd visited Papa at the asylum in a room with padded walls, where our voices had the same empty, deadened quality.

A prickly feeling raced along my spine, intensifying the closer I circled toward the center of the woods. Brambles snagged my skirt. A branch snapped somewhere in the gloom. My heart galloped as I strained to locate its source, but I saw nothing, and heard no other sound.

At last, I reached the middle of the forest with no sign of Papa. He'd disappeared from the woods as completely as the ghosts that supposedly haunted this place. Now I faced the other desire that had driven my return: confronting the well.

I pushed aside a drape of ferns. My feet dragged to a halt when I saw it. The well stared into the sky, a black, unblinking eye. I forced my attention down to the ground at the base of the rock ring. Stomach churning, I braced to see the pale figure of a woman laid out on the ground.

But the place beside the gray stone was empty.

Relief and disappointment clashed. I'd expected to find something here. If not the woman, then perhaps the silent little girl. Snugging my cloak tighter, I looked for any signs to indicate that a body had lain here. I came around to the side where I'd seen her—it?—and studied a depression in the leaves. Did I make out a space the size and shape of a body? I couldn't be sure. My fingers trailing through the damp earth stirred a musty scent of decayed plants. I crushed a fistful of dirt and let it crumble away, no closer to understanding what I'd seen here. The woods kept their secrets.

Dissatisfied, I rose to brush the rich, dark earth from my skirt. This had been a waste of time. If I hurried, I could clear the fallen tree from the fence and be back at the farm before I was missed.

Something moved at the edge of my vision. A flicker of black, like a tongue of dark fire, darted by. My head snapped to the left. Meager light struggled to reach the forest floor and lost its battle with the gloom. I peered into the dimness between the tree trunks, fixated on one large oak where the shape—had it been the hem of a garment whisking out of sight?—had disappeared. The rich scent of pines lay heavy in the still, silent air. I drew in a breath and held it.

Slowly, a small, white hand slid into view.

My breath cut off. Watching the pale fingers clutch at the bark, I couldn't think or move. I stared at the little hand and the face that gradually came into view above it.

The dark-eyed little girl leaned around the tree trunk, her black hair hanging over her shoulder. Her shadowed stare fixed on mine. Cold fog climbed up from the ground. Shivering, I looked down to see it snaking around my ankles. Chill seeped through my stockings. I expected to find the little girl gone when I looked back, but she remained.

A profound sadness hid behind her blank expression. The mists rose to the hem of her black dress, washing up her body like a wave of storm clouds. Before her face disappeared into the mists, she withdrew back behind the tree. Through the gray, I could make out the small hand letting go and slipping from view.

"No! Wait, please!" It was as if a trap that held me sprang open. I leapt into motion. She wouldn't escape this time. Cloak flying, I ran toward where the little girl had vanished.

And I found what I'd somehow known I'd find. Nothing.

No shaking leaves marked her passing, and the ground was free of prints. I ran my trembling hand along the tree where her fingers had been and found no hint of their warmth. I searched for a hollowed log, a hidden ditch or spring bed. Any place she could've ducked away to hide. Overhead, leaves whispered. I couldn't see any branches low enough for the child to pull herself up. My ears pulsed with the absolute silence.

Then, behind me, a branch broke.

My hand flew to my throat. I spun around to find myself facing—

Katherine Ausbrooks.

She froze in the middle of darting behind the well. A stricken expression flickered over her thin face. She hesitated, then threw back her shoulders and stepped boldly into view. Katherine regarded me with narrowed eyes, an open burlap sack dangling from her right hand.

I went to her and, before she could react, wrapped my fingers around her wrist. I had to know if it was really, truly Katherine. Her skin felt warm, and with her shout of alarm, her pulse picked up.

"Good God, are you mad?" Katherine wrenched her arm away, and the sharp motion sent a plant tumbling from her bag. The blossoms were an unappealing greenish shade that faded to bruised purplish black, growing from a stalk with dirt-smeared roots still attached. Katherine snatched it up and shoved the whole mess back into her bag.

"Did you see where she went?" I asked.

She darted a worried look into the shadows. "Who?"

"The little girl in the black dress," I said. "I was following her when I heard you behind me."

Katherine shook her head. "I've seen no one in the woods but you." She peered over my shoulder, gnawing at her bottom lip, looking about with the same jittery worry I felt. Whatever brought her to the woods today, she didn't relish being here. She caught me watching her, and the unease shifted to haughtiness. "What are you doing here, anyway?"

I opted for a partial truth. "When I came through the woods the other day, I saw a little girl. I wanted to find out if she was still around." I pointed to the bulging bag she carried. "And what about you? Doing a little amateur botany?"

"I'm gathering plants for our flower bed." Her eyes were shifty. Katherine was a terrible liar, but I doubted I'd get anything else out of her.

A shaft of warm sunlight broke through the canopy, incongruous with the gray fog that had so recently swarmed along the forest floor.

"Did you see the fog then?" I asked. "It came out of nowhere."

"Of course I did." She sniffed. "It probably had to do with air-temperature changes near the well. The spring water down inside is cold, the air up here's much warmer. Nothing special, really, now that I think on it." She sounded just like I had, the first time I'd seen the fog—like someone trying too hard to convince herself that nothing had unexpectedly come along to upend her views. "But there most certainly wasn't a little girl standing here. I would've seen her." Her conviction was sturdy.

I shook my head, equally as certain of my truth. "She was here. I've seen her three times now." How was it possible for

Katherine to have seen the fog, but not the child in the middle of it? She'd been only a handful of yards away when I'd watched the writhing mist pour over the ground to rise and swallow the girl.

Katherine seemed to waver, and for a second I thought she might actually believe me. Then she crossed her arms, suspicion all over her face. "We're too old for stupid little pranks. Shouldn't you be at the farm, doing your job instead of poking about in the woods? You know, my father's on the adoption committee with Sheriff Loftis." Katherine gave me a superior smile, and I felt my hands ball into fists. "One of his responsibilities is to call round to the families who got the orphans, make sure they're satisfied with their new wards." She wrinkled her nose. "I hope you turn out useful to the Weatheringtons. It would be a shame if you got shipped off wherever they send the ones nobody wants."

"Oh, Katherine, bless your heart." I'd stolen the phrase from Della, but where she used it with genuine warmth, my voice was frigid. "It's kind of you to be concerned. But my stay here is temporary. I'll return to New York in a few months and carry on with my plans."

Katherine tried to hide it, but I recognized the emotion that flickered across her face. Pure, wrenching jealousy. Katherine wanted to be the one leaving Wheeler for good. The mayor's daughter wasn't nearly as content with her small-town world as her brother or Della.

"I'll be sure to send a postcard," I said, turning on my heel and leaving the girl in the shadows.

18

The days wore on with no opportunity to go visit Lilah or arrange a trip to Argenta to see the Reverend and Mrs. Mayhew. Papa's whereabouts remained a mystery. In every idle moment, I speculated on where he could be, what to make of the strangeness in the woods, and how to account for Katherine's unexplained presence there. But those moments were few and far between.

The hay was ready to be cut and baled, and it took all of us—Big Tom, Hettie, Abel, and me—working together to accomplish the task. Long, sweltering days of forking hay into the press, helping tie it into bales, then lugging the cumbersome square bundles to the barn left me little time to do anything except eat, sweat, and sleep.

One evening, as I was feeding the chickens and stewing on how to approach my unsuspecting grandparents, the racket of hooves on gravel sent the hens into a flapping uproar. Abel galloped into the yard on Merlin, his voice carrying over the squawking hens. "I just came from Mama's place. It's Clara. The baby's coming, and Mama needs help. Get Aunt Hettie and come on." He wheeled and rode away without waiting for an answer.

Hettie froze for a moment when I delivered the message, then spun into a tornado of activity. Work forgotten, she saddled Lady May in a feverish hurry. "Get on," she said. "None of that sidesaddle business. We don't have time to be proper." I was only too happy to comply. We covered the few miles to Abel's homeplace at a breakneck pace.

The Atchleys' dogtrot house sat cupped in a shady valley between two hills. As we drew near, a little boy wearing cut-off overalls with no shirt underneath hopped out of a rocking chair on the front porch. He raced over the yard with bare feet flying and stretched onto tiptoes, catching hold of Lady May's bridle. "Clara's having that baby. They keep running me off, and nobody will tell me how they're gonna get it out of her." He turned wide blue eyes on me. "Do you know how?"

"In theory," I said, sliding off the horse's back after Hettie. We charged up the rickety front steps just as Abel came out onto the porch.

"How is she?" Hettie asked.

Abel shook his head. "I can't say. Mama hasn't come out in a while."

Hettie slipped into the cabin and disappeared through a doorway to the left. Abel turned to the little barefoot boy. "Hey, Jep, why don't you go see what Theo is up to?" He nodded toward another, even smaller boy, who was busily rolling a metal ring around the yard. "You haven't beaten him in hoop trundling yet, have you?" Jep ran off, Clara's baby forgotten for the time being.

The screen door banged shut as I followed Abel into the breezeway that cut through the middle of the house. Two small girls—twins, I thought—peeked out at me from a room to my right. Their small, freckled faces looked pinched with worry. Behind them, a door to the side yard opened, and another girl came in, a basin full of water balanced against one hip. I recognized her as the solemn-looking older daughter I'd seen with Mrs. Atchley at church. "Any news?" Abel asked.

"'Bout the same," the girl replied. "I'm Faye," she added with a glance in my direction.

"Verity Pruitt," I said.

"I know," she replied. "I've been wondering when you'd come around. Abel's told me all 'bout you." Abel's ears went slightly pink, and a little bolt of pleasure zinged through my chest.

Faye stepped past us and across the dogtrot into the single bedroom that made up the left side of the house. From inside, I could hear Hettie speaking in firm, soothing tones.

"Y'all take care of them, all right?" Abel said as a cry of pain split the air. His face turned pale.

I moved to the doorway Faye had gone through, trying to smile reassuringly. In truth, I wasn't sure I knew how to help either Clara or the baby if something went wrong. "We'll do our best," I said, stepping over the threshold and closing the bedroom door.

The scent of blood tainted the air inside the hot, dim space. Iron bedsteads lined both walls, three on each side. I found myself staring at the newsprint papering the walls, the rag rugs littering the floor, the faded patchwork quilts draped over the beds. At anything but the slight girl on the bed farthest from me.

Clara's labored breathing mingled with Mrs. Atchley's soft hushing sounds. Faye placed a wet cloth from the basin on

Clara's forehead, then stepped back, wringing her hands. She looked at Hettie, standing grim-faced at the head of the bed, then to me. "Do you need anything else?"

"Run along and check that fire under the big kettle in the backyard," Hettie said. The girl looked relieved to have an excuse to leave. "I've helped with a handful of birthings over the years," Hettie added for my benefit. "Always boil the rags and sheets. It helps keep the mama from getting childbed fever after the baby comes." She handed me a new cake of lye soap from the bedside table and gestured toward the basin. "Be sure to wash up real good."

Clara shifted her attention from Hettie to me. Sweat-darkened hair clung to her forehead, but her bright blue eyes were clear. Before she could speak, a contraction wrenched a guttural moan from her throat. I gathered every scrap of courage and stepped forward.

Mrs. Atchley offered me her seat by the bed. "Never thought anything could be more fearful than birthing my own babies," she said. "But watching my girl go through it is worse."

I took Clara's hand and wiped away the tear sliding down her cheek. "I'm Verity. You're going to be just fine." She nodded with a jerky, frantic motion. The mound of her belly shifted, like an earthquake inside her body. From her stool at the end of the bed, Hettie announced it was time to push. Clara breathed fast and shallow as another wave of pain washed over her. The bones of my knuckles ground together in her panicked grip.

For hours it went on. Clara would push until her strength was gone, then collapse back against the bed. Before she could stop gasping for breath, the next pain would crash over her. Hettie urged her on with all the tenderness of an army general, but Clara seemed to respond to the toughness. "One more. With all your might, girl," Hettie said. "You're almost done."

With a scream that vibrated through my skull, Clara gave a final push.

"It's a boy!" Mrs. Atchley shouted as Hettie lifted the newborn into her arms, directing me to tie off the umbilical cord with a length of crochet thread before cutting it with sterilized scissors. Clara's cries turned from exhaustion to relief.

A sudden, awful quiet filled the stifling bedroom. Under the blood and mire, the baby's skin was dusky. His soft breaths, fluttery and slow, grew fainter and farther apart.

"What's wrong?" Clara asked.

Mrs. Atchley's beaming face crumpled with worry. Hettie smacked the soles of the baby's feet, but there was no response. A blue line appeared around the tiny lips.

I acted before I had time to second-guess myself. With one swipe, I cleared the bedside table. Snatching the newborn from Hettie, I laid him down and grasped both his wrists in one hand. Then I extended the tiny arms over his head, and quickly brought them back down. My voice was steady as I counted to four, then repeated the motions. Stretch the arms, expand the chest, swing back down, apply pressure on the thorax.

One. Two. Three. Four.

Clara's soft sobs sounded distant. Her mother's worried questions barely registered as I counted. I couldn't take my eyes from the baby's rib cage, fragile as a bird's bones under my hands.

I leaned in close, listening. Praying. Arms up. Arms down. Press in, listen, count. From the corner of my eye, I saw Hettie, hands to her mouth, despair filling her eyes. No breath. No change. The room felt hollow, as though all sound had been siphoned away with the baby's breaths.

And then, a sigh. Petal-soft, delicate as a whisper.

I lifted his arms again and heard a shaky inhalation. A cough, and finally, a cry. Faint and wavering and miraculous.

Scooping the baby up, I held him to my face. Tacky blood smeared my cheek. I listened to his breaths gather strength. The mewling cry grew stronger as angry color flooded his cheeks.

Clara reached for her son. I handed him over, light-headed with relief. She pressed him close and his cries settled. He opened his eyes to peer at his mother.

"Hello there, little one," Clara said, voice trembling. She placed a kiss on the wrinkled forehead. "You gave us quite a scare."

Hettie and Mrs. Atchley hugged, spinning in a giddy circle. I burst out laughing in delirious gratitude that the baby boy lived. "How did you know what to do?" Mrs. Atchley asked.

I wiped blood from my cheek with the hem of my skirt. "My father taught me, in case I ever needed to resuscitate someone. He's a physician." The pride in my voice surprised me. The swell of joy that came with helping Clara's baby enter the world took me completely aback. Nothing I'd done before had ever felt this significant. A deep, settled peace rested over me. There were still so many things I didn't understand, there was still so much I couldn't do well, but in this one thing—when it counted most—my skills were enough. My work mattered.

From out in the dogtrot, Abel hollered, "Is everything all right?"

"It's a boy, Uncle Abel. And he's perfect," I shouted back.

"His name is William," Clara announced. While Mrs. Atchley persuaded her to hand the newborn over for his first bath, I washed up and ventured into the main room of the little cabin.

Exhaustion and elation swirled through my veins. I felt like I could take on the world. But maybe after a solid nap.

I collapsed beside Abel, who looked up from a stick he'd been carving into a whistle for his younger siblings. "It sounds like you did great in there. Do you think you've got a future in midwifing?"

"You know, maybe I do."

He reached over and gave my hand a quick squeeze. "Thank you for helping Clara. And William." The buttery light of a new day spilled over the five youngest Atchley children, all bedded down on quilted pallets on the floor. Jep sucked his thumb, one arm flung over Theo's shoulder. Faye slept with her curly-headed little sisters snuggled against her chest.

"It was an honor," I said.

Abel watched his siblings, looking thoughtful. "If you're going to have a child with no daddy to speak of, this is a good family to do it in," he said. "William won't ever lack for love or someone to watch out for him."

I leaned my head back and closed my eyes, thinking of my own mother. Her entire life would have been different if her family had treated her as the Atchleys had Clara. If she'd told them the truth, perhaps they would have.

Hettie opened the door, rubbing tired eyes with the back of her hand. "I'll stay to help out for a little while, but y'all can head on back." She looked to me, and the lines around her mouth deepened with a smile. "You did good in there."

"Thank you," I said. Getting to my feet, I looked out over the fields to the west, toward Argenta, only a few miles away. I could be standing in my grandparents' home in little more than an hour. "There's something I need to do in Argenta before I head back." I wetted my parched lips and rushed ahead. "It turns out I may have some family there."

19

Hettie must've seen something in my face that made her reluctant to ask questions. "All right," she said slowly. "But take Abel with you to drive."

We set out for Argenta in a light buggy borrowed from Mrs. Atchley. The seat was really meant for one, making the journey most distracting. Abel's leg pressed against mine, and even through my skirt and petticoat, I was aware of the contact.

When the little white church and parsonage came into view, my stomach knotted. "I hope Mrs. Mayhew is here alone," I said, just as Reverend Mayhew stepped out onto the parsonage porch.

"That's a shame," Abel mumbled, stopping the buggy.

The preacher scrutinized us from under the brim of his derby hat, a well-worn Bible tucked under his arm. Mrs. Mayhew came outside, wiping her hands on a gingham apron. I found myself searching their faces for any signs of my mother. Was she there, in the curve of Mrs. Mayhew's chin? Or in the preacher's thin build?

Mrs. Mayhew's gentle face lit with that same unexpected recognition her husband had shown when he saw me at the fair. "Can we help y'all?" she asked.

"I'm Verity Pruitt. I'm living with the Weatherington family outside of Wheeler. This is their nephew, Abel Atchley." Abel tipped his hat in greeting.

"I reckon y'all are here to get married," Reverend Mayhew said in a sonorous voice. "That's the usual reason a young pair shows up unexpected." His thin lips twitched as if he were in pain.

"No, sir," I said, hand lifted in protest. "I need to talk, that's all."

Mrs. Mayhew's light blue eyes flitted to her husband. "Certainly," she said, holding open the door.

Abel moved to follow, but I stopped him with a touch on his arm. "I think this is something I need to do alone." He searched my face for a moment, then nodded.

I followed the couple into their small parlor, settling onto a low sofa as the Mayhews took seats in two stiff-looking green-and-ivory-striped chairs across from me. While Reverend Mayhew laid his Bible down gently on the coffee table between us, I stared intently at a framed print of the Ten Commandments tacked to the chintz wallpaper. A breeze slipped through the open windows, ruffling the pink petals in the hanging baskets of geraniums.

Mrs. Mayhew smiled gently, waiting for me to speak. A piano stood behind her, with a hymnal propped open on its stand. I could just make out the title at the top of the page, a song called "Coming Home." "I'm sure this will seem outlandish, but I hope you'll hear me out," I began.

I picked my way along, as though the words were precarious stepping-stones in a creek. "I came here not long ago on an orphan train from New York. I think . . . well, as it turns out . . ." I stopped, took a steadying breath, and tried again. "My mother was from Argenta. And I believe you knew her."

Mrs. Mayhew peered at me, then looked to her husband. "You see it too, don't you?"

The preacher inhaled deeply. "Yes, there's no mistaking her."

Emboldened, I hurried on. "Mother never talked about her early years. I only just learned about her history here, so—"

"She was a good friend to our Mary," Mrs. Mayhew interrupted. "You've got to be Elizabeth Sutter's daughter. You look just like her. Liz was a kind, sweet young woman. She was Mary's closest confidante."

The silence stretched, long and thin, until my startled voice snapped it. "I'm sorry, what did you say?" I looked back and forth between them. Confusion roiled my thoughts into a muddy mess.

Reverend Mayhew leaned back in his chair, his face falling into shadow. "Elizabeth's people moved here a few years before Mary . . . left. They're all long gone now." His jaw worked as he struggled to hold back some strong emotion. Mrs. Mayhew fixed her tired gaze on nothing in particular. Both were too overcome by painful memories to notice my own turmoil.

My mother hadn't been the Mayhews' daughter, only the friend of their beloved child. Perhaps Mama and Papa really had lost a baby before I'd been born, and that part of my father's rant had been accurate. But equating my mother with the missing Mayhew girl based on Papa's cryptic words had been a bridge too far. I felt foolish, like a little child who'd insisted her daydreams were real.

Somewhere down the hall, a grandfather clock sounded its resonant notes. "If you'll excuse me." The reverend stood abruptly.

"I have duties to attend." His hasty steps echoed through the house. When the screen door slammed behind him, Mrs. Mayhew winced.

"It's hard for Franklin to speak about our Mary," she said. "Anything that reminds him of her . . ." She sighed deeply. "How much do you know?"

"I've heard about the baby," I said, quietly.

She pressed a hand to her heart. "Mary's life was far more than the way it ended, but that's all anyone recalls." Mrs. Mayhew swallowed hard, as though forcing down bitter medicine. "But you came here to talk about your mother, didn't you? I'm sure you want to know what she was like."

I nodded, glad to at least have this small consolation. "Yes, I'd like that. Mama passed away several years ago."

Mrs. Mayhew leaned across the table to press her warm, soft hands over mine. "I'm sorry. I was fond of Elizabeth. She and Mary were almost inseparable. For a time, anyway. Her folks were sharecroppers. Mary sometimes worried that Elizabeth worked too much." She paused, looking thoughtful. "Elizabeth wasn't cut out for that life, I don't think. She wasn't a weak person, mind you, but she never enjoyed farming." It seemed I had more in common with my mother than stubborn brown hair.

"Mary could be impulsive," she continued. "I hoped Elizabeth would be a calming influence on her. But they seemed to drift apart toward the end. We saw less and less of Elizabeth." She rubbed wearily at her temples. "I believe she knew about the trouble Mary was in. Elizabeth was such a sweet girl. It must've upset her to learn about Mary's condition."

I picked at a strand of horsehair poking through the sofa's upholstery. "I'd love to hear more about my mother's best friend, if you'd like to tell me about her."

Mrs. Mayhew's eyes lost focus. "Mary was spirited, but gentle, too. Motherly, you might say. All her life, she talked about how she'd have a whole houseful of children when she grew up." Mrs. Mayhew fidgeted with a tatted lace doily on the arm of her chair. "When Mary was small, she had an imaginary little sister. She called her Aurelia, of all things."

I recalled Miss Maeve's story of losing her family to influenza, and her sister having had the same lovely, unusual name. "It sounds like a character from a fairy tale," I said.

"Perhaps it was," Mrs. Mayhew said. "Mary always had her nose stuck in a book. It was hardly ever a religious text, and her daddy didn't like that. She loved her adventure stories and myths. Anything fanciful, really."

"My sister is like that," I said. "And my friend Abel." I gestured toward the front yard, where Abel waited. "I think they're opposed to reality."

Mrs. Mayhew smiled. "Mary especially loved old Celtic tales. My people came from Ireland. Mary took after my side, with that red hair of hers." She sighed. "And the temperament to match." I could imagine my demure, steady mother being drawn to the outspoken Mary, with her flaming hair and strong will.

"When she was born, I wanted to name her for my grandmother. Franklin insisted we choose a Bible name. Mary Eve was our compromise." She paused, her eyes roaming the room before coming to rest on me. "If you take out the r and y, you're left with the name I wanted to give her. Maeve. Such a pretty, magical name. She always seemed more like a Maeve to me."

Maeve. Mary Eve.

"She's been gone for nineteen years." Tears spilled down Mrs. Mayhew's cheeks, slipping unchecked from eyes so pale blue they were almost colorless. How had I not noticed the resemblance before? They were exactly like Miss Maeve's.

"If she'd only told me she was in trouble, maybe it would've ended differently. I feel sure all the worrying about her daddy and me finding out ruined her health and made the baby come early. . . ." Her voice trailed off. "I would've helped her run away. I never hated him like Franklin did." She waved her hands as if to wipe clean a slate. "I doubt there's anything more torturous than thinking on what might have been. That's why the Lord tells us to forget what is behind and press ahead." Mrs. Mayhew pulled a lace handkerchief from the sleeve of her blouse and wiped her tears.

Miss Maeve told me she'd been about my age when she'd arrived in Wheeler—the age Mary Eve Mayhew was when she left. I struggled to marshal my thoughts. "Thank you for speaking with me, Mrs. Mayhew," I said, rising on unsteady legs.

When Mrs. Mayhew stood, I scooped her into a hug. "I'm so very sorry." There was nothing else to say. Not yet, anyway.

She placed her hands on either side of my face, scrutinizing me. "You're quite like Elizabeth." She seemed to debate whether to continue, then added, "But I can see some of him in you, too. You favor both your folks."

"Did you know my father?" It shouldn't have surprised me. Argenta was a small town.

"I did. Matthew boarded with a local farmer, not very far from our house." She spoke with care. "When Matthew moved to Argenta, he began visiting our church. He, Elizabeth, and Mary were fast friends. But with Mary . . ."

My breath quickened. I didn't want to hear what I feared she would say next.

"Well, for Matthew and Mary, it became far more than friendship. Franklin said Matthew was no better than a vagabond, a Yankee boy drifting from town to town, never settling down. I think he feared Matthew would try to take our Mary away." She sighed deeply. "And he was right. They eloped one night in early summer, but Franklin caught up with them just over the county line before they could be married. I never knew what Franklin said to Matthew." She swallowed hard. "Or what he did to him, maybe. But I never saw Matthew again."

Mrs. Mayhew shook her head, the regret and loss still achingly fresh on her lined face. "I feared Mary would grieve herself to death. Elizabeth came to see her, brought her little gifts and things to cheer her. Nothing helped. I hoped Matthew would come back, and they'd try to sneak away again." Her voice rang with an unexpected ferocity. "I'd rather her set up house across the country, alive and well, than live here, caged like a broken-winged bird."

My pulse thundered in my ears. The idea of my father having loved another woman had never occurred to me. Mary Eve Mayhew had been his first love, not my mother. And now I wondered if I'd been right about at least one thing—that Mary's story hadn't ended as her parents, and the town at large, believed.

What if Mary Eve had taken the name her mother intended for her, invented a false history with long-dead parents and a deceased sister called Aurelia after her childhood imaginary friend, and moved one town over to become Miss Maeve Donovan?

My new theory was still speculation, but there was one undeniable fact in this tragic tale. Papa had fathered a child and left the expectant mother behind. Had he known of Mary's condition before he left Argenta, and deliberately abandoned her?

"My word, you've gone white as a sheet," Mrs. Mayhew said. She disappeared into another room, returning seconds later with a small glass of amber liquid. "Drink this," she said firmly.

The burn of whiskey and bitter herbs shocked me back to alertness. I choked down two swallows before Mrs. Mayhew took the glass from my limp fingers. "Thank you," I mumbled.

"My apologies, Verity. I only wanted you to know the rest of the story. Maybe that was wrong of me, but Matthew was a part of Mary's life, and mine. I don't hold ill will for your daddy. I forgave him long ago. I suspect he had"—her brow furrowed and her eyes darted to the door through which Reverend Mayhew had exited—"reasons for leaving. And I doubt he knew about the baby. Franklin and I certainly didn't."

"I'm sure he didn't know," I whispered, hoping I spoke the truth. I wished I had the glass of whiskey and herbs back.

If Maeve was truly Mary Eve, then Papa's first love still lived. And she had his youngest daughter in her home. An uneasy weight settled in my stomach. Miss Pimsler said she'd put us on the orphan train to Arkansas because Mama and Papa had a connection to the state. That might've been accurate, yet out of an entire state, the odds of us coming to this specific small town by pure coincidence seemed minuscule.

"I heard Elizabeth moved to New York shortly after that awful winter," Mrs. Mayhew said. "She and Matthew had been good friends, so I wasn't surprised at the news of their marriage." She patted my hand. "I was glad of it. They deserved a chance for a happy life."

They *had* been happy. For a while. Until Papa's mind began unraveling, and Mama spent her days worrying over what he'd do next and how far away the madness would carry him.

Mrs. Mayhew smiled sadly. "I'm sorry to hear Matthew's gone now." She assumed my arrival on the orphan train meant I had no living parents. I didn't correct her misapprehension. I had no room in my head for any words, any thoughts but these: Her daughter might still be alive.

"Thank you," I said at last. "For telling me Mary's story, and for your kind words about my parents." I stared down at my fingers. "I'd certainly understand if you felt bitter toward Papa."

"We must forgive as the Lord forgives us. Nothing kills a soul faster than bitterness and hate." Mrs. Mayhew put her arm around me. I wished I'd been right about my mother being her missing girl. Mrs. Mayhew would've made a fine grandmother.

I said my goodbyes and made my way outside.

"Well?" Abel asked, glancing back to where Mrs. Mayhew watched from the front porch.

I could only shake my head. "I was wrong. My mother wasn't their daughter."

Abel took my hand in his, helping me into the buggy. "I'm sorry, Verity." I wanted to tell him everything, what I knew and what I suspected. But I found I couldn't speak the words just then.

As we crested a rise in the road, I looked back. Reverend Mayhew stood at the edge of the graveyard behind the church. Hands clasped, head bowed, he looked down at a small stone marker.

I watched until the minister and the cemetery were lost from sight, swallowed up by the rustling grass. If Maeve really was Mary, I hoped time had softened his feelings toward his daughter. And that I'd be able to convince her to come home.

20

I bided my time until Saturday morning, thinking it would be easier to talk to Miss Maeve at her house than at the school. I'd worked myself to the bone, knowing Hettie and Big Tom would be more inclined to let me go visiting if my chores were done well.

Neither Abel, Big Tom, nor Hettie asked for more details about my visit to the Mayhews. Curiosity buzzed around them like flies, but they cared about my feelings enough not to pry for specifics beyond my vague "I was wrong about having family in Argenta."

The weekend dawned fair and hot, and after breakfast, I caught a ride to Miss Maeve's house with Abel. He dropped me off at the Lybrand property before heading into town to visit Jasper. "Tell Lilah I said hello," he called as I watched him ride away on Merlin.

Soon enough I'd be able to tell him this stop wasn't about seeing Lilah. It was about seeing the woman I thought could be Mary Eve Mayhew, and possibly bringing a family back together. I'd lost my mother to the grave and my father, at least as he'd once been, to the cruel torments of a broken mind.

Miss Maeve didn't need to live without her parents. That was one tragedy in her sad story that could be rewritten.

I found her kneeling in the dirt of a rose bed. Her fingers moved deftly among the thorns, breaking off withered blossoms faded to the color of old parchment. She stood as I crossed the shade-dappled lawn. Her face betrayed a flicker of confusion, and maybe a bit of annoyance, at my unexpected arrival. "Why, Verity, how nice to see you. I'm afraid Lilah just went inside to rest. We've been gardening since sunup."

Why had she chosen my sister in particular, and not any other eleven-year-old orphan girl? It struck me as strange that I'd never asked myself the question before. Did she know Lilah was Matthew Pruitt's child, and the connection appealed to her?

"I'm sorry for coming without an invitation," I said. "Actually, it's you I'd like to speak with, not Lilah."

She tilted her head, sending a lock of silvery blond hair slipping from beneath her kerchief. This decidedly not-red hair was enough to make me question my theory that Miss Maeve was Mary Mayhew. Perhaps, as with Marie-Antoinette before her execution, Miss Maeve's hair had lost its color during a time of extreme duress.

I hesitated, unsure of how to proceed. "Miss Maeve, was your hair red when you were younger?"

Her laugh sounded breathy, and a little nervous. "What an odd question. As a matter of fact—and I can't imagine how you guessed—it was. I believe it began turning light when I was around your age."

She picked up a pair of hedge clippers, avoiding my eyes as she turned her attention to the climbing roses. "I've been told it is the result of a rare medical condition. The name of it escapes me." Her knuckles around the handles were white. "I'll have to ask Uncle Reuben. I'm sure he remembers."

I watched her in profile. I could easily imagine her as a girl of my own age. In fact, she looked much younger than Papa, though they must be nearly the same age. When he left, why hadn't she gone after him?

Miss Maeve fixed me in an intense stare. "Surely you didn't come all this way to ask about my hair?"

"No. I went to Argenta this week and spoke with Mrs. Mayhew." Miss Maeve began deadheading the roses once more. "My mother, Elizabeth Sutter, lived there when she was young. She was good friends with the Mayhews' daughter, Mary."

The clippers went still. I had to force the next words from my throat. "Mrs. Mayhew told me Mary ran away from home nineteen years ago. Into a blizzard." I swallowed against the lump in my throat. "She said Mary had lost a baby."

Miss Maeve reached among the glossy green foliage to pluck away a crumbling brown leaf. "I've heard the story. Small towns do love a scandal."

"Everyone thinks she froze to death in that storm." The morning sun peered from behind Miss Maeve's shoulder, casting her face in shadow. I leaned closer, wanting to gauge the reaction in those pale eyes, so like Mrs. Mayhew's. Compassion swelled in my chest. "But I'm not sure that's true."

Miss Maeve's expression was bemused, as though I were a primary grade student spinning a clever story. "Oh, really?"

"It was a dreadful shock, but I learned that Mary's beau was my father. Matthew Pruitt." Miss Maeve drew in a sharp breath, as if the sound of his name were a knife between her ribs.

"At first, I thought she had run off to be with her suitor. But now I have a different idea. I believe Mary Eve *did* start a new life, but not with the young man she loved. And not so far away from her home in Argenta."

Miss Maeve went deathly still. A vein pulsed erratically in her temple, betraying the turmoil under her calm surface. Softly, I said, "Your mother misses you, Mary."

I braced myself for her to be furious that I'd exposed her well-tended secret, or to seem confused if I'd gotten it all wrong. Instead, her shoulders rounded, like she wanted to turn inward on herself and disappear. Her lashes dropped slowly, and her eyes stayed closed as she spoke.

"I named her Genevieve," she whispered. "She was so tiny"—Miss Maeve lifted her dirt-caked hands to measure off a small space in the air—"but she was perfect. She had hair just the color of Lilah's, just like her daddy's."

I wanted to look away from Maeve's anguish, but found I couldn't. It seemed my responsibility somehow, to witness the despair my father hadn't stayed to see himself.

She sank back to her knees in the freshly dug earth. "If I could've carried the baby longer, she would have survived. But the strain was too much. . . . I was terrified Mother and Father would find out, that everyone would know what we'd done." Her words gathered speed, rushing over one another. "I tried to leave, but I couldn't get away. Matthew went back home and never answered my letters pleading for him to come back for me. It was as though I never even existed. Like I wasn't alive at all."

The last remnants of her carefully crafted mask shattered. In her face was the suffocating hopelessness that had driven her out into the snow that night. "I was wild with the loss of him," she said.

She looked at me then, a question in her eyes. "Could you survive such betrayal? If you found yourself truly and utterly forsaken?"

I couldn't speak, struck mute at the mere thought. Losing

Mama to the grave and Papa to madness had been brutal. I couldn't fathom the hurt I'd feel if they'd left me by choice. "No," I whispered at last. "I can't imagine it."

Her smile was an upturned scythe, bright and sharp. "I'll tell you how it goes, then. You force yourself to get up, morning after blank morning. Alone. You make yourself swallow your tasteless food and remind yourself to breathe in and out. It takes all the energy you have just to keep living."

She leaned in, her face inches from mine, ice-blue eyes desolate. A shiver ran across my shoulders. "I barely survived Matthew's betrayal. Then I held our baby girl in my arms. I saw she wasn't breathing. I had no one." Tears glittered on her white lashes. "And there was no more of me." One hand rose to clutch at her heart. It was the same gesture Mrs. Mayhew had used when she spoke of her own lost daughter, of her Mary Eve.

"You let your parents believe you died all those years ago. Why?" My voice sounded weaker, more uncertain now.

Her voice held the finality of a crypt door closing. "Mary Mayhew is dead and gone."

I hesitated, aware that I'd never comprehend what she'd been through. I knelt beside her in the dirt. "I know your mother still loves you. And misses you. And I think your father might be happy to see you again, too."

There was a loud crash as Miss Maeve hurled the clippers against the house. "You know nothing!" Her laugh was bitter as vinegar. "I was their greatest shame. Do you think I care to bring a bit of happiness to my dear, aging parents? Father put the first nail in my baby's coffin when he stopped my elopement. Mother added another when she buried her head and wouldn't see my condition. I couldn't bring myself to tell her I was pregnant, but she knew. She let out the waist of my skirts, never letting herself face the fact that her daughter had played the whore."

"Miss Maeve!" Her words shocked me into speech. "Don't speak of yourself that way. You can't believe the people who loved you most in the world could be that unfeeling." I realized, though, that she did believe it. Her grief over the baby's death and my father's departure had turned to a scattershot blast of anger and blame.

And I understood too late that I was in the line of fire.

"I will not go back to being Mary Mayhew." Her lips twisted with scorn. "And how do you think the good people of Wheeler would react to finding out the girl from that cautionary tale, the one they pray their daughters won't become, is teaching their children?"

"No one thinks that, Miss—"

She struck like a snake, reaching forward to grasp my chin with cold, gritty fingers. I gasped as her nails dug into my skin. "I'd lose my position, my good name, then my home. It won't take long for them to work out that Reuben isn't really my uncle. What will they say then? 'That Mary Mayhew, she never learned to keep her legs shut.'"

My eyes went wide. Chills slithered down my arms at Miss Maeve's grim laugh. "No, he's not my lover. But no one likes to let truth stand in the way of a juicy, shameful story."

Miss Maeve eased closer, putting her lips to my ear. "You look just like your mother." Her breath stirred my hair as she spoke in a voice both hollow with hurt and brimming with hate. For whom, I couldn't be sure.

"You will not tell a soul about any of this." Her command carried the crackling charge that comes before a lightning strike. "Do you understand?"

When I managed a tight nod, she released me and patted

my face. A tear slid down my cheek. She'd do anything to protect her secret. Anything. She had Lilah, and I had much to lose.

Her gaze shifted to something over my shoulder. In the instant it took me to blink, Miss Maeve's demeanor shifted back to the kind schoolteacher. "Why, Abel . . . this morning is just full of pleasant company."

I turned to see Abel approaching, leading his horse. "Merlin threw a shoe before I got halfway to town," he said. "Do you mind if I leave him here while I fetch the farrier?" He looked longingly at Mr. Lybrand's Ford parked alongside the house. "Since y'all don't have horses, you won't have the supplies here."

"I'll come with you," I said, hurriedly. "Lilah is asleep, so I'll visit another time." The violent seesaw of Miss Maeve's emotions had rattled me to the bone. I had no idea if she'd once again turn menacing when Abel left.

Miss Maeve's laugh chimed like bells. She'd switched to this charming persona with practiced, unnerving ease. "Oh, don't be silly. I'll drive you both to town in the car. It's such a nice day, after all." She stood, gesturing to the cloudless sky, its blue so intense it hurt my eyes. "Uncle Reuben is inside reading his newspaper. He can stay here in case Lilah wakes up. I know how to drive the Ford. The only trouble is I can't crank it." She turned to Abel. "Do you think you could manage?"

Abel tied the horse to a tree and looked over to where the automobile stood, green and shiny as a holly leaf. "I've never tried it before, but I bet I can figure it out."

I stepped in front of him. "It won't take long to walk to town," I said, still eager to make my escape. "I hate to trouble Miss Maeve."

"Lucky for you, I'm in charge today, and I insist on driving y'all," Miss Maeve said, almost playfully, before switching to her authoritative teacher voice. "All you need to start it is a good grip and an arm stronger than my own."

I followed behind while they walked to the car. There was no trace of the venom I'd seen in Miss Maeve only moments before. She bent over the crank handle, showing Abel where to hold and which direction to turn. Anxiety spun in my chest. I'd seen the pure malice in her eyes, and I couldn't trust that side of her not to burst free again.

"Abel, we shouldn't trouble Miss Maeve," I said, but my voice was lost in the clank of gears turning. Abel wrestled with the crank, his shoulders straining. It turned, but not quickly enough. The engine choked, then sputtered. I breathed a relieved sigh. Once Abel failed to start the car, I'd force the issue and insist we leave.

While Abel kept struggling with the heavy crank, Miss Maeve slipped by me, stealthy as a cat, and climbed into the driver's seat. Her slim fingers adjusted something under the dashboard. She caught and held my stare. Miss Maeve smiled coldly, and my stomach lurched. A sound like gunfire shattered the stillness.

Abel's shout of shock and pain came a split second later. I whirled around just in time to see him collapse to the dusty ground.

21

Every moment stretched, each detail viciously sharp. Abel clutched his right forearm. Blood seeped from between his fingers, falling in violent red drops.

I flung myself down beside him. "Abel, are you all right?" The tremble running through my limbs didn't show in my voice, but my shaking hands gave away my fear.

He spoke through gritted teeth. "Engine must've backfired." Beads of sweat sprang up on his forehead. He struggled to catch his breath and tried to sit upright. The effort sent a widening track of blood coursing down his arm. He collapsed back to the ground.

"Let me see." I gently uncurled the fingers of his left hand away from the wound. Bones protruded through his ripped skin, two jagged spears of dull white spattered with red. I swallowed bitter bile. Abel's right hand hung at an angle so strange I hardly believed it belonged to the arm I cradled.

A shadow fell across his face. I looked up to find Miss Maeve standing over us. She gasped convincingly, covered her mouth with trembling fingers, then thrust a handkerchief my way. I pressed it to Abel's arm. Blood drenched the white silk, wicking up the swirling lines of a monogrammed letter *M,* turning it crimson.

"Did I hear gunfire?" Mr. Lybrand pounded down the front porch steps and across the lawn. Behind him came Lilah, trotting to keep up. Her face registered first confusion at seeing me on the ground over the prostrate Abel, then horror as she took in his condition.

"There's been an accident. The car backfired, and the crank hit Abel," Miss Maeve answered.

Mr. Lybrand's look of shock was gone just as quickly as it had come, replaced with an awful understanding. "What do you want me to do?" he asked. In that moment, I understood who was in charge.

"He needs a doctor," Lilah said. She slid her hand under Abel's uninjured arm while I grabbed his shoulder. Together we shifted him to a sitting position. The bloody handkerchief slipped to the ground.

"I need something to make a tourniquet, and water," I said to no one in particular. "And carbolic acid, if there is any."

"The Doctors Pruitt." Abel's voice was weak, and his brief smile morphed into a grimace.

"Uncle Reuben will get you to a doctor," Miss Maeve said. "I'll fetch something to stop the bleeding." The worried lines around her eyes looked so genuine as she whirled and fled to the house, I could almost believe my own memory lied, that she hadn't done this deliberately.

"The closest doctor any good at surgery is in Siloam Springs." Reuben Lybrand was careful not to look at Abel, who slumped against my side. Nor could he bring himself to meet my eyes. "We can have him there in about an hour."

Miss Maeve returned with clean linens, along with a jar of water and a stoppered bottle. She handed them to me with brisk efficiency. I tied a strip of linen tightly above the break, then diluted the carbolic acid with water, soaked the remaining linens in the mixture, and wrapped them around the wound. "This helps prevent infection," I said as Abel hissed in pain.

"Can I go with them to the doctor, Mama?" Lilah asked, worry crumpling her face.

"No," Miss Maeve said, just as I answered with a firm, "Yes."

My skin went hot and cold in quick succession. I didn't want Lilah left alone with this woman. Mr. Lybrand knelt next to me, examining Abel's wound. "There isn't enough room for three in the front," he said. "And Abel will need to lie down in back."

Miss Maeve wrapped an arm around Lilah's shoulder, steering my sister as she went.

"No, wait," I said, trying to stand.

Mr. Lybrand tugged me back down. "The girl is in no danger," he whispered urgently. He met my panicking eyes, and understanding passed between us. "For God's sake, don't press the matter. Don't make Miss Maeve angry. Just let her have what she wants." There were no other options, so I nodded my assent. For the moment, anyway, I'd play along.

He helped a woozy-looking Abel to his feet, and we got him into the back seat. "We need to hurry," I said, flinging myself into the passenger seat. Mr. Lybrand hastily started the car, then took the driver's seat, gunning the engine.

I glanced over my shoulder to where Abel lay, eyes closed, his face tight with pain. I doubted he could attend to anything, but I shifted closer to Mr. Lybrand and spoke in an undertone anyway. "Who are you really? You're not Miss Maeve's uncle." His gray eyes slid to meet mine, and I saw both defiance and fear. "And I know she's Mary Mayhew."

The color drained from his craggy features, but he held his tongue.

"She hurt Abel because of me, because I pried into her past," I continued. Dust whipped against my face, harsh as the fear scouring my thoughts. "Will she harm anyone else?"

Strangely, my frightened confession seemed to ease Mr. Lybrand's mind. The tension around his mouth eased as he examined my guilt-ridden eyes. "I don't believe so," he said, carefully, turning back to the road. He stomped on the gas pedal, slamming me back against the seat. "Not as long as you behave yourself."

22

The remainder of our trip to Siloam Springs passed in tense silence, broken only by Abel's groans of pain. Each one was a blade in my heart. I was never so thankful for anything as when the surgeon placed an ether chamber to his nose and rendered him blissfully unconscious. The doctor set the bone and issued a grim reminder that such a serious injury would take a long time to heal, and the arm might never be exactly as it was before. We left the office with a still-groggy Abel, who thankfully went to sleep almost as soon as the car started rolling.

Mr. Lybrand remained stonily silent on the ride home. Dread still twisted my gut when I thought of Miss Maeve. Her attack on Abel replayed in my head over and over. She'd proven herself dangerous, and capable of skillful deceit. As sad as I was for what she'd lived through, and as shameful as my father's role in it had been, I couldn't let her raise my sister.

When we pulled into the farmyard, Big Tom charged to-ward us, scattering a flock of indignant chickens as he came. He flung open the door and wrapped a massive arm around his nephew. Abel shook his head as if to clear it while his uncle helped him out of the car. "Easy. I don't need a broken rib to go with the arm," he mumbled.

Hettie pushed her way between them, her eyes falling to the heavy cast on Abel's arm. "Miss Maeve brought Merlin home and told us you'd been in an accident." She blinked hard. "The way she talked, we were afraid you might end up losing your arm."

"Nothing so bad as that, Aunt Het." Abel put his good arm around her shoulder, just as Della appeared around the corner of the barn, her wide brown eyes shining with tears.

"I'd just come for a visit when Miss Maeve brought the news. I was worried to death," she said, looking as though she badly wanted to hug Abel but wasn't sure how to navigate the cast. She settled for a peck on his cheek, then turned to Mr. Lybrand. "It's a mercy you were there and able to get him some help."

Big Tom extended a hand in thanks. "Much obliged to you, Mr. Lybrand." My pulse pounded in my temples. It was sickening, hearing Miss Maeve's loyal minion praised for helping clean up her crime scene.

"Let's go inside," I said to Della and Abel. We helped ourselves to the dinner Hettie had left on the table, though I had little appetite and couldn't keep from watching Abel with anxious eyes. Abel made slow work of the meal. After declining Della's offered help, he gave up an attempt to cut a pork chop one-handed and settled for forking black-eyed peas into his mouth. "You're going to have trouble climbing the ladder to the loft, too," Della remarked. She made an unnecessary adjustment to Abel's sling.

"I'll sleep in the loft until your cast comes off. You can have my room," I said, trying to ignore a twinge of annoyance at the way Della's hand lingered on Abel's shoulder.

Abel rose unsteadily, and shuffled to the kitchen to place his dish in the sink, grimacing when his arm jostled against his side. "I won't argue. Think I'll head on up to bed." His words stilled blurred at the edges, the lingering effects of the anesthesia the doctor used while setting the bones.

"Miss Maeve told me about the accident," Della said. "I can't believe you didn't have your hand open when you turned the handle. My grandpa had a crank tractor once, and he said the metal rod can break your arm clean off it you don't hold it right."

"I thought I did it just like Miss Maeve showed me," Abel said, shuffling to the foot of the stairs. "I guess I messed up somehow."

I gathered the other plates and retreated to the sink, my thoughts a tangle. Knowing how polished Miss Maeve's lies could be changed everything. When I'd sat with her in a sun-drenched schoolhouse to talk about what I'd seen in the woods the night before, she'd been so ready with an answer. But now I knew her concern was a clever façade. She was not only capable of skilled deception, but dangerous when backed into a corner. If Maeve lied so smoothly about her identity, it was likely she was concealing something about the goings-on in the woods as well.

I scowled up at the pressed-tin ceiling tiles. I needed someone with knowledge of what went on in the woods.

"Verity." My pulse quickened at the sound of my name on Abel's lips. I turned, hands still sunk in dishwater, to find him paused halfway up the staircase. "Thank you for everything you did today. You were calm when I got hurt, and it helped me not to panic."

Guilt threatened to overcome me. My interference in Miss Maeve's past had brought this accident about. "You're welcome," I managed. Our gazes stayed locked across the small room, and I had a sensation that each of us felt the weight of things unsaid. I knew what I wasn't voicing, but I wondered what his silent truths might be. He rapped his knuckles gently on the banister, then trudged upstairs.

When we heard the bedroom door creak shut overhead, Della joined me at the sink and dried the last pot. My thoughts drifted back to Maeve, and the woods. "If I wanted to know more about the woods, and . . . something strange that's happening there, who would I need to ask?"

Della peered at me, curious. "I suppose Granny Ardith would be your best bet. Her cabin is the only other house close to the woods besides Mr. Lybrand and Miss Maeve's place."

"You mentioned her that day I came to the store. Is she your grandmother?"

"No, it's more of a title, really. A granny woman is good at healing, with herbs and natural things. Some might lay a curse for the right amount of money, but Granny Ardith's not like that. She'll make a salve to clear your skin, pour herb candles to burn for luck, or string an amulet so you won't get lost. Things like that. Why do you need to know about the woods?" Her brow puckered with worry. "I've heard rumors and such. Did you see something out there?"

Footsteps sounded on the porch. I shook my head to tell Della we were done talking for now. She flashed me a questioning look, but said nothing as Big Tom entered, bending to avoid the wards still hanging over the front door. "Where's Abel?" Hettie asked, coming in behind her husband. "Please tell me that boy's resting."

"He is. But he's going to need something for pain, maybe to prevent infection, too," I said, thinking fast. "Della says

Granny Ardith could mix up something to help. Do you mind if we go see her? I'll be back before nightfall."

"That's a fine idea. Hurry on back, though," Hettie said, pressing a few coins into my hand.

"I will." I charged out the door with Della breezing behind me. We climbed into the fringe-topped surrey she'd driven over from town.

"All right, care to tell me what's going on?" Della asked.

I could see no way around it. I needed help to get information about Miss Maeve. And if I was honest, I wanted someone to take this perilous journey with me. I just had to find a way to do that without endangering anyone. "You have to swear you won't tell a soul." I paused. "If it gets out that I've shared this secret with you, you could be in danger."

Instead of fear, I saw only interest shining in her eyes. "I can keep my mouth shut."

I clasped my hands on my lap and willed her to believe me. "Miss Maeve is Mary Mayhew."

The reins went slack in Della's fingers. She turned her face toward me, lips parted in shock as we jostled down the rutted road.

"I had a talk with the Mayhews that made me think it might be so. When I confronted Miss Maeve, she made it clear I was not to tell anyone. Or there would be consequences." I took a breath. "And she hurt Abel on purpose to prove she was serious."

The surrey swayed and the horse's hooves thudded against the dusty road, a slower echo of my pounding heartbeats. Della didn't speak for an agonizing minute.

"All these years, Miss Maeve lied about who she was." She spoke slowly, as if trying words in a foreign language. "Why?"

Miss Maeve's failed elopement with my father, his abandonment, and the resulting death of their baby weren't easy to discuss, but I steeled myself and told the story. Then, into her stunned silence, I poured the tale of what I'd seen by the well that night, and how I'd been certain Miss Maeve was dead. "And now that I know she lied about so much, I want to find out what else she's hiding. And what's *really* going on in the woods."

When Della finally spoke, all she managed was a breathy "Lord have mercy." There was another long silence, filled only with the squeak and rattle of the surrey's wheels. "I believe you," she said at last.

"You do?" I hadn't realized just how badly I needed someone to share this burden with until that moment. "Even the part about her breaking Abel's arm on purpose?"

Della nodded. "Something didn't sit right with me about Miss Maeve needing Abel to crank the car." She worried her bottom lip with her teeth, thinking. "I've seen Miss Maeve crank that car herself before when she was leaving the store. Several times in fact, and she did it the right way. There's no chance she'd show Abel how to do it wrong by accident," Della said, steering us toward the wood's outermost fringes. "And Granny's a straight shooter. If something's going on out there, she'll tell you how the cow ate the cabbage." Della met my baffled expression, adding, "Sorry. She'll tell you the whole truth. Even if it might be hard to hear."

The path grew narrower. Gnarled branches like twisted fingers reached low, almost brushing our heads. I squinted into the mottled shadows, nervousness rippling in my stomach as we drew nearer the woods.

"There it is," Della said, pointing to a squat cabin tucked in an opening at the edge of the trees. Like Miss Maeve, Granny

Ardith made her home on the edge of the woods without being properly inside their reach. All around the little shack, wild gardens of herbs and weeds ran amok, giving Granny Ardith's home the look of an island floating in tangled green chaos. Rusted orange patches spread over the tin roof. The entire building listed to the side like a drunkard.

A figure in a tattered apron appeared on the sagging front porch. I couldn't shake the feeling she'd somehow been summoned by our approach. Della's horse whickered anxiously. "Granny Ardith's place makes her nervous," she said, cooing to the frightened animal.

The old woman rested knobby hands on her hips. Her head was covered in steel-gray hair thin enough to show patches of liver-spotted scalp. "What're you doing back so soon, girl?" she called in a rusted-gate voice. "I ain't half done with the bread you brought me last time."

"I'm not delivering food today, Granny," Della said as the carriage rolled to a stop in front of the shack. The mare stamped her hooves and snorted while Della stepped down and tied the reins to a gatepost. "We have a friend who needs a pain tonic." She thumbed over her shoulder at me by way of introduction. "This is Verity."

"How do you do?" I said, climbing down from the surrey.

Granny Ardith pulled a pair of wire-rimmed spectacles from a sewing chatelaine hanging off her belt and surveyed me from under sagging eyelids. "Can't complain, wouldn't help nothing if I did. I just got done making a fresh batch of tea. Y'all got time to sit a spell?"

We exchanged a glance. "Of course," Della said.

We picked our way through the riotous garden, passing under the blank gaze of a scarecrow, and stepped onto the porch. The window to the right of the screen door was covered in a woven net made of what appeared to be hair. An iron horseshoe hung above the threshold, with a crude cross made of twigs tacked alongside it. "Evil-spirit repellents," Della whispered.

Inside the dim one-room cabin, a pot bubbled on the cookstove. Clusters of drying herbs and flowers hung from the rafters, their petals crisp and brown. A mound of vines several feet high lay heaped against the wall. Some were spliced thread-thin and dried to a light tan. Others still dripped nectar, their honeysuckle scent golden and sweet.

Granny Ardith motioned us to sit at the table. She poured three steaming mugs of a yellowish liquid. "Dandelion-root tea," she announced. "Cleanses the liver, helps if you need to see into the future for a bit. And it's real good for constipation."

Della sipped from her mug, casting a sympathetic glance over the rim as I took a tiny swallow. Bitterness hit my tongue and tightened my throat. I felt my nose wrinkle in disgust, but tried to cover the reaction.

"What do you think of Wheeler?" Granny asked. "I wager it's a sight different than where you're from."

"It is," I said, barely keeping down a cough brought on by the stout drink. "Different, but beautiful."

Granny nodded in approval. "Ain't nowhere else I'd rather live."

"I like the open fields around the farm, but I can't say I'm entirely comfortable out here by the woods." I cut a look at Della, hinting with my eyes for her to be the one to broach the matter of the entity by the well.

She took the cue perfectly. "Verity saw something out there. Something awful strange, Granny," she said. "And I told her if anyone would know what to make of goings-on in the woods, it would be you."

Granny took a long drink. When she lowered the cup, a curl of steam wafted up, momentarily blotting out her wizened face. She turned a watery gaze my way. "Well, out with it. What's got you all stirred up?"

"I was walking through the woods at night," I began. Granny's lips compressed until her nose and chin nearly touched. "And I came across what I thought was Miss Maeve Donovan, lying dead on the ground beside an old well." I left out my encounters with the little girl, the one who might be the ghost of Della's little sister.

"Ahhh," Granny said. "I've heard tell of folks seeing such as weren't really there out in the woods. It's a place of power." She drummed stubby nails on the table. "But all power ain't good, to be sure." She shifted to look out the cabin's open door. Light flashed over the lenses of her spectacles. "Did you tell Miss Maeve about it?"

It was an odd question, and not the first that would've come to my mind if I were in Granny's well-patched shoes. "I did. She said there's a force in the woods, something dark that can trick people, and look like whatever it wants."

"Almost like a doppelgänger," Della put in. When I looked surprised at the German term, she blushed and said, "It was in a book Abel read to me when we were little."

"It weren't her, of course," Granny Ardith said, firmly.

"Yes, but what *was* it?" I said. "It was as solid as you or me, not some misty apparition. It looked exactly like her, right down to the clothes. When I checked for a pulse, I had to push back the bracelet Miss Maeve wears. Even that was precisely the same," I recalled. "A little square of gold, strands of red hair, and dried vine."

Granny stared at me hard. Dropping my eyes, I took another sip of the foul drink.

This time, I wasn't able to keep from choking on my dandelion-root tea when Granny Ardith said, "Sounds an awful lot like a charm I once made for your mama."

23

"What did you say?" I gasped.

"I would've known you for Elizabeth Sutter's girl anywhere. You're the spitting image of your mama. I did that working for Lizzie nigh on twenty years ago. She wanted a charm to keep somebody close," the old woman said. "A keeping spell. The kind that will tether somebody to a particular place so as they can't wander too far."

Della and I exchanged glances. "You can do that?" she asked. "Keep someone in a place against their will?"

I felt the color draining from my face. Why would my mother want such a thing? "That sounds awful," I whispered.

Granny waved her gnarled fingers, shooing away my protests. "It's real handy for wandering fellers who want to roam about. Keeps 'em tied to a particular location. Makes a nice, unseen circle they can't pass without getting sick as a dog." She sniffed. "There's too much gadding about these days, if you ask me. Course I'd never help tie a person to a place for spite. I only did keeping spells when there was real love involved, just to strengthen what was already there."

She pulled a snuff tin from her apron pocket and shoved a

pinch of the dark powder into her lower lip. "I never doubted Lizzie's intentions. She was a good girl, wouldn't hurt a fly." Granny Ardith nodded hard, as if her certainty made everything fine. "I told her I'd weave the bracelet, but she'd have to bring me some hair from the loved one, and a bit of something they held dear. She showed back up a few days later with a swatch of hair red as you ever laid eyes on and a little square of gold with a flower carved on it. I wove 'em up good, and told her be sure to call the magic to the surface or it wouldn't work."

"How do you do that?" Della asked.

"Got to leave the charm someplace where the earth's magic is strong, on the first night of a waxing moon." Granny spit into her empty tea mug. "Fork of an ash tree is a good spot, or by a stream. The stronger the magic in a place, the better the keeping works."

I thought about the inexplicable encounters I'd had in the woods. "So magical places exist, and you only have to know where they are to use their power?"

"Magic is scattered all over the place." Granny pointed a gnarled finger in my direction. "You've got them browny-greeny eyes, right? But if I look real close, I can see flecks of gold in 'em. Magic's like those speckles of gold—it's there, but only some folks ever notice it. If somebody's got the gift to know when there's magic around, they might can learn to make use of it."

Della considered this. "Our choir leader at church says most people can sing lead, because it's easiest to hear the melody of a tune, but if you don't have a gift for picking out the harmonies, it's not something you can learn. You've got it or you don't."

Granny snapped her fingers. "Right. And just like some

songs are harder to sing, some workings are harder to do. That keeping spell was one of the trickiest bits of crafting I ever learned, but I got it right in the end." She gnawed her bottom lip. "I might've even made it a little too strong. Once the spell comes alive, the person ain't able to leave the boundary, so long as they have their charm on."

Granny stood slowly and pottered over to a shelf full of glass jars. "I best get started on that pain tonic for your friend." The scent of crushed cloves filled the cabin as she went to work with a mortar and pestle.

I shifted closer to Della. "The bracelet Miss Maeve wears has strands of bright red hair. I don't know how or why it changed colors, but I'm positive it's hers, from when she was our age."

"Maybe so," Della said. "Magic can do strange things, I'll grant you." She tried to manage another sip of the bitter tea, but ending up spitting a neat stream back into her cup. I chewed my thumbnail, wishing I could ask my mother why she'd wanted such a spell cast over her best friend.

Granny Ardith proffered the tonic, waving off my attempts to pay for it. "I do what I can to help," she said. Given her history of making charms tying people to places they might otherwise leave, I wondered if we had the same definition of *help*.

"We should be going." I moved toward the door, a little shaky on my feet. My head spun with everything Granny had just told us. I couldn't say whether the revelations about magic or my mother were more startling. Della followed, saying her goodbyes.

Granny Ardith saw us off from the front porch. "It was good to meet you, Verity," she called in her raspy voice. "Come again and I'll mix up something for that hair of yours, smooth it right down." I proffered weak thanks as we rolled away.

Neither Della nor I spoke for a while as we each sorted our thoughts.

"Granny Ardith either doesn't know anything of substance about what I saw in the woods, or if she does, she's not telling," I said. Regardless, the information I had managed to gather was troubling in its own right. I swiped impatiently at a bead of sweat sliding down my temple and contemplated what could've possessed my mother to try and trap her best friend in Wheeler forever.

"Mrs. Mayhew said my mother and Miss Maeve were the dearest of friends, but they drifted apart before Miss Maeve—I mean, Mary—disappeared. Maybe Mama sensed the distance growing between them and hoped the bracelet would help."

Della's lips pursed. "Not to speak ill of your family, but it doesn't sound like something a true friend would do." She hesitated. "And then she married your father not long after Mary disappeared."

"They both thought she was dead," I said a little more sharply than necessary. "Were they supposed to stay alone forever? Besides, I think Miss Maeve keeping the bracelet all these years shows how much the friendship with my mother meant to her."

"I suppose," Della said at last, still doubtful but ready to drop the subject. "So, what do we do next?"

"I need to see the ring that was in the Mayhew baby's grave. Is it still at your house?"

Understanding sparked in Della's eyes. "Yes. I know exactly where it is."

I tucked myself into the foot well between the front and back seats of the surrey as we entered town. It wouldn't do for anyone to see me, pot-stirring spreader of lies about honorable citizens that I was, with Della and mention it to her father. I jostled about like an egg in a basket until Della stopped the surrey. "All clear," she said. "We're in the stable now, and Daddy's horse is still gone."

We hurried across the yard and onto the veranda of the Loftises' cheerful yellow house. I followed Della inside, through a parlor and into a large bedroom. A tall oak chest stood against the wall, a shiny keyhole winking from the center of the top drawer. "Do you know where the key is?" I asked.

Della slipped a hairpin from her black curls. "Who needs a key?" She set to work, her tongue poking from the corner of her mouth. "Mama and Daddy are private folks. And I've always been real nosy," she said candidly.

With Della explaining her methods, I watched her careful work. At last, the lock clicked open. She slid the pin back into her hair and stepped aside with a satisfied grin.

The drawer squealed in protest as I pulled it open. I riffled through tatted lace handkerchiefs and silk stockings until my fingers closed around a small black velvet bag. Della crowded in, breath held, watching me fumble with the ties.

I tipped the bag, spilling a single gold ring onto my palm. The wide band was dull, its shine dimmed from years hidden away without care, but the carved flowers were intricate and lovely. "Heliotropes," I breathed. The symbol of fidelity.

Lifting the ring closer, I could make out tiny, cleverly hinged panels. When I slid a thumbnail under the edge of one, it flipped back like the lid of a minuscule treasure chest. Underneath, carved in fantastically small script darkened with age, was one word: *Forever.*

I opened the other panels. *My. One. And. Only.*

The next-to-last panel lifted to reveal a shattering phrase.

I imagined a young Miss Maeve, pregnant, abandoned, and terrified, staring at the words, wondering if they were a lie.

I love you.

I slipped the band on my finger, feeling the gold slide against my skin. I turned it until I found what I was looking for: a single missing panel, broken cleanly away from the band. This was the bit used to make the charmed bracelet. There, exposed where the missing piece had been torn away, was a name. *Matthew.*

Della blew out a slow breath.

"I need to tell your father about Miss Maeve's bracelet," I said. "No one would have this missing piece from the ring except Mary. It helps make our case for Miss Maeve being the lost Mayhew girl." I slid the drawer shut, my confidence growing. "To adopt a child from the Children's Benevolence Society, Miss Maeve would've signed documents attesting to her morals and character. Even if we can't prove she attacked Abel on purpose, pretending to be someone you're not voids the contract. They'll have to take Lilah away from her just for that."

"Not to mention she's living with a man she's not married to," Della added. "She's really a Mayhew, so Reuben Lybrand isn't actually her family."

"Once your father hears our story and sees the bracelet she's wearing, he'll have to believe me." The hairs on the back of my neck prickled at the sound of another voice joining mine.

"We'll see about that." I whirled to find myself facing Sheriff Loftis.

24

My eyes dropped to the sheriff's boots. No spurs. He'd snuck in without the telltale jingle. Della's rosy cheeks blanched. I held my hands up, palms out. The sheriff's flat stare shifted to the ring on my left hand.

"We can explain." I winced, knowing nothing good ever came of a conversation starting with those words.

Della slid her arm into mine. "Verity needs to talk with you."

Sheriff Loftis jerked his head toward the back door. "Get back to the store, Della. Your mama needs help closing up."

"Not until you hear us out," she protested.

Sheriff Loftis swung round, his chest expanding with fury. "I told you about associating with her kind!" He advanced, and Della shrank against the wall. I placed myself between them, facing Della.

"Let me talk to your father, in private. I'm sure he'll see the truth. He's a reasonable man."

Della looked over my shoulder at her father. "Listen to her, Daddy. It may sound ridiculous, but Verity will make you see she's right." Not a ringing endorsement, but I knew she meant to help. She cast one half-defiant, half-frightened look at her father and scurried away.

Turning, I faced the sheriff. "I didn't come to steal from you. The fact is, I need your help." The glass knob of the dresser drawer pressed into my spine, and my heart threatened to beat free of my rib cage. "Miss Maeve Donovan isn't who you think she is. And this ring shows she's been lying about her identity. Will you hear me out?"

The sheriff shifted impatiently from one foot to the other. "Get on with it, then."

"I went to visit the Reverend and Mrs. Mayhew in Argenta. I had questions about their daughter, Mary. And now that I've talked with them, I'm convinced that she didn't die that winter when she disappeared. She moved to Wheeler, and she's been here ever since, going by the name Maeve Donovan. The time-line is right, and Maeve told me a story using the name Mary Eve called her imaginary friend." I spoke faster, never taking my eyes off the sheriff's flat expression. "My father . . . he and Mary Eve were going to have a baby. He gave her a gold ring before he left Arkansas. And part of that ring was broken off before she buried it with the baby. I had to see the rest of the ring, to see if it matched the bit of gold Miss Maeve wears on her bracelet. And it does. That's proof that she must've had the ring with her all along, ever since the baby was stillborn."

"How dare you dig up the past?" His voice was low and dangerous. "The Mayhews lost their daughter and didn't so much as get a body back to bury." He passed a hand over his mouth, agitated. "Nobody could help them." I blinked, stunned to understand that he felt responsible for the case remaining unsolved.

"You're nosing around where you've got no business, stirring up ghosts." He crossed burly arms over his chest. "I'll hear no more about this from you. The gold on her bracelet could've come for anywhere."

"But, Sheriff—"

"I deal in facts," he said, cutting me off. "Not the wild tales of a girl who will lie about innocent people for her own selfish reasons. As you've already lied about Miss Maeve once before."

My face burned with anger. "That's not what I'm doing. She's dangerous."

"Miss Maeve Donovan is a trustworthy, respectable member of *our community*." He stressed the last two words, hammering home that I was an outsider here. "You, on the other hand, have my property in your possession without permission. I caught you committing a serious crime, Miss Pruitt." His flinty eyes leveled with mine.

"I'm not stealing anything! I only needed to see the ring. My father bought it for Miss Maeve. His name is inscribed right here."

The sheriff cast a brief glance at the ring. "Matthew is a common enough name. Even if it was a gift from your father to someone long ago, that does not prove this harebrained story you've dreamed up."

Loftis stepped so close I could smell the tobacco on his breath. "As much as I'd like to, I can't arrest you for breaking and entering since my girl let you in." He grimaced. "She won't be so foolish in the future." His hand rested lightly on a pair of handcuffs hanging from his belt. "Return my property and we'll drop the matter. For now. But if you step one toe out of line again, I won't be so forgiving. Do we understand each other?"

"I understand perfectly." I dropped the ring into his open palm and brushed by him, heading for the door.

My hand was on the knob when the sheriff's voice reached

me. I imagined I felt his stare like an arrow between my shoulder blades. "I'll be watching you, Miss Pruitt."

"I'd expect nothing less. Have a good evening, Sheriff Loftis." Without looking back, I marched off in the direction of the farm.

Let the man think he'd won. He wouldn't silence me so easily. When I was out of sight, I doubled back into town. My sister's future hung in the balance. I was far from ready to make nice and keep quiet.

Bunching my skirts in my fists, I ran along the backs of the shops and homes that formed the heart of Wheeler. The little depot where our orphan train had stopped was less than a quarter mile north of town. A sharp pain knifed between my ribs, but I lowered my head and plowed on.

A weathered, flat-roofed building came into view. The rectangular sign nailed to the door read WHEELER TRAIN DEPOT and, underneath, in smaller letters, *Telegraph Office.*

A young woman with straight dark brows sat behind a desk, her nose buried in a dime novel. The garish cover showed a man on an inky sea, struggling to escape the grip of a sea monster. "How can I help you?" the operator asked, her eyes never leaving her book.

"I need to send a telegram." She handed me a pencil and a message form. I checked the posted fee schedule, laid out the coins Hettie had sent for Granny Ardith's payment, and began.

Miss Agatha Pimsler, Care of Children's Benevolence
Society, NYC, New York
    Must speak on matter both urgent and private. Take
first train to Wheeler. Reply with anticipated arrival time.
Please hurry, and keep confidential. Verity Pruitt.

The operator tapped out the message on the telegraph machine, her eyes flicking occasionally to the novel in her lap. "Is that a good book?" I asked, hoping the casual question would distract from the furtive nature of my telegram.

"It's excellent," the operator said, grinning. "The Brady Detectives series. You ought to try one. There's a new mystery every week, and there's always someone in peril who needs saving." She handed me a receipt and went back to her book. "But they all end well, and that's partly why I like them so much."

"I'll see if I can get my hands on a copy." I pushed open the door and inhaled deeply, filling my chest with humid air and hope. "That sounds like just what I need right now."

The fog-draped nights dragged on. For years she'd been conscious for each lonely second. Neither did she sleep in the day, when she played her role, smiling and putting on the mask to appear like everyone else. The old man who pretended to be her family knew the truth, as did the crone who'd done the working that trapped her. But no one else was the wiser. Fools, all of them.

She expected her spirit to wake as it always did to the blank nothingness. She expected to spend the seemingly endless hours 'til dawn alone. Always alone.

But tonight, a little girl sat cross-legged by the river.

She approached the child slowly, the hem of her gown dragging the black sand. The girl regarded her with recognition, unsurprised by her presence here. With a small hand, she skipped a rock over the obsidian water. It skittered to the far bank.

"I fell in the well, and I couldn't breathe," the little girl said.

She recalled the long-ago eventide when she herself had crashed through the surface of the water. She'd do it all so differently if she could. Every single thing. She would have stayed. And lived.

It was far, far too late now.

"I watched in the woods while some men with a ladder took

me out of the well," the child went on. "They couldn't see me or hear me, because I'm dead now."

Death had a way of making things so very matter-of-fact.

Over the girl's shoulder, hovering high in the air, the gate appeared. It came each night, and it was always closed. She didn't know precisely what lay beyond the gate, only that she should've passed into it.

The child lifted a small hand, pointing to the tightly closed wrought-iron panels. "Do you know how to open it?" Her dark brows drew together in a frown. "I'm supposed to go through it."

She knelt beside the child, placing her arms around the thin shoulders. Until this moment she'd never considered that anyone else could join her here, in the Hollow. She looked to the bracelet on her wrist, with its woven strands of hair. Sparks of understanding flickered to life. Plans began to take shape in her mind.

It was too late to change the past and the decisions that led to this forsaken existence. But perhaps there was a way to make it right, at least in part. Perhaps she could take back something of what was owed to her after all.

"No, I can't open it. But I'm glad you're here with me now." She stroked the child's dark hair, thinking of another little girl. "What if I bring us someone else to play with?"

25

Della was waiting just outside of town in her carriage, Abel's bottle of tonic in hand. In my tense encounter with the sheriff, I'd forgotten about it.

"I figured you'd have to head back this way eventually," she said, scooting over to make room for me on the small seat. "Come on. You'll never make it back before dark on foot."

"Won't your father be angry if he finds out?" I asked, hesitating.

"Oh, I'll catch nine kinds of hell," she said. "Now get in the buggy."

I filled Della in on my message to Miss Pimsler as we rode back to the farm. "You don't mind checking at the telegraph office for her reply, do you?"

"Not a bit. And I'm sorry about how awful Daddy was to you. I can't believe he just ignored us." She frowned, then added, "No, actually, I can." Della stopped the surrey at the edge of the Weatheringtons' yard. "Be careful, Verity." She pressed me into a hug before driving away.

I strode across the property with my back ramrod straight.

It seemed the only way to compensate for the crumpled feeling in my chest.

I replayed the day's events, and found them nearly impossible to comprehend. My sister's guardian was capable of horrific violence. I was no closer to understanding the mysteries of the woods and how Miss Maeve was connected to them. And a hissing suspicion crawled through my thoughts. I'd always believed my mother had been a kind person. Often sad, but always gentle. Was I as wrong about her goodness as I'd been about Miss Maeve's true darkness?

I wrapped my arms around myself and made for the barn, where I found Big Tom shoeing Lady May just outside the double doors. In the twilight, his hammer rang loud against the iron.

"Got some things to do before dark," he said, gesturing toward the sinking sun and the large shovel leaning against the barn wall. He looked almost apologetic. "Hettie brought your work clothes out to the loft. You'll want to change. The stalls need mucking out."

Of course they did. I took to the ladder, pausing on the second step. "How's Abel feeling? I got him something from Granny Ardith," I said, holding out the bottle. A sharp, almost painful desire to see him jabbed at my chest.

Big Tom took the tonic, his bear paw of a hand engulfing mine. "Abel's doing about as good as you can expect," he said, giving Lady May a pat on the flank to indicate her shoeing was done. The mare ambled out into the melting sunset and joined Merlin.

Big Tom came slowly over to the ladder. I found myself eye level with the farmer for the first time. "He's been talking about you." He scuffed his brogans along the dusty ground. "He bragged on how calm you were when he got hurt."

"That was good of him to say, but it's not entirely true. I only looked calm on the surface."

"Like a duck on a pond," Big Tom said. At my confused expression, he added, "You see them floating along, all peaceful. But under the water, they're paddling like crazy."

I smiled. "That sounds familiar."

He swept off his straw hat, leaving wispy white hairs standing up like a rooster's tail. "I know this life ain't what you wanted. But me and Het are glad you came. If you don't find a way back north, I hope you'll let this be your home. You're welcome for as long as you want to stay." He crammed the battered hat back on his head, smiling from behind the pushbroom bristles of his mustache before lumbering out into the sunset shadows.

I mucked out the stalls by lantern light, thinking over what Big Tom had said. As I fell into a steady rhythm, my mind relaxed. There was something calming about the simple, repetitive action. The slight burn in my forearms from lifting the heavy shovel reminded me of my growing strength.

The good feelings faded when at last I stepped into the loft to find that when Hettie moved my things, my nightgown hadn't made the trip. One of Abel's work shirts hung from a peg on the wall. I fingered the cotton of one sleeve and considered sleeping in it. It smelled faintly of hay and the warm sunshine smell of Abel's skin. The idea of his clothes against my bare body sent a jolt of heat through me.

I banged down the ladder and made for the farmhouse. A good, cold scrubbing in the washbasin was what I needed.

Laundry dried stiff from the day's heat hung on the backyard clothesline. I pulled down my gown and went inside to wash and change. Big Tom had gone straight to bed after leaving the barn, and Hettie was dousing the lamps, ready to follow him.

"I forgot to bring that to the barn, didn't I?" Hettie said, nodding at the gown flung over my shoulder as she handed me a lit candle. "I've been jittery as a long-tailed cat in a room full of rocking chairs today," she said, her tired smile fading to seriousness. "Thank you for taking care of our Abel. He may never use that arm like normal again, but if it weren't for you and Miss Maeve handling things like you did, it might've been a lot worse."

I could only nod as Hettie turned to head off to bed, my throat constricted with fury at Miss Maeve's attack on Abel.

It was only after I'd washed, dressed, and thrown the bathwater out onto the kitchen garden that I realized my comb was upstairs, in the room where Abel slept. I considered going to bed without retrieving it. But the wet tangle of waves that hung to my waist would be a bramble thicket in the morning if I didn't comb them out tonight. Slipping a housecoat over my gown, I began slowly climbing the stairs to the attic room.

I cracked the door and peered in, half expecting to see Abel awake and in awful pain.

Instead, he lay fast asleep, his good arm thrown over his eyes, lips slightly parted. Soft moonlight pooled over the rumpled bed, and only the gentle sound of his deep, even breaths filled the room. The injured arm in its heavy plaster cast rested on his bare stomach. I hadn't thought about whether Abel slept in a nightshirt before. I watched the plane of his chest rise and fall, taken by a sudden, fierce longing to touch him.

I shook away the brazen feeling. With quick steps, I crossed to the little dressing table, dropped my comb into my housecoat pocket, and turned to go.

"Verity?"

For three thunderous heartbeats, I couldn't move. When I turned around, Abel was sitting up, heavy-lidded and sleep-tousled, watching me. My eyes wandered of their own accord, taking in the length of his body. I wasn't quick enough in tugging my gaze back to his face.

He looked away and rubbed the back of his neck, then visibly relaxed when he spied a shirt draped over the bedpost. He slid one arm into a sleeve, leaving the other to hang empty over his cast.

It gave me a little thrill, knowing that my presence flustered him. "What, no remarks about me sneaking into your room at night?" I asked, grinning. "And not a single joke about your corrupting influence on my morality. I'm disappointed." I sat the candlestick on the top of the wardrobe, drew my hair over my shoulder, and began slowly working through the tangles.

Moonlight cascaded over Abel in a pale stream, grazing across the sharp line of his jaw, silvering the curls at his temples. "I'm sorry I woke you," I said.

His eyes met mine. "I'm not."

I pocketed the comb again and began twining my hair into a thick braid. The silence between us grew and changed, morphing into something charged and sparking with pent-up energy.

I should tell him good night and slip out the door. That would be the sensible thing to do. But I was sick to death of being sensible.

"And why is that?" I didn't intend to walk forward, but I found myself at his bedside.

The blanket slid to the floor as he stood. "Because I feel better when you're with me." The blue of his eyes had gone black with the night. I faltered under their intensity and looked down. Our bare feet were only inches apart.

Slowly, carefully, he slipped my braid back over my shoulder. His fingers lingered against my neck. "When we're together, it's peaceful, like evening coming down after a long day's work. But at the same time everything feels . . . brighter and newer." He paused, searching my face. "I don't want to feel any other way."

I closed my eyes and rose onto my toes. Abel's mouth was warm against mine, softer than I'd imagined, and sweet. I felt his startled breath slide over my lips, and for a dreadful second, I thought he'd pull away.

Then his hand pressed against the small of my back, pulling me close. Delicious heat started in my chest and spread through me. I wound my arms around his neck, fingers tangling in his hair. Our bodies aligned, as though we'd been designed to fit in each other's arms, our lips made for this seeking, searching, intoxicating moment.

Abel stepped away, his breaths quick. The familiar grin I loved spread slowly across his face like sunrise.

I pressed my little finger against the cleft in his chin, feeling delirious at my own boldness and a little bashful, all at once. "I think I've wanted to kiss you since the first time I saw you," I confessed.

"Same here," he said.

"Even when you thought I was a stuck-up Yankee girl with a chip on her shoulder?" My voice came out a bit shaky.

"Even then."

I thought of all the things I needed to tell him, and hesitated. If he knew that Miss Maeve had hurt him as a warning for my benefit, he could decide being with me was too risky.

Right now, the future blazed in my imagination like fireworks, bright and bold. I didn't want to let anything darken this moment.

But keeping these truths from Abel would spread like an inkblot until it blackened every interaction between us. And so I spilled the story of Maeve's past and my father's misdeeds, and the mysteries of the woods. He listened with wide, worried eyes, his lips pressed into a firm line. Then my eyes dropped to his cast. This was the truth I'd wanted most to conceal. And that made it the most crucial one to set free. "Abel, this morning at Miss Maeve's house, when you tried to crank the car—"

He pressed a hand to my cheek. I looked up at him, falling silent. "It wasn't an accident, was it?" he asked.

"No," I said. "I'd just told Miss Maeve I knew her secret, and she wanted to prove she'd do whatever was necessary to keep me quiet." The misery in my chest made it hard to breathe. "I am so sorry, Abel. If I hadn't confronted her, this wouldn't have happened."

Abel flexed his bruised, swollen fingers. "You were trying to help bring a family back together. Miss Maeve is the one who caused intentional hurt," he said. "This isn't your fault."

Tears began to slip down my face in earnest. "Thank you." I wrapped my arms around him, resting my cheek against the smooth line of his jaw. But the smallest of doubts crept in to mar the moment. Abel's recovery would be a long, agonizing one. Would he feel so merciful in a week? A month?

"You're going to hurt my feelings," he said, his breath stirring my hair. "Crying your eyes out right after our first kiss. I didn't think I did such a terrible job."

I laughed in spite of myself. "You didn't do terribly at all," I said. "To the contrary, I think we're *both* quite good at it." My cheek still pressed to his, I felt his smile bloom.

"We'll need to test that out, just to make sure," he said.

I sighed dramatically. "Oh, if we must."

When at last we stepped apart, I forced myself to say good night. Gathering my candle, I turned to look back at him, golden in its warm glow. I wanted to hang on to that moment, to tuck it away like a flower pressed between the pages of a book, precious and safe. "Good night, Abel."

His eyes shone. "Sleep well, Verity. I'll see you in the morning."

26

I wandered back to the barn in a blissful daze. Skimming up the ladder, I flung myself down in a patch of moonlight filtering through the window. My thoughts were a giddy kaleidoscope. They spun with hope when I thought of Abel, then fractured into dark shards when Miss Maeve's treachery and worries for Lilah whirled by.

My attention came to rest on Abel's tree-stump nightstand. A new candle and an open book sat on the rough wood surface. Curious to see what Abel had been reading, I found a match and lit the candle.

The page was open to a poem, "*Eros Turanos.*" I knew enough Latin to parse the title: "The Tyrant Love."

It was a mournful piece about a woman who chooses to stay with an unworthy man. Their love, even after it had soured and caused nothing but pain, felt inescapable.

> . . . like a stairway to the sea
> Where down the blind are driven.

I closed the book and stared uneasily into the candle flame. The fire shuddered, as though blown by a sharp wind, leaning sideways for a long moment, then shooting back upright.

I blinked hard. Again, the flame tilted, this time stretching toward me. A third time it repeated its mad dance, sending shadows lurching into the corners, reaching for me before righting itself. Certain my eyes were playing tricks in the late hour, I leaned forward to blow it out.

With a roar, the fire shot up, exploding into a whirlwind of flames. I flung myself backward as it leapt for me, hungry and alive. A spark landed in my braid. Screaming, I beat it out. In an instant, rivers of burning wax began pouring down the candle sides. One landed on Abel's book. The pages burst into flame.

A shower of sparks rained onto the straw-littered floor, igniting on contact. I snatched a quilt and flung it over the burning book, stomping to quell the blaze. The fire pounced like a hungry beast. I felt the flesh on the soles of my feet sear.

Shrieking, I leapt away as the inferno grew around me. My cries mixed with the loud crackle of flames. Fire forced me away from the opening in the floor that led to the ladder and safety. Sweat poured into my eyes. I blinked singed lashes and turned away from the unbearable heat.

Through black smoke, a small, unreachable window taunted me from far above. Darkness bloomed across my vision. Coughing, I sank to the floor.

Then a soft lowing carried over the crackling fire.

Edward.

I staggered upright and faced the firestorm. I wouldn't lie down and wait for death, and I wouldn't leave Edward shut in his stall on the ground floor to burn. I lowered my head and sprinted toward the wall of fire.

I burst through the other side and clattered down the ladder, gritting my teeth as the taut, burned skin on my feet tore. Hobbling to Edward's stall, I flung open the gate. Without waiting to see if he followed, I fled toward the house.

Only a few feet away from the barn, I stumbled at the pain in my feet and crashed to the ground. "Fire! Fire in the barn!" Trembling, I crawled toward the house. The pain of my burns began to subside. Perhaps I was going into shock. The relief was too precious for me to care. Shaking from head to toe, I righted myself and staggered on, screaming for Big Tom and Hettie.

When I crashed into the kitchen, Hettie met me at the door. "How bad is it?" She shoved on work boots, her hair wild around her face. Behind her, Big Tom fastened the strap of his overalls, eyes wide with alarm.

"The whole loft is on fire," I shouted, my voice cracking. Hettie pushed by, breaking into a run. I grabbed a metal pail and fumbled my way to the pump at the side of the house. Big Tom hurried to the kitchen garden to shovel more dirt into a half-full wheelbarrow. Our three-person fire brigade would never save the barn, but we had to try.

I heaved the brimming pail up, sloshing water down the front of my nightgown, and spun around, ready to run to the loft.

But the barn stood before us, whole and untouched, silhouetted against a calm, starry sky. Water washed over my bare feet as the pail slipped from my fingers.

Big Tom's wheelbarrow squeaked to a stop. His questioning eyes roved over the barn. A few yards ahead, Hettie turned. The confusion in her thin face shifted to anger. "What's the meaning of this?" She stabbed a finger at the barn. "Is this your idea of a joke?"

"I . . . Hettie, I would never do that. It was on fire, I swear."

I gripped my hair, panic and confusion warring within me. "I lit a candle, and it didn't make sense, but the flame burned sideways. Then it shot straight up like someone poured gasoline on it. The whole loft was engulfed." Hettie glanced at Big Tom, then hurried toward the barn.

The adrenaline coursing through my veins began to subside, leaving my insides quaking. Trembling, I followed Big Tom and Hettie into the barn. Edward peered at us through the open gate of his stall, mooing a greeting as we ascended the ladder to the loft.

We stepped onto the unburned hay and looked around. The candle sat atop the tree stump, its wick blackened. Abel's poetry book lay beside it, unmarred. I gathered the pallet of quilts into my arms, looking for scorch marks that didn't exist.

"I tried to smother the fire . . . my feet were burned," I said. "There was smoke everywhere." I gestured limply around me. "I had to run through flames to get out." My voice came out wispy and frightened. "Didn't I?"

Hettie watched me warily. "It must've been a dream. We all have those dreams that seem real from time to time."

Big Tom nodded. "Sounds like a bad nightmare."

A thin beam of light poked through the loft opening. "What's going on?" Abel's voice floated up from the ground floor. "I heard shouting and everyone was gone by the time I made it downstairs."

"Hold on, we're coming down," Hettie called. We all moved wordlessly back to the ladder.

"What happened?" Abel asked, latching the stall door I'd opened for Edward. The fingers sticking out of his cast were wrapped around a flashlight.

"I thought the loft was on fire. But I was wrong." I ran

shaking hands over my face. They came away wet with tears, proof that my fear had been real, if nothing else. "It was so vivid . . . the smell of smoke and the sound of the fire. I could feel myself burning." A cold sickness settled in my stomach. "It was the worst nightmare I've ever had."

"You must've eaten something that disagreed with you. Why don't you sleep on the sofa in the parlor tonight?" Hettie paused. "Abel will give you the flashlight to take to the loft whenever you come back." She spoke with her usual briskness as she stepped out into the dew-silvered grass, Big Tom at her side.

But I'd seen the worry in her lined face, and felt the pity in Big Tom's sad eyes. I knew their thoughts, because they were the same as mine. What if my father's condition was hereditary? What if the delusions that plagued him had been passed on to his daughter?

"Let's go," Abel said, handing me the light. Gently, he steered us toward the door. Tremors still ran through me. Abel tightened his grip and dropped a soft kiss on my hair. "It was just a dream, Very. That's all."

"Just a dream," I agreed. But in my head, the memory of my own deranged screams echoed over and over again.

27

Breakfast was a subdued affair. Hettie passed around a platter of fried ham with a side of worried looks. Big Tom's slow gaze shifted between my tired face and Abel's injured arm, a troubled line forming between his bushy brows. Abel looked as weary and worn as I felt.

After the incident in the barn, I'd spent the remnants of the night searching for the seam where reality and horrible fantasy met, trying to convince myself I'd fallen asleep in the loft and didn't remember it. The vision of the inferno had been only a nightmare. Hadn't it? I'd finally nodded off on the stiff parlor sofa just before dawn.

Big Tom cleared his throat. "Believe we'll all stay home from church today. Me and Hettie got up early and cut the cane down by the creek this morning." He glanced at Abel. "We'll make sorghum after breakfast. You and Verity can rest up for a while."

My heavy lids closed. Again, I saw the torrent of fire spreading over the floor, felt my skin burning. "No!" With a gasp, I jolted awake, jostling the cup of coffee at my elbow. Three pairs of concerned eyes turned my way. "No, that won't be necessary. I'll help with the sorghum." I gathered the cup with unsteady fingers. "Don't forget to take your pain tonic after you eat," I said to Abel, eager to divert attention from myself.

He bumped his knee against mine. "I wouldn't dream of it, Dr. Pruitt," he said.

Abel insisted on joining us at the far edge of the yard, where the sorghum press stood under the spreading bows of a live oak. "I'm not going to sit inside and go stir-crazy," he announced, settling himself carefully on the ground with his back to the tree trunk. His face was drawn with pain. Or perhaps it was something else? After my confessions and the fire delusion of last night, Abel had seemed unconcerned by all he'd heard and seen. Still, a nagging worry played at the edge of my thoughts. He could easily decide that stepping out with me would be too complicated, too precarious.

Big Tom, Hettie, and I began unloading the sticky cargo of cut cane stalks from the wagon. A brick oven, topped with a long stainless-steel pan, stood near an iron sorghum press. It looked like two huge, rusted gears stacked on each other. A wooden beam lay horizontally atop the press, with the long-suffering Lady May hitched to it.

At Big Tom's direction, I began feeding the stalks between the rollers, catching the bright green cane juice in a pail. We'd only worked for a few minutes when the sound of a bell vibrated the humid air. Wiping sweat from my brow, I looked up to see two bicycles approaching. Katherine and Jasper pedaled our way, with Della perched on the handlebars of Jasper's bike.

Jasper wobbled to a stop and Della hopped down, her sturdy boots flicking the hem of her calico work dress as she strode over. Katherine rolled to a halt nearby. She wore a split skirt made for cycling, and a frown made for me. It seemed my very existence needled the girl.

"The cavalry has arrived," Abel said. "I knew I was valuable around here, but I didn't realize it took three people to fill in for me."

"Pshaw!" Della scoffed. "Mama made a deal with Big Tom a while back to go halves on the molasses if I help cook it." She shot me a grin. "I've got permission to be here, but with strict orders from Daddy not to go off anywhere alone with you. Because you're a bad sort and all."

"And we wanted to come check on you," Jasper said to Abel. "Della told us about what happened. She's been worried to death." He pulled Abel to his feet and clasped him in a brotherly hug. "There're easier ways to get the ladies' attention. You don't have to go snapping your arm in half."

Abel's eyes were shadowed. "Trust me, no one's attention is worth this amount of pain."

I swallowed hard, keeping my face expressionless.

Bright green cane juice seeped out from between the rollers as Lady May pulled the press wheel. Della patted the horse as she went by. "When we were eight, Abel convinced me the green stuff was a witch's brew," she said with a laugh. A smile sprang to Abel's lips at the memory. I quickly looked away.

While Big Tom and Hettie unloaded the last of the cane, Jasper squatted by the brick oven, shirtsleeves rolled up as he fed logs into the fire. Katherine watched, arms crossed. "You'll need it hotter than that or the syrup won't ever set up right," she said.

"Sis, you're a wonder," Jasper said, straightening his lanky frame. "There are old-timers who've done this for decades and still don't have it quite right, and here you are, an expert on your first time." The remark earned him a glower from Katherine.

We worked on in companionable quiet, pressing the cane,

hauling pails of juice to the cooking pan, and boiling it until it thickened to a rich, brown syrup. Everyone took turns stirring, making sure to keep the sorghum in constant motion so it wouldn't stick.

"I need to start dinner," Hettie announced after a while, handing over an armload of cane for the press. "Stay here and help with the sorghum." I nodded, turning my back as she departed.

Hettie was a few yards away, headed toward the house, when I heard the screen door slam, followed by an exclamation. "Goodness, you startled me!" Hettie said.

The stalks tumbled from my arms with a clatter as she added, "What can I do for you, Miss Maeve?"

28

Miss Maeve stood on the back porch, hand in hand with Lilah. "I'm sorry for barging in," Miss Maeve said, her cheeks flushing rosebud pink to match her high-collared dress. "Our car is out front, and I suppose y'all didn't hear us drive up. I thought we'd find Abel inside. Lilah and I have been so worried."

Hettie looked both pleased and flustered, as if the Queen of England had stopped by for a chat. "That's mighty kind of you. Abel's at the sorghum press," she said, gesturing to where we all stood across the backyard. "Y'all will stay to eat, won't you?"

"I wouldn't miss a meal cooked by Hettie Weatherington for the world," Miss Maeve said, stepping down to the dusty ground. Big Tom, on his way to the woodshed to get more firewood, caught the full force of Miss Maeve's glittering smile as he went by.

Abel's good hand strayed to his cast. The teacher's crystalline eyes rested on his crushed arm. "Abel, I am so deeply sorry. I can't help but feel this is my doing." My breath caught. She pressed a hand to her heart. "It was my idea to take the car, after all."

Abel proved himself a fine actor. He assured Miss Maeve that of course it was nothing more than an accident. I tried to catch my sister's eye, to gather some clue to her state of mind. Did she have any idea what kind of woman she'd been handed over to? Lilah only peered curiously at Abel's cast.

"And Verity," Miss Maeve said, "I've never seen such a cool head under pressure. You're an outstanding young woman." Her words were like a kiss from a cobra, her mask of concern grotesque. Anger closed my throat, and I found myself unable to reply.

"I'm sure it was awful for everyone," Della said, a little breathlessly, filling the tense silence I'd created. "I would've fainted dead and been no help at all."

Lilah, still firmly held in Miss Maeve's grasp, reached forward to run her finger over Abel's cast. "Does it hurt a lot?"

He looked earnestly into her round face. "Yep. But I'll be right as rain soon enough."

Miss Maeve's blush-colored skirt swept the dusty ground. "Come along, Lilah. Let's go see if we can help Mrs. Hettie with dinner."

"May I stay with Verity for a while?" Lilah asked.

"I suppose," Miss Maeve said, glancing my way. "Listen to the older ones, and do as you're told."

I frowned at Miss Maeve's retreating figure, while Jasper shoved a stick into the coals, showering sparks onto the grass. I flinched.

"I should probably head for the house to help Maeve," Katherine remarked.

"Are you two close friends?" I asked, surprised at the familiarity. Everyone, even those far older than her, addressed the teacher as "Miss."

"When Mother died last year, Maeve was so kind. She lost

her own family as a young woman, too." Katherine stirred the syrup pan, looking moodily into the thickening liquid. "All this work, for little of nothing," she said, almost to herself, as she absently handed the paddle to Abel. "Sweating and slaving, just to get up and do it all again the next day."

I gave her a quizzical look. The mayor's daughter, with her smooth white hands, didn't strike me as overworked.

"One day, I'll shake the dust of this place from my shoes and be gone for good," she said. There was a familiar sourness in Katherine's complaining. She sounded like me during my first days off the train, consumed by resentment born of loss. It was illuminating and disconcerting, realizing how much of myself I saw in a girl I didn't like.

"Where would you go?" I asked.

"Anywhere but here," Katherine said, her mournful air evaporating into peevish annoyance. "We weren't all as lucky as you, to be born somewhere with real opportunities."

"Kat," Jasper said sternly. "It's hardly fair to say Verity's been 'lucky.' You know how we've grieved for Mother. Verity's been through that and more."

For a second, Jasper's intervention rankled. I was more than capable of speaking for myself. Then, like a lamp coming to life with a slow, spreading glow, I realized this was exactly what he'd do for Abel or Della. He was treating me like a friend. I'd somehow, almost accidentally, made friends in Wheeler.

"I'd say the worst of New York City is better than the best of Wheeler, Arkansas," Katherine retorted, but from the mottling of her cheeks, I knew Jasper's reprimand had hit a nerve.

"Parts of the city are grand," I said, looking to Lilah, who glowered at Katherine. "But much of what we saw in the last few years was certainly not anything you'd want to experience."

"You said yourself you'll go back there," Katherine said. "Maeve told me—" Her lips snapped closed, chopping off the rest of her sentence.

"Miss Maeve told you what?"

Katherine shook her head, her face stony. "Nothing." She stalked away toward the house.

"She's a sore-tailed cat lately. Don't know what's gotten into her," Della said, frowning. Before I could press her, Big Tom returned, his arms laden with firewood.

While Jasper and Della helped stack wood in a neat pyramid beside the oven, Abel leaned over the evaporating pan, steam rising around his face, curling the blond hair at his nape.

"Can I help?" Lilah asked.

"Sure," Abel said. "You can use the skimmer to catch any pieces of dirt or leaves that float up."

Lilah took the handle, her eyes narrowed in concentration as she watched the syrup begin to bubble.

"And I'll take a turn stirring." My fingers grazed across Abel's forearm, lingering against his warm skin. Scenes of us together last night in his room flashed through my mind. The flush that warmed my face had nothing to do with the nearby oven. Abel cleared his throat and shot a quick glance toward where the others worked. A worrisome little suspicion nipped at me, that perhaps he didn't want Della to know about us.

The screen door slammed. "Dinner," Hettie shouted in the same loud, lilting voice she used for calling the hogs to the trough. "Y'all come on."

I couldn't stomach the thought of sitting across the table from Miss Maeve, passing the butter dish as if nothing were amiss. "Lilah and I will keep working. Someone can bring us a plate later," I said as the others left.

"You know, I'm only missing dinner because you need my help," Lilah said when we were alone.

I laughed. "You and Katherine are instant experts."

Lilah rolled her eyes. "She comes to visit all the time. She's so snooty and she never, ever laughs. I can't imagine why Mama likes her. Probably because Mama likes everyone."

I swallowed the reply that rose to my lips. After loading a few more stalks into the press, I took Lady May by the reins and led her in a slow circle. The stalks crunched and snapped, like a crackling fire. Or a breaking bone. "Is Miss Maeve always so nice? Even when it's just the two of you?"

Lilah looked up, surprised. "Why do you ask?"

I stepped back, leaving Lady May to pull the press without me. "I worry about you, that's all. I want you to be happy. And safe."

Lilah's reddish brows creased. "Stop being such a worry-wart. Mama's wonderful. And she's waited a long time for me."

Despite everything, I felt a twinge of pain for Miss Maeve. She'd mourned her stillborn baby for longer than I had even been alive.

"I was meant to be her little girl," Lilah continued. "She said everyone has a family they're born to, but sometimes that's not who they *really* should be with." She paused, still gripping the paddle. "I should've been hers all along."

"Lilah, do you believe that?" I asked, stung. "Some children have parents who don't take care of them, but you meant the world to Mama. And Papa. I know you can't remember those days but—"

"What good is a dead mother and a father I never see?" She spoke without rancor, but the words still struck me like a punch to the gut. "It's for the best I came here."

"Did Miss Maeve tell you that, too?" I asked, voice rising. "That you're better off with her instead of with your family?"

With me.

"No," Lilah said, too quickly. She stuck the end of one braid in her mouth, an old nervous habit, then laid the skimmer carefully against the side of the pan. She wrapped me in a hug. She was still small for her age, and her head only came to my chest. "Please stop fretting, Very. I'm glad we came to Arkansas. I wish you could be, too."

I dredged up a smile full of lies. "I'm having a harder time settling in than you are. That's all. But I'm glad you're happy."

She sighed, and I felt her tension ease a little. "I'm hungry," she said. "I think I'll go get something to eat."

Lilah tried to leave, but I gripped her shoulder. The thought of letting her skip off to Miss Maeve made me ill. "What are you doing?" Lilah asked, annoyance mingling with concern in her voice.

"I can't believe you're leaving me to work alone," I said, forcing a teasing tone as I took up the stirring again. "Some sister you are!"

She bounded away, braided pigtails bouncing, dauntless as always. "I'm the best sister ever. And you know it!"

"I think you mean you *have* the best sister ever," I called after her. Lilah ignored me and hurried into the house as Jasper came out the front door.

"Hettie saved you a sandwich and a couple molasses cookies," he said. "Hurry, though, before Katherine takes them. You'd never guess it, but that girl eats like she's got a hollow leg."

"I can be pretty scrappy if cookies are on the line," I said, handing over the paddle. "No one keeps me away from dessert."

Jasper cleared his throat. "So that means you're coming with the Weatheringtons to the ice cream social?" He was suddenly intent on scooping an invisible bit of nothing from the pan. "If you are, I was hoping you might like to be my guest?"

I hesitated, and in the awkward pause, sounds of conversation wafted our way from the house. Abel, Della, and Katherine clustered together on the porch, talking. Della caught my eye and, with a knowing smile and a head tilt toward Jasper, leaned in to whisper something to Abel. His eyes found mine for a single heartbeat before he looked away.

"If you'd rather not . . . I mean, I hope you will, but . . ." The tips of Jasper's ears reddened. I could see no way to decline the offer without hurting his feelings. Later, I'd make sure Abel knew that I had no interest in Jasper, although I doubted he could think such a thing after our encounter the night before.

"A friendly outing?" I asked.

Jasper's answering smile was close-lipped, but not entirely discouraged. "Certainly. Meet me by the ice cream churns. I'll give you a tour of the finest sweets you've ever tasted in all your born days."

"I'll hold you to it," I said, moving away as quickly as good manners would allow.

Della bounded off the porch, intercepting my path. "He asked you to the social, didn't he?" She beamed in a way that made me worry she was silently choosing names for my and Jasper's firstborn child.

"And I agreed to go—as friends."

"You're so bashful about boys, Verity." She laughed. "You'll have to get a little braver if you ever want to find a beau."

I thought of my lips on Abel's, and realized I was rubbing the back of my neck just the way he did when he was flustered. "I'll keep that in mind," I said, tacking on a little smile.

"The best romances start as friendships, I think," Della added. My smile splintered. I knew her feelings for Abel were beyond platonic. Although he didn't return those feelings, it would hurt Della when she learned of what had grown between Abel and me. I needed to bite the bullet and tell her. As soon as we had a moment alone, I would. I didn't want Della to feel I'd deceived her in any way. She'd been too good a friend for that sort of treatment.

Della sighed. "I guess I should get back to work." Her gaze drifted to where Abel leaned against the white porch railing before she walked away. Katherine rose from her perch on the top step and came toward me with a hostile look, but brushed past without comment to join Della.

At last I could speak with Abel in private. I hurried over, noticing his guarded expression.

"Looks like you've been having some important conversations," he said, taking a drink of the tonic we'd brought from Granny Ardith's and returning the bottle to his pocket. "First Jasper, then Della."

I propped myself on the railing beside him. "I don't want there to be any misunderstandings, Abel. Jasper asked me to—"

"Thank you again for dinner, Hettie." Miss Maeve stepped onto the porch, Hettie and Lilah following. "I apologize for the intrusion, but I couldn't stand not seeing for myself that Abel is recovering. I still feel guilty for—"

"It's nobody's fault," Hettie cut in.

Miss Maeve laid a delicate hand on Hettie's forearm. "It means a great deal to me, hearing you say that. And Abel . . ."

I hoped I was the only one who saw his jaw tense before he spoke. "You have nothing to apologize for." Miss Maeve's eyes clouded with tears.

Hettie jerked her head in the direction of the sorghum mill. Abel clomped down the porch steps after her, work boots thudding on the wood planks.

"Lilah, we'll be going soon," Miss Maeve said, her voice wavering. "Would you go ask Mr. Weatherington if he'd come start the car for us?"

I waited until Lilah was out of earshot, then drew a furious breath. "You can drop the act now. It's just the two of us."

Miss Maeve's reply was a choked sob. A tear fell dark against the dusty boards. "Oh, dear. Where is my handkerchief?" she murmured.

She withdrew a balled-up handkerchief from her skirt pocket, and I recognized the monogrammed letter M at the handkerchief's edge. Now washed a snowy white, it was the same one I'd pressed against Abel's torn skin as his blood spilled over my hands and spattered the ground.

Fury washed over me. "Why are you doing this?"

"Doing what?" She stepped closer, her face a picture of bewildered innocence. She pressed the handkerchief into my hand. I shuddered, but couldn't pull away as she leaned in and whispered, "There's a gift for you inside."

I wanted to fling the thing away, but I had to know what she meant. Slowly, I unfolded the balled-up cloth.

29

A lock of hair the same midnight shade as a raven's wing rested in the center. The color gave away its origin. I pushed forward, my face inches from hers. "Don't you dare hurt Della. It's me you're angry with. Leave everyone else alone." My voice shook, but my fist around the handkerchief held steady. "Haven't you done enough already?"

"That's up to you," she answered. "I only wanted to remind you that I have . . . options, should you choose to disregard my request." She spoke gently, with precise calm, as though I were the unstable one.

"Don't you think I know that?" Hysteria crept into my tone. "How could I forget after what you did to Abel?"

She moved as if to grab my hand. "Don't touch me!" I shouted, reeling back.

It was then I saw Hettie across the yard, watching from beside the sorghum mill. She started toward us with hesitant steps. "Y'all ok?" she called.

Miss Maeve looked to me, her eyes still damp and red-rimmed from her earlier display, then to the handkerchief I clutched between us. "Best put that away. You can't explain it without sounding like a deeply troubled young woman," she whispered.

I shoved the cloth in my skirt pocket as Hettie drew near. "Good girl." Miss Maeve's lips peeled back in a grin. "We don't want the Weatheringtons to think your daddy's problems are showing up in his daughter, now do we?" My blood went chill in my veins.

Miss Maeve wiped her grisly smile away in a blink and turned to Hettie. "Verity is a bit overwrought, that's all." She glanced my way, her lovely face full of pity. Adding a hint of uncertainty to her voice, she said, "I'm sure that's all it is. She's had so many changes recently. I don't doubt any young person in her situation would find herself a bit . . ." Miss Maeve pursed her lips. ". . . off-balance."

Hettie nodded, wary. "Verity, maybe you ought to go inside and rest?"

"I'm fine," I said, iron in my tone.

The background clatter of Big Tom trying to crank the car ensured that he and Lilah hadn't heard my confrontation with Maeve, and it seemed Jasper, shoving wood into the fire, hadn't noticed either. But despite the noise that muffled our words, Katherine, Della, and Abel stood stock-still by the sorghum press, watching.

Even from across the yard, I could read Abel's stunned expression. He said something to Della, who shook her head, then shot me a worried glance. Katherine took it all in with a cold stare. The three returned to their work, but not before Abel cast one last troubled look my way.

Overhead, thick clouds rolled in, shadowing the farmyard. "Looks like a storm is on the way. I think it's time for us to leave," Miss Maeve said. She placed a gentle hand on my arm. "You take care, Verity." Fury and fear roiled in my stomach.

Miss Maeve called back to Jasper and Katherine. "Y'all can put your bicycles in the back seat and ride with us. I'd hate for you to get caught in the rain."

"I think I'll help finish up here and head home after the storm," Della said, quickly, before anyone could formulate a plan for her to fit into the car. Jasper and Katherine crammed in beside their bikes. Jasper gave me a wave and a smile. I couldn't fathom how he didn't notice the tension that crackled around me like heat lightning. Lilah dashed back to where I stood for a final hug, then fell in step with Miss Maeve.

Lilah settled a pair of driving goggles over her eyes as Miss Maeve wheeled the car around. I could only lift my hand in farewell as they jostled onto the dirt road, sure the anxious tremble in my limbs would show in my voice if I spoke.

I forced myself to walk calmly to the sorghum mill, where Della ladled syrup into jars. "Help me carry some of these to the kitchen," I said, gathering the full ones and spinning round before anyone could ask questions.

"What just happened with Miss Maeve?" Della demanded in a low voice when we were out of earshot. "You seemed . . . angry." I knew what she really meant: I'd sounded unhinged. I'd played right into Miss Maeve's hands.

"She gave me a warning," I said in a low voice, trying to appear casual in case the others were watching. "It had to do with you."

Della's steps faltered. "Is she going to come after me next, like she did Abel?" Fear limned her words.

"She's not going to do anything to you." I pushed as much conviction into my voice as possible. "Just be on guard, and keep your head down until Miss Pimsler arrives. Once she hears what we've found out, and about Miss Maeve's threats, she'll make your father understand the danger. There's no way Miss Maeve won't end up in jail for what she did to Abel."

"All right." Della didn't sound convinced. "It's strange. I know you're telling the truth, but I still find myself wanting to think none of it's real and Miss Maeve is who I always thought she was." The wind picked up, flinging grit into our eyes.

We ducked our heads against the gusts and carried our jars of sorghum into the house.

Sometimes people could tell you the unvarnished truth about themselves, and you'd still hope that, somehow, they lied.

❦

An hour later, we twisted the lids in place on the final jars of sorghum. Della looked up at the thick clouds, their underbellies shot through with streaks of lightning. "I think I'll stick around for a little while and see if the rain misses us," she said. "I'm not about to get caught in a downpour and have to take cover in the woods."

Reflexively, we both glanced in the direction of the wind-lashed trees. I'd taken to searching their perimeter after I did my daily check around the farm for any hints of my father's presence. I wondered if he had lingered among them long enough to encounter the little girl. Ghost, I corrected myself.

After everyone washed up from the hot, sticky work of the day, we settled down to supper in subdued silence. Thunder jarred the kitchen window. Shadows clung in the corners. I felt sure Hettie had mentioned my outburst with Miss Maeve to Big Tom. I caught the huge man studying me, worry tugging down the corners of his mustache. Hettie, never one for small talk, tapped her foot nervously.

Abel was quiet and withdrawn. He took an extra dose of his pain tonic. For her part, Della seemed determined to fight the oppressive feeling in the room. As the meal progressed, she managed to tease a laugh from Abel. She knew just the story to tell, the right memory to evoke, to draw him out. That only added to my jittery unhappiness.

"I need to go to the barn for a minute," I said, pushing back from the table and glancing outside. The rain had begun, light drops falling softly to darken the dust.

"I'll be there in a minute. It's my turn to feed Edward," Abel said. His words were for me, but his eyes fixed on Della as he spoke, with an expression I couldn't quite identify. "I think I can do it, even with the cast on. He's much gentler now." He looked my way at last, and must've seen the agitation in my manner. "Is something wrong?"

I shook my head and pushed open the screen door. A sudden gust snatched away Abel's next remark as I jogged toward the barn. Inside, the patter of rain on the tin roof grew louder. Jagged lightning shredded the air, followed by growling thunder. From his stall, Edward lowed softly. "Shhh," I murmured, leaning over the gate to stroke his forehead. "The storm will pass soon."

But the wind and rain raged on for what seemed like an age, just like the unwelcome thoughts battering my mind. I couldn't shake the image of Della sitting on my mismatched stool beside Abel. I envisioned my father, somewhere alone in the driving onslaught, and the picture changed to Miss Maeve's wicked smile as she delivered her warning.

Worry soured my stomach until I felt like I'd swallowed ruined milk. Abel should've come out to help long ago. His

brooding quiet at supper nagged at me. I mixed Edward's bottle and fed him myself, then paced and stared out at the sheets
of rain gusting across the farm. I had to get back to the house,
despite the storm. I needed to see Abel, even though Della was
still there.

With an empty feed sack held over my head as a makeshift
umbrella, I ran out into the storm. Puddles gathered in the
uneven hollows of the ground, and I splashed through them.
Muddy water soaked my stockings. I pelted across the yard,
my face turned down against the stinging rain.

Through the torrent, I made out the hazy outline of the
farmhouse. Wind ripped away the useless feed sack from my
hands. A bone-rattling clap of thunder reverberated through
my chest as a lightning strike dazzled my eyes. With water
pouring down my face, I passed under the eaves into the shelter of the porch.

Blinking away the lightning's afterimage, I saw two figures
silhouetted together just inside the screen door.

Abel spoke in a low, insistent tone, his words tumbling over
each other. Della looked up at him, her expressive face still. A
roll of thunder, and then her chiming laugh rang out, and she
threw her arms around Abel's neck. His hands slid around her
waist, pulling her closer. Della lifted her face as Abel pressed a
hand against her cheek.

I backed away, brushing the wards that were meant to fend
off bad things, moving from under the shelter of the porch
back into the rain. I knew what was coming, felt the approach
of the train on the tracks, the screech of brakes that would
utterly fail to stop the collision.

Their lips met.

I stood ankle deep in mud, unable to look away as the kiss
ended. They stayed entwined, Della looking up into Abel's

face. He rested his forehead against hers. Pain flared in my chest.

I was frozen for a moment, rain streaming down my face. My tears mingled with the storm, until I turned and fled back to the barn with the taste of salt on my lips.

30

After the storm tired itself out, I'd heard the wagon leave when Abel drove Della home. He never came to feed the calf, and for that I was grateful. I couldn't bear the thought of him finding me there in the loft, red-eyed and stunned.

Every encounter we'd had replayed in my head. He must have started second-guessing our kiss. A kiss that came just before I'd told him the grim injury to his arm was because of me, before I'd seen a fire that wasn't there. Later, with Della's steady, comfortable presence close by, it seemed Abel had spread out the cards, and decided I was a risky bet he wasn't willing to make.

I shifted onto my back and stared out the window high above. The hard, distant stars glittered in the black sky. Their silver light, so bright and cold, reminded me of Miss Maeve's eyes.

As night began to lighten to dusky dawn, I went to the smaller barn that housed the milk cow. Dragging the stool into place, I settled in and got to work. The rhythmic *shing-shing-shing* of milk hitting the tin pail filled the quiet barn. I finished faster than ever. My days here were numbered, and

I had to hash everything out with Abel before Miss Pimsler came to rescue Lilah and me.

Gathering my pail, I headed across the yard to the house, pulse pounding hard enough to feel in my fingertips. Abel would return from his pre-breakfast work soon, and I had to find a way to speak to him.

The clatter and bang of cast iron on the cooktop greeted me in the kitchen. Hettie, her back to me, scrambled eggs with agitated vigor. "Got the milk in early, I see. We'll churn some butter later," she said, half turning in my direction. A troubled frown flitted across her face.

I poured myself a cup of coffee from the percolator on the stove. "Have you seen Abel this morning?"

"He's gone into town." Hettie seemed even more taciturn than usual, but I decided against asking about her mood. She continued to scramble the eggs as though she wanted to disintegrate their very molecules. When Big Tom entered, we ate in silence, and I caught a few odd glances between the couple. After we finished, I cleaned the kitchen and went out to weed the kitchen garden.

I worked under an overcast sky, glancing at the road over and over, waiting for Abel's return. At last he came into view, riding Merlin at a jaunty pace. His crisp white shirt, with one sleeve rolled up over his cast, nearly glowed in the morning sun, and his trousers were creased sharp enough to cut. A little fancy for early-morning errands, I thought. The trill of a whistled tune spun through the air around him.

Nervous energy coursed through my veins. I nearly hoed through the toe of my boot while I waited for him to finish stabling Merlin. When he stepped out of the barn, I motioned him over. "Can we talk?"

Abel looked oddly relieved. "I'm glad you asked." He pointed to a path leading toward the apple orchard. "Why don't we go for a walk?"

We moved slowly, the space between us feeling miles wide. The winding footpath across the yard carried us into a small circle of trees. Apple blossoms, long-fallen and brown-edged, crushed under our boots. I spied a small wooden swing, motionless on a low limb. Sinking onto its seat, I wrapped my hands around the timeworn ropes.

Abel leaned against the tree's trunk, his face deep in shadows. "I need to tell you something," he said again.

"I already know about Della." There was iron in my voice.

"You do?" His light brows lifted. "How?"

I dragged my feet to stop the swing. "I saw the two of you." Standing, I stepped onto the seat so we were at eye level with each other. "On the porch. I just want to know why."

I left my other questions unspoken: Was it because of Maeve's attack? Because he thought I might be unbalanced? Because I'd wanted to leave Arkansas? Or because I simply wasn't enough somehow?

Abel rubbed at the back of his neck. "Everyone said Della and I would be a fine match, ever since we were kids. I don't know why it took me so long to agree." He took a bracing breath. "I've just come back from Della's. I asked for her hand in marriage. And she accepted."

My pulse exploded inside my ears. I gripped the ropes harder, feeling as though I were spinning.

Abel fixed his eyes on the trampled apple blossoms at our feet. "I know this is hard to hear, but I owe it to you. What happened between you and me . . . I shouldn't have let you kiss me. Or kissed you back. It was a line I was wrong to cross." He looked at me then, full on. "I hope this doesn't end our friendship."

I could feel myself crumbling from the inside. "Is that all I am to you now? A friend?"

"I thought maybe we were more," he said. "For a while, I thought there might be a future for us. But I know you'll be leaving for New York again as soon as you can. You've got a whole life planned out, and—"

The outrage that swelled in my throat threatened to choke me. "Does Della know about what happened with us?"

"Not in detail," he admitted. "I think she assumed you and I were interested in each other, but there's no misunderstanding now." He looked down, lashes grazing his cheeks. "She knows I love her."

My legs suddenly felt numb. Slowly, I lowered myself onto the little swing. "I see." My voiced flattened under the weight of humiliation and loss.

"I never meant to lead you on," he said. "But I know I did just that. You've got every right to be furious with me. Just please don't let this pull you away from Della." He clenched his hat in his hands, searching my face, waiting for my agreement.

In that moment, I buried any lingering hopes for a future with Abel. The final shovel of dirt showered down when I realized that, while he felt badly for me, my battered emotions were nothing compared to his worry that Della might be upset.

I wanted to rage at him. To let loose the tears that burned behind my eyes, tell him that I'd started to love him and a traitorous, unstoppable part of me still wanted to, in spite of what he was saying. But I did none of those things.

"I have no reason to hold a grudge against Della." The words were ashes on my tongue. "I only hope, for her sake, that you don't play her for a fool."

"I never would." His earnest expression made me want to be sick.

"Big Tom and Hettie are working in the hayfield," I said, realizing they'd known what Abel's outing to Della's had been about. That was the cause of their troubled quiet this morning. The Weatheringtons, at least, had cared about how this engagement would hurt me. "They're probably waiting for you."

Abel pushed away from the tree trunk, taking a hesitant step toward where I sat in the swing. Broken shade scattered shards of light across his face. "Very—"

"*Verity,* please." I twisted the rope until I faced away from him. Childish, perhaps, but I couldn't let him see my face contort with pain. "Tell Big Tom and Hettie I'll be there soon."

For an aching few breaths, I thought he'd say more. He didn't, and I listened as his footfalls faded and died. I untwisted the swing only when I was sure he'd be out of sight. Then, legs pumping and arms straining, I swung as hard and high as I could.

Closing my eyes and leaning back, I felt the strain of my muscles and the wind rushing past my ears. I swung as though I were still a carefree little girl, one who didn't know that the people I needed could ever go away. Higher and higher I went, until my hair brushed the leaves above, and at the zenith of each swing, I felt myself lift off the seat. For a split second, my body was weightless. I wanted to seize that perfect, airborne moment and fly away.

The feeling of freedom ended. I plummeted back toward the ground, hard and fast, the wind drying the tears on my cheeks.

31

Now more than ever, I had no reason to stay in Wheeler. Miss Pimsler couldn't come soon enough and free Lilah from Miss Maeve. Perhaps Papa, if he were still scouting the area for phantom dangers, would learn of our departure and return north, too. A twinge hit my heart at the thought of leaving Big Tom and Hettie behind. But it was nothing compared to the wrenching pain I'd feel having to see Della and Abel together every day.

Della came that evening to tell me about her engagement. "It seems silly now, but I was a smidge jealous of you over Abel," she confessed. "I was afraid he might've been smitten with you when you first arrived."

"No," I said, with a brittle smile. "He only ever had eyes for you."

Before she left, Della handed over a telegraph containing Miss Pimsler's reply. Because of my request, she'd gotten permission to do a welfare check for all the orphan-train children sooner than was her custom. She would be here Saturday morning, the day of the ice cream social.

As the week wore on, I kept up my flawless act. For Hettie

and Big Tom, I was an industrious worker. When Hettie asked if I was upset about the engagement, I'd managed to seem perplexed at the very idea.

And I treated Abel with the same bland, inattentive politeness I'd give a stranger I met on a sidewalk as I went about my day. It was a performance so skillful, even Miss Maeve would've been impressed.

At dawn on Saturday morning, I'd already been awake for several hours doing my chores by lantern light. I finished gathering eggs from the sleepy, baffled hens, and left the basket on the kitchen table with a note saying I'd gone back to the loft feeling ill.

Then I rode toward Wheeler.

I arrived in town just minutes before the train shrieked its arrival. Miss Pimsler stepped onto the platform, blinking around with weary eyes. I waved to her through the clearing coal smoke. Her tired expression changed to one of concern as she hurried over, dropping her leather traveling bag and taking my hand in her soft, plump one.

"I've been worried ever since I got your message, Verity. Are you all right, dear?"

"I'm fine. For now. But I need you to do something for me." I looked squarely into her eyes. "No, two things. First, I'm going to tell you a story that will sound incredible, but is entirely true. I need you to hear me out. And—"

"My goodness, you begin to frighten me," she said, looking nervously around the empty platform.

"And the second thing," I said, taking her by the arm and steering us toward the town, "is that you mustn't interrupt until I'm done with the story. All right?"

Miss Pimsler nodded, then steadied her large hat. "Of course. Where are we going?"

"To the church. It's always unlocked." And just as importantly, likely to be empty.

We nodded greetings to the few curious residents we met along the way and crossed the dirt road to the church. The sharp smell of wood polish greeted us as we entered. I settled onto the back pew, with Miss Pimsler taking a hesitant seat beside me.

I looked down at my hands folded in my lap, unsure of how to begin. Morning light filtered through the stained-glass window, shading my skin a deep red. Like Abel's blood covering my fingers after Miss Maeve's attack.

"Miss Maeve Donovan is not who she claims to be." Then I told Miss Pimsler of a young Mary Mayhew and my father, their failed elopement, and the birth of their baby, stillborn in the frigid winter. True to her word, Miss Pimsler listened silently. I explained Mary's flight to Wheeler and her assumed identity as Miss Maeve Donovan, false niece of prominent banker Reuben Lybrand, and how she wore a bracelet with a broken gold piece that completed the ring my father had given her long ago. "The ring is in Sheriff Loftis's house," I said. "I've held it in my hands. It has my father's name on it."

And then, with a huge breath of air and a prayer, I recounted my confrontation with Miss Maeve. "Abel Atchley's injury wasn't an accident. She wants me to keep her secret, and she'll do whatever it takes to make sure I'm too scared to tell anyone."

When I was finished, Miss Pimsler was quieter than I'd ever seen her. "And have you told anyone?" she said at last.

"Abel knows who Miss Maeve is, and he figured out on his own that she hurt him purposefully. I told Della Loftis everything. She's the sheriff's daughter. And my friend." I swallowed hard. "Miss Maeve doesn't realize Della and Abel know the truth. Yet."

"Have you spoken to the Weatheringtons about this?" she asked.

I shook my head. "The people in this town, including the Weatheringtons, adore Miss Maeve. She's wrapped them all in her web. Hardly anyone, especially the men on the adoption committee, will believe me over her. That's why I had to bring you here. Take Sheriff Loftis to her house, tell Miss Maeve you're there on a scheduled welfare check for all the children or something. The important thing is that you notice her bracelet. Ask the sheriff to show you the ring, if you must. You'll see they go together. If you doubt me, then confront Miss Maeve about her past. She'll crack, just like she did in front of me. She—"

Miss Pimsler held up a hand. "I believe you."

"You do?" That was far easier than I'd anticipated. I didn't trust things that came too easily.

"When Dr. Pruitt's belongings were delivered to the society for you and Lilah, we searched through them, as we do with all items sent to our children," she said. "As I was going through the trunk, I found this." She unclasped her satchel and withdrew a tintype. Miss Pimsler's small mouth drew into a bow as she handed me the image.

The hair was darker and the face more youthful, but it was definitely Miss Maeve. The muted sepia tones couldn't dim the fiery glint in her eyes. She stared boldly out at me, lips parted in a reckless smile. I could see why my father had been drawn to Mary Eve Mayhew. I flipped the tintype over. There, in a confident hand, was a message from the past:

Matthew,
My soul is paired with yours, now and always.
—M. M.

Miss Pimsler cleared her throat. "I thought it might be . . . upsetting for you to open the trunk and find this memento from your father's youth. He ought to have rid himself of it when he married your mother." She sniffed, extending her hand. I dropped the tintype numbly into her open palm. "In any case, when I met Miss Maeve, I thought she looked like the girl in the picture. But it wasn't until you told me this tale that I knew for certain."

"So, you'll help me?" I breathed. "You'll have Lilah taken from her?"

She stood, tugging at the bottom of her short jacket. "I'll figure something out. It might be tricky to find Lilah another home. I wouldn't want her to stay in the area, where Miss Maeve might come after her."

"But Miss Maeve will be in jail for what she did to Abel, won't she?"

"Only if the local authorities want to charge her with assault. And even then, she won't be away for long. It's in Lilah's interest to start anew elsewhere. The next train is going to Missouri and—"

"Take both of us back to New York." My hands clasped as if in desperate prayer. "The Weatheringtons will release me from the indenture, I know they will. If you'll let us both come back to New York, I'll find a way to support us. It's only four months until I'm eighteen now."

Miss Pimsler's small mouth tightened, and she fidgeted with the chain of her pendant watch. "I owe you that much,

Verity. And I also owe you an apology. I was untruthful with you about why you and your sister were sent to Arkansas."

I eyed her, wary. "It wasn't because my parents had history here, was it?"

She shook her head. "Mr. Lybrand made a substantial donation to the Children's Benevolence Society with the stipulation that the next orphan train come to Wheeler, Arkansas. He offered a home for Lilah. There was never a mention of you in his correspondence. I thought, however, it would be a comfort for you to find a new home near your sister."

Miss Pimsler's flower-laden hat trembled with the force of her agitation. "We had no idea the man was connected with a woman who would prove to be so grossly unsuitable. Mr. Lybrand said he'd known Dr. Pruitt's family years before, had heard your father had fallen on hard times, and hoped to do a good turn for his little girl by having his niece adopt her." Her pleading gaze roved the sanctuary before coming to rest on mine. "Surely you can understand. The money he offered helped us provide for our children. Each one in the orphanage is my responsibility. I couldn't turn down an offer that would help so many and, to my knowledge, harm no one."

She'd lied, but she'd done what she thought best for those in her care. "You couldn't have known what would come of it," I said, at last.

"I'll have to place you back in the Society Home until your birthday, but then I'll do my best to find you and Lilah a place of your own to stay. Together." Her eyes were glassy with tears. "And I'll make sure Lilah comes to no harm."

I felt my shoulders unknot a little. "Thank you. But please don't approach Miss Maeve alone. Take the mayor and the sheriff along when you confront her."

Miss Pimsler stepped through a pool of blue and green light shining in from the stained glass. "I'll find Mayor Ausbrooks and Sheriff Loftis right away. We'll speak to Miss Maeve without delay."

"I can come with you, if you think it would help," I said, catching up with her purposeful stride as we left the church.

She shook her head. "It sounds as though the sheriff has an ill opinion of you. He and the mayor will be more likely to listen if we talk in private, I think. After we sort the matter out, I'll come tell the Weatheringtons what's happened."

"We'll all be at an ice cream social on the courthouse lawn this afternoon. From what I understand, the whole town will be there."

Miss Pimsler nodded. "I'll see you then. Now, you should get back to Mr. and Mrs. Weatherington." She stopped abruptly, turning on her heel to face me. "I'm sorry you've had to go through this ordeal, Verity." She put her hands on my shoulders and looked hard into my eyes. "I'll put things right. This will all be over soon."

I watched Miss Pimsler march away toward the town center, off to find Mayor Ausbrooks and Sheriff Loftis. Then I returned to the station to retrieve Lady May, relief and anxiety mixing in a confusing rush in my veins. Overhead, the morning sun hovered in a sky the same summery blue as Abel's eyes.

I fixed my attention down the dirt road back to the farm. The next time I left this place, it would be on a train headed north, with Lilah at my side. And we wouldn't come back.

32

I worried I'd face an interrogation when I returned to the farmhouse, but Hettie only asked if I felt better.

"Much better, actually," I said, after taking a second to recall I'd left a note claiming illness earlier.

Hettie set me to canning green beans while she busily rolled out pie crusts. The jars sealed one by one with a popping sound, and she nodded happily each time. "We'll be glad for all the work we're doing now come winter," she said.

I didn't comment. I'd be long gone by then.

I conveniently made myself scarce at lunch, squirreling food away to eat in my solitary loft to avoid seeing Abel. I needn't have bothered. Through the barn's double doors, the crunch of Merlin's hooves drifted up to my hideout as Abel rode away for Wheeler hours before the social. Going early to spend more time with Della, I assumed. I pushed away my dinner untouched.

When I dressed for the social, it was with the enthusiasm of a mourner preparing to attend a funeral. Only the hope that Lilah and I would soon be free made the trip bearable. Hettie laced me into my S-bend corset, and as Lilah had suggested,

I wore the white lawn dress I'd been given when we left the Children's Benevolence Society Home. My attempt to put my hair up didn't yield the lofty swoop Della always managed, but it was tolerably smooth and tidy. I finished my ensemble with a simple hat circled with a lilac ribbon, adding a pearl hatpin Hettie had loaned me for the occasion.

"You look mighty nice, Verity," Big Tom said in his soft rumble as I climbed into the back of the buckboard.

"Thank you. I'm supposed to be Jasper Ausbrooks's guest," I confessed, "but I'm not feeling terribly social today."

Hettie looked over her shoulder as Big Tom flicked the reins and we started moving. "Try to enjoy yourself, Verity. Or at least look like you are." She handed me a pie to hold, adding, "When Abel's around, anyway."

I felt a smile creep over my lips. "Hettie Weatherington, I'm surprised at you."

She placed a hand on Big Tom's broad back. "I only stepped out with Big Tom to make another fellow jealous, truth be told. Best spiteful thing I ever did." Big Tom snorted, but the corners of his eyes crinkled with a smile.

We arrived at the square to find Wheeler buzzing with festivities. Fiddle music capered on the hot afternoon breeze. Apron-clad women swarmed around tables scattered across the courthouse lawn, spreading white tablecloths here, draping spring-green bunting there. Groups of children played tag, running circles around the spreading oaks. In the center of the merry chaos, a table at least thirty feet long groaned under the weight of dozens of pies, preserves, sauces, cookies, and other sweets. Big Tom meandered over to a group of men setting up chairs around the tables, while Hettie vanished into the crowd, a peach pie cradled to her chest like a newborn.

On tiptoes, I searched in vain for Miss Maeve's slim figure

or Lilah's strawberry-blond braids. Perhaps Miss Pimsler had made speedy work of her task this morning, and was gathering Lilah and her belongings from Miss Maeve's house right this moment. I glanced at the courthouse, looming large behind me. Could Miss Maeve be inside, being questioned by Loftis?

And though I hated myself for it, I looked for Abel among a group of shirtsleeved gentlemen cranking away at the ice cream freezers. I spotted Jasper instead.

I decided to take Hettie's advice. If nothing else, Jasper didn't deserve a dour companion. And though I knew I couldn't make him jealous, devoted to Della as he was, a mean little part of me wanted to make sure Abel saw me having a good time.

I hitched up my smile and wove through the tables. "Hello, Jasper. How's the ice cream coming along?"

He beamed from under a stiff new boater hat when he saw me coming. "It's not a job for anyone in a hurry," he said, turning the handle sprouting from the side of a wooden bucket. "Katherine brought chocolate syrup," he added. "She made it herself. Our mother used to do that every year." He dropped his eyes to the churning ice. "This is the first social since she passed away."

Without thinking, I reached out, resting my hand on his forearm. He looked up, surprised. "I'm sorry, Jasper."

He swallowed hard, then worked up a little smile. "I didn't mean to be gloomy. Today's supposed to be a good time." He sped up the crank as he spoke. "I think this is finally ready. Do you want to test it? There's a spoon here somewhere—Verity?" Jasper's merry words faltered as he noticed my distracted air. "Is everything all right?"

"I'm fine," I muttered over the quick heartbeats sounding

in my ears, tearing my attention from Abel and Della walking toward us.

Della's right arm was linked through Abel's left, and she rested her other hand on his biceps, keeping as many points of physical contact with him as possible. Jasper furrowed his brow, looking between the blissful couple and my rigid misery. His expression shifted from confusion to pained understanding.

"I hear congratulations are in order," he said, stepping forward to meet them. Jasper pressed Della's hand with genuine warmth before moving on to clasp Abel in a brotherly embrace, maneuvering around the cast as he hugged his friend. "I can't say I'm surprised. It was only a matter of time."

Abel slid his good arm around Della's slim waist and drew her to his side. As though I'd never pressed his body against mine, felt his hands at the small of my back as he pulled me closer.

Already, I felt myself fading from their lives, from this place. Soon I'd be a memory, a girl who passed through one summer and was never heard from again.

"Mama and me are already talking about the wedding dress," Della said. "I want a pouter-pigeon front, puffed out nice and full, and probably sleeves to the elbows. It'll be satin, of course, and we think maybe a lace overlay would be just the thing. And Abel's asked Big Tom for permission to buy an acre on the back of their place," Della went on. "We'll have a little cabin and—"

"Sounds like y'all have it all worked out," Jasper broke in. "Would y'all excuse us? Verity was just saying how parched she was. We're going to try some of Mrs. Sullivan's pink lemonade." He offered me his arm, and I took it gratefully.

"All right then," Della said, still smiling. "Save us a spot when it's time to eat."

Jasper led me toward the table laden with crystal punch bowls. We slid into place at the end of the line. I bit my lip while he stared fixedly at the ground.

"You're carrying a torch for Abel," Jasper said at last. "And it's pretty clear I've been making a jackass of myself."

"No, I think I'm the jackass here." An elderly lady ahead of us in line tutted at my language. I picked at the white tablecloth. "I was going to tell you today that Abel and I were . . . well, whatever I thought we were. I feel so foolish. I should've realized he loved Della from the start."

"Over the years, I think Abel and me both fancied ourselves in love with her, from time to time." Jasper took two cups of pink lemonade, handed me one, and gestured toward a table on the edge of the lawn. "When we were little, we used to fight over who Della would want to marry. I told Abel it would be me, and that he had to marry my sister."

I took a sip of my drink. Its sourness matched my mood. "I bet he loved that idea."

"It led to a few scuffles in the schoolyard." Jasper smiled, then sobered quickly. "Della's one of my dear friends. But just between us, I think Abel's making a mistake."

I settled on the edge of a white wicker chair while Jasper folded his lanky frame into the seat across from me. "How's that?"

"Della's a wonderful person. But she's not wonderful for Abel. People don't always know there's a difference." Jasper, cup handle pinched between long fingers, crossed one gangly knee over the other as Katherine came marching our way, a picnic basket in the crook of one arm.

"Have y'all seen Della anywhere?" she asked.

"Hello to you, too, Sis. Della's going around receiving congratulations on her engagement." Jasper didn't look in my direction as he said this, but Katherine did. Her words were for Jasper, but she kept her triumphant smirk on me as she spoke.

"I figured. I'm glad Abel Atchley finally had enough gumption to propose. Lord knows he's had plenty to distract him lately."

I held her gaze over the rim of my crystal cup, making sure to slurp in a most distracting manner. Katherine inclined her head and swept away. I frowned as I watched her disappear into the crowd. "She's not usually so horsey," Jasper remarked, sipping his lemonade.

"I think I bring out the worst in your sister."

"I hate to admit it, but I believe you're right. I'd hoped spending time with Miss Maeve would sweeten her up a little. There's nobody kinder than Miss Maeve." He sighed. "Truth be told, Kat's seemed even more mean-spirited than before they started visiting with each other."

"I can't imagine," I murmured, my attention focused on the crowd. Miss Pimsler should be here any moment, hopefully with Lilah in tow. But try as I might, I couldn't see her amid the milling townsfolk.

Instead, I found Mr. Lybrand. Hands atop his brass cane, he stood at the edge of the crowd, scowling at the gaiety swirling around him. With his dark suit and black homburg hat, he looked like a crow skulking in a field of songbirds. His attention was fixed on the courthouse steps. I followed his line of sight to find Mayor Ausbrooks, looking pleased as punch. The tall, handsome man didn't seem unsettled, which he surely would have been if he'd already spoken to Miss Pimsler.

I shifted uncomfortably in my seat, noticing Sheriff Loftis not far away, shaking hands with passersby, looking not at all like someone who'd just found out the schoolteacher had attacked his future son-in-law. My fingers knotted together in my lap. Had Miss Pimsler delayed in her plans to speak with the men on the adoption committee? Why wasn't she here?

Della and Abel slid into the empty chairs beside Jasper and me just as Mayor Ausbrooks stuck two fingers in his mouth and whistled. "Welcome, everyone, to the annual Wheeler Ice Cream Social," he said. Cheers rose from a knot of small boys. One familiar whoop lofted above the rest. Lilah stood on a chair, clapping wildly.

"Would all the members of the Ladies' Aid Society join me on the steps so we can recognize y'all for your hard work in getting this together?" Mayor Ausbrooks continued. A dozen women, including Hettie, eased their way forward to pattering applause. The mayor hooked his fingers in his suspenders. "And let's not forget our chairwoman, Miss Maeve Donovan."

A lump of ice lodged in my chest, and I watched Miss Maeve ascend the courthouse steps.

Her attention roved over the crowd, searching, until her pale eyes locked on mine with a gleam of triumph. Then she melted back into the crowd, disappearing amid a sea of plumed hats and smiling faces.

I pushed back from the table, shaking. "I need to go home. I'm not feeling well."

"Hettie said you'd been under the weather this morning," Abel said, oblivious to my agitation.

Della frowned, her eyes flicking to where Miss Maeve had been standing. "Is that all that's wrong, Verity?"

I pressed a hand to my middle. "I think the lemonade was too much for my stomach. I'm so sorry to leave early," I added to Jasper. "Abel, do you mind if I take Merlin?" He barely finished nodding his agreement before I spun around and pushed through the milling crowd.

Worry for Miss Pimsler knotted my thoughts as I unhitched the horse from his post. I couldn't explain the dread certainty that gripped me.

I spurred Merlin forward, gravel flying in our wake, and rode straight for Mr. Lybrand and Miss Maeve's house.

33

Fierce sunlight poured down on the house, bleaching it bone white, draping black shadows over the flower beds around the porch. Merlin snorted, shying away with nervous side steps as I tied him to the wisteria arbor.

I approached the stately home, heart thundering in my ears. When my hand touched the brass knob, I stopped. There was a charge in the air, a hum, the way there was just before a lightning storm. Fine hairs on my arms lifted. My heartbeat stuttered.

I forced down the wild impulse to flee and shoved my way inside in a rush.

Hand shaking, I pulled the door quietly closed behind me. The curtains were all drawn, casting the entryway into a murky twilight. At the foot of the staircase sat a small leather satchel. A shiver traipsed down my spine. I recognized it as the one Miss Pimsler had been carrying at the station.

"Miss Pimsler?" My voice echoed off the high ceilings. I jogged up the stairs, checking the bedrooms in a breathless hurry. All empty.

In Lilah's room, I fought to control my trembling fingers

and unlock the door to the secret room. I shoved it open and leapt back, expecting something dreadful to lash out at me.

Instead, I stared into a vacant space. A tangled mass of greens and browns were heaped on a table to the right, but I hadn't the time to consider what they were, or why the smell in the hot air seemed familiar. I must find Miss Pimsler before I gave in to the urge to run away that itched along my nerves.

Back downstairs, I stumbled into the empty parlor, then on to Mr. Lybrand's sitting room. I called for Miss Pimsler again and again. Fear swelled, rising into my throat, threatening to suffocate me. Each step felt like forcing myself over the edge of a cliff.

A long, narrow hall led toward the back of the house, the only place I hadn't checked. My fingers trailed along the textured wallpaper as I peered into the dark. "Miss Pimsler, are you here?"

Dread thrummed through me. Eyes on the floor, I pushed myself ahead, watching my boots sink soundlessly into the deep blue rug. Flickering light seeped from under a door at the hall's end.

I pushed it open and peered inside at a candle burning atop a round mahogany table. The thin finger of blue-hearted flame did little to push back the black of the windowless room. The fire called to me with its dancing light. I drifted toward it.

Something soft gave way under my boot. I stooped and my fingers brushed against feathers and velvet. With the other hand, I reached up and gripped the candlestick. Slowly, I brought it closer to the floor, until I saw in the feeble light what I'd trodden on.

A lady's hat, covered with plumage and silk flowers. One I'd seen earlier that morning. I shifted the candle closer.

Miss Pimsler's hair had come undone, and a swath covered

her round face. I pushed it away. Her eyes stared into mine, dull and sightless. Dead.

A memory unburied itself, clawing its way into my consciousness. I watched myself as though from outside my own body.

I followed Miss Pimsler down the sidewalks of Wheeler, trailing her to this house. Fury radiated like heat waves as I stalked her. Everything was her fault. She'd sent us here. She'd let Miss Maeve take Lilah from me. She was the reason Papa decided he had to escape the safety of the asylum and search for us. Because of her, I had lost what remained of my family. If not for Miss Pimsler, I wouldn't have met Abel and been forced to watch him fall in love with someone else.

I'd trailed her here, into Miss Maeve's empty house. She'd screamed, but the sound had died quickly after I wrapped my hands around her throat.

That was how I had murdered the woman who came to help me.

I dropped the candle. The light went out, and I turned away from the corpse, vomiting on the polished wood floor.

Insanity had come for me after all, just as it had for Papa. But unlike my father, I didn't merely suffer from visions of monsters. I had become one.

Sobs racked my chest and scorching tears blurred my sight. I fled through the house, throwing open the front door. And careened straight into someone.

Reuben Lybrand, Miss Maeve's faithful servant, gripped my upper arm. His eyes were dark voids. He yanked me upright, and I felt the bones in my shoulder grind together.

A hysterical cry burst from me as he dragged me away from the house.

34

Anguish rent my mind, blew apart my reason. I didn't want to die, but in my panicked grief over Miss Pimsler, I wasn't sure I deserved any better.

Mr. Lybrand dropped me on a stone bench and turned away, breathing heavily. His shoulders rose and fell in jerky movements, and his hands clenched to tight fists. Dimly, I knew I should take his moment of distraction to run for my life, but my body and mind felt leaden, too heavy for clear thought or action.

As though from a great distance, a familiar voice punctured my stupor. "Have you got her?" Mr. Lybrand lifted his head and looked toward the woods.

Through blurry eyes, I watched my father stride out of the trees.

"Deep breaths, Verity." Papa cradled me to his chest, as though I were a little girl, and carried me through the wisteria vines into the arbor. "There now," Papa muttered once we were inside. "Feeling better yet?" he asked, setting me on my feet.

The bleak guilt and terror rolled away like fog burned off by the sun. The scent of wisteria tickled my nose. I drew a deep breath and felt a mental haze I hadn't recognized before lift. It left me feeling weak, weary to my core, as though I'd just woken from a long illness.

"Something happened in the house," I said, rubbing my temples. "I was sure I found Miss Pimsler dead, and that I killed her. It seemed so real, but it couldn't have been. . . ." I paused, sifting through images of the day.

Reuben Lybrand stepped through the curtain of vines, a black blot against the vibrant leaves. I reached for Papa, dragging him back. "Stay away from us."

Mr. Lybrand lifted a hand as if to show he meant no harm. "Matthew, we don't have much time. We'll have to explain on the way." He retreated, making for the Ford sitting beside the house.

"Can you walk, Verity?" Papa asked, his voice wire-taut.

"I think so. Where are we going?" Papa was already trailing after Mr. Lybrand, motioning for me to follow.

Mr. Lybrand stopped when he reached the gleaming automobile. "Miss Pimsler is dead," he said, abruptly. "That much is real." He wrangled the crankshaft handle into place. "You brought her here to expose Maeve's secret, didn't you?"

"Yes," I breathed. "But I begged her to go to Sheriff Loftis and Mayor Ausbrooks first, and not approach Miss Maeve alone."

He began twisting the crank. "Maeve can be very persuasive. She saw Miss Pimsler in town, likely just after she'd spoken with you, and convinced her to come here to talk things out. I expect it took the poisoned tea less than an hour to do the poor woman in. Potions mixed in teas are some of Miss Maeve's specialties. She's used them for all sorts of things. To induce madness, and for less drastic things, too—to make someone sleep, change their mood. This is the first time I've known her to brew something deadly."

With a start, I realized that I had likely sampled one of Miss Maeve's concoctions before. I thought back to the Sunday dinner, saw her stirring something I'd assumed to be sugar into my tea. I'd been so at ease, so relaxed throughout the meal. Unnaturally calm, as I now realized. She could just as easily have mixed my death into that swirling amber liquid and I would've had no forewarning.

The motor of Mr. Lybrand's car roared to life. My heart raced at the memory of Miss Pimsler's vacant eyes, the dark tinge around her lips. "What happened to me in there?" I asked, looking back toward the house.

"The sense of dread you felt and the urge to flee were crafted by a magic working," Mr. Lybrand said as he climbed into the car, motioning for me to join him in the front seat. Papa gave my arm a reassuring squeeze and moved to the back. "Miss Maeve designed them to keep anyone from entering and discovering her handiwork until she can dispose of the body tonight."

"But why did I think I'd killed Miss Pimsler?"

Mr. Lybrand looked hard at me. "Maeve is also adept at candle magic. She likes to make people see things that aren't there."

Things like a loft engulfed in flames. My jaw clenched. Making me seem unhinged was the perfect way to cast doubt on my claims about her identity and her attack on Abel, should I ever go public. "She tried to make me, and the Weatheringtons, think I'd lost my grip on reality."

I glanced at Papa behind me. In his lucid states, he understood that his mind at times betrayed him. He appeared clearheaded right now, leaning forward, the wind whipping his copper hair. "I know who she really is, Verity," he said.

"I've seen Miss Maeve several times. I've been watching Mr. Lybrand's home for days, looking for a chance to speak with Lilah." His eyes darkened. "It took me a while to recognize her, changed as she is, but she's Mary, without a doubt." The wounded look on Papa's face as he said her name was more than I could bear.

I shifted my attention to the grand Lybrand house fading into the woods. "Where's the horse?" I asked, realizing that Merlin was no longer tied where I left him.

"I let the animal go," Mr. Lybrand said as the car swung around a bend and the house was lost from sight. "He's likely halfway back to the Weatherington farm by now. When Miss Maeve comes, we don't need her to know that you were here." His lips pressed to a grim line. "And it would help if the law has no reason to think you've been at the scene where a body will soon be discovered. I'm still not sure what Miss Maeve plans to do with the corpse, but—"

"She'll try to set me up, make it look as though I killed Miss Pimsler," I finished. Papa and Mr. Lybrand exchanged weighted looks.

More questions bobbed to the surface. "I don't understand how the two of you met, and for that matter, why Mr. Lybrand is helping us at all."

"I spotted your father lurking in the woods recently, and recognized him," Mr. Lybrand said.

I shook my head, frowning. "How?"

He shifted uncomfortably on the leather seat. "I'd seen him in New York, many times. At first, I didn't tell Miss Maeve he was here, for fear of upsetting her. She is . . . unpredictable when caught off guard. But today, when I found out what she'd done to Miss Pimsler . . ." Tension radiated from the man, and there was an anguish in his eyes I thought I recognized. Guilt.

"I have been complicit in Miss Maeve's wrongs for years. I aided in her attempt to harm your father's mental state. Without my travels to New York to plant her potions and workings, it would've been impossible. For that, I will be held accountable by God. But I cannot stand by this time. She's killed an innocent person, and I fear she will again."

My blood ran cold. "What do you mean?"

We passed out of the trees. The hot sun beat down without mercy. "This nightmare began, as so many do, with the death of a dream. I was once a husband and father, but a negligent one. I made no time for my family and spent my days traveling for business, gaining money and all the while losing my real treasure," Lybrand said. "One day, my wife decided to bring my son to visit me, since I was so rarely home. They died in a railway crash on the way."

The self-loathing in his words was so thick I could almost taste the bitterness. "I retreated to this lonely place, intent on living out my life in solitude." Gears clashed, and the car picked up speed. "One winter night, I helped Granny Ardith rescue a young woman from the old well in the woods." I felt my eyebrows lift in shock. Granny Ardith was involved, too?

"I began to see helping the girl as a chance for redemption. During her recovery at my home, she shared a horrible story of how she'd run away from her life, and her true identity," Mr. Lybrand went on. "Maeve's grief, her deep loss, spoke to my own anguish. I promised her a home and vowed to protect her secrets. Perhaps for the first time, I felt like a father." Wind whistled by, and he tugged his hat lower. "Soon, I began to realize she was hiding something.

"One evening, near dusk, I caught her sneaking into the woods. I followed her, saw what happened at eventide . . ."

A shudder passed through Mr. Lybrand's body. "She

confessed all then, weeping as though her heart would crumble. She told me how a gift from her supposed best friend had trapped her, making her unable to track down the young man who'd left her." He shot a hard stare at my father. "In despair, she'd tried to end it all, only to find her body pulled night after night back to the well, and her spirit into a terrible, lonely place she called the Hollow."

Dreadful calm settled over me like a shroud. "I was right, then. She really was dead when I found her in the woods. Then somehow, she came back to life."

"It happens every night," Mr. Lybrand said. "The well calls her back each evening at sunset, the time when she died. The universe—or Heaven, or Hell, perhaps—tries to set things right and send her on. But she remains ensnared by the keeping spell. In life, she couldn't leave its perimeter. And now in death, her spirit can't depart, try as it might. With the dawn, her spirit returns to her body. The spell has her kept, body and soul."

We barreled toward a flock of crows squabbling in the dirt lane. I turned toward my father as the birds took flight in a flurry of black wings and croaking cries, their shadows sweeping over his face.

"It's true that Elizabeth had a bracelet made to keep her dearest friend—her only friend—close, but that was all she intended," Papa said, his fervid eyes on mine. "Mary was the sole comfort in her difficult life. When Mary told Elizabeth we planned to elope, she was distraught." Papa's cheeks went red. "After I left, she didn't want me to return and take Mary away, so she didn't send the letters Mary gave her for me. I didn't know about the baby, and neither did Elizabeth. Mary hid her condition well. After she was . . . gone . . . Elizabeth appeared one day on my doorstep in New York, sobbing so hard she could barely speak. She blamed herself when Mary disappeared, and she bore that guilt to her dying day. She'd only wanted her best friend to stay with her. She had no idea Mary would try to end her own life. Elizabeth was young and rash. We all were! She was jealous of Mary for planning to escape Argenta and leave her behind, with no hopes for a future beyond a sharecropper's life."

Understanding dawned. "But Miss Maeve thinks it was all a ploy to steal you from her," I said. "And that's why she hates me so much. I remind her of my mother."

"Being with me was the furthest thing from Elizabeth's mind," Papa said, wretchedly. "We came to care for each other in that way only after Mary was gone. Both of us, tormented by her loss . . . it drew us together, in the end."

I stared at my father, watching the wind tug at his hair. "I can see why Miss Maeve hates you both, Papa."

His shoulders slumped. "As can I."

Mr. Lybrand cleared his throat. I had to strain to hear his gravelly voice over the roaring engine. "And no one, of course, had any idea that the keeping spell would increase in strength when she drowned herself in a powerful magic well. I brought Granny Ardith back into the matter once I realized Miss Maeve's unnatural condition had something to do with the keeping bracelet the old woman had crafted. Year after year, Granny searched for a way to grant Miss Maeve's request, to free her spirit from its caged state. She felt it her duty to fix the mistake she'd made in working that bracelet for Elizabeth to give Maeve. While Granny Ardith sought to break the spell, I set out to fulfill Miss Maeve's other deepest wish—to right the wrongs done to her by Matthew Pruitt."

My fingers tensed around the back of the seat. From Papa's

resigned expression, I realized Mr. Lybrand had already made these same confessions to him.

"I thought I was an agent of justice . . . taking trips to New York, using Miss Maeve's potions to cast illusions over your father with spells and conjurework she'd learned from Granny Ardith. The magic destroyed the life he'd built. But over time, as I watched his sanity break, I began to doubt." The man's brow creased with agonized memories. "Did anything merit this retaliation?

"Miss Maeve changed, too. With each of Granny Ardith's failed attempts to free her, Maeve grew more bitter, and more cunning. She'd taught herself to work magic of a darker sort than Granny Ardith's."

"The secret room," I blurted. "She was working spells in there." The familiarity of the smells came to me at once. Miss Maeve's hidden workshop smelled like Granny Ardith's cabin.

Reuben Lybrand's grip on the steering wheel tightened. "Everything changed when the Loftis girl died. Miss Maeve encountered the girl's spirit, trapped in the Hollow." He slid me a sidelong look. "Miss Maeve told me you came to the schoolhouse after you saw the girl's shade in the woods."

I snatched at a wind-tossed tangle of hair that flew across my eyes. "Yes, I did."

"When Josie drowned in the well and her spirit became trapped in the Hollow, it gave Miss Maeve the missing puzzle piece she needed to understand her own captivity. She'd thought it was the charmed bracelet that snared her, but that was only *partly* right. When Miss Maeve drowned in the well while wearing the bracelet, the keeping spell mingled with the well's own power to create a greater force than either source possessed on their own."

"The well and the bracelet together magnified each other's powers," I said.

Mr. Lybrand nodded. "It was the bracelet that allowed her spirit to return to life each daybreak, and the well that called her soul back each night. Their strengths are at once melded together, yet also opposed to one another." My head spun, and I gripped the polished metal door handle, needing something solid to hang on to.

"Miss Maeve spoke to Josie Loftis, there in the Hollow, and a twisted idea took root," Mr. Lybrand said. "But you must understand, Verity, I had not an inkling of this at the time. I thought Miss Maeve had turned toward the good. She no longer wanted to destroy Matthew's sanity or tear his family apart. She had me seek information on Matthew's health, nothing more sinister, although I was sad to report the years of meddling had taken their toll."

My gut twisted. "Miss Maeve ripped our lives apart, and you made it possible."

Mr. Lybrand's craggy face blanched. "I carried out evil, thinking I was doing good. Even after she stopped sending me with the spells, his decline continued. When Miss Maeve showed remorse for what she'd done to Matthew, I thought perhaps we'd both atone for our sins. And when we learned several months ago that Lilah had been brought into the state's care, she wanted to take the child in."

"What about me?" I asked. "Did she have a plan for me all along, too?"

Mr. Lybrand shook his head. "Miss Maeve knew of your existence, naturally. But she never thought they'd send someone so close to adulthood on the orphan train when we arranged for Lilah to come. Your arrival threw her plans into a state of confusion."

"What plans?"

"I didn't know what she intended until very recently," he said, his words tumbling out with feverish heat. "She began talking about wanting Lilah with her always . . . a daughter of her own kind. She sees Lilah as the cure for her sorrow, the righting of every wrong done to her." He clenched his jaws, bracing for what came next. "She's going to trap her. In the Hollow."

Terrible understanding blazed through me. "She's going to—" I choked on the words and the bile in my throat. "—drown her."

I twisted in the seat to face my father's pale, drawn face. He nodded grimly. "From what Mr. Lybrand has told me, I believe that is Mary's plan. And we believe it will be tonight."

"This is the summer solstice, the night when magic is at its strongest," Mr. Lybrand said. "The boundaries between the here and the hereafter will be thin. She's made a keeping-spell bracelet for Lilah, so the girl's spirit will return each morning, as her own does. Miss Maeve has aged at half the normal human rate, given that she is dead from sundown to sunup every day. Lilah will do the same. When it becomes obvious the child isn't growing into an adult at the usual pace, she'll hide her away on some pretext of illness, never to leave the house again. Eventually, they'll retreat completely into a life of solitude. Maeve will cut all ties with the outside world. She plans to keep Lilah in the house by day and the Hollow by night. Should anyone drop by, they'll have her secret room as a bolt-hole. They'll live as recluses in our home, never making contact with anyone else."

He leveled his black eyes on mine. "Lilah will be imprisoned, day and night. Always."

35

Rushing wind caught my shallow breaths and flung them away. I reached out to grasp the dashboard, trying to steady a world gone sideways. Papa reached forward to place a hand on my shoulder. "Reuben said the keeping spell prevents Maeve from going outside its boundaries, just as it was meant to. She can travel only in a rough fifteen-mile radius from the well during daylight hours. And it forces her to return there each night."

"I only need to get you three outside the perimeter of the keeping spell, and she can't follow," Mr. Lybrand said.

My understanding of reality had unraveled in the few minutes it took us to drive back to Wheeler. As the town drew closer, Mr. Lybrand's voice grew more urgent. "Both of you need to stay out of sight. I'll park the car in the alley behind the bank. I believe you know how to drive an automobile, Dr. Pruitt?"

"I do," Papa said, then ducked into the back foot well. "I took a car when I fled from New York."

Mr. Lybrand seemed unruffled by the admission of theft. He motioned for me to get down, and since the Model F had no doors in the front, I crawled over the seat to join Papa in his hiding spot.

When we'd entered a shadowy alley, Mr. Lybrand killed the engine. I struggled out of the car. "I'm going to get Lilah."

He nodded, straightening his tie nervously. "I'll do my best to distract Miss Maeve, but her attention is never away from the child for long. Get as far from Wheeler as possible before Miss Maeve discovers you and Lilah are gone." Mr. Lybrand fished in his pocket and pulled out a small bag. "There's enough money here to get you wherever you're going."

I mumbled my thanks and shoved the purse in my pocket, still reeling from the things I'd learned.

Papa clasped Reuben Lybrand's hand, looking into the eyes of the man who'd carried out Miss Maeve's crooked schemes, who'd worked for years to unseat his reason and demolish his life. "Whatever wrongs you helped create, you've saved my family today, Mr. Lybrand. May God bless you."

"I will need those blessings a great deal, I think." His eyes were somber pools under the brim of his hat. "I'll rejoin the crowd at the courthouse and occupy Maeve's attention for as long as possible." He looked at me, and I thought I saw a trace of tears in his eyes. "Verity, be quick. And Godspeed." He turned on his heel and vanished up the alley.

I watched his progress toward the court square. Then, creeping through the shadows behind the buildings, I crossed to the other side of the square unseen, at last stepping out onto the sidewalk to approach from the opposite direction.

A dance had broken out on the open space in front of the courthouse. Raucous fiddle music set my nerves jangling, and I jumped with every whoop and holler from the dancers. Everyone's attention was fixed on the couples spinning and reeling at the center of a ring of onlookers. Through the gaps in the standing watchers, I spied Abel's wheat-colored hair and Della's raven locks whirling by. A little pinch in my heart acknowledged that this was the last time I'd see either of them, but I couldn't linger over the emotion. Fear for Lilah drove me forward.

When I laid eyes on her, clapping along to the music, I nearly melted with relief. I edged closer to where she stood with a group of children, then stepped behind a sweet gum tree. Plucking a prickly sweet gum ball, I tossed it at her.

"Cut it out, Cecil," she said, turning with a playful frown. Her eyes widened with surprise when she saw me, and I put a finger to my lips, gesturing for her to follow. Miss Maeve stood across the circle, conversing with Mayor Ausbrooks. Lilah stepped behind the tree, curiosity lighting her eyes. "What are you doing, Verity?"

I took her hand and started across the street toward the line of businesses and the alleys beyond. "I've got a surprise for you," I said. "But we need to hurry." I glanced over my shoulder again and again, praying Miss Maeve hadn't seen us.

Lilah stumbled a bit, but still I quickened our pace. "What is it?" she asked.

"It's more of a *who*."

Papa sat behind the steering wheel of Mr. Lybrand's car. Lilah's wide eyes locked on him, and her lips opened in a startled *o*. "Papa's come to visit us," I said. "Isn't that wonderful?"

Before she could speak, he flung himself out of the car, wrapping us both in a hug. The rank smell of sweat and fear clung to him, and I felt his shoulders shake with suppressed sobs.

Lilah tensed at my side. She tentatively patted his back, then pulled away. "Can we all go back to the social now, Papa? I'm sure Mama would love to meet you."

"First, let's take a ride," I said. "Mr. Lybrand and Papa are acquainted, and he lent us the Ford. We'll talk in the car." I gestured toward the front. "Would you like to sit with Papa?"

Lilah climbed in. She leaned over the seat to where I sat in the back and spoke in a low, rushed voice. "Is he right in the head now, Verity?" Her eyes were earnest and worried.

"Yes," I said, hoping she'd believe what Papa and I had to tell her.

We drove along the back sides of the row of shops and over an open field, avoiding the crowd at the town's center until we were far enough away to take to the road. Papa accelerated smoothly, and allowed himself a careful smile. "Come here, Lilah," he said.

She slid closer, with a tentative movement that was almost a question, before letting her head rest against his shoulder. I imagined I knew her thoughts. Was it worth the heart toll to let herself be close to him, even for a second, knowing he'd soon slip away into madness?

I felt the weight of what we'd lost to our papa's manufactured illness. Once we were free, I'd find out how Miss Maeve had exacted her revenge on Papa, what foul magic she'd used, and how to fix it. Tenacious hope sparkled in my heart. Papa was here, and sane for the time being, and we were safely on our way. Together.

The car breezed along, slicing through the sticky, humid air. I glanced behind me, watching Wheeler grow smaller against the expansive sky.

"Lilah, I need you to listen to me," Papa began. "We aren't going back to Wheeler. We're going to find a place to stay in New York."

Lilah leaned away from him. "What do you mean?" She

turned to me for the answer, as if Papa's word couldn't be trusted. "Are we going to get Mama, too?"

Gently, I said, "Miss Maeve isn't coming with us." I couldn't bring myself to tell my sister the stark details, how the woman she adored had planned to drown her and trap her very soul. "Papa and I found out she meant you harm. That's why we had to get you away from her, and quickly. To protect you."

The confusion in her expression turned steely. "I don't believe you." She scooted to the far side of the car, as far from Papa as she could get. "Mama told me you envied how happy we were. She said I shouldn't be mad at you for it. But this is mean, Verity. You can't take my mother away just because you're jealous."

"That's not . . ." My words trailed away like a vapor. I *had* been jealous. Of Lilah's easy transition to her new life, of her genuine happiness while I struggled through my work on the farm and longed for the life I'd planned. "That's not true anymore," I finished. "I'd never do something like this for spite. How could you think that?"

Papa tightened his grip on the steering wheel. "Lilah, we must—"

"You know we can't believe him, Verity," she cried, pushing wind-whipped hair from her face. "Is he the one who told you Mama was bad?"

"Lilah, I understand you're confused and upset," Papa said, gently. "But Mr. Lybrand told us what was going on, and now we must get you to safety."

"Mr. Lybrand never wanted Mama to have me. He's tricked you both into getting rid of me for him." Lilah's chin trembled as she looked rapidly around, seeking a way to escape the speeding vehicle. "Very, you've turned out like Papa. You can't tell what's real and what's not anymore."

"No, Lilah." I reached for her hand.

She pulled away. "You can go back to New York if you want," she said. "But you'll go without me."

In a blink, she flung herself toward Papa, interposing her small body between him and the steering wheel. She slammed her foot on the brake.

The sudden stop rammed me into the seat divider, pushing the air from my lungs in a painful gust. Papa's forehead hit the steering wheel with a thud. He went motionless.

A cloud of dust engulfed the car. Lilah shifted out from under our father's still form, rubbing her right shoulder where it had slammed into the steering wheel. "Is he all right?" she whispered.

I pressed shaking fingers to his neck and found a pulse. "He's alive," I said, and Lilah sprang into action. I reached for her at the same moment she scrambled out of the car.

She stood in the swirling dust, her chest heaving. "I'm sorry, Verity. I love you. And Papa, too. But you're both ill. And no one is taking me away from Mama."

She turned and ran.

I vaulted out of the car. "Lilah, stop!" My legs still shook with adrenaline from the crash, and Lilah was faster than I remembered. She ran back toward town, toward certain death.

I closed the distance between us, breathing hard. Then I saw her goal. She wasn't making for the town at all. Barely visible, but drawing quickly nearer, the black-clad figure of a man on horseback galloped our way. Miss Maeve must have sent him after us right away, almost the minute we left.

The afternoon sun glinted off a gold star on his lapel. Sheriff Loftis had found us.

36

Lilah stumbled to a halt as the sheriff reined in his horse and dismounted. She looked to the sheriff, then me.

She turned and went to Sheriff Loftis.

"Lilah, don't!" My voice cracked, along with my hope.

The sheriff drew his pistol low at his side, unsure if I was the villain or victim in this strange play. "Miss Maeve Donovan reported her daughter missing, and stated that she left the ice cream social early. Who is that man?" He gestured with his gun barrel to Papa, still unresponsive with his head on the steering wheel.

"He's our father, Dr. Matthew Pruitt." I looked desperately to either side, as though someone might come to rescue us, but found only oceans of waving grass.

The sheriff's sharp eyes slid over Mr. Lybrand's highly recognizable green Ford. "He's a thief for certain, and maybe a murderer as well. Miss Maeve asked my deputy to go to her home and check on the well-being of Miss Agatha Pimsler. He returned, right as Miss Maeve told me her daughter was missing, to report that the Pimsler woman was dead."

Lilah let out a short gasp. "She was fine when she came to see Mama this morning. What happened to her?"

"We can't say yet," Sheriff Loftis said, "but Miss Maeve assured me the woman was lying down for a nap and in good health the last time she saw her."

"That's a lie," I blurted. "Ask Mr. Lybrand. He knows what really happened."

Loftis scrutinized me from under the brim of his cowboy hat. "I plan to talk to everyone who set foot in that house today, Lybrand included. My deputy has him waiting at the courthouse for questioning as soon as I return. Miss Maeve said he's been behaving strangely of late.

"Then again, Lybrand could have nothing to do with the woman's passing." The look he gave my unconscious father was one of contempt. "Matthew Pruitt's name was mentioned when Mary Mayhew disappeared from Argenta all those years ago. Now here he is, back in the area just as this nasty business happens."

Lilah's alarmed stare fixed on Papa. "He didn't do anything to Miss Pimsler, Sheriff. He isn't a bad man; he just thinks things are real when they aren't sometimes." She wet her lips, and knotted her hands together. "Right now, he believes Mama is going to hurt me. He thought he was rescuing me."

Loftis flicked a sharp glance at me and laid a hand on Lilah's shoulder. "What about your sister? Does she have a similar affliction?"

My breath went solid in my chest. *Please,* I silently begged. *Please, Lilah.*

A tear slid down her cheek. "Verity needs someone to help her. They both do."

"We'll see to it," Loftis said with oily ease. "Why don't you climb on into the car? I'll drive us all back to town. Your mama's waiting for you."

Lilah seated herself in the Ford, averting her eyes from Papa's slumped form. I made to follow, desperate for her to hear me out.

The sheriff gripped my forearm. "Before we go, let's see if you've helped yourself to anything else that doesn't belong to you." Without waiting for me to respond, he reached inside my pockets. The pouch of money from Mr. Lybrand appeared in his fist. "Can't say I'm surprised," he said.

I had far worse things to dread than being thought a thief. It was late in the afternoon now, the day of the solstice. My sister would die at sunset.

"Mr. Lybrand gave me the money pouch, and he let Papa take the car," I said. "He knows that Miss Maeve is dangerous. She killed Miss Pimsler. You can't send Lilah back to her." I looked to Lilah then, her face ghostly pale against the black leather of the car seat. "I'm sorry, Lilah. I wish you didn't have to hear these awful things, but they're true."

"Very, don't." Her voice broke. "Please, stop."

"That's enough out of you, Miss Pruitt," Loftis said, letting go of my arm. "Until we get back to the courthouse for questioning, you'll do well to keep your mouth shut." With a metallic rattle, he unhooked the handcuffs from his belt.

I bolted. Legs churning, I sprinted into the field, through the windswept grass. I had no plans, no idea of where I could hide. My only thought was of staying free so I'd have a chance to somehow rescue Lilah.

Heavy footfalls pounded behind me, speeding up to match my racing heart. I dodged a swiping hand, stumbled, and kept going.

The sheriff's arm hooked around my waist. I crashed to the

ground, roaring my frustration. Loftis rolled me onto my back and pressed me to the ground with his knee. I landed one solid punch to his jaw. His head jerked to the side. I heard Lilah calling my name, running to us.

The sheriff captured my hands. My screams dissolved into a sob. "You're sending my sister to her death," I wailed.

Lilah halted a few feet away, face pale. "Don't hurt her!"

"I'm not going to," Sheriff Loftis barked. The iron bands of the cuffs snapped around my wrists. Panting, he pulled me to my feet and led me back to the car. Papa lay with his eyes still closed. A purplish knot bulged on his temple.

"Papa! Help me!"

He roused for a moment before his head dropped again, chin resting on his chest. Sheriff Loftis let me go, pulled a length of rope from his horse's saddlebag, and bound Papa's hands. With a grunt of effort, he hauled Papa across the bench seat to the passenger side.

Lilah watched her rescuer shove me into the back seat, then tie his horse to a tree to retrieve later. Sheriff Loftis took the driver's seat, and we sped back toward Wheeler. Frightened tears streaked the grime on Lilah's face, but I knew it wasn't from fear of Miss Maeve. She was scared of me.

When we arrived, only a few dozen people lingered on the court square. Ladies in pale dresses dotted the courthouse lawn like clouds run aground, drifting about folding table-cloths. Men hauled the chairs and tables onto wagons to be taken away. I scanned the faces for a glimpse of Hettie or Big Tom. With a sinking feeling in my gut, I remembered telling Abel to let them know I'd gone home feeling sick. In the time it would take them to get back to the farm by wagon, find me missing, and return to town to make inquiries, it would be too late. The sun would set and Lilah would be drowned.

Our roaring arrival drew the attention of the little crowd. All around the lawn, hands fell still. Curious stares turned to confusion, then shifted to worry, as the onlookers took in my father, slumped unconscious in the front seat, and me cuffed in the back.

The Ford bounced over the sidewalk. Loftis eased it to a stop next to the redbrick jailhouse. A deputy loitered nearby, smoking a cigar in the shade.

"Help me get him out," Loftis ordered. Together they dragged Papa from the car. Sheriff Loftis nodded to another deputy, then toward me. "Her, too."

The man approached, thumbs hooked in his gun belt. This was my final chance to make Lilah understand. Cuffs jangling, I clutched the sleeve of her party dress. "You have to listen to me. This isn't one of your stories, Lilah. It's real, and the bad guy isn't who you thought. Miss Maeve truly means to hurt you. Don't let her take you into the woods. Please."

Lilah's hazel eyes searched mine. Quick as a breath, she pulled me close and pressed her cheek to mine. "When Papa said frightening things, you always told me I shouldn't be scared," Lilah breathed into my ear. "You taught me to hold on to what was real. Now you must try to do the same." A tear slid down my cheek. I couldn't tell if it was mine or hers. "I love you, Very." She stepped out of the car, arms folded over her chest as if against a bitter wind.

The iron-barred door of the jailhouse gaped open, showing a cramped, bleak cell. Loftis and his helper hauled Papa inside. Whispers hissed through the crowd. The other deputy loomed over me. "Come on then. Don't be difficult."

I looked at my hands, heavy with iron shackles. There was no escape. I was surrounded by men with pistols and a knot of curious townspeople. Tilting my chin up, I gritted my teeth and allowed the deputy to assist me out of the car. He let go of my arm only when I stepped into the dim jailhouse.

Loftis finished untying Papa's hands, then removed my cuffs. "My sister's blood will be on your hands if you don't stop this," I said. He couldn't meet my fiery stare as he returned the cuffs to his belt.

The jailhouse door slammed shut with a clang. I rushed forward, gripping the iron bars, and watched Sheriff Loftis take Lilah's hand with surprising gentleness. "Come on. Deputy Finley will take you home." He escorted her to the car and helped her climb in beside the officer who waited behind the wheel.

"Someone stop them!" I shouted, desperate. The people watching the scene edged back, some looking wary, others frowning in my direction. No one was willing to buck the sheriff for the sake of an unhinged-looking girl ranting from behind prison bars.

They drove away. Lilah looked back, her eyes holding mine until the car rounded a corner and she was lost from sight.

Among the scattered observers, a flash of gold hair caught my eye. Abel watched the scene from a short distance away, his eyes shadowed, his brow creased with . . . what? Contempt? Disappointment?

Della was at his side. I motioned for her to come closer, but she shook her head. The rejection felt like a punch in the gut. Abel leaned down, saying something in her ear, still looking at me with that grim expression. I gripped the bars with bloodless fingers. "You have to help her. Please. Miss Maeve is going to kill her at sunset," I shouted.

Sheriff Loftis barked at me to hold my tongue, then stalked

over to where Della and Abel stood. He spoke to the pair, arms folded. Della nodded once. They didn't so much as glance my way as they left.

Something in my chest caved in. My friends had decided I was crazy after all.

The sheriff watched Della and Abel go, and the final stragglers who'd lingered to take in the show followed their lead, until only Sheriff Loftis remained on the courthouse lawn. He marched to the cell door, spurs jingling. "I'm going to interview Mr. Lybrand about Miss Pimsler while we wait for the coroner to come from Siloam Springs. I'll talk to you next."

He looked at Papa, slouched like a sack of potatoes in the corner. "And I'll contact the asylum your father escaped from, let them know we've got him. There are similar places for women with your—" He stopped to search for the word. "—tendencies. If you don't end up in a prison, I'm sure we can find a spot for you in one of them." With that he retreated to the courthouse.

I smacked my palms against the rough walls of the jailhouse over and over again. Bits of brick ground into my skin. At sunset, Lilah would be dragged into an endless half life. And I was locked up within sight of the woods where Miss Maeve would drown her, trapped as surely as my sister would be. I clenched the bars and screamed, blood from my cut palms flecking the iron.

"Verity, stop." Papa's slurred voice drew me up short. I turned to find him staring blearily around the cell. "Where are we? Where's Lilah?"

I sank to my knees in misery. "Sheriff Loftis found us, and we're in the jailhouse. He's taken Lilah back to Miss Maeve."

The news seemed to blast away Papa's stupor. He rose, a bit unsteadily, eyes darting wildly from one corner to the next.

He sprang onto the bench that sat against the back wall under a tiny window. Papa's long fingers searched the edges of the rusted roof for any weak spots.

I joined him, but the effort proved futile. Outside, the sun scraped the treetops. It would set in little more than an hour. "There's no way out, Papa."

The jail's tin roof trapped the heat, and I reached absently for my hat to fan myself. My fingers closed on Hettie's pearl hatpin. I pulled it out, staring first at the pin, then at the lock on the door. Papa followed my line of sight and caught on. "Brilliant, Verity," he whispered, taking the pin and bounding over to the door.

Papa maneuvered it into the lock while I cast wary glances around the blessedly empty court square. Only a few straggling shoppers meandered along the storefronts across the road. None of them looked our way. "Almost there," Papa muttered through clenched teeth. The delicate metal bent in his fingers. I held my breath.

The pin snapped, ringing in my ears like a gunshot blast.

"Damn it," Papa said, flinging it aside. "Do you have anything else?"

"That was the only hatpin." I tugged a hairpin from my coiffeur. "Will this work?"

Papa tried it. "No. Too short." He leaned his forehead against the bars and closed his eyes.

I slid back to the ground, head to my knees. To lose hope somehow felt far crueler than to have never had it at all. A sob built in my chest. I struggled for a deep breath against the biting pressure of my corset.

Gingerly, I traced the hard ridges of flat metal strips running the length of my torso. I exhaled sharply as the idea struck. Papa lifted his head. "What's the matter?"

"Just a minute," I said, scuttling into a shadowy corner, where I stripped off my dress. Standing in just a chemise, I fumbled over the laces of the corset and wrenched it off. Then I laid into it with teeth and fingernails, shredding the seams, until the first bit of metal boning poked out. At last I held the thin piece of metal between my fingers.

"Make sure no one's looking our way," I said, edging Papa away from the lock. He scanned the empty square, then hurried to the window in the back wall to check the street before giving the all-clear.

With the precision of a surgeon, I slipped the metal into the lock. Thank Heaven I'd paid attention when Della explained her technique for breaking into her parents' chest of drawers. But hearing how to pick a lock was a far cry from having practice myself. Seconds stretched, and the sun sank ever lower. Despair started to rise in my throat.

Then, without warning, I felt the metal slide into place between the tumblers. Not daring to breathe, I pressed down. A small click. The lock fell open.

Papa moved to open the door. "Not yet," I said. I stepped back into my dress and did a quick check of the sidewalk. Under a red-and-white-striped pole, the barber swept the day's cuttings onto the sidewalk with maddening leisure. Finally, the man sauntered back inside his shop, unaware that his peaceful evening routine was delaying a prison break.

"All right. Let's go." I slipped out first, Papa following a split second later, and pulled the barred door carefully closed behind us. The urge to run rose like a flood tide, but I forced myself to walk across the road and down the sidewalks toward the edge of town.

Papa took my arm. "We are only out for a stroll," he said, raking hair over the swollen bruise at his temple.

As we passed the bank, a young man stepped out in front of us. My heart scrambled into my throat. "Evening," he said, tipping a hat to me and nodding to Papa. He must have missed our arrest, or else he would've recognized us on sight.

"To you as well," Papa replied. The clerk settled the hat on his head and started down the sidewalk, glancing once over his shoulder at us. I gave a tight smile and, when he turned back, we ducked down the alley.

"Hurry," Papa said, breaking into a run. Together we sprinted toward the woods.

My lungs began to ache, but I willed myself on, legs churning, skirt balled in my fists. All the while I tensed for the sound of pursuit. I heard only the whipping of grass against my legs and Papa's pounding steps beside me.

The woods drew closer, the shadows of the trees reaching for us. Papa broke through first, and was swallowed almost immediately by the gloom. My heart thudded in time with my racing feet.

I ran as hard as I could into the darkness.

37

Night consumed me. The canopy choked out all lingering light. I stumbled to a halt beside Papa. "Keep moving," he said, his voice hushed.

We headed in what I hoped was the right direction, but before we'd gone a hundred yards, a cold wind whipped by. The chill of the fog began to rise around me. "Not this," I said, voice quaking. "Not now." The fog pressed in and seeped through my clothes, leaching all warmth until my bones felt brittle with cold. I clung to Papa for support, struggling against the freezing, creeping feeling of confusion that came with the fog.

"Which way?" he murmured.

"I don't know," I said. Tears threatened. We couldn't come this far only to lose Lilah to the dark and the fog. But the blank grayness ahead gave no hint at which way to go.

A weak light appeared, casting an uncertain circle of illumination. In its center stood the silent little girl I'd encountered the day I'd found the well.

Josie Loftis, Della's sister.

Papa went stock-still. "A spirit child," he breathed, awed but unafraid. For once, his readiness to believe in what should be impossible wasn't a hindrance.

"We need to find the well," I said. "Will you show us the way?"

The ghost girl's face shone eerily in the strange, watery light. The edges of her form blurred, like a charcoal drawing smeared by a careless hand. I feared she'd fade away. Instead she crooked a finger, beckoning us to follow.

I took Papa's hand, and together we followed Josie's spectral light as it wavered through the fog. Dread clenched my insides. With no way of following the sunset, I couldn't be sure we weren't too late. I picked up my pace, ducked under a limb, and drew even with our guide. "How much farther is—"

In an instant, she was gone. Darkness crashed down. Papa's hand in mine stiffened, but he whispered calmly into the black woods, "Thank you for guiding us." Then, speaking close to my ear, he added, "I think we're right where we need to be."

Just ahead, through the trees, tepid lantern light pushed at the dark. We peered into the fog-smothered clearing. At its heart stood the well. And beside it, Miss Maeve.

She knelt in a pool of light, her white nightgown and silvery hair almost glowing. Lilah lay motionless on the mossy ground before her, face deathly pale in the hovering fog. "Is she alive?" I asked in a strangled whisper. I could see in Papa's terrified eyes that he wasn't sure.

Miss Maeve tied something around Lilah's wrist, humming the uncanny lullaby I'd heard Lilah singing to her doll. "We're going to run at her on the count of three," Papa whispered.

Tensing, I dropped his hand and prepared to spring. "One . . . two . . ." We rushed forward, silent on dampened leaves.

Miss Maeve rose with the swirling mists and leveled a pistol at us.

We slammed to a halt. Papa lifted his hands, palms out. I looked to Lilah, small and still at Miss Maeve's feet. The little finger on one hand twitched.

Papa risked a glance at Lilah, then focused on the woman who had once been his true love, the woman now holding us at gunpoint. "Mary." He said her name like an apology, an accusation, and a confession all at once.

And in it, I heard the lingering love for the girl she'd been.

"It really is you," she said. Her voice was flat, but a tumult of emotion gleamed in her pale eyes. "I suspected Reuben had betrayed my trust, but I couldn't be sure you were the man I'd seen him talking with." Her grip on the gun tightened. "It's a shame, after all his loyal work. He helped me ruin you, and he played the hateful miser so everyone would pity me." A vein pulsed at her throat, but the hand that held the pistol was steady. "It's my own fault, for deciding to toy with you. I should've killed you and been done with it, before Reuben had time to go soft."

Papa edged forward. "Put the gun away, Mary. Let's discuss this calmly."

Miss Maeve cocked the hammer. "The time to talk is long gone, Matthew. Dead and buried, along with our baby. All that remains are debts to pay." She tilted her head toward Lilah. "I'm taking what's mine." Miss Maeve's voice began to quaver. "She is my recompense. She is my payback for the suffering I endured at your hand."

Papa stood before her, racked with remorse. His once-handsome face was gaunt and twisted with guilt. "I harmed you greatly. But I didn't know about the baby. That night we tried to elope, your father told me you were better off without me. He made serious threats. I was young, and frightened."

"Do you think I wasn't?" she asked, her voice rising.

"Mary, I'm sorry. We should've had a little girl together. A life together." The sincerity of his words showed in every tortured syllable. "But hurting Lilah will not bring our baby back."

"I would never hurt my own daughter." The gun began to tremble in her hands.

"You plan to drown her," Papa said, almost gently. Even in my terror, I marveled at his calm.

"It's the only way to keep her with me always. She's not safe without me." Angry tears slid down Miss Maeve's fair cheeks. She kept the gun trained on us. The snub-nosed barrel gleamed oily black. "I'm taking care of her."

"This is not how a parent cares for a child," Papa said. His words rang through the clearing.

"What do you know about it?" Miss Maeve shouted. "Nothing! She is owed to me, and I'm taking her."

Papa shook his head, taking another step forward. I tensed, waiting for Miss Maeve's reaction. She only stared at Papa, her eyes gone suddenly forlorn. "That's not true," he said. "You know it, deep down."

Her shoulders slumped. "She's mine," Miss Maeve said, but a hint of doubt edged her words. I risked a glance at Lilah, who lay so unnaturally still, surely drugged with one of Maeve's concoctions. "Mine," Maeve repeated, and this time it was almost a question.

Slowly, Papa reached for the pistol handle held in Miss Maeve's white-knuckled grip. His fingers wrapped gently around hers. "She can't replace our lost little girl, Mary. Lilah isn't that child. She's my daughter, mine and Elizabeth's. Nothing you do will change that."

I saw the flash in her eyes a split second before I heard the shot. Smoke billowed out, mixing with the fog.

I froze, torn between rushing to Lilah, or to Papa.

Through the smoke, I saw him stretched full-length on the ground, one hand draped over his chest. Bright blood spread across his grubby shirt. I flung myself down at his side, moved his fingers, and saw the dark hole in his chest. So small and so brutal.

"Papa, stay with me. Keep your eyes open." I ripped the bottom of my skirt and pressed the wad of fabric to the wound, my thoughts and emotions thrashing in a frenzied jumble. "I have to keep pressure on the wound," I said in a steady voice. Amazing, because I felt like I was shaking apart from the inside out. "Lie still. We'll get the bleeding under control and then I'll—"

Papa placed a hand over mine. Blood pooled on the ground beneath him, staining the torn hem of my skirt. I watched it spread.

My heart turned to ash.

His eyelids fluttered, but he forced them open, and touched my cheek. His blood was warm on my face. "I love you, Verity. Tell Lilah the same. You girls were my second chance to be a father. I'm sorry for . . . not being . . . for . . . letting you both down."

I quieted the panic roaring through me. I would be calm for him. "You did no such thing." My smile wobbled, but held. "I love you, too."

The pained lines around his eyes lessened, and he looked, for a moment, young again. Then a thin trail of blood snaked from the corner of his lips. His breathing frayed. Papa's hand slipped from my face, landing heavily on his ruined chest.

I watched a girl's fingers reach out to wipe the blood from his face and close his eyes. My fingers, I noted. Strange, because I was far away, huddled in the moment between a razor's slice and the hissing pain that follows. I held still in the stretched instant, feeling nothing.

A blast of bitter wind cleared my head. My senses returned. Every nerve vibrated with warning.

Where was Miss Maeve? I sprang up. The gun lay on the ground near her lantern, but Miss Maeve and Lilah were gone. The well loomed only feet away, shrouded in fog. I snatched the light and staggered toward it. A double pulley and ropes came into view below a crossbeam, all new additions since I'd last seen the well.

The pulley turned, spooling the rope down into the well.

Far below, I glimpsed Miss Maeve's white gown. She sat in a rope hammock, Lilah's body in her lap.

I reached toward the pulleys and ropes, desperate to stop their movement, but they were out of reach. At the same instant I heard the distant splash of Miss Maeve reaching the water. I screamed as she plunged Lilah beneath its black surface.

Without even stopping to unlace my boots, I climbed onto the side of the well. I took a deep breath and stepped out into nothingness.

38

I hit the frigid water and plunged into utter blackness. My heart stuttered in the cold. Panicking, I kicked upward, fighting the weight of my clothes and shoes, clawing through the water until my fingertips grazed rough rope.

With a gasp, I hauled myself up. Tremors racked my limbs. I swiped dripping hair from my eyes. In the near dark, I could scarcely see more than a few inches. But the lantern high above on the well's edge gave enough light to show the stomach-twisting sight before me.

Lilah lay alone in the hammock, her body and face submerged. Her arms floated gently at her sides, one wrist wrapped in a woven bracelet. It was made of twisted vine and strands of hair. The gold nib from her fountain pen—an item she held dear—was trapped within the vines.

I reached a shaking hand to pull Lilah's face above water.

There was a splash from behind, and Miss Maeve's fingers wrapped around my throat.

"Just like your mother," she said smoothly, her breath warm in my ear. "Neither of you could stop meddling in my life." I scrabbled at her fingers, choking, gagging. I slammed my head backward, trying to break her nose.

She dodged, and her grip tightened. Black encroached on the corners of my vision. Then, inexplicably, her hold on me released.

Icy water pulled me down. Struggling with all my might, I fought for the surface again, coming up across the well from Miss Maeve. Before she could react, I threw my upper body over the side of the hammock.

I struggled to lift Lilah's face above water. My muscles were leaden with cold, and the angle was all wrong. Splashing and cursing, I wrenched myself further into the hammock and gripped her under the arms. Miss Maeve, treading water effortlessly, lurked at the far side of the well, making no move to stop me.

Desperation gave me strength, and one final pull brought Lilah's head and shoulders above the water. There was no gasp for air. No sound at all. My breath plumed in a frozen mist around her face as I slapped her bloodless cheeks. Her lashes didn't even flutter.

Miss Maeve spun a carefree circle in the water, fingers trailing along the surface. The gold charm on her bracelet swung beneath her slim wrist. "Lilah is safe now," she said with sudden, dreadful calm. "She'll be with me every moment, forever."

Lilah's limp hands floated just under the water's surface. The bracelet, twined with the coppery hair I'd brushed and braided since she was a toddler, stood out like a slash against her white wrist. Lilah might be gone, but I would not let her spirit be trapped. She'd be free to move on, to find our parents. To be at peace.

My energy surged back and I scrabbled with both hands at

the cruel trinket, wrenching and twisting with all my might. The woven vines and hair bound Lilah's wrist as tight as the cuffs I'd worn to jail. My cold, wet fingers couldn't slide underneath.

Miss Maeve wrenched both my arms behind my back. I began to kick harder, fighting to stay above the surface. With one last desperate effort, I tried to tear the bracelet off with my teeth. Miss Maeve forced me under water.

I gasped at the cold flooding over my face, felt the water rush down my throat. This was how it ended, then. My sister and I would die together in this well, drowned in freezing water.

But no. Miss Maeve hugged me from behind and pulled me back to the surface. "It had to be done," Miss Maeve explained, almost regretfully. She rested her chin on my shoulder as she spoke, as though we were old friends, comfortable with one another. Her breath misted around my face. "I'm saving her," she said. "I'm the only one who can save her, Verity. I can protect her from this vicious, hateful world. Even you couldn't do that. But when she's with me, she'll always be safe. I will never fail her."

I felt my mind begin to drag, slowing down like a clock unwinding. Safe. I'd promised Papa I'd watch over Lilah. They were both gone now. The violent shaking in my body stopped. Miss Maeve propelled me gently forward. She draped me across my sister's still body. My head lay across Lilah's chest, just as she used to lie on mine at night when she was little, talking away until sleep overtook her. I couldn't fathom a world without Lilah's voice. My eyes dropped shut. It wasn't so cold now. I'd be asleep soon, and nothing could hurt me anymore.

I heard a thump. Faint, from a long way off. Then a second

one. An impossibly long wait. Another thump. Another heart-beat.

Lilah's heartbeat.

It wasn't too late. While she lived, there was hope.

Angling my head, I could see Miss Maeve, mere feet away. Her silvery blond hair swept over her face like seaweed, bedraggled from our struggle. She ducked under water to smooth it. With the only strength I had left, I ripped Lilah's bracelet off and slipped it down the high neck of my dress. It rested there, broken and close to my heart.

Miss Maeve resurfaced and moved toward me, chin skimming the water as she approached, pale hair flowing out behind her.

I knew this would be my last chance to fight her off. And to save Lilah's life. But my limbs had locked up. Each breath grew shallower. Miss Maeve dragged me from the hammock with ease. Whatever the cold's effect on me, it seemed not to trouble her at all. I grasped at the slick rope, barely keeping myself above water.

"Lilah will be waiting for me in the Hollow when I arrive this evening. And every one after," she said. "We can't have you—"

From far above came the sounds of a commotion. A new light appeared, darting back and forth across the opening of the well. Yelling voices drew nearer.

"Help!" I called. My voice was frail. I knew it didn't carry all the way to the surface. I tried again. "Down here . . . in the well!"

Miss Maeve looked up, annoyance darting across her face. "Whoever it is, they're too late." The flickering light glittered in her ice-chip eyes.

She gripped my shoulders, her face only inches from mine. I tried to push her away and failed. All my energy was gone. Our skirts tangled as she kicked us away from the hammock. Away from Lilah.

"If you drown in this well, your spirit becomes trapped in the Hollow," Miss Maeve said. "Lilah and I can't have you spoiling our sanctuary." My head lolled to the side. She pressed her cheek against mine, righting me.

"You do remind me of Elizabeth," she whispered, placing a hand on either side of my face and looking hard into my eyes. A feeble hope sparked. Maybe the bond she'd once shared with my mother would be enough to save me.

"Please," I whispered.

Miss Maeve slammed my head against the wall. "I can't let you *drown*," she said again, almost apologetically. "Drowning in the well is essential for bringing a soul to the Hollow." Light burst in my vision, red fireworks of agony. Blood ran hot down my neck as she bashed my skull into the rocks again. "So I can't let the water be the death of you. But you're not getting out of this well alive." A third blow, though I felt this one less.

She hauled my limp body back toward the well's center. The shouts from above and the lap of water against rock grew distant, as even the searing pain in my head receded. Miss Maeve placed me over the hammock, draping my torso across Lilah's legs. She adjusted my body so my face was clear of the water.

"You'll bleed to death soon enough. Or freeze, although that might take longer." She looked up, searching the distant circle of dark sky. Then her focus shifted back to me, and the merciless bite in her voice turned almost sad. "Goodbye, Elizabeth."

The light in Miss Maeve's eyes vanished as the sun fully set.

With her soul departed for the night, her lifeless body sank under the black water.

I lay there, unable to move, my life ebbing away. I closed my hand around Lilah's wrist, feeling her faint pulse.

Dimly, I became aware of water droplets landing on my back. I looked up to see the long rope used for raising and lowering the hammock being pulled up and out of the well. Then the hammock began to move. Someone was trying to hoist us to safety.

A frantic voice reached me. "He's already gone, you can't do anything for him. Come help me pull!"

Even distorted by the echoes in the well, I knew the voice.

"Again!" Abel's words shook with strain. I wondered distantly how he managed to move us at all with only one good arm. "Can you see her? Is she all right?"

The bottom of the hammock lifted above the waterline. Drops cascaded from it with the sound of a summer rain. The well shaft brightened. With a half-open eye, I saw an arm far above, holding a lantern.

"It don't look good, son," said Granny Ardith's creaky voice. "We might be too late, but—Good Lord! Verity's with her!"

There was a shout of fury and fear from Abel. We dropped a few inches, until I was again waist deep in the icy water. Granny's face vanished and the pulling resumed. Abel shouted desperate encouragement, urging Granny on.

They fought, freeing us from the water in slow degrees, only to lose what they gained as Abel's single working arm tired and Granny's feeble strength waned. Over and over, Abel and Granny pulled us up, only to have the hammock slip back down. Beneath my ear, Lilah's heartbeats began to fade. "Try again," Abel shouted, despair disguised as anger in his voice. "We're running out of time."

My spiraling, weaving thoughts coalesced into a single certainty. I knew what I had to do. And it would cost me my life. But with a settled peace, I knew this was as it must be.

I fumbled with leaden fingers for Lilah's hand and pressed the cold skin to my lips. "Goodbye, Lilah. I love you."

I let my sister go.

Shifting my body, I slid off the hammock. Freed from my weight, it glided skyward, twirling slowly as it went. I watched Lilah float away as I fell.

The splash came much sooner than on my first drop into the well. As I sank, there came a second, quiet sound. I felt the brush of icy metal against my outstretched hand, something descending into the depths with me, following me to my death.

My death would save Lilah.

Breath rushed from my mouth and nose, sending delicate bubbles over my skin. Then the water flooded my lungs. Strange how it burned despite being bitingly cold. I sank further, until suddenly the black in my vision turned to a pure, blinding white.

My last living thought was of my sister.

39

Dark water rippled at her feet. In the living world, rolling waters had a song. Here, there was only and always silence. She bounced slightly on her toes. They left no impression in the gray sand. The fog swirled around her white gown, stirred by her anxious pacing.

Maeve forced herself to fold her hands and be still. She exhaled. She didn't have to breathe here, but it felt like a comforting reminder that her time in the Hollow would end at dawn, and her body would live again. For a handful of hours, anyway, until she was forced back to this awful place. But now, she would have her little girl with her. She only needed to find Lilah, and everything would be as it was meant to be.

Tonight, the fog was especially thick. It rose and fell, tumbling down the low hills on either side of the dark river, all at the will of an unseen, unfelt wind. Lilah could be here right now, waiting, obscured from view. Maeve worried the bit of gold hanging from her bracelet and tried not to think of Matthew. It wouldn't do to dwell on such things. This night was for Lilah and her. It was time for them to begin anew.

"Lilah?" Maeve pitched her voice low, lacing it with loving reassurance. "If you can hear me, come here."

On the far shore of the black river, the fog stirred. The mists thinned to reveal a blurry figure, motionless in the cloaking haze.

"Lilah, I'm over here." Victorious joy warmed her. "Follow the sound of my voice." The figure turned in her direction, but didn't advance. It stood silent. Still. Watching.

Maeve stepped closer, until her toes were nearly in the water. Swirling clouds of consuming fog hovered thick over the obsidian surface. When they shifted, the watcher was gone. Maeve scanned the riverbank, barren save for a stand of blackened, skeletal trees. "Lilah?" she called again. "It's me. You don't have to hide. Come to your mother."

A flash of white flickered between the trunks, followed by a sound she'd never heard in the Hollow—laughter. But it wasn't Lilah's usual giggle. This was a low and mirthless sound, almost bitter. "Lilah, this isn't funny," Maeve said, suddenly tense. Something was wrong. "Come here at once."

The hazy figure of a girl stepped out from the dead woods. She seemed almost to be carried by the mists to the river's edge. Then, with the grace of a prowling cat, she stepped out onto the water. The mist began to part, like curtains drawn back, as she moved closer, ripples spreading under her boots.

Maeve felt herself go rigid with shock as the face came into focus. A face so very like Elizabeth's.

Verity stepped onto the near shore. Her eyes glittered, fearless and full of anger. In her hand, she clutched a pair of silver shears like a dagger.

Maeve took a halting step backward just as the fog swept down. She couldn't stop the cry of alarm that crawled up her throat. She was blind in the swirling clouds.

The girl began circling her. Maeve spun. She tried to see where Verity had gone, tried to quell the rising worry she felt. Not only worry, but—and she was stunned to realize it—dread. Maeve reminded herself that she had no one to fear. What greater harms could befall her than the ones she'd already suffered?

And yet, there had been a look of pure vengeance in Verity's face. If there was any way Maeve could be called to account for the things she'd done—tormenting Matthew's mind and ultimately killing him, taunting Verity and testing her sanity, taking Lilah—the fire in Verity's burning gaze said she'd find it.

For the first time in a very long time, Maeve felt that she might not be in control.

She turned another disoriented circle, then stumbled. A hand shot out from the fog to grip her arm. She found herself wrenched around. Maeve let out a gasp as she came face-to-face with Verity.

The girl's eyes were full of pain and steel.

"Hello, Miss Maeve."

40

I woke to fog. The light here was wrong, flat and dull, coming from nowhere in particular. Overhead, in a tin-colored sky devoid of sun or moon, the mists circled and swirled. I paced the dark sand, reliving my last moments. Slipping from the hammock so that Lilah could be saved, the splash as I went under, the consuming silence as I sank. Something solid and smooth sinking next to me, brushing my fingers just as I died.

As I died.

My right hand coiled into a fist. In it, I clenched a pair of silver shears. I examined their intricately carved handles, the wickedly sharp tip.

From across the water, a voice cut through the silence. Maeve, calling for Lilah.

My grip tightened around the shears. I felt the tip bite into my palm, just as though I were alive. In a flash, I knew where I'd seen them before. And some instinct, some knowledge that came with death perhaps, told me what I had to do.

I would end Maeve Donovan, once and for all.

And, with that thought, I laughed.

I stepped out onto the water, intending to wade or swim to

reach Miss Maeve. But just like the sands, the water showed no sign of my passing. It bore me up as though I were no more substantial than the billowing clouds around me.

I swept toward Miss Maeve, tracking her through the fog as she called for my sister again. A smile snuck over my face at the worry creeping into her voice. I could pinpoint the second she realized that her plan had gone awry, that whoever was coming toward her now was not Lilah. And I savored the hint of fear in the way she gasped as I reached from the fog to pull her to me. She brought her hands up, as if to ward me away, but I grabbed her right wrist in a merciless grip. "Hello, Miss Maeve."

She struggled, but the strength I'd lacked in the well had returned. I only tightened my hold. Her pale blue eyes flicked to the long blades of the shears.

"Whatever you're thinking about doing with those, it won't work," she said. "I've tried everything you can imagine to end it all. It's impossible. Both of us, we're beyond help or harm now."

I opened the shears. "We'll see about that." I slid the open shears between her skin and the woven vines of the bracelet. There was a soft snick as the blades closed.

The bracelet fell away, lost to the fog.

Maeve went still. Shock washed over her beautiful face.

She'd expected me to stab her, but I was confident that the shears had been sent for the purpose of cutting the bracelet. They were from Granny Ardith. She'd bespelled them to accomplish this very task. "It's time for you to move on, Mary Eve." I prepared myself to see her vanish before me.

We faced each other by the dark river, watched by the gnarled, black trees. I waited. . . .

A slow, delighted grin lit Maeve's perfect face. "You thought you broke the keeping spell, didn't you?" She shook her head, and her pearly laugh was gentle. "Don't you think I've tried cutting it?" she asked. "I've done it over and over again. With those very shears, even."

Miss Maeve leaned close. "The Hollow can't be escaped. You'll soon find out," she said, with complete assurance. "The bracelet will return in a few seconds." She peered at me, serene and smooth as glass. "I can't have you roaming this place, disturbing my time together with Lilah. There's a pit in the center of the woods, just where the well is in the aboveground. I think it would do nicely for holding you. And I'll finish what I started with Lilah tomorrow evening," she said. "You gave your life—and your afterlife—to delay my plans by one night." Maeve shook her head. "I thought you were smarter than this, Verity."

The shears dropped from my fingers as I sank onto the dark sand, numb with defeat. I'd been wrong. I'd failed. There was nothing and no one left for me.

All at once, I knew what Maeve had felt when she'd walked away into the snow.

Then a subtle change began to warp the gray air. I squinted into the dimness over Miss Maeve's shoulder. The fog drew together, growing solid. A black wrought-iron gate formed behind Miss Maeve, looming in the air above our heads. Its panels scrolled and swirled in an intricate, almost lacy design, up and up. I could just make out the wicked points at their tips.

Miss Maeve saw my gaze shift upward. She turned, and we watched the massive gate swing soundlessly open. In the next instant, I felt the wind's movements for the first time since my arrival in this eerie land.

Miss Maeve whirled, towering over where I slumped on the riverbank. "What did you do?"

Wind howled down on us in a flood of sound and sensation.

I staggered to my feet, hands clapped over my ears, squinting against the flying sand. Miss Maeve's mouth opened in a scream, but her voice was lost in the wind's rage. She stumbled, dragged backward toward the yawning maw of the gate.

Then, as suddenly as it had come, the gale stopped. Silence slammed down. An expectant hush settled over the Hollow. The mists stilled. I felt a presence draw near.

A small figure in the shape of a little girl floated toward us through the black trees. She was even less distinct than she'd been in the woods, when she'd led Papa and me to the well. The shade of Josie Loftis rose into the air like a feather borne on a breeze. She passed over our heads, her wispy voice trailing after her. Her words echoed in my mind. "Tell my family I love them."

She vanished through the gate.

I was close enough to see the silvery lashes framing Miss Maeve's eyes as her frightened expression changed to one of understanding. She looked down at her still-bare wrist.

Maeve turned, tilting her head to look through the open gate. I felt sure she was seeing something I could not perceive. She opened her arms, as if to receive an embrace.

The melting started with the hem of her skirt. It dissolved into a hazy nothingness, becoming part of the swirling mist. The fog made its winding way up her body as the edges of her silhouette softened and faded. Miss Maeve neither looked back nor spoke as the fog unmade her. She stared fixedly through the open gate, as though she saw far beyond it, and into whatever waited for her.

The wind returned. This time, it was a soft, welcoming pull. What was left of Miss Maeve floated up and through the gate.

As gently as a sigh, she was gone.

I held my breath, waiting for the wind to draw me upward, too.

But instead, the gate began to close. The black scrollwork turned red as a blazing furnace, then sunrise orange, before softening to a gentle gold. Then they vanished back into the fog.

I was completely, endlessly alone. I couldn't tell how long I lay there, weeping on the sands. It could've been hours or years. I knew nothing in my disconsolate state.

And then a flash of incandescent white blasted over me.

I felt myself engulfed in radiant light, and I dissolved into nothing.

41

The wild, pungent smell of sage hit my senses. My eyelids felt like they'd been welded shut, my entire body was stiff and sore, and I had a vicious headache. With effort, I opened my eyes to find myself looking up at rough-hewn ceiling beams. Bundles of drying herbs swayed over me. I was awake. And I was alive.

I lay on Granny Ardith's kitchen table, beneath a small window opened to a daybreak sky.

"About time you came around."

I turned my head to find her withered face close to mine. She passed a hand over her sparse gray hair. "I was afeared you wasn't coming back," she said.

A thousand questions flitted about in my cloudy mind. How did I get out of the well? And how had I survived? The one I gave voice to was the most important: "Is Lilah all right?"

Granny Ardith inclined her head to indicate a blazing hearth on the far side of the cabin. Lilah lay sleeping beside it on a narrow cot, her cheeks pink. "Nothing some restoratives and some warming won't fix."

Lilah lived.

Our father was dead.

I felt ripped in two with the strength of the opposite emotions. Racking sobs burst out, shaking my shoulders, throbbing in my head. I couldn't have said whether they were born more of joy or grief. Perhaps both in equal, overwhelming measure.

Granny seemed to understand the source of my tears. "Reckon we'll bury your pa as soon as you and Lilah are well enough to attend a funeral. It didn't seem right to do it without y'all."

"Miss Maeve killed him," I said, barely believing this conversation was real, that I was discussing my father's murder. My head was a muddled mess as I tried to work through the events of the previous night. "There's so much I don't understand."

Granny Ardith stuck a pinch of snuff in her lip, then studied the snuffbox as though it could help her explain. "I'm bound to tell you what's what, but it's hard to know where to start. Probably when Della and Abel showed up here yesterday afternoon wanting my help to try and stop Miss Maeve." Her eyes darted to mine, then away. "And Della was hell-bent I break that love spell Abel was under real quick while I was at it."

"Love spell?" I asked.

Granny nodded. "Seems Miss Maeve concocted one to make Abel chase after Della. To hurt your heart, like your mama hurt hers. I never should've taught her how to do any workings." Granny wiped at her nose with the back of her hand. Her voice sounded unsteady. "I've been eat up with guilt for years now, 'cause I made the bracelet that caused her to get stuck. She hated me when I couldn't fix it and let her go. And I was scared she'd get my spirit trapped neither here nor there, like she always said she would, if I didn't do what she wanted."

Granny Ardith looked at once both ancient and like a guilty child. "I was hoping you'd figure everything out and find a way to stop her. That's why I told you the truth about where her bracelet came from. I was too yellow to give you all the story, in case she found out I'd been running my mouth, but I hoped I gave enough to help."

I let Granny's confession hang in the air, not sure if I was quite ready to tell her all was forgiven. "Did you know she was going to hurt Lilah?"

"No." Behind her spectacles, Granny's eyes sparked. "I wouldn't have abided that." She spat a stream of tobacco into a tin cup and continued. "Della and Abel heard what you was hollering there in the jailhouse, about Miss Maeve and the well. They came and gathered me up, and then Della went back to the courthouse, trying to convince her daddy to stop Miss Maeve. Me and Abel went straight to the well. That boy was undone to find you in the water, I don't mind telling you. We fished you and Lilah out and brought y'all back here."

She rubbed her eyes, the loose skin around her lids bunching under her fingers. "It's been one thing after another the whole night long. Had to go tell Big Tom and Hettie what happened. The sheriff is still holding Reuben Lybrand, trying to sort through this mess. Loftis didn't want to listen to Della, but he did show up in the woods after he found y'all gone from the jail. He don't know what to make of it all, what with that woman dead in Miss Maeve's house, Abel pulling you and Lilah out of the well, your daddy . . ."

I cut her off. I couldn't talk about my father right now. "And what about Miss Maeve?"

"Loftis took a man to help, and they got her body out sometime during the night."

I blew out a wavering breath. "The shears I used on Miss

Maeve's bracelet, the silver ones that came with me to the Hollow. You threw them into the well, didn't you?"

"When I saw you slipping, I knew you wasn't gonna make it to the top. Had to cobble a charm together with the shears right there on the spot. I wasn't sure it would work. I'd tried the same thing with them shears for Miss Maeve a dozen times when we were looking to break the keeping spell. No matter how many times we cut it off, the bracelet always came back. Nothing could break its power." A shadow passed over the withered face. "And all this time, the shears needed someone drowning in the well to carry them over to the Hollow. Thank the good Lord Miss Maeve never thought to try that."

A shiver coursed through my body, and Granny tucked another quilt over me. I did my best to let go of the anger I felt at her for helping Miss Maeve. Like Mr. Lybrand, she'd tried to aid a young woman who'd been deeply hurt, without first stopping to consider a wronged person could do a great deal of wrong herself.

I pulled my hand from beneath the covers and grasped hers. As Granny Ardith looked at our joined hands, her eyes widened. When I glanced down, cold spread through my chest.

The bracelet Miss Maeve had crafted to trap Lilah, the one I'd torn from her wrist and tucked away before Maeve's final attack, now coiled around my wrist. The strand of strawberry-blond hair woven in with the vines had changed to a dark brown. Even though it was braided and wound with the honeysuckle, I recognized it as my own.

Granny's voice dropped to a nervous whisper. "When they pulled you out, it was there on your arm. That was the well's doing, not mine," she added quickly. "I reckon when you cut the one off of Maeve's arm, all that keeping power had to go somewhere. And it found this other charmed bracelet right there, just waiting . . ." Her thin lips pinched together. "It seems like the well didn't want all that power to drift away into nothing."

Truth hit me like a tidal wave, tumbling my thoughts. I tried to sit up, but the motion set my head spinning. I propped myself on my elbows instead. "When I broke Maeve's keeping spell, the charm transferred to me."

Visions of endless fog and a blank sky, of black trees and a desolate riverbank, swam before me. I had to swallow the panic clawing its way up my throat before I could speak. "Will I be pulled back to the Hollow every night? Am I like Maeve now?"

Granny Ardith's bleak stare confirmed my fears.

I lay back on the table, stunned as surely as I'd been when Miss Maeve tried to crush my skull in the well. "Miss Maeve wanted to follow my father when he left her and went back to New York. But the keeping spell ensured she couldn't get too far away from Wheeler."

Granny Ardith's wrinkled lips worked. "That's right. Once the well's power got her bound up when she drowned in it, we couldn't get the bracelet off. She was trapped, day and night."

My breaths shallowed, and my newly beating heart pounded. "And so am I." A spark of understanding for the desperate, dangerous woman Miss Maeve had become glowed in me. I'd never condone her cruelty, but I could at least comprehend how she'd eventually chosen her dark path.

Big Tom's hulking form appeared in the cabin's doorway, turning slightly to fit through. Hettie pushed her way past him and rushed over to me. She glanced at the sun, now fully over the horizon, glowing through the open door. "It's true, then. What Della said about the keeping spell and the well . . ." Her voice trailed off, and she pressed me in a tight hug.

I closed my eyes, resting my head on her bony shoulder.

"We prayed you'd come back with the morning, but we weren't sure." Her voice hitched. Big Tom fished a handkerchief from his overalls, dabbed at his own eyes, then handed the damp cloth to his wife.

"Granny told us about Miss Maeve, about her past and the well," Hettie said, wiping her nose. "I can hardly believe it, even now." She stood up, running a shaky hand over her apron.

"And we know about your daddy," Big Tom said. He twisted his battered hat, looking miserable. "We're real sorry for your loss," he added in his slow, rumbling voice.

I reached for his and Hettie's callused hands. None of us knew what to say, but making that small circle lifted some of the weight of my sorrow. The aching in my chest eased, if only a little.

My attention shifted toward two figures approaching through the herb garden. Hettie followed my line of sight through the open front door. "Lord have mercy, it's hotter than blue blazes in here. Why don't we all step outside for some air?" Without waiting for their consent, she herded Big Tom and Granny out as Della entered.

Della's hands flew to her mouth to stifle a cry. She charged in, slid onto the tabletop where I lay, and crushed me in a fierce embrace. "I can't believe it worked. When Granny Ardith told us about Miss Maeve and the well and the keeping charm, and how you might come back, too, I thought she'd gone off her rocker." She dropped a kiss on my cheek, her laugh wobbling. "You're more trouble than you're worth, Verity Pruitt. To think, I stayed up a full night bawling over you dying."

"Your father was right. I'm a troublemaker," I said. My smile felt unsteady as a newborn calf. There was a question I feared, but had to ask. "When the sun came up, Miss Maeve didn't—"

Della shook her head. "She's gone, Verity. Truly gone." She blew out a long breath, both relieved and sad. "I hope wherever she is now, she's with her baby girl," Della said. And I knew it was time for me to tell my friend about the other spirit that had been freed from the Hollow last night.

"I saw Josie's ghost," I said. Della's pink cheeks blanched. "She was in the place where Miss Maeve's spirit went at night." The place I'd be forced back to with every eventide.

"But she's free now," I went on. "When Miss Maeve's keeping spell broke, it opened a gate, and Josie was able to move on. She wanted me to tell you, and the rest of your family, that she loves you all." Della's tired brown eyes, still red-rimmed from crying, filled with tears again.

"Thank you," she whispered at last.

I spoke around a lump in my throat. "When you and Abel left me in the jailhouse, I thought that was the end. I thought your father had convinced you I'd lost my mind, and you'd given up on me."

"Verity Pruitt, do you really think I'd listen to my daddy?" Della asked. "I'm sorry I couldn't get him to the woods sooner." She dropped her gaze from mine and swallowed hard. "Maybe if he'd gotten there faster, he could've saved your father."

"You did what you could," I managed. It would be a long time before I could think of Papa with anything but wrenching pain, I knew. I reached for the closest good thought, and found myself saying, "You are the greatest friend anyone could ever have, Della Loftis."

"It's a tie between me and Abel, I think," she said, an odd half smile on her lips. "When the two of you step out together, promise you won't make me feel like the third wheel?"

I took in the sincerity in her dark eyes. "Della, he's your fiancé."

"Was," she said. "He *was* my fiancé. And I loved having one, sure as shooting. But deep down, I always felt something wasn't right. I'd heard Granny mention that she used to make love potions before. It took me a while to realize that Abel was under one." She sighed and looked out the window. "The strangest thing is, I could've been happy with Abel. I'm certain of that." Della looked back to me, her expression open, the honesty of her hurt unconcealed. "But I'm just as certain I can be happy with him as my dear friend, like he's been all my life. I'll need some time, but I'll get there."

I placed a hand over Della's, and we sat together for a time in silence.

"All right," she said at last, "you can come on in now."

Abel stepped into the little cabin. Emotions cascaded in his blue eyes. Wonder, confusion, worry, relief, something I couldn't quite name, all shifting and mingling together.

Della motioned for him to come closer and he sidled over, regarding me with a look of awe that bordered on fear. Della slid off the table and, as she passed Abel, turned her face up to look into his. "Thank you for giving us a minute to talk. I know you've been as anxious to see her as I have." She laid a hand on his forearm before she left.

Abel stood before me, his tired eyes fixed on a spot just over my left shoulder. He scrubbed a hand through his hair, making it stand up at wild angles. "Granny told me I was under a spell. Della figured it out." Abel's cheeks went pink. "I had no idea until she asked Granny to undo it. Della decided it was either Miss Maeve who dosed me with the potion, or Katherine working on Miss Maeve's orders," he said, looking at me at last. "So, she roused Kat out of bed at about two in the morning to make her explain."

I let out a startled laugh. "Y'all had a busy night."

One corner of his mouth twitched up, but his blue eyes remained troubled. "I think that's the first time I've heard you say *y'all*."

I shrugged. "It grows on you."

"Della wore Katherine down until she got the whole story. Miss Maeve had promised her money to move away, get out of Wheeler like she'd always wanted. All she had to do was run Miss Maeve's nasty little errands for her. Like gathering some Adam and Eve root from the woods to make a love potion. She got Katherine to put it in my pain tonic while they were at the farm for the sorghum making."

"Miss Maeve had a way of making people take her side," I said. "And Katherine not liking me to start with didn't hurt, I'm sure."

Abel searched my eyes. "Verity, I'm sorry. Miss Maeve convinced Katherine that your mother had betrayed her years ago, and this was her way of getting retribution. And Katherine thought she was helping Della, too. Making sure me and Del ended up together."

He took a breath, like someone about to jump from a great height. "Miss Maeve thought it was the perfect payback. Elizabeth took the boy she loved. She thought you wanted me, and she saw a chance to ruin it." His voice was low, tentative. "She might've overestimated how much you cared about me."

I lifted my hand, ran my fingers lightly over his cheek, across the stubble on his chin. "No, she didn't."

He captured my hand and pressed it to his chest. "I pulled you up from the bottom of the well. You were *dead*, Verity." A tremor rippled through his voice. "I knew it, but I held your face above the water anyway. I carried your body back here." Tears filled his eyes, making them blue as the ocean. "You were so cold."

Slowly, I slid off the table. He steadied me as I stood on shaky legs. My arms twined around him. Resting my chin on Abel's shoulder, I looked beyond him to where Lilah still slept soundly. "You saved my sister's life. She has a future because of you."

Abel ran his hands down my back, circling my waist. "I hope she grows up just like her big sister," he said.

"Oh, do you mean stubborn? Or nosy and outspoken?"

"All of that," he said, drawing me even closer. "And smart. Determined. Brave."

This time, his lips met mine first. He tasted of mint and clear water. In the cramped little cabin, wrapped in his warm arms, for a moment I felt freer than I could ever remember.

When we broke apart, I leaned my forehead against his. Lilah's voice drifted from inside a mountain of blankets. "You're all right, I guess, but I'll never be half as bossy."

My legs almost buckled as I tried to rush to her. Abel maneuvered an arm around my waist and helped me across the little room.

"What happened to your hair?" Lilah asked, apprehension in her voice.

I swept my hair over my shoulder, and suppressed a gasp. The strange twist of magic that had taken the color from Maeve's auburn hair had done the same to mine. I dropped the silvery locks and lifted shocked eyes to Abel's face.

He shrugged. "Nobody wanted to be the one to bring it up," he said, almost bashfully. "Granny Ardith reckons it has something to do with being tied to the Hollow. Maeve always told her it's a colorless place."

Abel pulled up a chair, and I lay down beside Lilah. Hot tears filled my eyes as I thought of Lilah's deathly cold hands, her blue lips. Gratitude and aching love overtook the words I meant to say. I thought to ask how she was feeling, what she remembered of the night before. She needed to know I wasn't losing my mind, and what had become of Miss Maeve. And Papa. The tale I had to tell her was one full of dark moments, with more sadness than anything she'd read in a book.

But not right now. Those words came later in the story. Instead, I heard myself say, "I love you."

"Love you too, Very."

"You should rest as much as you can," I said, taking in her pale face and shadowed eyes. "We'll talk more later. For now, try and go back to sleep."

Lilah's freckles bunched together as she wrinkled her nose. She looked at Abel, then put her head on my shoulder with a sigh. "See what I mean? Bossy."

EPILOGUE

September tempered the summer's heat to mellow warmth. Still, my bracelet stuck to my sweat-dampened wrist as I shielded my eyes and looked around the Argenta train station. In the other hand, I gripped a worn leather suitcase. The station wasn't busy today. For that I was grateful. I didn't want a crowd witnessing this goodbye.

"Hand it over, Very." Abel reached for the bag.

I swatted him away. "It's heavy. I'll hold it so you won't tire your arm." I had cut his cast off myself months ago, but I knew the old break still hurt him a good deal.

"The convenient thing about arms is that they usually come in pairs." He reached around me to take the bag. I took the chance to hug him, crushing the brim of my Sunday-best hat, one of the many I wore to help cover the pale roots of my dyed-back-to-brown hair.

Abel smelled of mint leaves today, and he wore his hair neatly combed. I fussed with his tie, though I'd already straightened it twice. "Merlin's going to miss you," I joked.

"He won't even notice I'm gone. You know he's smitten with you lately," he said. "I put some dried apples in Lybrand's carriage house for him." I nodded, finding it hard to speak. Each night, Abel's horse carried me to the woods when the well called to me. Abel had turned the carriage house where Reuben Lybrand once kept his car into Merlin's makeshift barn. Every morning, when dawn pulled my spirit back, I'd find the chestnut stallion waiting patiently in the burgeoning light, ready to carry me back to the farm. Those rides back home wouldn't be as eager, now that neither Merlin nor I would have Abel waiting to greet us.

I cleared my throat, hoping the quaver in my voice wasn't too apparent. "I'm doing a terrible job at being your steadfast, cheerful girl back home, and you haven't even left yet. I promise my letters will be nothing but lighthearted notes about how excited I am for the next school break when I can see you again." I straightened my shoulders and looked into his morning-glory-blue eyes. "I'll miss you."

There was no question of me traveling to Fayetteville, where Abel had been accepted to the University of Arkansas's College of Education. Granny Ardith had been right. The bracelet that gave me the gift of renewed life had indeed come with a price. There was no use trying to travel beyond the daylight boundaries of the keeping spell.

Abel pulled me close. "I'll be done with school and back here teaching before you know it." He slid a hand under my chin and tilted my face up. "And I'll be home to visit as often as I can until then."

I reached up and clasped his sun-warmed hand in mine. "If you don't, I'll send Hettie to fetch you. And nobody likes an angry Hettie." The afternoon sun winked off the tiny sapphire in my engagement ring. "I need you here as much as possible."

His lips brushed my ear as he whispered, "You'll probably change your mind after a few years of coming back from the well and finding me in your bed. I'll always be waiting for you. Morning after morning, for the rest of our lives. You'll be tired of me before long."

My pulse quickened. With a quick glance to make sure we were still alone, I lifted onto my toes and kissed him. "You're handsome when you're wrong," I said.

Hettie and Big Tom had taken Lilah inside the terminal, ostensibly to check the schedule and see if Abel's train would be on time, but I knew it was so Hettie could gather her emotions and give Abel and me a chance for a private goodbye.

I caught the eye of a lady from church who was in her eighth month of pregnancy. After news of my helping with Clara's delivery spread, a few mothers-to-be had approached me with tentative requests that I attend the births of their little ones. I was far from experienced still, but I found midwifery suited me. And it gave me a reason to dust off a few of Papa's medical texts. Leafing through their pages gave me a sense of connectedness to him. I was the next link in a chain of Pruitts practicing medicine, just not in the way I'd imagined.

The few other locals waiting for the train gave us tight, sympathetic smiles. It was the usual reaction we got since that fateful night in the woods.

The general consensus was this: The widely disliked Mr. Lybrand had indeed formed an unseemly attachment to the woman who'd pretended to be his niece. He'd gone into a fit of rage upon finding her former lover in town and killed them both, with Miss Pimsler being an unfortunate victim in the wrong place at the wrong time.

In the court of public opinion, it hardly mattered that Sheriff Loftis had come to a far different conclusion, one much nearer the truth. In his estimation, Lilah and I were the unfortunate bystanders. Miss Maeve Donovan had concealed her past for years and, when faced with exposure by Miss Pimsler and the reappearance of the man who'd wronged her, she'd gone completely mad. Insanity was the reason she'd taken Lilah to the well that night, and Providence had seen fit to thwart her plans in the form of me and Papa arriving in time to rescue Lilah.

The sheriff didn't try to deny that Miss Maeve had killed my father, to my surprise. Mr. Lybrand convinced him of the truth before the banker quietly left town under a cloud of black suspicion. We never learned where he went, and the beautiful house on the edge of the woods was abandoned. Even though no one in town knew of the otherworldly aspects of what happened, of trapped spirits and the Hollow, no one tried to buy the Lybrand house, even when months passed and it became clear its owner wasn't coming back. The lore of the woods held sway over the town still.

The sound of boots on the plank walkway called me back to the present. Big Tom, Hettie, and Lilah returned. My sister stepped between Abel and me, taking our hands in hers, lips pressed in a solemn line. Abel's departure was a loss not only for his aunt and uncle and me, but also for my sister, who loved him nearly as much as I did.

Well, not nearly as much, but she did love him a good deal.

"You'll be back, won't you?" Lilah bit her lip, and I knew she was trying to hold in tears. It was a sadly familiar look.

Lilah's memory of the night at the well was almost entirely missing due to the sleeping potion Miss Maeve gave her and the trauma of her near drowning. I'd filled in the gaps as gently as possible. Still, the reality of what Miss Maeve had tried to do to her, and of our father's murder, affected Lilah to the core. My once optimistic, spirited sister was now prone to bouts of melancholy. For a time, her stories had a dark bent and dismal endings. Of late, they'd tipped toward the bittersweet. With time, I hoped she'd find her way back to happily-ever-afters.

"Of course I'll be back," Abel said. "And Mr. Johnson is only teaching in Wheeler until I have my degree, and then the school board has promised me the job." He tweaked her nose. "You'll have to practice calling me Mr. Atchley."

The downcast look lingered for a few seconds before a small smile tilted her lips. "And you'll have to practice calling me Sister Dearest." In her estimation, my engagement to Abel would never have happened if she hadn't given me solid advice regarding his merits. After all, she'd been the one to point out what nice teeth he had.

The screaming of a train's whistle made us all jump. A deep bass chugging could be heard as the black engine came into view. We watched it grind to a halt with a shriek of brakes and a billowing cloud of coal smoke. Passengers began filing out of the depot, bags and trunks in tow.

Big Tom clasped his huge hand on Abel's shoulder. His mustache trembled a little, and I thought for a moment he wouldn't muster any words. "Make us proud. Like you always do."

Abel nodded, swiping a hand across his eyes. They both knew Abel's crushed arm would never be the same, and the intense labor of running a farm would be too much for him. The injury had been savage, but it had also given Abel a practical reason to further his education.

Hettie moved in to give Abel a quick hug. She stepped back hurriedly and set a hand on her hip. Her eyes were misty as she said, "Take care of yourself. Eat right. And don't stay up all hours reading, you hear?"

"Yes, ma'am. And please tell Mama I'll write as soon as I get there." Abel's mother hadn't been able to come see him off, as two of his siblings were sick. We were the only ones still on the platform now. The porter came to take Abel's bag and reminded us all that the train was about to depart.

With no more goodbyes to say, Abel shoved his hands in his pockets and turned to go. Instinctively, I tried to follow. And I hit the end of my tether.

The pulling sensation in my chest was intense, as though my sternum were trying to collapse inward. I stumbled back a step. The feeling subsided. I'd encountered several points on the invisible boundary that kept me from leaving the area. Here, it seemed, was another. I could try to force myself forward, but I'd learned that would lead to crushing pain, and, if I persisted, falling unconscious for hours. Living with the confinement of the spell was at times mildly frustrating and, at others, nearly devastating.

The limits of the keeping spell seemed to stretch from Wheeler to Argenta, and that had proven helpful. I'd been able to answer Mrs. Mayhew's invitations to dinner. And although I'd never be able to give her the joy of a reunion with her daughter, I thought in some small way my company made her happy.

A great gust of smoke blew from the stack as the train began to roll. Abel leaned out the window, one hand lifted in farewell. I blew him a kiss and was relieved to find I could smile.

Despite it all, I lived. In a world much smaller and simpler than I'd planned, but in one at the same time far fuller than I'd known before.

This afternoon, I'd check on Abel's siblings; then Lilah and I would help Hettie stack more firewood for the approaching cold. Later, Della was coming over, set on another attempt to use the curling tongs on my unruly hair. I'd told her to bring Katherine along this time. My hard feelings toward the girl had softened when she'd come to the farm to offer a stiff, but sincere, apology for her role in helping Miss Maeve, and condolences on the loss of my father. Perhaps Della's relentless quest to bring us all together as true friends would eventually win out.

Della had released Abel from their engagement with grace and, to my mind, an unimaginable lack of bitterness. She'd taken what came, unfair as it seemed, and carried on. Perhaps all the extra time she'd been spending with Jasper lately helped. He'd once said Della was a wonderful girl, but not wonderful for Abel. I strongly suspected now that Jasper's childhood insistence that he'd be the one to end up with Della hadn't only been boyish bragging.

I rubbed at the bracelet that I, like Miss Maeve, could never remove. Granny Ardith said that when I grew old and full of years, I could return to the Hollow and use the shears to cut the bracelet for the final time. Because I'd had them with me when I died, they'd stayed in the Hollow. Waiting for me. But unlike Miss Maeve, I wasn't going to try and escape my uncanny half life for a long while. I had things left to do, and people left to love.

I squared my shoulders. "We should go," I said to Lilah. "We've got another calf to raise on a bottle, and it's nearly feeding time. I'll show you the trick for getting him to drink."

She slid her hand in mine and we started back toward the buckboard. Big Tom and Hettie followed, Hettie sniffling slightly behind a smile, and Big Tom standing straight and tall with pride for his nephew.

"I've got a new story to read you," Lilah said. "I'm not done with it, but I think it's going to be my best yet."

"What's it about?"

"Two sisters who have to save each other from a wicked witch," she said. I cut a sidelong look at her. "The younger sister does the saving," she added.

"Obviously she does."

We climbed into the wagon and I looked back at the station. It seemed an entire lifetime ago when Lilah and I first came here, unaware that we'd be torn apart, and that we'd lose our father once and for all in this tiny town. I was sure that I'd never stop missing him, or my mother. Their absence hung over me still, muting the happy days, taking a touch of their color away. But as time passed, I found my memories of them no longer held only pain. The ache of loss was still there, but somehow less acute, and mingled with gratitude for the life we'd shared together. Twilight faded from our spirits, and joy edged back into my life and Lilah's like sun rays bursting through clouds.

I put my arm around Lilah's shoulders. Against all odds, we were together. And this time, we would stay that way.

Big Tom eased into his seat beside Hettie. "Y'all ready?" he rumbled. I tugged off my hat, letting the brilliant sun shine down on my face. Lilah did the same, grinning.

"We're ready," I called. A welcome breeze slid over my skin. I breathed in, filling my lungs with the sweet, fresh air. "Let's go home."

ACKNOWLEDGMENTS

I owe more than I can express to my outstanding agent, Hannah Mann. Your ceaseless enthusiasm (and meticulous charts!) kept me sane throughout the submission process. There's a reason my author friends are jealous that I get to work with such a rock star. And sincerest thanks to my editor, Melissa Frain, for taking a chance on a strange historical fantasy from a debut author, then helping me shape it into what I'd always hoped it could be. You deserve all the ice cream socials in the world.

My warmest appreciation to the team at Tor Teen: Matt Rusin, Lesley Worrell, Peter Lutjen, Laura Etzkorn, Melanie Sanders, Anthony Parisi, Isa Caban, Eileen Lawrence, Lucille Rettino, and Devi Pillai.

Thank you to Eva Fuell (my Senior Sister), Kristen Tinsley, Jenn Wojcik, and Jane Nickerson for the insightful beta reads, and to Jessica Lamb, whose sharp editorial eye helped get this book query-ready.

Small Town Café in Poyen, Arkansas: thanks for the endless tea and letting me hog the corner booth for hours.

For my parents, Jerry and Thelma Crutchfield. Remember how I talked for the entirety of my childhood, except when I was reading? Well, I finally put that wordiness to good use. And to my in-laws, Don and Deronda Goodman, who for twenty years have been nothing but wonderful to the odd girl their son married.

Lauren Allbright, my brain-twin/possibly me from the Berenstain timeline: I'm so glad you asked me where I got that Coke at DFWCon years ago.

To Dr. Johnny Wink, who once said if someone cut me, he believed I would bleed stories. That remains the most graphic and meaningful compliment I've ever received.

And to Hannah West Penick, who will be unsurprised to learn I'm typing this with teary eyes: I knew your writing was beautiful before I knew it flowed from an equally lovely soul. I could not have done this without you, CP.

AJ, Silas, and Caroline—y'all are my heart outside my body. I am fiercely and endlessly proud of you three.

And for Jeff. "Many waters cannot quench love; rivers cannot sweep it away." I love you.